CURSEBUSTERS!

Visit us at www.boldstrokesbooks.com

CURSEBUSTERS!

by

Julie Smith

A Division of Bold Strokes Books

2011

Credits
Editor: Greg Herren
Production Design: Stacia Seaman
Cover Art by Gun Brooke
Cover Design by Sheri (graphicartist2020@hotmail.com)

Acknowledgments

Thanks first to Cooper Fleischman, who gets my vote for Rookie Editor of the Year, and who came out of nowhere to say, "Hey, how about a curse? And maybe a few more kids." In case Cooper ever needs a job, let me mention here that you should hire him. Big fat thanks also to Paloma Tripp and Mittie Staininger, who did the research and shared the intel; my first guinea pigs, Emaline, Macy, Thad, and Coco Pryor; Mary Jean Haley, who shared esoterica; Leanne Heywood, an early supporter; Juan and Robbie, the only people in the world who could live with the real A.B.; Maryann Walker, Mayan food consultant; my sensational agents, Vicky Bijur and Charlotte Sheedy; and three magical ladies so talented they could probably levitate a jaguar—Brianna, Isanna, and especially Charline. Then the Bold Strokes home team—my stupendous editor Greg Herren, my splendiferous publisher, Radclyffe, and the hyper-talented Gun Brooke, whose cover design scares even me. Finally, as always, my husband, Lee Pryor, who will probably complain that he didn't get a fancy adjective like everyone else. That's because there isn't a strong enough superlative.

Dedication

Can you dedicate a book to a cat? Especially one you've lost track of? I'm going to. I'm pretty sure if I didn't, he'd hunt me down and take me out. This is wholeheartedly for Mojo. Moji, I hope you're still with Juan and Robbie and on your 900th life. Here's what I know: You're still in charge. (Shut up, please, I'll call you Moji if I feel like it.)

Chapter I: Fall Of The Fingerton

L ook behind you," A.B. said. In a rare act of rebellion, I ignored His Bossiness. Why should I look away when the most beautiful sight I'd ever seen—and the strangest—was right in front of us?

"Do as I say, girl-face."

Slightly annoyed, I turned—and forgot all about the beach with the ships that looked like the *Pinta* and the *Nina*. In the distance, a city that looked like something from another galaxy glittered like Oz.

"It's a Mayan town," A.B. said. "I've never seen one, either."

How to describe it? It was zany. Bizarre. Totally whacked out. So crazy and colorful and creative it might have been built by artists. (Or stoners.)

I loved it on sight. "Oh my God, let's go there!"

A.B. cocked an ear. "Quiet. Before it's too late."

It was his get-out-of-my-way voice, and would have gotten my attention even if three men and a woman hadn't suddenly stepped into view and begun walking toward us. I stopped dead, staring rudely. Two of the men—obviously Mayan—were short and tattooed, their hair in Flintstones ponytails. The peculiar way I see people, one was kind of a shiny terra-cotta, the other gunmetal gray. The third one, who looked European, wore cotton sailor's pants and shirt, about five hundred years out of style. He was light blue, the woman pea green.

All three men started shouting and elbowing each other, looking at me in a distinctly familiar way. They were giving me the all-too-universal once-over. The way they were yelling—and the little clicking noises they made—were the ominous sounds of construction sites everywhere.

"Male bonding," I said nervously. "You can't get away from it."

They were nearly upon us now, and one man broke from the group, one of the Mayans. He got up in my face, saying something I didn't get, but there was a look in his eye I did.

"A.B.," I quavered. "Do you understand Mayan?"

"He said, 'nice rack,' girlkin. You don't need Berlitz for that one."

"I was afraid of that."

Very afraid. Because it wasn't like I could just dial 911 on my cell phone. Where we were—Cozumel, Mexico, to be exact—it was 1519. This was shaping up like a scene from some cheesy History Channel movie—*The Quest for the End-of-the-World Book*—only it was starring me, Reeno Dimond, fifteen-year-old citizen of 2011. And it wasn't a TV movie.

This was real, Lucille. I was about to be cruelly murdered, no doubt after suffering unspeakable torture.

And whose fault was it?

A.B.'s, of course. As usual.

❖

A.B. is a monster and a beast. Literally. He's so self-important he actually calls himself the Alpha Beast. He's meaner than Freddy Krueger and trickier than James Bond.

He will do anything to get his way, and he gets away with it because he's invisible. Sort of. Meaning you can see him, you just don't notice him, which is why he's so dangerous. "Who else," he says (with glee, I might add), "has fangs and access to your neck at all times of the day and night?"

Kind of chilling, isn't it? And it's true, LaRue. He can find you, he can get in your house, and he can take you out before you can spell c-a-t. He'll enjoy it too. He'll revel in it. He has neither mercy nor conscience.

I ought to know. Despite his dirty tricks and snarky remarks, I count him among my dearest friends, which just shows you what a forgiving person I am. Besides, he's the only assassin I've ever personally hung with.

Before A.B., it was mostly burglars.

This is because, before the beast destroyed my life on the night of my crew's Big Hit, I was among the most accomplished teenage burglars who ever lived.

I remember confirming with Jace the night before the hit, the little flutter of excitement when I said, "Tomorrow. Seven sharp." We were going in in twenty-two hours.

Just as I clicked my cell phone shut, Mom poked her head in the laundry room, where I was folding clothes. "Forget it, Deb. Tomorrow's a school night."

I played along. "Mom! It's a study date. Jace and I have this big project due at the end of the week."

My sister Haley's voice floated through the open door. "Mom! Mom, my nose is bleeding."

Mom's expression turned from irritated to frightened. I usually saw her as dirty ivory, but lately she'd been getting muddy, kind of grayish. I had no idea why I saw her that way, or why I saw colors around everyone, but I always had. Dad had once said something about "auras," but not enough to make it make sense. Mostly what he'd wanted to convey was that I shouldn't tell too many people I saw them.

I noticed that whenever Haley bled, Mom's gray deepened. That is, whenever she bled badly. The bleeding almost never stopped. Haley was nearly always leaking through her skin or bleeding internally, into her muscles and joints. She was only eighteen and had barely even been able to walk for two years.

"I'm coming." Mom blinked tears and headed for Haley's room. Without a miracle, Haley was going to die soon. I was trying to make one happen for her.

❖

Tonight, Jace and Morgan and I were going to lift Michelle Zunger's diamond studs and whatever else we found—cash, with any luck. All we ever took was cash and stuff like studs and gold chains, things lots of people had that couldn't be identified.

We called this one the Big Hit, but for me, it was going to be a piece of cake. As it happens (she said modestly), I was, at a mere fifteen years of age, a near professional.

At 7:00 sharp, after I'd set the table and left a casserole in the oven for Mom and Dad and Haley, I heard a horn honking. Excellent. Perfect. My crew knew I demanded punctuality.

I gave my dog Curly a good-bye pat, told her I was sorry I couldn't take her along, and ran down the driveway dressed in black jeans and T-shirt, a cap in my backpack. This last was important, because my hair's very distinctive.

"Right on time," I said. "Everything good?"

Jace was sweating. "You really think we can unload those studs?"

"Nervous, huh? You're such a wimp!"

Morgan said nothing, just drove.

We parked in front of the Zunger house and waited for the family to leave. The school play was that night, and Michelle played the lead, so we knew they'd all be going. At 7:15, the four of them came out: Michelle, her sister, and their parents. Coast clear. We'd be counting our loot in ten minutes.

The thing is, most burglaries take only about forty seconds—you could look it up. But this time, we could afford to take a little longer, because we knew they'd be gone awhile, and we knew for a fact there was no alarm on the house—Morgan had cased it on a sleepover.

We did what we always do. Jace and I got out of the car, and Morgan parked around the corner, all three of us with cell phones in hand. We were a well-oiled machine if ever there was one. Jace started walking immediately and hid behind a tree. I slipped like a shadow into the backyard and skinked to the back door. There were lights on in the house, but I didn't worry about it. People think lights keep burglars away, but that means amateurs, which is not us. We'd cased this place outside and in. Morgan had drawn us diagrams and floor plans. I knew exactly what to do.

I reached in my pocket for the picks Jace had lifted from his dad, easing the door open in seconds. I'd done it before, last Sunday night while they were at church. Hadn't gone in, just made sure I could.

Right away, something felt weird. Kind of *alive*. Like maybe this wasn't an empty house after all. And yet we'd seen everyone leave, so it had to be. Maybe they had a pet.

I sneaked up the stairs, headed straight for the parents' room to look for money, fingertoned fifty bucks—good haul!—and then skinked into Michelle's lair. It was all pink and flowered, such a happy room, so unlike the one I shared with Haley, cluttered with bloodstained pressure bandages and medicines that didn't work. It reminded me of the way it used to be at our house. For a moment, everything got all blurry.

When I'd blinked away the tears, I opened Michelle's jewelry box, which was in plain sight right on her dresser, and fingertoned the earrings, which I slipped into my pocket along with the cash. Perfect.

Nothing to do now but skink back downstairs and out the door. But as I crossed the threshold, I tripped over something—something I knew hadn't been there before. A big, ugly orange cat. Oh, yeah, the pet—the live thing I'd sensed when I came in. It produced a completely hideous and utterly deafening yowl.

Me, I fell flat on my face.

I looked up in amazement, just in time to see the thing leap onto the windowsill and jump out the second-story window. My first thought was, Oh no, I hope I haven't killed it—no cat could survive that! My second was, I knew there's a reason I hate cats. Because by that time a person was yowling too, and it wasn't Jace.

Someone else was in the house!

An old lady, by the sound of her. "Is somebody here?" she yelled, and she sounded scared out of her skin. I thought of my grandmother, how awful this would be if it happened to her, how terrified she'd feel. I wanted to go down there and tell the old lady everything was okay, but you know how that would have gone over.

"I'm calling nine-one-one," she hollered. And then there was a lot of commotion, and I heard her talking, her voice coming in little puffs. "I think…(gasp, breathe)…I'm okay, but I think there's someone in my house. Okay, I'm going. I'm not hanging up." And the lights went on in the stairwell.

I was on my feet now, standing in the hall. When the place lit up like City Hall, I jumped back into Michelle's room. But too late—the old lady saw me.

"Omigod!" she yelled at the phone. "Omigod, I saw him. Yes, I'm out now. I'm okay." But I didn't hear the door close.

My cell phone vibrated. "Jace!" I barked into it. "Somebody's here."

"No kidding. An old lady in a wheelchair, with something in her lap."

"With what in her lap? A gun?"

"I…gosh, Reeno, it could be. I'm too far away to tell." His breath sounded a lot like the old lady's. He was as scared as she was, and I was right behind them. "She turned the chair around and she's looking at the house. Watching the stairs like a hawk."

Pretty brave old lady, I thought. I could barrel down and run past her, but not if she had a gun. I'd have to try the window. But first I had to think of my crew. "Jace, listen to me. Get out of there. Go! Now. And don't go past the old lady. Call Morgan and tell her to drive around the block and pick you up at the far corner—not the one where we're supposed to meet her."

"Reeno, no! What about you?"

"I'll go out the window."

The cat had done it—maybe I could. When I got there, I saw how he'd worked it—there was a tree there that a cat could probably reach in a leap. But I knew I couldn't. I was trapped.

I looked again, just to be sure, and I could have sworn that, just for a split second, I saw him hanging upside down by his tail. Like a monkey.

And then I had some kind of weird auditory hallucination. "Tough luck, girl-face," some guy said. I mean some guy's weird, British-sounding voice. Or something in my head.

Definitely not the cat. As soon as I blinked, the hallucination vanished. When I looked down at the ground, the beast was there, staring up at me with big nasty eyes. The light from the house glinted off them, creating an eerie effect that unnerved me more than the sirens that now reached my ears, faint at first, then louder and louder.

Panicked, I tried to find a place to hide, finally deciding on a bathroom hamper. Eewwww! Stinkerama. It smelled kind of like rotten cheese. But you don't get to be a crime queen by being a wuss. I climbed in and covered up with Michelle's dirty underwear, realizing too late that the hamper was really only a canvas bag that slipped onto a metal frame. It was definitely not meant to hold a human.

Fortunately, it did, though—through a few minutes of calming the old lady, a thorough search of the downstairs, and a good gander at the parents' and sister's rooms. It held absolutely perfectly until the precise moment when heavy footsteps crossed into Michelle's room, just across the hall from the bathroom.

And all of a sudden, RRRRRIPPP. A sound like fabric tearing, really loud. And then a thud. Me hitting the floor. And then a soft "oof," which I couldn't contain.

I could picture the cops looking at each other. A female voice said, "Dominick, I think we've found him," and I abandoned hope. How many Dominicks could there be on the Santa Barbara police force?

When he spoke, I knew it was the one I knew. "Put your hands up. Get them in plain sight."

"Wait a minute," I said, "I've got to get right side up first." Once again, I pictured the officers, staring at each other in disbelief, thinking, a girl?

"Officer Dominick, don't shoot, okay? It's just me, Deborah Dimond. I'm not armed, okay?"

"Deborah?" I heard the amazement in his voice, and I felt kind of proud, thinking, How many tenth graders could have pulled this off? And then thinking, Uh…I didn't pull it off. I am seriously busted.

"Deborah, what on God's green Earth are you doing here?" Frank Dominick was the same cop who'd popped me once before. Why do I have all the luck?

I rose from the wrecked hamper like a cobra, thinking I must look pretty scary in my black cap and clothes (though of course I did have my hands up).

But the female officer, far from shaking in her boots, was about to pop her bra, she was laughing so hard. "Hey, Dominick, we got a fashion victim here." To me, she said, "Honey-babe, check out your head."

I was seething over "honey-babe," thinking how embarrassed she'd be if she knew her essence was baby blue, but I turned to the mirror anyway—and suffered the worst humiliation of my entire life. A pair of Michelle's bikini panties had stuck to my baseball cap—pink ones! Oh. My. God.

Dominick wasn't even slightly amused. "Deborah, I am so disappointed I could cry." Big six-foot cop with bags under his eyes and he's talking about crying.

I was the one who ended up actually doing it.

But not right away. I did feel bad for Officer Dominick, and, well, for my parents. If this guy who wouldn't even know me if he hadn't arrested me could be disappointed, that was nothing to the way they were going to feel.

Here's the thing, though—it shouldn't have happened. Just shouldn't have. Wouldn't have if it weren't for that big orange furball (and a visiting grandma, but I couldn't really blame the old lady). This is what went through my mind: Reeno the Crime Queen brought down by a stupid cat! Forced to hide in some substandard hamper with panties on her head. I was so mortified I lost my mind.

I should have been devising a clever way to talk my way out of this. With fifty bucks, a pair of diamond studs, and a set of picks in my pocket, that was going to take some serious focus.

But I was mainly furious at that ugly hairball. All I could say was, "Stupid cat got in my way."

"What cat?" the old lady said from downstairs, and for the first time I saw her sitting in her wheelchair, a great big soda bottle in her hand, full of Coke or something. That must have been what Jace thought was a gun. "We don't have a cat."

"Big ugly orange one," I said. "Didn't you hear him complain?"

I saw the old lady shake her head, looking bewildered.

"Deb," said Dominick, "you are a piece of work, you know that?" And without another word, he handcuffed me and marched me out of there.

Well, due to my parents' position in the community, they were able to make a couple of phone calls and get me home by about midnight, but I might have been happier at Juvie. Mom was capital "M" mad. "Deborah Dimond," she goes, "for God's sake, what is wrong with you? You have everything you want and a family who loves you—why on Earth would you burglarize a house? I swear to God I don't know what to do with a kid who acts like this. First that backpack thing, and then you come home with those horrible tattoos!" I thought I'd never been so humiliated in my life, but that's how much I knew.

"Now this! Don't you think this family already has enough trouble?"

That hurt. We Dimonds had more than enough trouble; I was trying like hell to help, just in a slightly illegal way.

Dad was like Dominick, all disappointed and down in the dumps.

Mom wouldn't stop. "I just can't handle you anymore. I'm going to have to find someone who can."

"Like who?"

"You tell me. We tried therapy and that didn't work. What do you think is next? What should we do with you?"

Dad gave her this look like he knew but wouldn't say, and I knew what he was thinking—that we'd be okay if we could just be normal, if Haley didn't have a mysterious disease no one even knew how to diagnose, much less cure.

If we didn't live day and night with the threat of losing her.

If Mom would agree to let her see some non-Western doctors. If we had enough money to send her to this amazing hospital my dad found on the Internet. (Dad knew a lot about stuff like that—it was part of his job—and he was much more open to things than Mom.) The hospital was in Thailand, and they had specialists in Oriental medicine as well as psychic practitioners and shamans, the very thought of which made Mom start yelling at the rest of us.

Mom was a doctor, and that was why she felt that way. It was probably also why she felt so responsible for Haley's illness.

But it just wasn't her fault.

Our house was so horribly sad, a place where all we did was wake up every morning and hope Haley wouldn't die that day. She had transfusions several times a week, and after all these years was still undergoing diagnostic tests.

She didn't have hemophilia, which affects mostly men, or von Willebrand disease, which affects women. Both of those are caused by the absence of some clotting factor. Haley's disease didn't seem to be, so they couldn't just add the right chemical thing and get her blood to clot.

Just about all Mom's time went to taking care of Haley, and I tried to take up the slack. I did the best I could, and Mom did the best she could. I just wished she'd given me more credit for it. I mean, I did all the laundry and cooking, and with all that blood, you can imagine the laundry alone! But I couldn't do anything right around here any more. I know Mom was frustrated—did I mention she's a pediatrician? She had to give up her practice to take care of Haley, and the worst part was that she couldn't really do anything for her own child! I knew how close to the edge she was.

But this is how it was: All Mom's attention went to Haley; all Mom's frustration landed on me. And she wouldn't even talk to Dad and me about the only thing in the whole world that might help Haley. So I'd made a vow: By hook or crook (mostly crook) I was going to get Haley to that alternative hospital Mom didn't want to hear about. So what if my method was a tiny bit felonious? It paid really well.

"They have places for girls like you, you know."

She meant boarding schools.

I knew all about them. She'd already threatened and shown me brochures and made me look at a website so I could see what they looked like, which was grim. The kids looked like robots. Ken and Barbie robots.

But she did it just to threaten me. I knew perfectly well my dad wouldn't let her send me to a place like that, and most of all wouldn't send me away from Haley. Who knew how long we had with her?

"Meanwhile, you are grounded until doomsday."

That night, when we were in bed, Haley whispered to me. "Deb? Reeno? Don't leave me, okay? Don't let them send you away."

All I could think was, Don't leave *me,* Haley! Don't die on me.

She didn't get this thing till she was twelve. It had come, as so many things do, with puberty. Before that, she'd been my rock, my big sis who took care of me and taught me games and grooming and never let anyone bully me. Oh, and read to me when I was really little—that might have been the best of all.

I am aware that crime queens do not cry, even if they get arrested and grounded till doomsday. But when Haley said that—my poor sister who couldn't even move without leaking out part of her life—this one bawled. I went into the living room, where she couldn't hear me, and all night I sobbed like a sissy, shaking and squirming and getting everything wet.

In the wee hours I finally fell asleep, but I had The Dream, this recurring dream I have that involves bleeding from my tongue. How demented is that? Except that part didn't come from my imagination. That's how Haley's ailment first started—with her tongue bleeding.

When I woke up, eyes still burning, I took this mental vow to give up my life of crime, and I really, really meant it. I was through with all that. I was so, so sorry for what I'd done to my family, and I told everybody I was over it forever.

Mom remained stony-faced.

Dad said, "Now, Patricia, don't be so hard on her," and gave me one of his sad looks. He took me aside later and said why didn't we go somewhere together, just the two of us, to talk about things. Maybe next weekend.

I could hardly believe what I was hearing. My dad and I had never been anywhere together. "I think you need a break from all this. I know how much you love Haley, but it's just too much to ask…"

I threw my arms around him. "Dad, you're the greatest! I mean it. The greatest dad ever."

Mom said, "She's not going anywhere if the Zungers press charges. I swear to God, I'm not even going to get her a lawyer. Let the 'system' handle her. They can send her to kingdom come for all I care."

Like I wasn't even there.

CHAPTER II: THE BELL RINGS

Mom had a positive genius for making me feel bad. All week I was extra good, using a whole lot of bleach on Haley's sheets, sitting with Haley so Mom could have a little time to herself, making sure our dog Curly had plenty of water, even making chicken Caesar salad for dinner.

Everything I did, Mom complained about. I didn't spend enough time with Haley, I overcooked the chicken, I spilled bleach and got a white spot on one of Dad's blue shirts, I didn't arrange the pillows right when I made up my bed.

And there was no escape. I was grounded till doomsday.

Mom even took away my cell phone as part of the punishment. My only time outside—except for school—was walking Curly once a day, but Dad had to go with me, for fear I'd sneak over to Jace's. I didn't have a moment to myself the entire week after the Big Hit.

I was pretty worried about going to Juvenile Court and maybe getting sent to some gnarly reform school, but there were a lot of phone calls and meetings that week, and somehow or other, my parents got the Zungers to drop the charges and chalk it all up to a "misunderstanding." Or so they told me at the time.

Even though I was a perfect model citizen now (except in Mom's eyes), Dad said there was still a lot to talk about and was I still up for a picnic on Saturday? He knew this great place near Ojai, less than an hour away. We could pack a lunch, hike a little, what did I think?

Oh, man, was I up for it! I'd never been to Ojai and never, ever, since Haley got sick, had time alone with my dad.

But I should have known the trip would come to no good. Because the night before, I had The Dream again, only with embellishments. I dreamed I was bleeding from my tongue, as usual. My tongue was bleeding and the blood was falling on paper, and then I picked up the bloody paper and put it in a little bowl and set fire to it. And the smoke from the fire somehow turned into a snake. Out of the snake's mouth came a huge cat, a cat like that big ugly one that tripped me at the Zungers'.

And then the cat somehow grew, turned into a jaguar with spots and everything. And I started to run, knowing it was going to tear me limb from limb. But instead it got small—it shrank before my eyes. And then it lost its spots and suddenly turned into a housecat again, but this time a real pussycat, a normal little ordinary cat, not a big ugly orange one. And I was suddenly huge, like Alice when she ate the mushroom.

But when I woke up, I didn't feel huge. Just really creeped out.

❖

We left Santa Barbara about eleven that Saturday, and on the way, Dad talked about the town we were going to, regaling me with its completely wacko history. The average Californian knows it's a colorful town where they have a film festival, a rock festival, a poetry festival, stuff like that. But my dad—who also is a Unitarian minister—happens to be one of the world's leading experts on New Age Religion, which he teaches at UC Santa Cruz.

According to him, Ojai's got "something about it" that attracts believers in the occult, the psychic, the spiritual, and the downright weird. First there was some offbeat religion called theosophy, an import from England, then this guru guy named Krishnamurti and another called Meher Baba, followed by Buddhists and spiritual healers and people who founded "retreat centers," whatever they may be. Yeah yeah yeah, fascinating.

But despite the semi-dryness of the subject, Dad's a famously riveting lecturer, so I was pretty far into it, not thinking about much except the sound of his voice, and the beauty of the road we were on, seemingly in the middle of nowhere. I was feeling so close to him, I ran my dream by him, thinking since he was so smart and all, he might have something to say about it. He looked at me kind of funny.

"That snake thing…" he said, and then shook his head. "I don't know, kid. Maybe it's about leaving your childhood behind." He looked significantly at my snakes, the gorgeous red and green ones tattooed on my upper arms. "About growing up, you know?"

Leave it to adults to dis your tattoos. I said, "But, Dad, I didn't grow up. I was still me. I just got bigger."

He still had the snakes on his mind. "Deb," he said. "Why snakes?"

"I thought they were pretty." And they make me feel powerful. But I left that part out. I couldn't really have explained it.

I was so focused on bonding, on really having great conversations with Dad, that I didn't notice anything odd until all of a sudden I realized we'd just passed through a gatehouse onto a more manicured stretch of road, an elegant, tree-lined one that didn't lead deeper into the woods.

What lay ahead were stone buildings in a gothic style, ostentatiously decked out with gargoyles and bell towers, and scattered around were kids my age. Lots of them. We were on a campus of some sort. Cold dread settled on me like a giant bird.

Dad pulled off the road, stopped the car, and reached for his cell phone. And I knew immediately what this was. It was a kidnapping.

Life as I knew it was over.

I drew a hot, furious breath. This trip was no happy, daddy-daughter day to "reevaluate and talk things over." And this place was definitely no scenic picnic area.

It was my punishment. Bad Girl School.

Furious, I lunged at Dad, fists flying. "You lied to me," I shouted, "My own father! You betrayed me."

He grabbed my fists, not even fazed. "Deb! Listen to me! There's no other way. We had to make peace with the Zungers."

"What are you saying?"

"They're not pressing charges, they feel sorry for you. If you want to know the truth, they probably feel sorrier for Haley than you, but somehow we talked them down. This is the deal, though—no contact with them or their precious Michelle."

He spat out Michelle's name as if he were a teenager himself, and I felt a burst of warmth for him. No matter what, Dad was still on my side! But he'd still lied to me.

"Why didn't you tell me where we were going?"

"Oh, please. You'd have just gotten in the car and come quietly?"

Okay, I could see his point, but I that didn't mean I had to stop being mad about it. "I didn't get to say good-bye to Haley! And Curly."

"I know." He looked down at his hands on the wheel and I could see he was sorry about that. "But you can come home in a few weeks… for a weekend, maybe."

"Why couldn't I just go to some other school in Santa Barbara?"

"Honey, you're only an hour away. What's the big deal?"

What's the big deal? What was the point even talking to him?

I twisted away and started to open the car door, intending to make a run for it, but someone was standing on the other side, grabbing for the door handle himself.

He was a middle-aged dude in Saturday attire—khakis and polo shirt—and to me, he looked yellow. But other than that, he was white, as in Caucasian. He had the sandy hair, the blue eyes, the all-around doughy look, the arrogance.

"Mr. Dimond?" he said to my dad. "Good trip?"

Dad said, "Deborah's a little upset."

The man leaned into the car. "Hi, Deborah, I'm Hal. The headmaster. Welcome to St. Joan's."

Welcome, you believe that? Like welcome to hell.

I was too furious even to answer.

The man and Dad looked at each other. Dad shrugged.

Hal said, "Okay, let's get your things."

Huh? I didn't have any "things."

Dad surprised me by pulling out my favorite bag—a little yellow one that I usually used when I slept over at a friend's. That was how small it was. He gave it to Hal. "Here you go."

Can you imagine the depth of deception that went into this? He'd actually sneaked around and packed a hell-bag for me. I started to cry.

"It's best," Hal said, "to make the transfer as quickly as possible."

Dad nodded, looking as if he were going to cry too. "Deb, can you look at me? Deb? Okay, I understand. But please know that if we could have done it any other way, we would have."

"You lied to me!" I screamed again, not caring who heard.

He turned back to the headmaster. "Give us a moment."

Silently, Hal stepped back.

Dad said something so mysterious and, I'll admit it, appealing, that I almost forgave him. "Your mom doesn't know about this."

Well, in that case, I thought for a moment, how can it be all bad? But only for a moment.

"I mean, she knows I'm taking you to school, she just doesn't know what this one's like. I do, because one of my students did a paper on it. And it's our only hope, Deb. Listen, babe, I understand things about you that your mother doesn't. The way you dream, for one thing. And that color thing you've got going. What do you think that is?"

"You know what it is?"

"I think they might here. Just keep one thing in mind, will you? Before you close yourself off. The name of this place."

"Huh? St. Joan's—meaning it's Catholic? What's the big deal?"

"Deb, listen to me—this place can help us. And so can you. You're our only hope." I had no idea what he meant, but I saw the tears in his eyes. "Give me a hug?"

I gave him a look like the North Pole. "No way," I said, "in hell. 'Cause that's where I am."

"I'm sorry," he said again. "Your mother and I love you. We all love you." He turned away, shoulders drooping.

You've got a dynamite way of showing it, I thought, but I didn't say it. Instead, I screamed again, and I was amazed at what came out of my mouth: "Daddy, don't leave me!" I grabbed for him, but he pushed me away, saying not another word, not even another "I'm sorry."

I watched him get in the car and turn around, and then I just stood there bawling, tears flowing freely, raw sobs coming out of my chest. I was shaking, I was so scared. And so mad.

When the gate closed behind him, I was left with Hal, the headmaster. More like the warden.

This was so goddamned unfair. I was completely reformed! How come I was being punished for it?

I was humiliated. That and betrayed. And momentarily flummoxed. But I reminded myself that I was still Reeno, and started pulling myself together.

Whatever, I thought. I still rule. I am still one tough cookie. And by the way, I am no longer reformed. That Good Girl thing didn't work out.

They are *not* going to break me.

CHAPTER III: ORIENTATION

I trudged up the steps after Hal, into a building that looked more like my idea of a British prep school, equipped as it was with leaded glass windows, leather furniture, and lots of dark wood, than a convenient cooler for embarrassing offspring. Oddly, there was a certain air of luxury here—not what I'd expected at all.

Hal's office was lined with books, and he had some plants in there. It was nice, with sun pouring in, pictures of his family on the desk, church art on the wall. But I noticed it was church art with a strange twist—it kind of looked contemporary. I was sure the student quarters were going to be a lot more primitive than the headmaster's little palace.

Hal smiled at me. "You like the paintings?" he said. "They were done by a former student. That's St. Joan there, and St. Malachy—you'll like him—and Simon Magus next to St. Francis of Assisi."

I stared at the last two. "They look like they're flying."

"Levitating, yes."

"So this is a Catholic school?"

"We…" Long pause. Way too long. "We have Catholic support. But actually we're nondenominational. Now." He turned businesslike. "We have two units here. You'll be in remedial."

Remedial! I was insulted. "I'm crooked, Hal, not stupid. Believe me, I can keep up."

He smiled. "This isn't about levels of accomplishment, Deborah. Remedial is…well, let's just say St. Joan's wasn't the first choice for our remedial students."

"Oh. It's the prison unit."

He was smiling again, with little eye crinkles. I could almost have liked the guy if he wasn't so damn superior, like he had some big secret that I wasn't in on. "Sometimes you don't choose a school. Sometimes a school chooses you."

What kind of cheesy-cheerful crap was that? Like "you make your own reality" or "there's a reason for everything." I can't stand that kind of bull.

"Your adviser will explain more. Evelina's on her way."

A young Latina bustled in, as gorgeous and exotic as Hal was blond and bland, maybe a little heavier than average by Santa Barbara standards, but that could only be good. She had fabulous, thick curly hair, a round face, and a big smile. And she was a fantastic fuchsia color. I couldn't help it, I liked her.

"Deborah Dimond? I'm Evelina Gonzalez." She pronounced my name DiMOND.

"DImond," I corrected, saying it right. "Reeno Dimond."

She ignored me.

"Let me show you your room. Bring your suitcase, please."

Well, I was right about the kids' quarters lacking the luxury of the headmaster's office. But, that said, it wasn't a bad room. Actually, it was really cool and totally unexpected, furnished with two white beds with really fun sunflower sheets, one a tangled mess, the other one mine, I presumed; also one chest of drawers, white as well; two white desks; and even a couple of polka-dot bean bags. Truth to tell, it was better than my room at home.

Except for a highly disturbing development. On the made-up bed, curled like a rattlesnake and looking just as deadly, lay a big, evil cat. A really familiar-looking cat.

"That's your bed," Evelina said. "The one with the cat."

"I can't sleep there," I retorted. "I hate cats."

"Oh, don't worry. Jag ignores everybody. It's the first time I've ever seen him in here."

She made shooing noises until the cat left, shooting me a glance of disdain on his way out. He had ugly yellow eyes and a too-long tail that stood straight up in the air and curled at the end like a monkey's.

"Your drawers are that one there and the one below it. The top one has your uniforms in it—shorts for gym, long pants for everything else. The other is for your other clothes. Unpack and change, please."

I put my suitcase on the bed and opened it. It contained seven pairs of white cotton panties, four white cotton bras, five pairs of white cotton socks, two pairs of pajamas, and a pair of sandals in a plastic bag. In a little hanging bag that I'd never seen before were a hairbrush, toothbrush, tube of toothpaste, bar of soap, contact lens supplies, and shampoo. That was it in the way of grooming aids.

Just like Dad, I thought. He hadn't packed a razor, tweezers, makeup, any of the stuff I needed just to make it to breakfast.

I said to Evelina, "Is there a little store here? Where I can get some, like, lipstick and mascara?"

"Cosmetics aren't allowed here."

"Oh."

"Neither is money."

"This sucks, you know that? Why don't you just go ahead and call it a prison?"

She said, "I don't think of it that way. You could look at it as a great opportunity."

Opportunity for what? I thought. To turn into a robot?

"You know what?" I said. "That's the whole problem with the adult world. You think we're idiots."

And then, to my humiliation, I started crying again.

Ignoring my complete and utter anguish, Evelina said coolly, "I need you to change, please."

"What if I don't?"

"You get a consequence."

"And that means?"

A storm blew in and threw her books on the disheveled bed. She was slightly heavy and looked okay at first glance, with this cool black bob and a scorpion tattoo on her ankle, visible because she was wearing gym shorts. But there was something strange about her energy, something weirdly hostile, I thought. And she was a muddy mustard color I didn't much care for.

Evelina stood up. "Kara, Deborah," she said. "Your new roommate."

"Reeno," I said.

"Huh?"

"What people call me."

"I beg your pardon," Evelina said. "Reeno." That was just about the last thing I expected to hear. I was actually going to get something I wanted? It had been so long I didn't know how to deal with it.

"Kara, could you take Reeno to the dining room for orientation?"

"Do I have to? I've got to—"

"Yes, you have to," Evelina answered, so perfectly catching Kara's whiny tone I snickered. Kara shot me the evil eye.

At the same time, blinding pain ripped through my head. I grabbed my face in my hands. "Ow!"

"Reeno, what is it?" Evelina sounded frightened.

I pulled myself together as the pain began to subside. "I don't know. I must have moved wrong. Sudden headache, that's all."

Evelina looked from Kara to me, then back to Kara. "That'll be five consequences," she said to my roommate.

"For what? I didn't do anything."

"Really?" She said it that sarcastic way people have. And Evelina didn't strike me as a sarcastic person.

If they were going to fight, fine. "Never mind," I said. "I'm sure I can find the dining room," and I left both of them standing there speechless.

❖

It felt great to be outside and on my own—so great I considered making a run for it. But where was I going to go? I was contemplating that when I ran smack into a tall skinny dude walking ahead of me. He turned around, looking bemused, an expression that quickly changed to something between kindness and appreciation. Like maybe he liked my extremely eccentric appearance. Or felt sorry for me or something, I couldn't quite read him. At any rate, he seemed perfectly nice, even gave me a little smile. And promptly began spewing vile poison at me. "What the hell are you doing out of uniform? You are so pathetic. What a crybaby!"

I was on the verge of tears, and that tipped me over. I felt my cheeks go wet, and the skinny kid turned slightly pale. "Oh shit!" He was clearly horrified, definitely one of those guys disgusted by female tears. "That way," he said, pointing. Then he turned and ran—exactly in the direction he'd pointed.

What the hell to make of any of that?

But there was something even more puzzling. He was a color I call oily olive, a color I'd seen only once before. It was Haley's color.

The boy'd steered me right. The building he indicated housed a giant room with a vaulted ceiling and gothic windows, furnished with heavy wooden tables and chairs like you might find in a monastery. Very nice, actually. Some kids were eating in the far left corner, where the skinny kid was just sitting down.

I was still trying to get my bearings when a lavender girl called my name. My real name: Reeno. Evelina must have called her. I was pleased with that—maybe I had one friend here, even if she was faculty.

"Orientation, right? Come over here." The lavender girl beckoned me to join her and an orangey dude with a truly excellent build, but kind of shy-looking. "I'm Rachel, Level Four. Carlos, meet Reeno, fellow Level One." Rachel had green eyes and long wavy brown hair, parted on the side and a little messy. But nothing else about her was messy. She was so completely 100 percent Good Girl material. I couldn't imagine how she'd come to be at Bad Girl School. Maybe she was a perfect example of how brainwashing works. A major prissy lips, not remotely my type, but Carlos was definitely my type—kind of rough-and-tumble, with a couple of macho tattoos, very spiky and tribal.

While I was assessing my tablemates, someone brought us lunch: one hot dog, one small cup of chili. No mustard, ketchup, or other condiments. Gingerly, we picked at the meager fare while Rachel filled us in on the set-up.

"There are six levels of progress in the remedial unit. You are Level Ones. As such, you will operate under a stringent set of rules and you will receive consequences for breaking them."

I was dying to know what a consequence was, but I knew enough to keep my mouth shut.

"You will reach the next level by earning points. A consequence removes five points."

Oh.

"You may receive mail only from parents and approved family members. Your incoming mail will be monitored, and anything inappropriate will be withheld. You will receive e-mail in the form of printouts from your adviser. All letters you write to friends or family will be read first by us, and then sent to your parents, who may then withhold any they wish."

As if that didn't suck enough, she started in on the "no's." No makeup and no money was the least of it. It went like this: No phone calls, period; even from parents.

In fact, no phones—which meant no texting.

No visitors.

No weekends at home.
No Internet access.
No care packages.
No food or beverages, except what you got in the dining room.
No gifts, except on birthdays and Christmas.
No sharp objects.
No mirrors!
No tweezers, nail files, or nail clippers.
No matches.
No music.
No television.
No mustard.
No ketchup.
No salsa.
No salt.
No pepper.

Do I need to mention no drugs, cigarettes, alcohol, guns, gum, or explosive devices?

I didn't think so.

But I could have lotion. And one stuffed animal. Both of which Dad had forgotten.

CHAPTER IV: HOMEROOM

I was totally freaked. The only thing I had left were my snakes. Well, those and my hair, which is a total disaster, according to Chief Patricia Dimond of the Fashion Police (aka my mom), but which actually rocks. She's always trying to get me to cut it, have it straightened, thin it, preppy-chick-it. Forget that. Nobody has hair like mine.

I wear it kind of like a lion's mane, and it's a totally fabulous color. My dad calls it pink, but it's actually raspberry, the exact color of the ice cream. My mother ranted for two hours when she saw it, but it's been this way for months. She would have grounded me, but she got distracted. That was the day Haley cut her hand and hemorrhaged.

After the initial rant, Mom just kind of forgot my hair, so I figured it was safe to get the snakes. Now that I did get grounded for, and cried over and yelled at too, but it blew over like I knew it would. These days Mom had bigger things on her mind than me. So for the moment I had my snakes, each winding sinuously around one of my upper arms.

And I had my green nail polish, but that would grow out. At least emery boards were allowed. I could request some through Evelina, I learned, and my parents could send them. They couldn't send care packages, but they could send a last-minute cache of things they'd forgotten. And I needed stuff. Where was my lotion? And my one stuffed animal? I felt very forlorn.

But just the same, I was through with crying. Instead, I was going to fight.

You don't even know how to fight.

I heard it as clearly as if Rachel had spoken. But it was a man's voice, an older man's, a smug kind of voice with maybe a slight British accent.

Only it couldn't be.

One thing, the speaker would have had to read my mind to know what I was thinking. Another, there wasn't a speaker. We were in the hall at the time, the three of us, on our way to Evaluation, whatever that was. Just us and that fat, ugly cat lying across the doorway in front of us, sprawled out like Jabba the Hutt.

I don't notice you getting any modeling contracts, the voice said, just as Rachel shooed the cat. It was the same voice I'd hallucinated in Santa Barbara, exactly the same! But it couldn't be, right?

"Jag. Out of the way."

Must be lack of sleep—The Dream had awakened me at four o'clock and I'd never dozed off again.

Evaluation meant tests, it developed.

And after the tests, I had my schedule: English, biology, gym, and my two electives, second-year Spanish and Latin American history, which went nicely together. Plus, I figured Carlos, who had a slight accent, would pick those two as well. So far he was the only person on campus I liked, if you didn't count Evelina.

He walked me back to the dorm. Woo-hoo, I was scoring! "So," I asked, "is it bad form to ask what you're in for?"

"I don't know, I just got here. But I don't care who the hell knows. The calico's unbagged anyhow. I'm here because my parents don't want me at home. They trumped up something and got me in on a technicality."

I was kind of amused. "You were framed? Don't they all say that?"

"Uh-uh, I wasn't framed. I did exactly did what they thought I did. But St. Joan's wouldn't have thought it was grounds for admission. They could care less."

I was mystified. "What did you do?"

"Took a guy to the homecoming dance."

Oops! Not scoring after all. But I had to laugh. He was so matter-of-fact about it.

"It's not funny. Ted and I can't see each other till I get to Level Five."

"Forget about Ted. You can be my girlfriend."

He stopped and stared at me. "Hey. Nobody in Bakersfield talks like that."

"This ain't Kansas, Toto."

"All right, Miss Thing!" He paused, like he'd surprised himself. "Hey! I've been waiting my whole life to say that to somebody." He raised a hand for a high five and just like that, I had my first friend.

"I had a feeling about you," he said, "the minute I saw you."

"Yeah, well, I had a feeling about you—only it wasn't the same feeling."

He laughed, but only to be polite. He had something on his mind. "That's not what I mean. I just feel like…"

"What?"

"I don't know. Like we have something to do together."

"You mean like…a science project?"

"Go on, laugh. It's weird."

"You get these feelings a lot? I'm pretty sure they've got a campus shrink."

"I'll tell you what else. Somebody in that dining room was thinking about you."

"I didn't even know anyone in there!"

"Yes, you did. Tall dude? You know, that preppy-looking type with the clothes that always look ironed even when they're wrinkled? Hair like a Kennedy?"

"Oh, him! Probably thinking up murder methods. He hates me."

"I don't think so."

"Something funny about that guy."

"Yeah. Like he's crazy. And mean."

"Uh-uh. He's sad. Just really sad. Like you."

I stared at him. "It shows, huh? Want to grab something to drink and talk about it?"

"Where? The dining hall's only open for meals, right?"

"My room. The lady's choice: Red Bull, Vitaminwater, some kind of peach tea thing…"

"You've got Red Bull?"

"And some delicious bottled coffees."

Oh, man! Not only a friend, but one with contraband.

So we drank forbidden elixir and showed each other our tats and poured out our sad stories, his about being a gay kid in a working-class family, mine about Haley. And stealing, of course.

❖

I hated the idea of going back to my room, but finally there really wasn't any choice. I was going to have to face the bitch with the evil stare, the one who'd hated me on sight. With luck, she'd be out torturing puppies or something.

But no, my luck, she was there, sitting on the floor with another girl, wearing a black leather skirt and fishnets, an odd choice for a Saturday afternoon. The other girl, looking equally eccentric in desert fatigues, was the color of coffee, no cream—so far the only black kid I'd seen—but to me she was eggplant. She looked good with Kara's muddy mustard.

Kara had her legs drawn up under her so as not to show panties, and the other girl was cross-legged. Midway between them lay a deck of cards, but they didn't appear to be playing a game. Their eyes were closed.

I watched from the door a moment, trying to figure out what was going on, and saw Kara peek. "Is it working?" she murmured, and then, spying me out of the corner of her eye, "Eeeeeeeee!"

The black girl opened her eyes. And the weirdest thing happened—the cards flew all over the place. I mean it. Literally flew. Like someone had picked up the deck and flung it.

I stepped into the room, expecting to see a window open. "Hey, is there a windstorm in here?"

Kara said, "What the frick did you just do?" and with that I went over the edge.

"Listen, Headache Eyes, I think we missed a few beats. Could we go back to the beginning? 'Hi, Kara, nice to meet you.' 'Hi, Reeno, welcome to St. Joan's. Anything I can do to make you miserable?' 'Nice of you to offer, Kara, but that won't be necessary today. *I just got abandoned by my family and dropped off at St. Psycho's School for Losers. Everything's just craptastic, thanks!*"

I screamed that last part so loud someone started running down the hall, no doubt to check on the murder-in-progress. Slightly ashamed of myself, I went out to apologize, nearly running smack into an old lady about half my size, Mexican-looking, wrinkled as a prune, and hair in a bun.

"Everytheeng okay?" she said, surprisingly unruffled at coming face-to-face with Psycho Girl.

"Sorry. I've just had kind of a bad day."

"Okay." She gave me a big smile and turned away, like this kind of thing happened all the time. We didn't really talk, but something about her just seemed nice. I couldn't put my finger on it, but I knew she had my back, I just knew it somehow. I wanted to stop her, do a more flowery apology, but she was already halfway down the hall.

I turned back to Kara and the black girl. "I think I scared that lady."

"Nothin' fazes Abuela. She's our housemother," the stranger said, "Used to way worse stuff. Usually before breakfast." She got up and offered to shake hands. "I'm Sonya, by the way. Tell you what—why don't I take Kara to my room, give you a little space?"

Kara got up too and almost looked at me. Not quite—she kind of focused a little past my left ear—but I could tell she was addressing me because she too, stuck out her hand. "Peace?" she said, and we shook, me wondering what would happen if our eyes actually met.

Okay then: alone at last. I needed a nap the worst kind of way, but who could sleep? My brain felt like a pretzel.

I just lay there for a while, crazy twisting around psycho, sad twining with miserable.

Already I was missing Dad and Mom and Haley. Well, maybe Mom not so much, but Dad and Haley a lot. I fought off tears, thinking about it. Every day with Haley meant so much more than a day with anyone else.

Because there probably wouldn't be that many.

So I needed to get out of there as soon as possible. I saw it as clearly as if I'd read it in Wikipedia: What I wanted was to get back home, and if I had to play their stupid game to do it, I was going to. Level One through Level Six, what could be so hard?

Okay, then, that was that. I was doing it. Instant Suck-up Girl.

What would it cost me to do what they wanted? As long as I had my snakes—and they couldn't take those away—I knew who I was. Right now I had nothing else to do but earn points and avoid consequences. Why not do it?

My dad used to really irritate me by saying, "When the going gets tough, the tough get going." An old marine thing, I think. Major league annoying. But the first week of Bad Girl School, I said it over and over to myself, like a mantra.

Where I come from, I am famous for getting going if I totally want something. Like the time when I was ten and Mom offered me five dollars to clean up my room. I hadn't touched it in a month and I had it spic and span in an hour. I filled up four garbage bags with junk and had those babies ready for pickup in about twenty minutes. After that, it was just a matter of putting on my iPod and scurrying.

Well, I was going to get going now, and put my mind to it and whatever other clichés you want to haul out. I also had a saying of my own—or mostly my own. I borrowed it from my cousin Howard, a truly disgusting parent-pleaser: all As; stratospheric SATs; citizenship awards; the whole thing. Like you could puke.

I pretty much hated him until one day my dad asked him how he managed to do so well at everything he touched. And Howard said, "You mean school? Easy. I just figured out what those clowns wanted and I gave it to them."

That was my new motto. Figure out what the clowns want and give it to them. Brothers and sisters, I am here to testify that at that precious moment in the sight of the powers that be, I was born again—as Reeno Dimond, double agent: by day a mild-mannered model student at St. Psycho's; by night a freewheeling woman of the world, an outlaw goddess who made her own rules and lived by them. They couldn't control my dreams, right?

Meanwhile, I had to get points. All you had to do to get points was the usual suck-up stuff—make your bed, keep your mouth shut, eat everything on your plate, go to class, make good grades, keep your journal, write your parents, and act like a robot.

It only took a hundred points to get to Level Two, which seemed like practically nothing. Of course, that was because it *was* practically nothing. The sole difference between Level One and Level Two was access to condiments. That was it; the whole deal. But it was the first step on the way to freedom.

I could make a hundred points, easy. I'd already gotten ten in Evaluation—they gave us those just for going through it. Do that nine more times and I was eating hot dogs with mustard.

From there, it ought to be a piece of cake to move up. At Level

Three, your parents could call you, and I was pretty sure that, given my special circumstances, I could talk the clowns into letting me talk to Haley as well.

At Level Four, your parents could take you off-campus—Dad had lied when he said I could come home when I wanted. Or maybe he'd just implied it. Who cared? I could get to Level Four in about three weeks, I figured. And then I could see Haley!

On that happy note, I finally did fall asleep. Nothing like getting thrown into prison and undergoing a complete attitude transplant to wear you out. I slept away the afternoon, through dinner, and into the night, but all the same, the day held one more horror, and when I say horror, I do not exaggerate. This was a big, hairy one, and I don't mean that awful cat. When Kara came home, none too quietly, I opened my eyes only to behold four ginormous black spiders—like the size of my hand—hanging on the ceiling; and not in webs, either. Just lurking there upside down. Now if there's anything I hate worse than cats, it's spiders.

So the tough cookie screamed, prompting Kara to shrug. "What's the big deal? They're here every night."

That made me feel so much better.

I couldn't sleep for hours, contemplating what would happen if they came crawling down the walls. What if they slunk down and decided to skulk onto my sunflower duvet? And then walk on me, with their thirty-two hairy legs, and munch me with their eight hideous mandibles?

That was so scary I cried myself to sleep.

I dreamed of my parents, only they didn't look like themselves. They were young. Mom wasn't so thin and worried-looking, and her color was good, meaning she was ivory, not dirty ivory. Dad had more hair and less heft, but, oddly enough, his color wasn't as strong. Dad is bright, robust pink. Not very masculine, you might think, but you would be wrong. He practically glows. Not so much in my dream, though. He was lighter, almost pearl-pink. Calmer-seeming, maybe.

They were young and they were on a deck, having cocktails and talking, though I couldn't hear what they were saying. Then Dad got up, knelt in front of Mom, as if he were about to propose, and then the whole picture cracked into tiny pieces, like a jigsaw.

The pieces rearranged themselves and this time they were on the same deck, but their drinks had spilled and flowerpots had turned over, as if a storm had blown through. Mom was still sitting in the same chair, but she was crying and crying and Dad was still on his knees, trying to comfort her, it looked like. But she was brokenhearted and couldn't stop.

The scene changed—you know how that happens in dreams?—and I was looking at a movie. Old-time scary movie music came up as the screen announced in huge Gothic letters, THE CURSE OF THE JONESES. That was the name of the movie! And guess what—Jones is my mother's middle name. The movie began.

Suddenly I was looking at my grandparents, only not younger, pretty much as I've always known them, in a church with a little girl. There was a casket at the front of the church and now there was solemn church music. Then a minister stepped up and began intoning about a young boy who would never see adulthood, who suffered so horribly... and even in my sleep, my stomach clenched. This was what we all feared so much. For Haley.

Then there were other scenes—other parents, other dead children, first in 1940s outfits I recognized from old movies—those sexy long skirts and rolled-back hairdos—and after that, clothes from other periods. The reel speeded up, and the clothes kept going further and further back in history, and I began yelling in outrage, yelling for the movie to stop. But it didn't stop. Instead, it flipped through a slide show of children, beginning with me! Then the little girl with my grandparents, who I realized must have been my mother, and I knew the boy in the casket had to be her brother, who had died when she was still little. Then other kids, once again in outfits that kept going back in time.

And then the scene switched to a two year-old Chinese girl, baby Haley, clearly adopted, and terrified, yelling for Mom.

Blood dripped from her poor little baby tongue.

I woke up screaming. I didn't know if it was from the dream or because I was in bed with something horrible, something my hand was resting on. Something fuzzy and hairy, from the outer reaches of hell. The world's biggest spider leg. Omigod, the worst had happened!

I screamed again. And again and again. I couldn't stop screaming. But in about two seconds, Abuela was there, patting me, soothing me in Spanish. Telling me "there, there" or something like that, calling me *chica* and *niña*.

She hugged me, all soft and...sweet. Nice. Like my mom, back in the days when she could remember I was there. That could have made me sad, but instead, I felt better. And I noticed something. That feeling I'd had the afternoon before, that this woman was someone I could trust, someone with a great heart, was somehow connected to her color. She radiated pure white. I'd never seen anyone else who did.

Abuela rattled on some more, partly in English, partly in Spanish, and finally I woke up enough to realize that she was asking what was wrong. I tried to explain about the huge spider leg, but that just made her laugh in a way that actually managed to be reassuring. I didn't catch everything, I guess I was still too out of it to penetrate her accent, but the words *gato* and *Jag* were all too clear, and so was this: "He must have been sleeping with you."

Kara said, "Ha! That cat doesn't sleep with anybody."

So what was worse? Carnivorous spiders or a killer cat?

Abuela got me out of bed and into the hall, where she had a chair set up so she could watch the whole floor, and a lamp for her embroidery, which she kept in one of those big Mexican shopping bags. She hugged me and patted me a little bit more, and it was so nice I thought it was almost worth it to have a nightmare. And then she asked if I was okay to go back to bed and sent me to the bathroom to wash my face.

And guess what was in the little round sink? A big, ugly, orange monster who'd somehow squeezed his corpulent form into it, and whose tail was flicking ominously on the counter.

Well, enough already. This was night. At night, I was the real Reeno, the one who was master of her fate. "Scat, Jag," I said, trying to sound bored. But my heart was pounding. What if he jumped me?

Instead he stood up in the sink, stretched, descended delicately to the floor, and ambled elegantly out, his unhandsome tail three feet up in the air and curling like a question mark. As he rounded the corner, he said, "As you wish, girl-thing."

I mean, he didn't say it, he couldn't have. It was that voice again, the one I heard when I was feeling crazy. But it sure sounded like he said it.

CHAPTER V: STUDY HALL

I figured I could make about eighteen points a day, just by going to class and doing my homework and stuff. No biggie—Ketchup City in about a week and a half.

Sure enough, I had four points before breakfast my second day. All you really had to do was show up and go through the motions.

And a funny thing—it turned out I kind of liked the classes. I had history and Spanish with Carlos, which was great, and Kara was also in Spanish, which was tolerable, and two kids I sort of knew were in my English class—Kara's friend Sonya and the weird preppy guy, who I now knew as Cooper Allingham. Sonya was okay. She was someone who gave people little shout-outs in class, very supportive. Cooper, on the other hand, was plain mean.

"I was right the first time," I told Carlos. "It's like he zeros in on the most vulnerable millimeter of your psyche and sinks the knife exactly...there. Bull's-eye every time."

"Uh-huh. More?"

"There's this blond chick, Julia. I can't warm up to her, either—mall rat material, very shiny—but everything he says to her somehow manages to disparage her tiny brain."

"You're not doing so bad yourself."

"Well, I wouldn't say that to *her*. I'm not even sure she's dumb—but she thinks she is, people have been telling her that all her life. You can tell that from the way she reacts. And Sonya! He can't speak to her without calling her fat. Major, major assweed."

"All righty, then, the main event. What about you?"

"Me? Nothing. He never talks to me."

Except the time he asked me if I felt guilty about being the healthy one in my family. That hurt so bad I couldn't even repeat it. Plus, it begged the question of how he knew about Haley. Was he mean enough to steal people's files just to insult them? Had he somehow hacked into some secret student database? Did he know someone I knew? It just wasn't something I preferred to spend my time thinking about. I changed the subject.

"You know Rachel? That girl from our orientation?"

"Oh, yeah. Good Citizen Barbie."

"And a Level Four, as she never fails to tell you in the first thirty seconds of any conversation. She filled me in on my roommate. Know what? She's been here six months and she's still a Level One."

Carlos whistled. "What the hell's up with that?"

"I don't know. World's biggest loser? Off the top of my head."

"Wonder what that Cooper guy would do with that one."

"Let's hope they don't know each other."

"Do you find him attractive at all?"

"Eeeeeeew."

He gave me a sidewise squint. "Methinks the lady doth protest too much."

But it wasn't that. It was that creepy color he was—like Haley. I couldn't shake the thought that maybe he was dying too.

❖

I was in the library, working on this essay for English when Jabba the Cat turned up again. He jumped up on the table and settled himself like the King of Abyssinia. Maybe there was a reason that country—if it even is one—came to mind. I think an Abyssinian cat's one of those fancy breeds, and, trust me, Jag was anything but that. But he had an aristocratic look to him, one of those triangular heads like Siamese cats have. He really wouldn't have looked so bad except that he had ears like a bat—great big funnel-looking things that he could turn around on his head like radar—and a nose almost as big as a human's.

He was about the size of an ocelot. I mean *huge*. If he got up on your chest and purred, like normal cats do, you probably couldn't breathe. He had a muscular body, but not thin, definitely not wiry, and he had one of those belly pouches like tigers have. I read somewhere

that that's where cats carry their fat. Jag had a pretty awesome supply
of it. He could probably live off his pouch for a month. Yeah, I may
have called him fat before, but he wasn't really. He was just a great big
hulking monster.

And he wasn't exactly orange, either, although I may have called
him that as well. Well, he sort of was, but he was really more a peachy
kind of color. Sandy, you might say, but with a lot more red in it.
Strawberry-blond? On a person maybe, but this was a cat. He had faint
stripes on him, in some kind of broken-up tabby pattern.

His eyes, except for a weird little blue halo around the irises,
pretty much matched his fur. They were kind of gold, that color that's
technically known as "amber" but isn't anything like real amber,
because cats' eyes have a scary sheen to them.

Everything about Jag was scary.

Especially his feet. They just did not compute on a housecat. They
were about twice the size of Curly's—maybe more like a boxer's paws,
except with these machete-like claws on them.

And I've already told you about his tail.

That was the creature that was now pretending to sleep on the
table while I was trying to write my essay. Having him there was
working my nerves. He had his great big evil eyes closed, but I figured
he was laying a trap of some kind—maybe getting ready to tear my
face off. I intended to get up and move quietly to another table, but for
some reason I sketched him first, all curled up like a little kitten. "Cat
Position One," I called the sketch, "Fur Grenade."

I was just finishing up when he opened his eyes.

I thought, "Close your ugly eyes, Furface. You looked a lot better
before."

His eyes snapped shut.

That went so well I turned back to my essay. But I'd only written
a couple of words when I felt something grab my wrist. Before I could
even register what had happened, my hand streaked down the paper,
still holding my pen. Jag's tail was wrapped around my wrist. That
voice, that kind of know-it-all, seen-it-all, slightly British one, said,
"Better furred than freckled, Novice."

I bit my lip to keep from screaming—the last thing I needed was
another consequence. I tried to pull away, but that scary tail gripped
me like a pair of kitty handcuffs. Two more strokes quickly joined

the diagonal line my imprisoned hand had made with the first assault. Leaving a giant "A" scrawled on the page.

The thing finally let go.

Freaked didn't begin to describe. I was, like, in another world, shaking and sweating and scared as hell.

But what was I going to do—call for help? Say a talking cat had grabbed me with his tail?

"Your sister's adopted, isn't she?"

"Duuuh! She's Chinese." Damn! I thought, Why did I say that? I mean, think it? I will not be drawn into a telepathic chat with a kitty-cat.

A completely different voice, a head-of-state type thing, suddenly said, "You will not call the Alpha Beast cute names!"

With an effort, I kept myself once more from having a screaming fit—this was getting old. "Hey, Jag," I stammered. "Chill, okay? Use that other voice again."

"Certainly, my dear," the Jag voice said. And then a growly one inquired, *"Parlez-vous francais?"* and then a young but very cultured English one, kind of like Hugh Grant, said, "Pardon me, do I unnerve you?"

I'll admit it—I was kind of fascinated. "What's your real voice?" I asked.

And the thing did a perfect puddytat imitation. "Meow."

Every head in the room turned. There's a strict rule against talking in the library. But someone said, "Hey. Jag spoke. He never talks."

And there it was—independent evidence that the cat was talking to me. Somebody else had heard him meow.

"Do that again," I said silently.

"Meow," said Jag, and rubbed up against me.

The librarian whispered, "Look. He likes you."

"Did you hear him meow?"

"Sure. Didn't you?"

"Twice, I mean."

"Yep. A first—and then a second—all in the same five seconds. We all thought he was mute."

"Oh."

"Well, girlet," the Beast said blandly, "have I finally managed to convince you?"

Okay, I was convinced. For whatever reason, he could talk to me—and weirder still, I could answer.

"Excellent," he said. "I'm delighted to have that out of the way."

"Quit reading my mind. It's rude."

"As it happens, I'm not reading your mind. Surely you're aware of the hypnotist's claim that you won't do anything you wouldn't ordinarily do while you're in a trance? This form of telepathy is like that. I can't get into your mind unless you want me to. I can only hear what you're sending me. In short—we're simpatico, embryo."

"We are not simpatico—you're some kind of monster!"

He preened a little. "True. True. I am a monster. But if you're talking to me, you're in no danger. I can only talk with one human at a time—my assistant—and, more's the pity, you appear to be in line for the job. My handmaiden of the moment is very seldom on my hit list."

Hit list. Here was a pussycat talking about a hit list. All right, I was willing to concede that this was no ordinary pussycat, but the question remained: What was it?

"I told you," Jag said. "I am the Alpha Beast."

"You want to expand on that?"

"I am a Planet Guardian," he said grandly.

I was utterly in the dark. "Well, that's a lot of help."

"Permit me to go back a step or two. You've heard of the Gaia theory?"

He had me there. "Uh, I think I saw a special on it once—"

"No doubt. In a word, it holds that the Earth is a system of interrelated parts. Humans and plants and animals—even canines—are all part of that system. And Gaia must have a network of protection, the same as God does. That is, if you believe in God."

I nodded, just to show I was following.

"Angels are Heavenly Guardians. And cats are Planet Guardians. All cats. The Alpha Beast is the Supreme Commander of the Feline Guard." I was completely speechless. "Every cat in the world is under my command. The Egyptians knew about us, of course, but they got it slightly wrong. They thought we were gods."

I think I may have snorted.

"You may also have heard us called witches' familiars."

Now that sounded more like it.

"Witches are part of the protection system too—rather like superheroes, but not nearly so advanced. We work closely with them, and indeed some of them are guardians. Planet Guardians exist in many species. But the only beings who have yet developed unusual powers are feline—the Alpha Beasts down through the ages."

"Do tell," I remarked, but that animal simply could not recognize sarcasm. He was on some kind of kitty roll.

"There is only one Alpha Beast on any continent at any given time, and it's a very long time. In fact, its existence gave rise to the primitive notion that a cat has nine lives. The Alpha Beast has not nine, but 999,999 lives, of which he uses 999 per year. He needs every single one and does not expend them carelessly."

"You're telling me you're immortal?"

He rose to a sitting position—*Cat Position Two*, I thought, *Egyptian Temple Cat.* "Not exactly. But I'm not exactly mortal, either."

"Hoo boy." He was seriously unbalanced. "So what does His Kittyship find to do for a thousand and one years?"

"I really thought you'd never ask. But since you did—the Alpha Beast is the avenger of the Guard, the executioner, and the dispenser of punishment, but also the first line of defense in times of danger—he is a ninja for Gaia, so to speak. When the planet is threatened, he is often expected to carry out certain special missions."

"Using your 'unusual powers,' I suppose. What powers, exactly, might we be talking about?"

"Well, we're talking, aren't we?" he said, "I'd call that a trifle unusual."

"So what else?"

He grabbed my wrist with his tail. "Then there's this one." Startled, I stared at my trapped hand. "And I command troops. Every cat, whether house or wild, tiger or kitten, must obey the Universal Mandate, which means he must relay any intelligence that threatens Gaia (AKA the planet) or the least of the planet's interconnected parts, to the Alpha Beast. AKA *moi.*

"We are able to field this network because no one notices so 'insignificant' a beast as a cat. Perhaps you know the expression, 'fly on the wall'? It may surprise you to learn that the original was 'cat on the pillow,' but I myself personally quashed that one. It was far too close to the truth, which is that we are welcome anywhere, from the most squalid hut to the most magnificent palace."

"For the simple reason that you're so adorable." My voice dripped sarcasm.

"Exactamento, girl-flesh. We are literally everywhere. And when one of my troops sends intelligence that requires it, it is my duty to formulate a plan, issue orders, and act upon it."

"Oh, right, Bond. I suppose you have a license to kill."

He groomed the fur on his neck. "Actually, it's more of a mandate. And you must admit I am uniquely equipped for it. Think about it. A cat is the most efficiently designed killing machine on the face of the Earth. Have you ever watched one of us hunt? We stalk; we pounce; we claw, we bite, we disembowel, we do not rest until our prey is brought down. And we enjoy every second of it. You know perfectly well that if a cat were a person, humans would call him a monster."

My blood ran slightly cold.

"The Alpha Beast is actually a kind of super-monster, as ruthless as any other highly trained commando, yet equipped with unusual tricks and talents. I've only mentioned a few of them."

I was really tired of his bragging. "Excuse me, but didn't you say something about an assistant? If you're so all-powerful, why would you need one?"

For the first time, he sounded regretful. "Alas, the cat has not been born who can open locked doors. And alas again, I can talk to only one human at a time. Sometimes I need a pair of hands. And a mouthpiece." He stood and stretched, giving me a much-needed break. This was starting to get ugly. I had enough trouble without playing "handmaiden" to a monster.

When he had settled down in his Jabba the Hutt position, he said, "And there's another 'alas' out there somewhere. Alas for me, the current mission is a job for two—you and me; it might as well be written. Why do you think I brought you here?'

And then I got it. Finally. I remembered how he'd grabbed my hand with his tail and knew I'd seen something like it before—seen him hanging upside down like a monkey. Sure I knew he looked like that cat, but it hadn't yet sunk in that they really were the same. I mean, it was too crazy to handle, right? How would he get from Santa Barbara to Ojai? So I'd just smashed it down. It hadn't dawned that he'd actually tripped me on purpose.

"You were at Michelle Zunger's that night!" I shouted (ever so silently). "You're the one who screwed up the Big Hit."

"Well, aren't you a quick little study?"

I was blown away. This animal had ruined my life. He was the next thing to the devil, and now he was telling me he was some kind of commando for truth and justice?

"You are psychotic!"

"Oh, come on, Human. It's not like there's nothing in it for you. But something odd's going on here. You haven't even asked, 'why me?'"

"All right," I said, sighing heavily. "Why me?"

"Tell me something. Why do you have those snakes tattooed on your arms?"

I certainly wasn't going to tell him the truth. "You know everything," I said. "You tell me."

"Because they are the mark of the Vision Serpent."

I gasped. On the one hand, it was gibberish, but on the other, I had had a vision—my dream the night before Dad brought me here—that did involve a snake.

"The Mayans," he said, "spilled blood onto paper to invoke the serpent. The serpent showed you a jaguar, did it not?" Without waiting for an answer, he continued. "The jaguar is the classic shamanic companion, the witch's spirit guide, so to speak."

This was way out of control. The jaguar wasn't the only cat in the dream. The other one looked a lot like someone I knew.

His ear twitched and it was almost like a wink. For a moment he reminded me of some debonair con man. "I can help you get what you want."

"Well, doesn't that just suck for you. Because I'm stuck in a place where I'm not even allowed to have anything." I paused. "And I don't want anything, anyhow."

"Oh, yes, you do." He let it hang in the air.

Oh, yes, I did. There was something I wanted so bad it hurt. I knew if I spoke, it was going to start the waterworks, and I was not going to cry in front of this furball.

"You want your sister to get well."

My eyes were swimming. I didn't know if I could hold it together.

When he spoke, his voice was much softer, actually containing a hint of a quality remotely resembling gentleness. But only remotely.

"I can help you with that," he said.

I didn't believe him. I knew he couldn't help me. Nobody could. Who was I kidding? I was probably hallucinating the whole thing anyhow. I didn't trust myself to say a word. I mean, to think one.

"There's just one thing," the beast said.

Okay, that I could deal with. It was what I'd been expecting, the thing that reinforced my faith in the universe as I knew it. "Right, con-cat. Here comes the catch. The part where I become your little servant girl."

"You needn't get so huffy. It's only for one assignment."

"What kind of assignment?"

"Oh, the usual kind. Save-the-world sort of thing. Shouldn't be much to it if we work it right."

Well! Some bait I could resist—did he think I was six? That I was going to look at him adoringly and say, "Really, Mr. Kitty? Save the world? Me?" Uh-uh. I wasn't going there. Exasperated, I blurted, "Oh, please. You're out of your fuzzy little mind."

"I'll take that as an affirmative."

"Hold it, here—"

"You are now my apprentice and my handmaiden. I generally call my students novices."

"That's what they call nuns."

"Oh, really, child. Feel free to conduct your personal life as you see fit. A novice is simply someone new to a discipline."

I couldn't resist mocking him. "A novice is simply someone…"

"Very well." He turned and glided haughtily away, curling that demonic tail like a lasso.

And leaving me wondering: *What the hell was that?*

I was so deep in thought I guess I was in a kind of trance, because I absolutely didn't hear anyone coming, I just heard, "Watch it, Cotton Candy!" before I collided with Cooper Allingham on his way to the library.

"Sorry!" I blurted, looking up at him in apology, in fact really looking at him for the first time. He had that kind of beautiful skin that tans very gently and still looks slightly pink. I hadn't seen that before—all I saw was that awful oily olive. And his hair was brown, but fine and shiny, almost like fur, hair that was so well nourished it practically glowed. He looked like a kid who ate nothing but vegetables and drank about a gallon of water a day. Not sick at all. Certainly not dying.

His eyes were a kind of goldy green, and I was looking right into them. They were slightly amused, and they were soft, not even slightly angry or arrogant, completely belying what came out of his mouth: "The hell you're sorry, Candilocks. You were dying to talk to me."

Which was true in a way—I was both repelled and fascinated by the way he reminded me of Haley. But he couldn't possibly know that. "You arrogant assweed," I retorted wittily. "You know what you just did? Turned an apology into an insult. I swear to God you're the rudest individual I've ever met in my life."

"I know! I mean, I'm sorry, I just...well, I could tell you wanted to talk and..."

"You could *what*? I don't want to talk. I want to leave the building, but I can't because you're standing in my way. And why are you calling me names, by the way? Because it's in your genes to be an asshole? It's like, congenital?"

I was furious. I must have been shooting lightning bolts out of my eyes. But out of his came...tears!

Huh? I'd made the campus douchebag cry?

He was nodding, it seemed, as if actually answering the question, about to say, yeah, it really was genetic, and then, somehow, his chin jerked in mid-nod, like he'd suddenly changed his mind. "The thing about your hair—it was a compliment, you know? I just never thought the Chosen One would have a fro that looked like something you'd buy at a county fair. But, hey, it's all good. You're destined."

He stepped aside and went ahead into the library, leaving me in even worse shape than the Beast had. Had I misheard something? I could have sworn he'd just said "Chosen One." Which was something like what the cat said. But I sure as hell wasn't Buffy, and even if I'd hallucinated the conversation with the monster, how could Cooper have known?

I was shaking. This was way too much weirdness for one day. The best thing was to go back to my room and pull the covers over my head.

I scurried swiftly across campus, keeping my head down, trying not to think, just to get through space and time till I'd slipped back into reality as I knew it. I breathed a sigh as I grabbed the doorknob—though I probably should have wondered why the door was closed—and stepped through to safety.

Whereupon something hit me hard in the shin.

"Ooof!"

"Don't you ever knock?" said Kara. She was sitting on her rumpled-up bed in the lotus position, back as straight as a broomstick. But she didn't look good. There was something off about her color.

On the floor, freshly bounced off my shin, was my own Spanish book. This really had to stop. "Kara. I'm your roommate. I know you resent me, but we're both stuck with it. What can I do to make it better? I really need you not to throw things at me."

She unfolded her legs. "I didn't throw anything." She was all sulky-voiced, like a kid trying to get out of detention.

"Right." I turned away, intent on just lying the hell down, when I realized how bad she really looked. I turned back. "Do you feel all right?"

She looked at me like I was crazy. "Yeah. Fine. What are you talking about?"

"I guess it's nothing." But here's what it really was: She was usually the color of French's mustard with a pinch of Worcestershire; she was now tending toward Dijon.

I read for a while, just for escape, while Kara dressed to go somewhere, somewhere other than dinner, apparently, because you had to wear your uniform to the dining room. She hauled out the leather skirt again, probably what she'd been wearing when her dad dumped her here. And when Sonya came to pick her up, she actually spoke in a halfway friendly tone of voice. "See you later. We're going to our club meeting."

"Really?" I was interested, despite myself. "What kind of club?"

Instead of answering, Kara looked at Sonya, as if in surprise. For a moment, their eyes locked, and then they burst out giggling.

"You'd be surprised," Kara tossed back as they went through the door.

"Yeah, slightly," Sonya added, and the two of them laughed all the way down the hall. Maybe not at me, exactly, but then it was me who'd asked the stupid question.

Ws it possible to feel any more left out?

I felt so sad and lonesome I actually missed the cat. And my family—I missed my family so much. Especially Curly. Now there was an animal!

Which reminded me. Where was my stuffed animal when I needed it, the one frivolous thing they let you have here? My family didn't love me—couldn't even be bothered going through the motions. Everybody else in the whole remedial unit had their one stuffed animal, and neither my mom nor my dad had managed to dredge up my old teddy bear and pack it with my clothes. How hard would that have been?

I needed it so bad! Because there they were again: the four arachnids of the apocalypse. Oh, God, they were so scary I almost wished I hadn't run Jag off. I covered my head with the sheet and cried; cried because I was about to be chewed to bits; cried because nobody cared about me; cried because I didn't even have a stupid stuffed bear to feed to the ceiling monsters.

Jag pounced on the bed. "They do love you, Novice. Why, I couldn't say. But they seem to."

"Go away."

"I'll prove it to you."

Could he? I didn't think so, but he was distracting me. That was good. "Okay, prove it. Work your magic."

"Ah, the m-word. Well, this is a form of scientific magic. Do you partake of science fiction?"

"I've seen a few movies."

"Perfect. Think *Back to the Future*. *Time and Time Again*. Even *The Time Machine*. And hang on to my tail."

"Not my hat?"

"Grab it, girlo."

I reached for it, but he flicked it away. "One thing—promise you'll keep quiet."

"Okay. Sure."

"I mean it; not a sound."

"Whatever you say, kittykinx." Right.

"I'm trusting you." The tail flicked into my hand and I gave it a hostile little pull.

And wished I hadn't. The world as I knew it dissolved, along with my body, and this ear-splitting noise, like a spaceship taking off, took over the universe. I was falling, falling, falling, bodiless, into space, and the noise stopped and then there was none at all, only silent, black, terrifying nothingness.

Worse, it was anything but a smooth fall; it was jerky and it hurt, even without a body. Jag and I jerked and jumbled for what seemed like several centuries, and then there was a terrible grinding, and I was standing in the second-floor hall of my own house in Santa Barbara, which has what they call "a great room," a kind of two-story living room, overlooked by the hall above. I was looking over the banister into that room, holding an orange cat in my arms.

My father was down below, and Haley was lying on the sofa. Dad hauled something out of a bag and showed it to my sister, who took it and examined it. "Wow, Dad, that's amazing."

"I had to go to L.A. to get it—I must have gone to ten different stores before I found exactly the right one. Think she'll like it?"

Haley hesitated. "Well…she'd like Curly better."

"I know, honey." Dad sounded sad. "I feel really bad for her—and for Curly. That dog misses Deb so much she's been sleeping in her laundry basket."

Haley said, "I miss her too."

Dad was fooling around with a box. He took the object from Haley, crammed it in, and said, "Okay, it fits. Have you got the stuff Mom got her?"

"The lotion? Yeah. It's this special stuff Mom uses—Debbie's always wanted some, but Mom said it was too expensive."

She pulled a plastic container out of a bag on the coffee table, and Dad stuffed that in the package too.

How to explain what I was seeing? The thing was, it wasn't like watching a movie. I was right there. They could only see me if they looked up, but I felt so close I could have touched them. I was so disoriented I didn't even think to do the sensible thing—run down and fling myself in my dad's arms. I was overcome with grief. And love. I couldn't move. Finally I found my voice. "Dad!" I said, or meant to, but all I could get out was a whisper.

Suddenly, I heard the rocket-noise again, and I felt my body dissolving and I heard my dad say, "What was that?"

The noise got louder, so loud I could barely make out what Haley answered, "Just Curly. Whining to come in."

Dad said, "It almost sounded like Debbie."

And then I was out of my body again and falling, jerking, twitching through black, infinite, silent space, and then the grinding. I woke up in bed at St. Joan's. Jag jerked his tail out of my hand, jumped off the bed, and pranced away.

I was furious. I knew he'd somehow sent me the dream, and I didn't appreciate it. All it did was make me feel bad. And tired—really, really tired. I was totally out of it for a couple of days afterward.

But then, Sunday, at mail call, I heard my name. "Deborah Dimond. Package."

It was childish, but I hoped...I hoped against hope...

I tore the package open. In it was a plastic tube of Mom's special lotion (which I used to steal from Saks because she wouldn't buy it for me) and something else—the other thing I'd seen Haley and Dad packing. It was a stuffed dog that looked so much like Curly I'd have done a double take if I hadn't already seen it.

The Beast was on my bed when I returned to my room, all curled up and practically spitting canary feathers. I was in such a good mood I didn't even give him his much-deserved ration of sarcasm. "Okay, A.B., so you can see into the future. Would you mind telling me when I can go home for a weekend?"

"A.B.?" The Thing inquired.

"Alpha Beast. That's your name, right?"

"My title, actually. But the Novice may certainly give me a nickname. Quite healthy, actually. Part of the bonding process."

"Thanks so veddy much," I said, thinking I wouldn't bond with him if he were smeared with superglue. "Spill, please—how'd you know about the dog?"

"Excuse me. You're the one who knew about the dog. You saw it time-traveling."

CHAPTER VI: FIGHT CLUB

I was so blown away I couldn't even answer the monster. But I saw what he meant—that dream about seeing my dad and Haley. There were things about it that weren't very dreamlike.

"And then," said the Beast, "there's the fact that they did send the dog and the lotion. But you've got it wrong, Novice. I can't foretell the future. I took you back to the past."

"Somehow, you figured out I was going to get the package—"

"Think about it. You got it three days after we saw them packing it. Mail takes at least a week to get here. They had to have mailed it already—by the time we traveled back, I mean. As it happens, we saw them packing the dog four days, thirteen hours, and three minutes after they actually did it."

"You mean that horrible dead quiet…"

"Was time, not space."

"But you can't do it that way. You need a time machine."

"According to whom? All the great fiction writers? Let me tell you something, Human—they've never time-traveled. You have. If you would care to know how it's actually done, I suggest you read *A Brief History of Time*. Then talk to me again."

"My dad read that book. Stephen Hawking, right?"

The Beast flicked his tail. "Mr. Hawking more nearly understands the concept than most humans—however, your reading will still need supplementing. But that's for another time. Meanwhile, are you quite ready for your first magic lesson?"

"I said no, remember?"

"Funny, I don't."

God, he could be annoying. "Go away!"

I swatted at him with my Curly dog, nothing dangerous, just a statement, but for some reason, it set Kara off. Did I mention she was in the room? Oh, yeah, and Sonya too. The great thing about telepathy is no one knows you're doing it. But it seemed I'd unwittingly spoken aloud.

"Do you have to be so cruel to that poor cat?"

I spoke without thinking. "Oh, shut up, Loser Girl. If I'd sat here like a lump for six months without even making it to mustard, I'd be pretty careful who I criticized."

As it happens, I'd made Level Two that day, so maybe I was feeling the teensiest bit arrogant. If ketchup was this easy, could a weekend at home be far behind? But I was sorry as soon as I said it.

Kara didn't cry, she just seemed to fold into herself. I felt bad. I felt really awful about it. But it was clarifying. Whatever it took, I most certainly did not want to be a total lameoid like Kara. Who now unfolded and sat up on her bed.

"You hate me, don't you?" she shrieked. "You think just because you have those stupid snakes on your arms you're Queen of the Damned or something."

"I don't hate you," I said. "You're the one that hates me, remember? I just think it's stupid to waste your time and your parents' money."

"What do you know about me?" she shouted, and she jumped me. Sprang off the bed, grabbed me by the collar, and started shaking me, like I'd gone unconscious and she had to wake me up.

"Get off me, lameoid!" I hollered, and slammed her as hard as I could.

"Abueeeeeela!" Sonya hollered.

Apparently, Abuela had some kind of alarm button she pressed. Security came running. Next thing I knew, one guy had my arms pinned behind me and another one had Kara.

"Welcome to my world," said Kara, with a smile so malicious I was sure it must mean something. And boy, did it. Oh, yeah. Oh, joy.

Here's what it meant: At my dear alma mater, St. Psycho's, fighting is what they call a Category Four offense. The only thing worse is running away, which is Cat Five, and which causes the whole school to get punished. Know what you get for Cat Four? All your points removed! That's right, all of them. So I was now literally in Kara's world; I didn't have a point to call my own. I'd lost my ketchup before I even got a hot dog.

Not only that, they have this other thing they do to you, the high school version of a "time-out." They send you to a language lab cubicle, and make you sit up straight, staring straight ahead while listening to educational tapes. If you slump, someone taps you on the shoulder. The tape I drew that day was one about the Spaniards coming to Mexico— majorly boring.

But no problem, I wasn't alone. It was a perfect set-up for a private session with a little Yoda wannabe. "Nice regressing, Novice."

"Shut up, flea-farm. I don't need your sarcasm. I blew it, okay? I shouldn't have picked a fight. Are you happy?"

"That was no fight. You don't fight."

"Are you kidding? I fight with my mom night and day. I'm famous for fighting."

"Repeat. You do not fight. You quarrel, like a kid, as you Americans say. Lord, how I hate that word!"

"I *am* a kid, fuzzfest."

"I rest my case, child. You pout. You flounce. You lose."

"I do not!" I said, pouting.

And knowing I was totally busted.

"I could teach you to win," he said.

That word "win" glittered before me like a Christmas snowflake— something beautiful that you just couldn't catch. He'd baited the hook and I was about to gulp it down like a guppy. I knew what he was doing, but I couldn't stop myself. "Okay," I said. "Forget about magic. Give me fighting lessons."

The cat actually reached out his paw and swiped at my hand. Inadvertently, I pulled back. "Don't be afraid. That's the way I nod. If I did it like you people do, think how much attention I'd attract. You're on to something, Human. Magic starts at the mundane level. 'As above, so below' is one of the first magical principles.

"Magic is nothing more than working with energy. Learning to fight properly is a very good use of energy—although they probably call it something else in this school, like standing up for yourself. You don't need me to teach you that. That's what your parents are paying these people for."

He rubbed up against my leg like a normal pussycat.

"Stop it, A.B.," I said, "Someone might get the idea you like me."

"Heaven forefend." He jumped up on the little table that held the tape recorder and, if you were actually there for language lab, your Spanish book. "You baited Kara. You practically invited her to jump you."

I sniffed. "She's a little mouse. I didn't think she was the jumping kind."

"Okay, Novice, here's your first fighting lesson: Never underestimate your enemy."

"I never thought of her as an enemy."

"You treated her as one."

I felt ashamed. "Okay, I shouldn't have said that stuff to her. Although she did have it coming. She probably had no idea how lame she is. I probably helped her."

"Oh, really? Like your mother helps you by getting in your face? As you young people say."

"What?" I wasn't sure I'd heard him right. Nobody had ever understood about my mother before.

"Chew on it," he said. "At the risk of uttering a dreadful cliché, live and let live."

I winced. "I really expected better of you." But the demon-cat was gone.

I got it.

All right, I got it. I'd done something stupid and kind of cruel and not even realized it. But I wasn't about to concede anything to the Beast of Beasts. I found him fuzzing up my pillow as usual. "So what was the lesson, A.B.?" I said. "I think I see what you're getting at, but I don't exactly call that a fighting lesson."

"Here's the lesson, Novice: Don't get blindsided."

Like it was that easy.

"Not underestimating your enemy is a strategy, Novice. And strategy's what we're going to be learning in our informal little classes. Take boxing if you want to know how to hit. What I teach is the Twelve Tactics of Magical Combat. You'll find the same things work both for physical and psychological battles. You just learned Tactic Three."

"And Tactics One and Two would be…?"

"Tactic Two is obvious: Know your enemy."

"Right."

"Tactic One is this: Fight smart, not strong. Chew on it."

❖

I had plenty of time to chew. Nothing much happened the rest of the week, unless you count my mad scramble to win back the points I'd lost, and a letter from my dad.

Dear Deb, he wrote. *Your mom and Haley and I miss you so much. Sometimes it seems as if you haven't really gone at all. A week or two ago, when Haley and I were mailing your lotion and your dog—did you get them, by the way?—I had the feeling you were actually in the house. It was eerie, but I shook it off, and then I thought I heard you say, "Dad?" as if you were trying to call me. I wonder if you were thinking about us then.*

There was a lot of other stuff too (mostly of an inspirational nature), but that was the part that really freaked me out. I didn't tell junior fiend about it. Just filed it and did what the clowns wanted—did it so well, I'm happy to say I went into my third week with exactly 100 points—once again a Level Two.

When I got back after dinner that night, I was surprised to see that Abuela wasn't there. Rachel, aka Good Citizen Barbie, was in her place.

Abuela had never not been there, and I missed her, missed knowing someone nice would be there if I had another horrible dream. But I was tired that day, and once again a little full of myself—like the first time I made Level Two.

So I let it go. I figured A.B. would come slinking around, and I could ask him where she was.

But that didn't happen. The Fur Grenade was missing too.

Chapter VII: Violation Cat Unknown

I got through the first part of the next day okay, and actually enjoyed my language lab tape, which was about the Mayans, in whom I was suddenly deeply interested, now that A.B.'d told me they did the kind of stuff that happened in my dreams. They also bound their babies' heads so they'd be flat. They hung little beads over their kids' noses so they'd be cross-eyed (which was considered attractive). They filed their teeth into points. They pierced their penises and pulled thorns through them, in order to get closer to God, thus reinforcing the theory that God was to be avoided at all costs.

They were majorly weird.

The only thing that seemed normal about them was that they loved tattoos and chocolate. To them, chocolate was like gold—or like spices were to the other ancients I knew about.

Precious.

Valuable.

Possibly addictive.

I could follow their reasoning.

So the tape was okay and the classes were perfectly normal. But after that, Evelina called a meeting of the girls in my dorm. Sonya and Kara were already there, and they were kind of agitated and quiet, like something was wrong. Evelina looked like she hadn't slept in a month.

"Girls," she said, "I'm sorry to say I've got some bad news."

My heart started pounding. Bad news. What was bad here, where nothing was good?

"Abuela was attacked by someone on her way home early Sunday. I'm afraid she's in the hospital—"

Julia, the mall-rat girl with the ironed blond hair, was the only one who could speak. "Attacked? What kind of 'attacked'? What happened?'"

Evelina looked like she might cry. "She was beaten. We don't think she's coming back to work."

"You mean she's going to die?" I said, thinking that the end of the world was probably on its way. Also thinking I was going to have to hurt whoever did it. Very very badly.

"No." Evelina was trying to be soothing. "No. She's not going to die. She's tough, but she's old. It's just not safe for her to be out on the streets at her age. She's going to be all right, but another man was killed in the attack. And Jag." She looked straight at me.

Had I heard right?

"Jag?" Julia wailed. "Who'd kill an innocent pussycat?"

Something funny was going on here. Something very strange indeed.

"Wait a minute; hold it," I said. "Jag doesn't leave the school, does he? He sleeps with me every night." Too late, I realized how pathetic I must sound. Jag hadn't slept with me since Saturday.

"We don't really know what happened." Evelina sounded like a mom explaining that Daddy wasn't coming back from the war. "All we know is that Abuela was found unconscious, and a man a few feet away was dead. Jag's body was there too."

Mine might as well have been too, for all I could feel it—I was having an out-of-body experience, unable to feel or process anything. I didn't feel sad, I felt panicked; I was absolutely sure none of this could be true. I kept asking questions, like a wind-up toy that couldn't stop. "How did he die?"

"He was shot to death."

"Abuela shot the man who attacked her?"

Sonya hollered, "Way to go, Abuela!"

Evelina's face lost a little of its tension. None of us were falling apart; she might get through this. "Oh," she said, forcing an almost-smile. "Sorry, Reeno. I thought you meant Jag. I know you were very fond of him."

Were. She'd used the past tense.

Jag was dead. This wasn't some crazy misunderstanding. There was no such thing as the Alpha Beast. The whole story was just a nutty acrobatic routine my pathetic little mind had performed to get me through Bad Girl School; I'd just been a kid with an imaginary friend.

Evelina kept talking. "Jag was the one who was shot to death. We don't really know how the man died."

"Did he have a gun?"

"There was no gun at the scene. Only a tire iron."

We winced collectively, realizing that must be what the man hit Abuela with.

Evelina was quiet. No one said anything for a while, which gave me time to think. Or would have, except that thinking was out of the question. The panic was getting worse, and there was something mixed with it, something I didn't want to think about. I dug my fingers into the seat of my chair, willing myself to stay in it, stay calm, try to understand what had happened. But my brain just wouldn't take in information—couldn't grasp the fact that Abuela had really been beat up, and the cat was dead, and there was really no Alpha Beast, and A.B. and I weren't going off to have an adventure and save the world, and, except for Carlos, I was really, really truly all alone at St. Psycho's, where I'd probably rot, because I sure wasn't going to play their stupid games anymore.

"What did they do with him?" I finally said.

"The cat? I don't know—buried him, I guess. He's gone, Reeno. I'm sorry."

I lost it. I got up and ran out of there before she could even call security; ran straight for the principal's office, my sandals flapping on the stone floors. "Hal! Hal! Hal, I've got to talk to you!"

Hal let me in, looking curiously sympathetic. "Reeno, come in. I know you're upset—"

"I have to say good-bye to him."

"To the cat? We know you loved him. Listen—"

I wanted to say, I did not love that stupid furball—I believed in him!

"I was the one who found Abuela—I was coming to school as she was leaving, I guess, or shortly after. She regained consciousness while we were waiting for the ambulance, and she asked me to bring Jag back for you and have him buried on campus. It was weird—she didn't say what happened, wouldn't even talk about it, wouldn't identify the man. The important thing is this—she was thinking about you, Reeno. I didn't even know you knew her that well."

"You mean he's here? I want to see him."

"Well, ah—"

"What?" I demanded. "What?"

"We had to go ahead and bury him. In this heat, he would have..."

"Noooooo!" I screamed, sounding like some chick in a movie whose boyfriend has just been killed before her eyes. This wasn't my boyfriend. It was only a stupid cat.

Hal took hold of both my hands. "Reeno? Reeno, are you all right?"

"Of course I'm all right." Crying a little, that was all. "I just want to say good-bye. I want to—uh, put a flower on his grave."

"Well, I can understand that. Come on. We'll go pick some bougainvillea."

So we went and got the flowers from a vine that grew by the side of the classroom building, and, sadly, miserably, I went with Hal to the little mound behind the kitchen door that was Jag's grave. I wanted to be alone with him, but fat chance of that.

I wanted to cry a little more. I'd really had no idea how much I was going to miss the fuzzfaced little liar. He couldn't talk and he couldn't time-travel, and he certainly couldn't save the world, but he'd gotten me through the first few weeks of the worst time of my life, and that was a lot for a cat.

I knelt down with the flower and planted it.

"Blast! I thought you'd never get here," the Jag-voice said. "I've been digging for a day and a half. Get me out of here, and be quick about it! I've got permanent dirt in my fur."

"A.B.!" I shouted, "I'm here, A.B. It's okay!" and I started digging with my hands. Hal, who evidently thought I was the teenage equivalent of one of those widows who leap into the casket with their dead husbands, stepped forward and grabbed me.

"Meow, Beast!" I shouted again, forgetting that A.B. could hear if I only thought it.

It was an order, but Hal evidently took it as a sign of panic. "He's beyond meowing, Reeno," he said, "I'm sorry."

And finally the fuzzbrain caught on. A tiny, weak little "mew" issued from the grave.

"He's meowing, Hal! Can't you hear it?"

"Reeno, you're just going to have to accept it. Jag is dead."

"Could you put a little feeling into it, Your Furriness?" This time I thought it, and for once, the stupid cat did what he was supposed to.

A full-blown "Meeeeow!" came out at us.

Hal said, "My God, she's right!" as if he had an audience. "I'll get a shovel."

But by the time he found one and got back with it, I had one filthy paw unearthed, and I was pulling hard on it.

"Don't pull, Novice. Gently, blast it all."

Hal elbowed me aside and started to dig. "Wait! Wait!" I yelled. "You'll hurt him."

"Get out of the way, Reeno!"

"You get out of the way!" I kept pulling on poor A.B.'s paw, and when he meowed this time, I was sure it was for real—real pussycat pain, none of the usual con-cat talk. "You're going to hurt him."

"Let me do this!" Hal shouted and shoved that shovel way, way down, right in A.B.'s midsection. Actually, his aim might have been better if I hadn't been trying to shove him out of the way, but he was hurting the poor old thing. A.B. emitted a screech like a hoot owl. I couldn't stand it any more.

I kneed Hal in the balls.

The kitchen staff, who'd come out to watch the proceedings, let loose with a collective "ooof!" and Hal, grabbing his crotch, went, "Aieeyyeeeeeee!" and fell down writhing, the little knot of Mexican workers closing sympathetically around him. But what do you do for a headmaster who's lost his dignity and proceeded to roll around on the ground?

He'd gotten over the initial shock and was now hollering all the words that got the rest of us consequences.

Me, I was digging like a gopher. I finally got A.B.'s head out, and I've rarely seen a sadder sight. He had dirt in his ears, his eyes, his nose, just about everywhere it could possibly cling. Horrified, I tried to brush it off, and he sank his teeth in the soft place between my thumb and forefinger.

I couldn't believe it. "Judas!" I screamed.

"Later for the beauty salon!" the monster bellowed. "Just get me the bloody dickens out of here."

I have no idea why I wanted to help the ungrateful Beast, but my finer instincts got the better of me, and I managed to work my hands around his shoulders so I could lift without pulling his ugly head off.

He got some purchase with his back feet and pushed while I pulled. For a while, nothing happened. And then all of a sudden he came out so fast we cracked skulls.

I'd been squatting on my heels, precariously balanced at best, and I fell over backward, bouncing my head off the dirt, which was hard! No wonder it was so tough to pull the Beast out.

It took me a minute to get my bearings and sit up, by which time A.B. was sitting up in Cat Position Number Two (Egyptian temple cat), applying his little pink tongue to his matted, dirt-caked coat, absolutely as if nothing had happened. I think Hal had regained a little composure by that time, and may have also been on the verge of sitting up, but I had eyes only for my little fuzzy buddy.

I grabbed him and hugged. "Let go, Novice," he hissed. "I'm an assassin, not a play-toy! If you want to hug something, go find that egregious stuffed canine and squeeze the life out of it."

I was stung. "A.B., I was just—"

He turned his evil eyes into slits and said, "Listen, Novice, and listen well—today you violated the first rule of fighting. I simply cannot work with an incompetent!"

He stood up and seemed about to stroll grandly away, dirt and all, but by then Juan the handyman and Maria the cook had abandoned Hal and come over to witness the miracle of resurrection. They spoke in Spanish, evidently thinking no one could understand, but with my two years' worth, I could just get the gist of it. It went something like this:

"What's going on here? That cat had a hole in him the size of a quarter—this isn't Jag, it's some other cat."

Maria had fallen to her knees. "Holy Mother! It's a miracle!"

"Get up, stupid! It's no miracle, it's a stray."

Hal dusted himself off and joined us, though I noticed he now had a slight limp. He knelt, but it had to hurt. "Jag? Come here, boy. Hey, Jag, nice kitty."

A.B., who took orders from no man and no woman, walked right over like somebody's sweet little Fluffykins and rubbed up against the headmaster. "Let me see your side. That's right, boy."

He examined the Beast's substantial rib cage, which now sported a half-healed sore—a quarter-sized scab that could have resulted from a run-in with a barbed-wire fence or a nip from a fellow feline. "Juan? Juan, look at this—he wasn't shot. They probably gouged him with that tire iron."

Even I knew a tire iron wouldn't tear fur, but I kept my mouth shut. A myth was being made here and I didn't want to interfere.

Juan went, "No. No! It's not Jag."

Okay, I did interfere. I said, "Did you ever see another cat with blue-green circles around his irises? Show him, Jag."

The Beast might obey the headmaster (if it suited his agenda), but he sure wasn't going to listen to his humble handmaiden. Hal had to grab him by the chin and hold up his head so we could see his creepy-looking eyes. "Humph. Never noticed that," he said, and Maria crossed herself. As well she might. Because I knew what had actually happened. Once again, the Alpha Beast had used up one of his lives, and what we'd witnessed was exactly what she said—a resurrection of sorts, though not exactly a holy one.

"Two, Novice," the creature said.

"I beg your pardon?"

"Thanks to your damnable slowness, I had to give up two lives—once when I was shot, and once digging out—couldn't do it fast enough, so I smothered. This thing could have cost me another three lives if you hadn't come along." He paused. "At long last."

I was overcome with guilt. It was pure accident that I'd come along at all. It was only because I missed him. I thought he was really dead, once and for all, like normal mortals. I'd decided all that Planet Guardian stuff was so much bull and my imagination was just playing tricks on me. In other words, I was really thinking about me, not all the stuff he'd said. Some handmaiden I was. But I wasn't copping to it. When in doubt, be sarcastic.

I said, "I would have thought the great and grand Alpha Beast could manage the simple of trick of resurrection without the aid of one so unworthy as myself."

"Oh, stop talking like me," he said. "I'm furious with you, do you realize that?"

"What, for not rescuing you in time? I told you, I didn't know you needed it."

"No. Not for that. For what you did to Hal. Don't you ever listen? Never underestimate your enemy."

He was right. I said only, "I guess I'll have to work on that."

"What? Do I actually hear an admission of imperfection?"

"I said I was sorry."

"Actually, I don't recall that. But you have passed a test of loyalty, even if you failed miserably in certain other areas, and you have proved useful, however imperceptibly. Therefore, I'm promoting you."

"Promoting me?" You could have knocked me over with a cat whisker.

"From novice to soldier. We have work to do and we really must get to it. Just as soon as Hal's through with you."

I didn't have to ask him what he meant by that. Running away was a Cat Five Violation, the most severely punished of all—up till now.

They didn't have a category for nearly kicking the headmaster's nuts off.

CHAPTER VIII: THE ASSIGNMENT PART I

Well, Hal made the punishment about as bad as he could. And he didn't have to, he really didn't. I begged him, I got down on my knees and pleaded with him just to let it go as fighting, which is only a Cat Four.

Majorly wrong move. It gave Hal a chance to point out that I'd recently had a Cat Four for fighting and seemed to be escalating, which meant he'd have to escalate too.

"That just sucks, Hal," I said, and got five consequences for it. They wanted me to be honest, didn't they? You couldn't win.

For a Cat Five, everybody—yep, everybody in the whole remedial unit—got busted down one level. And everybody had to spend two hours a day for a whole week walking around the exercise yard.

Oh, boy, oh boy, did they love me for that!

And there was more for me personally. Since this was considered even worse than a Cat Five, I got hours and hours in the language lab cubicle, listening to tapes.

Two things were really bad about my personal punishment—one was getting busted back to Level One (it was almost enough to make me pull a Kara and just give up) and the other was all that hatred directed against me. Ouch, ouch, and ouch! Now, that sucked. Not that I had any two-footed friends there, except for Carlos, but now it seemed like I was never going to make any.

I hated being hated. I mean, I guess I'd sort of experienced it before (my mom never seemed that crazy for me), but at least at home I had Jace and Morgan. I decided just to hang on to the memory of them— Jace, Morgan, and Curly, my three true friends—and meanwhile try to be some kind of pals with the kind of cat who'd bite you when you tried to rescue him.

And worse, I felt horribly guilty because just after the fight with Kara, she began to go downhill. I mean, physically. She wasn't just sick, she was scary sick, and no one knew but me. Not even Kara. I knew I didn't cause it, but maybe the stress made it worse. Can you imagine how guilty I felt?

That muddy mustard color she was got muddier. In twenty-four hours she went from the light side of Dijon to something like Worcestershire sauce. I literally thought she was going to die, but I couldn't get her to go to the infirmary. If only Abuela had been there! I knew for sure she'd have helped. Finally, in desperation, I told Sonya.

"Listen, you're going to think I'm crazy, but there's something seriously wrong with Kara."

Sonya glared at me, evidently holding a grudge about the fight. "I'd say so. Last thing she need's a roommate make her feel like dog vomit."

"Her color's off, Sonya. I know it sounds crazy, but I can tell when people are sick."

"Huh?" She actually seemed to perk up a little.

"I see colors around people—like my mom, when she's really beaten down, she turns completely gray. I know it sounds crazy, but Kara's gone from mustard to brown overnight. You've got to help me."

Sonya's stone face suddenly crinkled in alarm. "Wait a minute. Let me see something." She closed her eyes and moved her lips, as if praying. Then she sat still for a moment, looking alert, like someone listening. And out of the blue she bounced to her feet, yelling, "Oh, my Lord! Let's go." She started running, me right behind her.

By the time we got to our room, Kara was passed out on the floor. Before I could even panic properly, I heard pounding footsteps and Carlos blew in, breathing heavily, looking as spooked as I felt. He took one look at Sonya, on the floor trying to rouse Kara, and knelt beside her. "Let me. You get Evelina."

But Sonya didn't leave. Without a word, Carlos lay down on top of Kara, like some pervert groping a sick person. And he truly did look like he was doing something obscene, pressing his body to hers, winding her hair in his hands. Sonya started to beat on him, but he didn't budge. Not until Kara rolled her head back and forth, black hair flying, and spat, "Get off me, freak!"

And then Sonya did take off.

Rolling off, Carlos patted Kara gently. "Okay, babe. Okay, we're gonna get you to a doctor. Gonna be okay now." He was soaked in sweat, shirt and hair sodden, face slick.

"What did you do?" I squeaked, shocked at the shrillness of my voice.

He was panting. "I need to hold her hand, okay? Just till Evelina gets here. Could you hold the other one?"

I got down and grabbed the other, which felt half-broiled, and tried to smooth her hair. Carlos kept talking to her, "Take it in, babe, be still and take it in and you'll be okay. Just keep awake, keep breathing. Talk to me, okay? Can you say something?"

And to my utter amazement, Kara said, "Thanks."

The long and short was this—it turned out she had some kind of bacterial infection, but wasn't yet showing symptoms. (That is, before she collapsed.) The details are boring, but the off-campus doctors said she was in the early stages of septicemia, and easily could have died without immediate treatment.

Which she wouldn't have gotten if it hadn't been for me. Well, Sonya, Carlos, and me.

But it sure seemed to me the timing on the amazing rescue was a bit on the eerie side. The first part was logical enough—I could see Kara's color was off and I went to get Sonya. But what was up with Carlos being in just the right place at the right time? And what the hell was the perv thing?

"I don't know," he said when Evelina had called an ambulance and Kara had been whisked to a hospital. "I just knew you needed me. I could feel you. Really, really strong. Does that make sense?"

"Not a lot."

"It might," Sonya said, returning from escorting her friend to the ambulance. "It just might. Mind telling me what the hell you were doing on top of that poor girl?"

Carlos flushed, his handsome face taking on a lobster hue. "I'm not too sure. It was…uh…what got me kicked out of school."

"Hold it! I thought that was your homecoming date."

He shrugged. "Well, yeah. That too. I don't know how to talk about this other thing. It started when I was playing football. Guy got injured, I fell on him in the pileup, and I just started feeling something."

"Yeah," I said. "They call it tumescence."

"No, no. No!" Was it possible to get any redder? I was pretty sure he was going from lobster to strawberry. "I mean something, like, flowing from me to the other kid, and it felt, I don't know, so smooth and gentle I just went with it—like it was kind of holy, you know? God, do I sound like a perv! I know! I know what it sounds like.

"But, see, next thing you know his knee quit hurting. And after that, every time someone got hurt, they always wanted me to…you know." He shrugged. "But then somebody's parents got pissed off."

Sonya's forehead was so furrowed you could farm there. "That the only time it worked or what?"

"Oh, no, it always worked."

I was thinking. Thinking back to a few minutes ago. "Hey! You know when we were holding Kara's hands? I think I felt something like that. That flow thing."

"Y'all had an energy loop going!" Sonya was so excited she was yelling.

"Huh?" Carlos and I spoke together.

"Carlos, you know what? You might be a healer." We were both about to protest when she said, "No. For real. Somethin's funny here. 'Cause then there's you, missy. You ever heard the word 'aura'?"

"My dad said it once. About the colors people are."

She nodded. "You got it. They're the energy fields around people. You might not know the word, but you see 'em. Me, I hear stuff."

That was so not a good time for the bell to ring.

But it did, and upon hearing it, Sonya stood up and hollered, "Aw right, then! Let's get out there and walk that yard. (Thanks so much, Reeno.) But listen up, you two—y'all are coming to our club meetin' tonight."

Sonya tried to outrun us—she was playing with us, building suspense. Which was fun! Almost like being teased by a friend. What a concept! Maybe I was making one of those. A slightly chubby girl, however, is no match for a perfectly-in-shape running back, so Carlos had her almost before she got started. A little tickling and she spilled the salsa: Kara and Sonya's club was called the Ozone Rangerettes.

Big help that was.

❖

The Beast even found a way to make the super-punishment work to his advantage. Or I should say, for The Assignment, which was the grandiose name he'd started calling the job he wanted me to do. He figured out immediately that while I was walking around and around with the others, he could sit in the yard and he and I could talk without anyone knowing.

So today of all days, he happened to say, "So. Know anything about the Mayans?"

I frowned at him. "Funny you should ask. That was the tape I heard today. Mayan History and Culture."

"Possibly not so funny. Would you care to summarize?"

"Okay," I started out, "the Mayans were Indians who lived in Mexico along with the Aztecs and others before the Spanish got there. They were extremely weird and bloodthirsty, but also very advanced for their time. They built up a huge, very grand civilization by 600 A.D. Do you know how long ago that was, A.B.? Europe was barely in the Dark Ages."

"Before my time."

"Oh, yeah, I forgot—even you weren't around yet. Well, anyway, they had these giant cities with amazing pyramids all over Mexico and Central America—and then all of a sudden, around 900 A.D., their civilization started to disappear. Just like that. They abandoned their cities and disappeared. No one knows why or where they went."

He interrupted. "Plenty of them are still in Mexico, you know."

I didn't.

"Oh, yes. Many. Only they don't live like the kings and nobles who inhabited those palaces in the cities. They live very simply, much like the Mayan peasants did in ancient days. And they still practice the old ways, some of them. They still have shamans who can still do the magic. Do you know anything about that?"

"A lot of the stuff on the tape is about the religion, if that counts. They were big into human sacrifice. Guess they're kinda off that these days."

"Indeed," he said. "They farm a little, mostly. Sacrifice goes with war."

"Yeah. Plenty of handy humans you're not related to. They liked to tear their captives' hearts out. Did you see *Apocalypto*? Extremely realistic movie. Also, they had these ballgames—like soccer, you know? And if you lost, say good-bye to your heart—or maybe your head."

"Some think it was the winners who were sacrificed."

"Some Olympic medal. Why would anyone want to be sacrificed? They liked tattoos, though. I get that."

"Well, your parents don't, do they?"

"Okay, okay, I see your point—everybody's different. But these guys were off the charts."

"Pah. If you live as long as I have, you see everything. Continue, however. What were they like culturally?"

"Awesome! They knew all about astronomy, and they had fabulous clothes and jewelry and incredible feathered headdresses, and this very advanced calendar. Oh, and writing and math, and even books that they made out of bark."

"Very good, Soldier. Excellent. Tell me about the calendar."

"I'm promoted?"

He said nothing.

"Well, it was complicated," I continued. "There were three parts to it."

"Never mind. About the books."

"Well, uh, they were in the Mayan language—"

"I hardly expected English."

"Do you have to be so sarcastic?" I said. "I'm really trying here."

"You're a soldier, Soldier. Back to the drawing board. Tomorrow I want a full report on the calendar and the books."

I gave him a pained look "Do I have to?"

I didn't want him to know it, but this was kind of fun for me. I'd gotten really interested in the Mayans. It was like my destiny was somehow mixed up with theirs, you know? My Vision Serpents and all. And my dreams.

Anyhow, I was rooting around, having a merry old time, as A.B. would say, all full of my own importance. But you want to know the truth? I really had no idea just how big The Assignment was going to be—and how much might hang on it. I just wanted to annoy the Beast. So I pretended the whole thing was a big fat pain and that I had to be bribed to do it.

Also, there was something I wanted to know.

"Look, kittywhompass," I said. "I might do it, okay? But there's a condition. I want to know what really happened out on the street. With you and Abuela."

He tried to shrug it off. "Nothing worth telling. Nothing at all, really."

"Don't tell me it was nothing. Hal said you were shot, and so did Juan. So you must have been shot—but there was no gun. What went down out there?"

"Very well, if you really want to hear it. Blast, I wish I could sigh! To begin with, Abuela is old, not unlike your faithful servant."

I hooted mentally. He was neither faithful nor anyone's servant.

"Thus, I have great respect and sympathy for the elderly. Owing to that, I usually try to see her home." He flicked his tail, as if the next part didn't matter. "So Sunday I was doing that when someone mugged her before I could stop him. I interceded before he could damage her further."

"What about the gun?'"

"There were two men, not one. The one with the gun left the scene prematurely."

"'Prematurely.' I love that. What should he have waited around for?"

"What was coming to him, Soldier Girl. What was coming to him." His tail flicked in anger.

"I don't think I want to know."

"Then don't ask."

But I couldn't help it, I had to know. "Tell me."

"I've told you before and I'll tell you again. No one hides from the Alpha Beast."

"Meaning—"

"Meaning I tracked him down and took him out. End of story."

"Wait a minute. Before or after we dug you up?"

"After, of course. Even I can't be in two places at once. I did it this morning." He paused, annoyance written all over his little puddytat face. "If I could sigh, I would."

"What are you trying to say here?

"It's so tedious, really. It's just that today the town will be full of the usual vampire and werewolf stories. I never leave blood in the bodies, you see—and now there are two of them."

"Two?"

"I killed the tire-iron artist as well, of course." He punctuated this with a decisive tail-thunk. "You didn't seriously think Abuela did it?"

"And I thought the *Mayan*s were bloodthirsty."

Again, he flicked his tail—this time gently, more like shrugging. "It's nothing to do with that. It's just my mandate."

"But that blood thing—"

"Do you really need the details?'

"Uh. I think I might let it go." I was actually pretty freaked out.

But one thing about A.B.—he might be a pompous ass, but at least he didn't brag for no reason. At lunch, everybody was going bananas about the "murders." Even Evelina and Hal were walking around with worried looks.

Chapter IX: Riding the Ozone

Ozone Rangerettes?" said Carlos. "I might be gay, but still."
Sonya said, "You're gay? Had me fooled, and I'm psychic. Listen, nobody's asking you to join. It's a big deal for us even to have a guest. We are super, super, super secret, okay? Absolutely no one can know about us! Understood?"

We both shrugged. "Uh, sure."

"How many members does this exclusive club have?" I asked.

"Three. And Kara's out tonight. So it'll be just the four of us. Oh, and our mascot. Jag always comes."

Huh? What was this? Jag was the Alpha Beast, not some stupid club mascot.

"And for the moment, Aura Girl, keep that to yourself," said the Beast himself, who was already curled up on the table of the room Sonya led us into. It was one of the so-called "study rooms" on the third floor of the library, and it was furnished something like a mini library—walls lined with books and a big table to put your books on and pore over them. In fact, it was such an exact replica, I thought to A.B., "As below, so above."

"Quite correct, Student. There are moments when I do not absolutely despair of you."

The Beast not only wasn't alone in there, the other two occupants were even more surprising, if that's possible. Even Sonya was shocked by one of them: "What's he doing here?"

Seated at the table were Julia, the blond mall rat, maybe the last person on campus I expected to see if you didn't count her companion, the dread Cooper Allingham. Did I mention she's kind of a dusty rose? Not one of my favorite colors.

Though Sonya had addressed her question to Julia, trust Cooper to dive in first.

"Great question. Mall rat, Chicano jock, fat black chick, and Candi-hair. This is the Outcasts Club, right? My lucky day or what? Hey, Carlos, you on steroids? Even half those biceps, you'd be out of proportion. And, Reeno, where do they even *do* tats that tacky?"

"Believe it or not," Julia said, "he may not be a complete and total asshole."

Cooper said, "Hey, I didn't mean to, I just…" Once again, I saw his chin jerk some crazy way, as if he were somehow unsure of himself, and then he shut up.

"These the two you mentioned?" Julia said to Sonya.

"Uh-huh, Aura Girl and Healer Boy. Maybe. On the other hand, he could just be a perv."

Carlos and I exchanged glances and, as if by unspoken decision, sat down at the table.

"You mind telling us what this is all about?"

"Kara and I were the first ones," Julia said. "We were in a class together and realized we were picking up each other's thoughts."

"Huh?"

"Yeah, that's what we thought. Great big huh. So," she shrugged, "we started meeting and, you know, practicing. Seeing exactly what we could do. Oh, and we might have told each other a couple of secrets."

Cooper said, "Like what, Mall Rat? How much each other's sweaters cost?"

"One of Kara's stress reactions is throwing things."

I was puzzled. It's not exactly civilized, but who hasn't done it? "So she's got a temper," I said. "Big deal."

"Well, see, she doesn't use her hands." Julia waited for it to sink in. "She does it with her mind."

I remembered the book that hit my shins. "Oh. My. God. She threw something at me the other day. But, now that I think of it, I don't think it was on purpose."

"See, that's the problem. She can't control it yet—that's one of the things we're working on." Suddenly I remembered seeing Kara and Sonya doing something with a pack of cards, and when I came in, the cards started flying around the room. I must have made them lose focus. And the same with the book; I'd disturbed her and she'd lost control.

I was starting to get this now—maybe not understand it, but at least I knew what I was seeing.

"When she was living at home," Julia continued, "stuff would just start flying. Sometimes really dangerous stuff. She only figured out it was her that was doing it when she got mad in math one day."

"What happened?"

"An eraser rose up and hit Mr. Aldrich in the head."

We all laughed, even Cooper. Who hasn't dreamed of doing that to their least favorite teacher? In fact, we couldn't stop laughing. Cooper picked up a book and pretended to sail it at me. And then we were all tossing imaginary missiles.

"So," Julia finally said, "does this mean the ice is broken?"

She was so serious that set us off again. And then the ice really was broken. I could actually feel something like warmth starting to creep into the room.

"Okay, Mall Rat," Cooper said, "what's your big secret?"

"I know too much," Julia said. "I'm clairvoyant. I see things I'm not supposed to." She turned to Cooper. "Like what I said about you. You know what I told you? That I don't think this is your fault—you know, the way you always have to be an asshole." She turned to the rest of us. "Carlos, you've got a secret, right? Okay if I mention it?"

Carlos shrugged.

"The picture I get is of you kissing a boy. But here's the weird thing. You're in, like a locker room, and you're both wearing football uniforms."

"Big deal. I'm gay and I play football. I haven't exactly hidden either earthshaking fact."

"You're number eighteen, right? Who's twenty-one? Blond kid, taller than you—built like a quarterback."

Carlos put both hands on the table, eyes bugging. "Jesus Christ! Nobody knows about that. It could get him kicked off the team."

Julia ignored him. "And, Reeno, you're sad. You're just really sad. Something horrible's going on in your life, isn't it? I don't know what it is, but here's what I see—blood. An Asian girl and—"

I put my hands over my ears. "Stop!" I didn't want to hear what she had to say. Maybe something awful had happened to Haley.

"It's okay. Right now she's okay." She spoke as if she'd...well, read my mind.

"See, Julia sees things. She's clairvoyant. Me, I'm clairaudient," Sonya said. "Means I hear things. Sounds jus' like somebody's talkin' to me. Always thought I was crazy till Kara caught me in the bathroom, talking to my angel—that's what I call my…you know, my spirit. Whatever it is tells me stuff. Kara took me to her room and showed me how she can make stuff move, say she and Julia been workin' on it. So I teamed up with 'em."

"Hence," said Julia, "the birth of the Ozone Rangerettes."

"Ta-da!" I said, unable to stop myself. I was kind of fascinated, no question. Though I absolutely had no idea where I fit in.

"Excuse me, miss," said a familiar voice, "but do you from time to time engage in meaningful colloquy with someone of another species?"

Before I could stop myself, I laughed.

"Not," A.B. said, "that I would encourage you to mention it just yet. I fear it would strain even a psychic's credulity."

"What's so funny?" Sonya asked.

"Nothing, I just…" I seized on something A.B. had just said. "I guess I'm just realizing what this is all about. You and Kara and Julia—you're all psychic."

"Give that girl the Firm Grip on the Obvious Prize," Cooper said.

"And we think you three might be," Julia said.

"Well, you know about my two," Sonya answered. "One knows Kara's sick before even Kara does, the other knows how to heal her. Think we got a couple of candidates here. But what's up with Trashmouth over there?"

"Okay, let me ask you something," Julia said. "He says these really awful things, right? Do you notice that it's like he somehow zeroes in on the millimeter of a subject that's the most painful for you?"

"Aha," Carlos said. "Like he can read your mind, kind of."

"Well, I can't, Jock Itch, or I'd be beating you up right now—because I'd know all the ways you want to Kama Sutra me."

Carlos looked at him like he was a specimen in biology class, flattened, pickled, and laid out for dissection. He pushed his chair back on its two back legs. He spoke to Julia, not Cooper. "Yeah. Yeah, I get what you're saying. It's not like he sees what's in your mind, necessarily. He goes for your worst fear."

"What?" Sonya said. "He's not that bad looking. Why would it be your worst fear to have sex with him?"

Carlos came down on all fours again. "I wouldn't be afraid to have sex with him. I'd be afraid he'd think I wanted to."

"Oh." Sonya and I spoke together.

"Okay," Sonya said, "maybe he's got some sick telepathy thing going, but he's still an asshole. He doesn't have to mention how fat I am every time he opens his mouth."

"You're not fat!" This time everyone who wasn't Cooper answered at once—me, Carlos, and Julia.

"This is getting spooky," Carlos said.

"Maybe he's got Tourette's," I suggested. "You know, that thing when people blurt stuff they don't mean to? Cooper, have you been tested?"

"Does the pope molest little boys?"

"Hey," Sonya protested, "I'm Catholic."

"He knows," Julia said patiently. "At least on some level. That's the whole point. Look, I found out he hates talking, so I'm going to talk for him. We've got a class together and what happened was, I started picking up some stuff about him. Like, maybe that he was really hurting inside, that everything he said hurt him as much as it hurts the person he says it to. And some other stuff. So we had some talks. Here's the bottom line—he's been tested for Tourette's and every other neurological disorder. His family's convinced he's just a bad seed— that's pretty much why he's here. But he doesn't want to say those things; he just can't help it. And not only that, he can't even say that. That he can't help it."

That sounded right. I remembered the strange little chin jerk, as if he wanted to speak, but couldn't. But I was curious. "How do you know this stuff?"

Julia wrinkled her nose at me. "Did I mention I'm psychic? I just had a hunch, okay? And then of course we had a few long talks." She gave Cooper a look. "*Very* long talks."

"I can imagine. Insults every breath."

"Yeah, but…" Long pause, as if she was trying to decide whether to say it or not. "Every now and then I'd see tears."

"Yeah." I nodded. "I've seen that."

Julia said, "I just think there's more going on than we can see."

Carlos shrugged. "Okay. So what's next?"

"We ride the ozone."

"Huh?" The three newcomers all spoke together.

Sonya spoke up. "You know. We troll for what's out there—and the ozone's *way* out there. Tha's how come our name."

"All very fine," I said, and Cooper finished for me: "But what the frick does 'ride the ozone' mean?"

"We're going to go into a trance and figure this thing out."

"Yeah?" Cooper said. "Have pigs sprouted wings or something?"

"Look, we're trying to help you." Julia was getting miffed. "You don't have to go there if you don't want to. Just sit here and wait, I really don't give a flying, uh, pig. Is everybody else in?"

I couldn't see any down side and neither, apparently, could Carlos, although I didn't have a clue what they actually meant. Maybe Carlos didn't either. It just sounded cool. Like something that happened in movies, not real life. I, Reeno Dimond, was about to go into a trance? Wow. I was all over that. I just wasn't sure what it actually was.

"A trance," Julia intoned, "is nothing but a focus."

"Bullshit!" Cooper said.

"Uh-huh," Sonya said. "Cowboy know everything. As usual. For your information, the Ozone Rangerettes have done extensive research."

I was puzzled. "Why is he a cowboy?"

"Raised in a barn." She sat back in her chair, arms crossed on her chest, clearly pleased with herself.

Carlos fired a finger gun at her. "Good one."

Julia kept on as if nothing had happened. "So a trance is a focus, okay? The deeper the focus, the deeper the trance."

Cooper said, "We just sit here and focus? That's it?"

He sounded hostile, but I noticed he said "we."

Julia said, "First I'm going to light a candle." She produced one from her purse, along with matches. "And maybe a little trance music." She turned on an iPod in a dock that sat on one of the bookshelves. (Where had she gotten the matches and the iPod?) "Now I'm going to turn out the lights."

So there we were in the dark, with this spooky music playing, like Indian flutes or something. Very haunting. She said, "Everybody close your eyes. And by the way, Cooper, if you say one word until we come out of this, you are completely dead."

Cooper, for once, had no answer. I could imagine him clenching his jaw so tight it must hurt the top of his head.

What happened next was unbelievably weird. But what made

it weird was that it started out really ordinary. And, except for the weirdness, it kind of stayed that way.

"Just breathe for a while. In…and…out. Very deeply."

So we did that, and the next person who spoke was Sonya. She told us really ordinary stuff, like leave the rest of the day behind, and the school, and our lives and relax our toes. I'm serious. Relax our toes, but first clench them. Then came every other body part. You not only had to relax, you had to contract first, so you got this big *burst* of relax.

After that, we had to send these roots down and connect with the Earth. And then we went down a ladder to a river where we got in a boat, counting each step as we went. And then the boat went somewhere, I'm not quite sure where, but I think it might have been out in the ozone. We were in the boat with Cooper, and while we were in the boat, we focused on his "energy," whatever that was. Nothing magic there, right?

But at some point, Sonya, stopped talking—or maybe she didn't, maybe I just stopped hearing, and that's when things got weird. I was focused like crazy on Cooper, and all of a sudden, his oily olive aura started to twist and curl and grow into all kinds of smoky shapes. Until they settled on one: the shape of Haley. As if Cooper and Haley were the same person. But what was up with that?

Okay, I could do this focus thing. I focused on Haley. And I got… me. I was in a really weird place, stone, with dark rooms and lots of steps, and I was riding an animal, but not a horse. I couldn't actually see the animal, I could just feel the ride…you know how some dreams are like that? The most important details get left out.

Except that this wasn't a dream; I didn't know what it was, maybe some kind of waking dream. I was riding this thing and I was inside a building. Maybe it was a bull. Anyhow, I was riding it and I was about to fingerton something. I was stealing something, I had to steal something, my life depended on it, but maybe not just that—maybe something else depended on it as well. Something really, really important. Haley's life?

It felt like Haley's life.

But what did all this have to do with Cooper?

CHAPTER X: ALL ABOUT ME

S tart slowly to retract your roots," said Sonya. "You are at the center of the Earth. Go up very very slowly, through the white-hot layer to the red-hot layer, to the molten lava above that; and then into the cool, hard rock of the crust. Come up gradually; come through any rivers that may flow beneath us, and then through the basement of the library, through the first floor…"

And I had the strangest sensation—as if all that stuff was actually happening to me, like I was floating back through layers. When we were back in the room, we had to start feeling our fingers and toes and everything again, making sure they were still there, and finally, finally, when Sonya said we could come back to the meeting, we got to open our eyes.

I was toast.

Not tired, exactly, just disoriented.

Sonya said, "Everyone okay?" and Julia turned on the light. Colored bars and stars and snowflakes dotted the room.

Cooper was slumped over, apparently still out. Sonya laughed. "So much for pigs flying."

"I'm here," Cooper said. "I just can't move."

Julia reached into her backpack for water, which she made him drink and then passed around, along with a protein bar: "Everyone break off a piece." Evidently, she was a mistress of contraband—first the iPod and matches, now this. I chewed my portion. And gradually, very gradually, I stopped seeing colors, started feeling less spacey. Like I was actually present.

"Let's talk," Julia said. "Anyone get anything?"

I didn't say anything. I was too embarrassed that I was supposed to be focusing on Cooper and my vision had been all about me.

"I did," Carlos said, "but the weirdest thing. It was really about Reeno. It was this pied piper kind of thing. She was going somewhere and she had all these people following her. It looked like she was giving them something, but I couldn't tell what. They were, like, in love with her."

"That's it?" Cooper said. "Why in the hell did I bother coming here anyhow?"

I was so sick of his negativity. "See, there you go. You know Carlos is going to be upset because he didn't get the right psychic vision, so you zero right in on him."

"I didn't mean…I was just…"

He looked so upset I was almost sorry for him.

"Wait. That wasn't all," said Carlos. "Cooper was with her. Only not really. Kind of like some shadow. A ghost, maybe." He paused and looked away. "I could see through him."

Nobody spoke, not wanting to give voice to what the vision might mean. Finally I said, "Like a spirit? Like Cooper was there in spirit, maybe?"

Sonya nodded. "Our research shows that psychic visions are all about metaphor." I must have been staring because she followed that up with, "What? Just 'cause my English is bad, you think I'm stupid?"

It wasn't worth answering, although she was wrong. Her speech patterns were the furthest thing from my mind. I was thinking about the research she'd mentioned. These three crazy girls—Sonya, Julia, and Kara—had somehow turned themselves into near experts on psychic abilities. That seemed kind of great to me, to have a cause; to care enough about something to really learn about it.

"And there's one more thing," Carlos said. "She was with Jag."

The Beast opened one eye, as if he were a normal pussycat who happened to hear his name dropped into the conversation. "What in Gaia's name," he said, "made him think it was *you* those people were in love with?"

"Know what?" Sonya said. "I saw Reeno too. I mean, I think I did. Seein' isn't really my thing. But I saw her face, real clear, and she looked real scared. And I saw somethin' else too. This guy yellin' at her. He was standing at the top of some steps, like a pyramid, kind of, and he had on some kind of crazy Indian outfit, like with a big ol' headdress. Except not American Indian."

"You mean, like someone from India?"

"Uh-uh, no. Like an Aztec or somethin'. I don't know what he said, but I can tell you one thing—he was flat-out cursin' her out."

At that, Julia perked up. "Whoa! Let's get back to that. Reeno?"

"Well, I feel kind of weird, but I saw myself too. I mean, Cooper was in the vision at first, but then he turned into my sister Haley. So I focused on Haley and then she turned into me..." I told them the rest of the vision.

By the time I'd finished, Sonya was shaking her head. "Somethin's off-base here. Way, way off-base. Whassup with all the Reeno trash?"

"Oh, man," Julia said. "I am so weirded out by this."

She was weirded out. That had to be nothing compared to how Cooper was feeling. I looked to see how he was doing and saw that he'd slumped down, kind of crumpled into himself like a cold popover.

I addressed him. "So," I said. "What was I doing in your vision?"

He seemed dejected. "About the only good thing about my vision was it wasn't about you, Flosshead." He was shaking his head. "Bad news is, it wasn't about me, either."

"Huh?" someone asked.

"It was about my father. I saw someone yelling at him. Like in Sonya's vision. Cursing him out."

"In a Halloween Indian costume?" Carlos asked.

Cooper shook his head again. "Real ugly dude." Long pause. "He looked like you."

Carlos went from half-there to bolt upright. "He looked like me? Or he was me?"

"He could be you in fifteen or twenty years. Much older dude, thirty, maybe even thirty-five, but already gone to seed. His face, I mean. His body was out of line—'roid monkey if I ever saw one. Like you, Flamer. Hispanic too. Weird thing, though. You play football, right? Guy was wearing a baseball uniform."

"Oh, man!" I put my elbows on the table and rested my face in my hands. "Where the hell does all this get us?"

"Well," said Julia timidly, "guess I'm the only one."

Cooper said, "The only one who what, Mall Rat?"

"Who saw you."

"Huh?"

"You were up against a wall."

"Whoa!" Sonya interrupted. "Watch out—heavy metaphors headed your way."

"And there was this crowd all around you. No one was saying a word, or even moving, but you were writhing, like in pain, and getting down on your knees and twisting and turning like someone was sticking pins and needles in you."

"What the hell does that mean?"

Sonya had come alert. "Psychic attack!"

Julia nodded. "That's what I thought too."

Cooper repeated: "Psychic attack." As if the words were Chinese.

Carlos was clearly struggling with it. "You mean like...a curse?"

A curse?

"That's really weird," Julia said. "Two people already used that word."

"Huh?" I said. My mind wouldn't stay still.

"Yeah. In Cooper's dream, someone was cursing his dad out and in Sonya's you were getting cursed out. Three times that word has come up—coincidence?"

"Oh, My. God. A psychic attack is, like, when someone attacks you with their mind?"

Sonya and Julia nodded.

"And a curse can be a psychic attack?"

"Uh-huh."

"And a metaphor. Run that metaphor thing by me again."

"It's like poetry," Sonya said. "You know—when you use one thing to represent another—'my bright star' for 'my sweetie pie,' maybe. Dreams do that all the time. As in 'cigar' equals 'penis.'"

Julia turned red. "Sonya!"

"What? That's the most famous example."

"Hang on here." I was struggling. "What about this curse thing? I mean, we might have hit on something big. If Cooper's under psychic attack, how do we get it to stop?"

"Hmm." Julia was clearly thinking. "We could treat it as an illness."

Illness? My mind was all over the place.

Sonya nodded. "Maybe try a healing."

But that didn't satisfy Julia. "You know what, though? Maybe first try to pull the energy off him."

Cooper stood up. "Bunch of psychos. I can't even believe I'm listening to this crap."

He started to walk out the door, but for some reason, I stood up too. "No! Sit down." We stared at each other. "Do it!" I said.

Without a word, he sat. I had no idea I was going to do that. But truth to tell, for my own reasons, I was suddenly deeply, deeply interested in his case. "How do we do it?"

"We need to go back into a focus," Julia said. "I don't think we can do it tonight. It's too tiring."

"I'm not tired." Carlos and I spoke together. We were doing that way too much.

"I'm good," Sonya said. "Cooper?"

"Why don't you work on Reeno instead? Tonight's all about her, right?"

"Interesting point," Julia said, "and one we're going to have to get to. But later. Let's fire up the candle."

So we went back into the Earth and into our individual trances, and then Julia started in on something new. "Let's start with the idea that Cooper is being attacked by a cloud of negative energy. See it now! See the energy around Cooper." Well, that was easy for me—it was almost all I saw when I looked at him.

"Give it a color if it doesn't already have one." Right. Oily olive.

"Now make a space for that negative energy, right above the candle flame. Kind of an astral basket. Do you see it?"

This was like a kid's game, but, okay, I saw it. And I saw it getting bigger as other people visualized it. I was literally "seeing energy," a term I'd heard a few times, but not really understood. The thing was like a wicker basket, oblong, about eighteen inches long and half as deep.

Whoo! This was seriously fun.

"Sonya, you've had the most experience with this. I'm going to appoint you to keep the discarded energy from leaving the basket.

"Everyone else, start now. Begin stripping off the negative energy and putting it in the basket. Use your strong, fighting psyche to pull off the energy, from the tips of Cooper's head to the tips of his toes. And don't forget his back. Cooper, you relax. But focus gently on giving it up.

"The rest of you do whatever you have to do to get it in the basket. Strip it off piece by piece, or all at once, like pulling a garment over his head. Get it in the basket any way you can. Compress it if you have to."

And then she was quiet while we settled down to an old-fashioned energy pull.

Damn, that stuff was stubborn. The more I pulled, the more it clung, like chewing gum stuck to the floor. At first, I got a little to peel off, but these big nasty tendrils hung on. I put out a little more of my own energy, and pulled, pulled, until my astral wrists hurt. And I broke them off him! But then when I tried to transfer the pieces to the basket, they dissipated into a nasty cloud. Aaaaarrrgh!

Okay, now what? Got an idea. I imagined a whirlpool, a vortex of that oily olive energy, all of it spinning together, and then when I had it going about the speed of light, I did what Julia suggested—compressed it. Put it in a psychic zip drive. Zipped it. Shrunk it to the size to a pea. And dropped it in the basket.

Sweet!

Now to get the rest of it off. I went back for seconds, and then thirds. Weirdly, I found it got easier each time. Was it possible I was getting good at this? Or were we actually making a dent in the psychic attack?

Eyes still closed, I glanced at the basket—it was almost overflowing!

"Okay," Julia said, "let's put on one last big push. Or pull, I should say. Let's all visualize a huge siphon, a giant funnel hanging over Cooper with a long tube at the other end that empties right in the basket.

"On the count of three, let's lift the last of that stuff into the funnel and funnel it into the basket. One…two…heave!"

Omigod, I could actually see it happen. The last of the oily stuff really did go over his head and into the funnel, still shaped like his body, looking like the icky-olive ghost of Cooper Allingham.

"Whoosh!" said Sonya, "It's in there."

And I knew she'd heard it land, just as I'd seen it.

Julia said, "Everyone, open your eyes. But stay grounded. Leave your roots in place."

I opened my eyes and I was looking at a different person, a person starting to glow a bright neon lime-green. The new aura was just starting to shimmer around Cooper's body, not yet formed, but the oily olive was definitely gone.

"Cooper. How do you feel?"

"Great! Fantastic. Like…it's a beautiful day and everything's really nice and you're all really great and…"

"Hold it," Carlos said, "did I just hear you say we're all really great?"

"Carlos, listen, I think you're a really brave, truly fine person." He stumbled over the words, as if they were really hard to say. "I mean… the way you take care of Reeno…"

Huh? What was this?

"I'm sorry if I ever said anything rude to you—it's like some other person did that. I don't think those things at all…" He paused, a look of delighted astonishment spreading over his features.

"Hey! Hey, I'm talking. I'm talking like a regular human being! I don't believe this."

Suddenly we were all on our feet, all but Sonya, holding up our hands for high fives, slapping each other, laughing, in Cooper's case crying too.

And then Sonya yelled, "Help! Help me! It's getting away!"

Instantly, my focus went back to the basket—presumably everyone else's did too—and I saw the thing rising, spreading out like some kind of toxic cloud. I tried to get my energy around it, but the minute I did, it compressed itself and shot itself through my fingers—metaphorically speaking—exactly like a spitball.

It landed in the middle of Cooper's chest and the millisecond it hit, it started to curl like oily smoke around his body.

Cooper felt it, I guess. Anyhow, he must have known it was happening because he yelled, "Reeno! Great tats! Cool hair! I just wanted to say that."

But the next words out of his mouth were, "You blew it, you incompetent fat bitch! What a pathetic bunch of retards."

Sonya wasn't even fazed. She just shook her head sadly. "He's gone."

CHAPTER XI: THE MAYAN CONNECTION

That night I dreamed. I desperately needed to lie awake awhile, trying to connect various dots, but Julia had been right—the double trance was draining. I fell into a deep sleep and dreamed so hard I flung my hand out and all eighteen or fifty pounds of A.B. landed on the floor. That made me fear for my entire arm—but all he did was climb back in with me and cuddle. Maybe he could read my mind even when I was asleep. Because this dream I'd been having was in living color and Dolby sound, with special effects from the far side of hell.

Also, it was a double feature.

In the first feature, I dreamed I was a Mayan. I was kneeling and a man, who I knew was my husband, stood over me holding a torch. He was dressed in an outlandish outfit—mostly elaborate jewelry, strange little boots that tied, a kind of intricate belt around his waist that was big enough to cover his privates, yet small enough to show his all-over tattoos—and he had the sweetest, kindest expression on his face, as if he loved me more than his kingdom. Yes, his kingdom. He was the king.

I knew it as well as I knew I was a woman in the dream—and I was the queen. He and I were carrying out a tableau in front of the whole city, which looked, quite frankly, like something I'd made up. A whole array of pyramids and palaces with thatched roofs rose from a cleared plain where the jungle had once grown. And every single weird, peculiar, absolutely bizarre building was painted and carved with amazing designs—it was nothing like the pictures you see of Mayan cities in which the buildings are mostly white. This one looked like the whole population did some drugs one day and got down and dirty with a bunch of paintbrushes.

We weren't in the main square, or courtyard, we were kind of off to the side, but there were about a million people there, all about half-dressed, some wearing only loincloths.

My hair was tied back in something like a ponytail, and on my head was a hat so elaborate it may have been a crown; in my ears were huge earrings that covered nearly half my face, and I wore a necklace as big as a Masai collar, and bracelets nearly to my elbows. For clothing, I had on an embroidered cape-type thing—a royal robe. As I mentioned, I was kneeling. At my knees was a basket with a codex in it, one of those folding accordion books the Mayans invented.

And I was doing the weirdest thing—I was pulling a rope with thorns attached to it through a hole in my tongue. I was drooling blood; I mean, totally leaking Yosemite Falls. Like in my other dream! But I could barely feel the pain. It was like I was in a trance, and the people were cheering or chanting or something. I could smell incense—copal, I think, that resin you get back at home that comes from Mexico.

The heat was vicious, but it felt good, and the light was kind of gold. Everything was gorgeous, almost heartbreakingly so. I don't know how else to describe it. Colors were brighter than usual; the chanting was like the most beautiful singing, but it wasn't singing, just chanting. There was shouting too, and even that was beautiful. My skin was extra sensitive, in a good way, and I felt kind of sexy, like I was getting off on the pain, which wasn't really pain at all, just this very intense sensation. I've got to say it felt good, pulling those thorns through my tongue. Call me crazy, but I was in this very peaceful, serene frame of mind, and I felt that I loved everyone and everything—all those chanting people; that mean, relentless sun; even the thorns themselves.

And then I felt the worst pain I'd ever known, somewhere around my midsection. I was screaming and moaning and I was lying on some kind of stone thing that was killing my back, and a woman was doing something to my most personal tissues, but I hurt so bad I didn't care. "It's coming, it's coming!" she yelled, and a head popped out of me. Once again I felt that calm, serene peace, but there was still pain. And then this naked, slimy, bloody little human fell out into the woman's hands, and I realized I'd just had a baby. I was just starting to get happy about it when the scene switched again.

I was wearing all white, but I was tattooed on my chest, and I had big plugs in my earlobes again. Only this time I was a man. I had really messy hair tied with a scarf, and I wore a sarong. But I guess pockets hadn't yet been invented because I had a bunch of quill pens tied to my forehead, and I was writing with one on this kind of accordion thing—a codex—spread out in front of me. It wasn't easy because I had a pet monkey that kept getting in my way. What I was writing was something about the thirteenth Baktun. I didn't really have much sense of what I was putting down, but I was aware of a very queasy feeling in my stomach, a sense of imminent doom.

Which proved to be prophetic. Next thing you know, I was on my knees in front of this stone where they sacrificed people—don't ask me how I knew what it was, but I would have found out anyhow, because they made me kneel with my head on it. My last thought was how beautiful the day was, and I took a good long breath, my nostrils filling with copal.

Then the scene shifted to some kind of soccer game, and they were using my head for a ball.

I woke up spooked—so spooked I grabbed for the stupid cat like he was a teddy bear, but he was out stalking mice or perps or something.

Kara was there instead, just walking in, looking almost Dijon again—a definite improvement. "Hey."

"You feel better, huh?"

She shrugged.

"I know you do because I can see your aura." I gloried in the new word.

"Yeah. I saw Sonya on the way up. Okay, you were right. I should have gone to the infirmary." She sighed, as if I'd just said I told her so.

"I see auras, you throw books with your brain. Does that strike you as a little strange? That we're both here. I mean, what's the likelihood?"

"I'm going to bed if you don't mind, probably for days. I'm still on antibiotics and I still feel like...well, whatever color my aura is."

That was by far the longest conversation we'd ever had. She undressed, got into her unkempt bed, and pulled the covers up. But just as I was dashing out for breakfast, words came from the depths: "Sonya said to tell you there's a meeting tonight. Be there or beware."

❖

I couldn't wait. Last night I'd had way too much information way too fast. And then that dream! I needed to debrief the worst kind of way. I also needed some answers form a certain furry fiend. But A.B. was nowhere to be found.

Until that evening. I arrived for the meeting straight from the dining hall to find him curled up in the same spot he'd been in the night before. As if he'd never moved.

To my amazement, Kara was there! I hadn't been back to the room all day, and I could see why antibiotics were called miracle drugs. She'd gone from Dijon halfway back to muddy French's.

I'd had cleanup duty so I was slightly late, and the meeting was already in progress. "I move," Julia was saying, "to accept the three new members."

"Second the motion," Sonya said.

"All in favor…"

And they voted us in. "Hey, wait a second," Carlos said, "I'm a member now, right? I move to change our name to the Ozone Rangers."

Cooper said, "Think that'll make you feel more normal, Carlette?"

Carlos ignored him, the motion was carried, and boom, we were Ozone Rangers. Sweet! I hadn't thought about it before, but Julia must be the president. "Let's check in and see how everybody is," she said. "Last night was a pretty heavy evening. Reeno, you want to start?"

I was dying to start. It was like she was psychic or something. "Sure. Love to. I think I realized something really really important about my life."

"Duh," Cooper said. "It's all about you, right, Pinkoid?"

I looked straight at him, repelled by the vile, toxic cloud of his aura, yet for the first time understanding how trapped he was, that the vile and toxic Cooper wasn't the real person at all, was instead a layer of evil someone had covered him with.

"Well, see, the thing in my life? The sad thing Julia said she could see? It's that my sister has a horrible disease no one can diagnose." I looked straight at Cooper. "Except that it's not psychic Tourette's. It's a lot worse. She leaks blood. She's going to die if we can't find a way to stop it."

Gasps went round the table, but Cooper pressed on, nasty as ever. "And your point is?"

"Your aura is exactly the same as hers."

"Jesus, Reeno," Carlos said. He reached across the table to take my hand.

"Oh, Lord, they're both cursed!" Sonya looked as if it was her mom we were talking about. I'd never thought much about her because she was the best friend of the dread Kara. But I was starting to realize what a kind person she was.

I nodded. "I think that's why so many people had visions about me instead of Cooper. I think that's what our psyches were trying to tell us.

"And I've been having these dreams. I had a dream that I think was about my parents talking about getting married. Then there was this movie and…I don't know, the gist was that they couldn't because there was a curse on my mom's family—the kids died early, only not all of them. And now my sister's dying!"

"The Curse of the Dimonds," Cooper chanted. "Dum de dum dum." Then he pulled a laptop out of his backpack and started searching the Internet. Real feeling guy.

But wait. He had a laptop! How had he gotten it?

Julia said, "Reeno? Are you there?"

"Sorry. Got distracted. So I had that dream about my parents and then I started dreaming about the Mayans."

"Huh?" Carlos said.

"Mayans. Indians. You know, the guys with the pyramids. Like in *Apocalypto*."

"And 2012," Kara said. "They're the ones who predicted the end of the world."

"Not exactly," said A.B., his first words of the evening; though no one heard them but me.

"Wait a minute," Sonya said. "that Indian guy who cursed you…"

"Yeah. Maybe not Aztec."

Cooper looked up from his laptop. "Here we are. Retrocognition. AKA postcognition. It means you know about events in the past."

"By dreaming?"

He shrugged. "You just know."

Well, I didn't know if I knew, but then I hadn't known the word "aura" till yesterday. But I could ask Dad about the curse dream—that is, if I could ever talk to him.

"What about the Mayans?" Sonya asked.

So I started telling them the Mayan dream and when I was finished, Cooper showed me an image on his laptop from a website he'd found on Mayan art. It was the first part of my dream! A woman pulling a rope of thorns through her tongue—same guy with the torch, Masai collar, the whole thing. Identical in every detail.

"Oh. My. God."

"Maybe you've seen the picture before," Julia suggested.

"Are you kidding? I'd remember that."

"Maybe it's you, maybe it's a past life dream."

I shook my head. "Uh-uh. I don't think so. Because of the other dream—I dreamed about my parents, and I definitely wasn't either of them in a past life."

"Uh-oh," said Cooper. "Bad news. You know that thirteenth Baktun thing? Where you were the scribe and you felt a sense of doom?"

"Uh-huh."

"Well, the thirteenth Baktun's when the Mayan calendar ends. In the Gregorian calendar, that would be…"

"Oh, shit," said Sonya. "2012."

"Wait a minute," Julia said. "All that happened was the calendar ended? They didn't actually predict the end of the world?"

"No. That was it." I knew that from my Mayan tapes.

"Then the big question is why did the calendar end."

"And now, Student," said A.B., "we are, at long last, getting somewhere. Extremely Important Assignment? Curse on your sister? Are things coming together yet?"

Chapter XII: The Assignment Part II

I let that one go for a while. A.B. and I had a lot to talk about, but one thing at a time. We had a curse to remove.

And it was very important to me to remove Cooper's curse, because if we could remove one curse, we could remove two, right?

"Wait a minute," I said to the group. "Could we get away from the end of the world for a minute? And maybe focus on what we're actually trying to do here?"

"As above, so below," Sonya said.

I almost fell off my chair. No one talked like that—at least no one human. "What did you say?"

She shrugged. "Found it in a book. It think it means, look at the little stuff first and then you can understand the big stuff."

"For now," intoned A.B., "that definition will have to suffice."

"Well, okay, back to us and our little stuff. All the visualizations we had. Julia saw Cooper get cursed and Sonya saw me get cursed, right? But something's funny here. If I'm cursed, then how come my sister's sick instead of me?"

"They could have cursed your family," Cooper said. "A lot of curses are like that. 'First child in each generation'—you know, stuff like that."

"Oh. My. God. My mom's brother died really young. And my sister's the oldest child in this generation—but she's adopted. That's what my first dream must have meant. That my parents adopted Haley because they were afraid to have children."

"So what are you doing here, Raspberry?" Cooper asked.

Kara said, "It only happened to the oldest child." She shrugged.

"So it was, like…safe." She looked around nervously, like she was afraid everyone would ridicule her. But it sounded right.

"Yeah. Yeah, that must have been it. But see, there's a problem here. How can I be the one who's cursed? I mean if this is a family thing that's been going on for generations. Is there some kind of metaphor here that I'm not getting?"

"Oh, I don't think so, Human." A.B. flicked his tail. "Chew on it."

And Julia said, "Must be something. Otherwise, you'd have to time-travel."

The room started spinning. "Omigod."

Carlos grabbed for me. "Reeno, what is it? You look like you're going to faint."

"A.B.," I said, "A.B., is it time? Can they know about you?"

"No!" he roared. Perfectly silently.

All righty, then. I'd have to go it alone for now. But I stated the obvious. "I'm not exactly sure we can rule that out."

Blank stares.

"But could we come back to that? Because Cooper's curse sounds like the same thing. Maybe some guy cursed him through his father—'may your firstborn son,' I don't know, 'insult everyone he meets.' That doesn't make sense. I man, what *was* the curse exactly? Why this weird, um, communications glitch. Or whatever it is."

"Hey!" It was Cooper. "Good one, Pink Cloud. I mean for a bimbo. Wait a minute."

He already had his laptop out. His fingers moved over the keyboard until he'd brought up the website for Allingham Communications. "That's my dad. Mr. Communication." AKA Bertrand Allingham, a name so famous everyone in the room recognized it.

A few of us gasped. Kara went further: "Holy shit!"

This was like saying your dad was Rupert Murdoch. His dad was a media king. A communications god. If you were going to curse Allingham's offspring, this made perfect sense—you'd make them unable to communicate.

Sonya was trying to think it through. "So let's say somebody got mad at him and cursed him. But for what?"

Carlos spoke up. "Had to be a news story."

"Of course!" I could see exactly how it happened. People who got bad grades were always threatening my dad. "A revenge thing. But who'd do that?"

"Somebody really really mad," Julia said. "Like a person whose career was ruined. Or who went to jail. Or lost their kid. Something really serious."

"Oh, just brilliant," Cooper said. "My dad's only the investigative journalism king of the universe. He probably takes down an assweed a day."

"Hmm," Carlos said. "Which would be three hundred sixty-five a year, and he's been in business how long? About twenty-five years?"

I had an idea. "Hold it. Not everything's a metaphor, right? Isn't there this saying about that—'sometimes a cigar is just a cigar'?"

"Huh?" asked Kara.

"Oh. Forgot you missed last night. We talked about how in dreams a cigar is supposed to represent a penis."

Julia winced. "Do you have to use that word?"

"Well," Carlos had this big naughty grin on his face, "considering the alternatives…"

But I was too impatient for goofing around. "Why don't we take Cooper's vision literally? Look for a Hispanic baseball player?"

"Now that," said Carlos, "is a thought."

Cooper's fingers were already flying over the keys. "This could be it! Know how I said he was a 'roid monkey? Look at this freak."

As advertised, the guy in the picture looked overmuscled, as if pumped up on steroids.

"He was involved in a steroid scandal that ruined his career. Got all of his sports commercials canceled. And guess who broke the story?"

"One of your dad's papers."

"Yeah, but that's not all. There was this Tiger Woods thing too."

"What? You mean he was like some Mr. Clean who cheated on his wife?"

"Uh-huh. That came out as a result of all the publicity. All these women came forward. Lost his career, lost his wife, lost his kids. Manny Diaz. Anyone remember him?"

"I b'lieve," Sonya said, "I'd want me some revenge too. 'Bout when did this happen?"

"Good point," Carlos said.

And Cooper replied, "Let me look. Uh-huh. Three years ago. And I've been…uh, like this…for almost three years."

Julia nodded. "Timing's right."

"Hey, wait! He came back—he played baseball for a while and then retired. Now he's a sportscaster."

"Probably remarried. Just no sports drink commercials. So what's the big deal now? Maybe he's mellowed. He'd probably be really sorry if he knew he was ruining Cooper's life."

I suddenly had an idea. "Hey, why don't we ask him?"

"Huh?"

"You know, call him up and just appeal to his better nature."

"Are you nuts?" Cooper said.

"I'll do it. What harm can come of it?"

"Yeah? With what phone?"

"You got a computer. I'm sure you can get a phone."

❖

"A.B.," I said when the meeting was over, "I'm walking home with Carlos. Could you please meet me in my room?"

He groomed a paw. "Student, you cut me deeply. Surely you mean *our* room."

It was weird, but that made me feel kind of good.

He was there when I arrived, as usual curled up on my pillow like a sweet little allergy-machine. I was about to explode with curiosity—and naked need. "A.B., what *happened*? Some Mayan cursed me, right? It's my fault Haley's sick. But it has to be your fault I got cursed—you're the time traveler here. What did you do to me?"

At that point, Kara came in. She'd walked home with Sonya and probably dropped by her room for a few minutes. "What the hell are you doing?"

I must have been staring at Kitty-Poo like he was some sort of oracle, which kind of made me feel like a dork. But her tone was so hostile I actually interrupted my conversation to throw her a zinger: "Nice to see you back to normal."

She didn't say another word, just grabbed a towel and headed for the bathroom. Well, later for her. Like maybe a hundred years.

A.B. dropped to the floor and assumed Cat Position Two, his

favorite. "It hasn't happened yet, Traveler. I didn't hear you agreeing to The Assignment."

"But I must have! I had to have time-traveled for that to have happened."

"Time is rather a tricky thing. More a loop than a path, they say."

"Don't feed me that garbage. You know perfectly well…"

A vise gripped my ankle. His tail. "Do you forget to whom you speak?"

"Oh, for heaven's sake. I'm sorry, Your Fuzziness. Would you mind explaining what in the name of Dante's Eighth Circle you're freakin' talking about?"

"Dante's Eighth Circle! That's your father speaking, right?"

"A.B., talk to me!"

"Actually, it's more your conversation, I believe."

I lay down, to let my brain settle. "Okay, let's start from the beginning. The Assignment—the Thing—it's about the 2012 problem, right? Like I'm supposed to single-handedly prevent the end of the world?"

He held up a paw and examined it, evidently trying to decide whether it needed cleaning. "Certainly not. Your faithful servant would be charmed to provide the brains. Also the muscle."

I didn't even bother remarking to myself that he was neither faithful nor anybody's servant—he'd just have read my mind. Instead I just sighed. "I don't really have a choice, do I? I mean, Haley's already sick—there's already this family thing with the oldest kid that goes back generations. So I'm already cursed."

"That's an interesting philosophical question, Student. No one is quite sure how time travel—or the lack of it—changes history."

Oh, hell. I must have done it. So that meant I had to do it. The question was, what was it?

"Please," said A.B., "research this phrase: 'Mayan Codices.' And report tomorrow at lunch." And then he proceeded to hop back on the bed and stretch out full length—horizontally.

When I got back from my shower, I asked the question that was nagging me most. "A.B., I don't get it. Why would anyone want to curse me?"

"The Zunger family probably wanted to." He paused. "Chew on it. And for Gaia's sake, get some sleep."

Okay, if the Zunger family wanted to curse me, what would it be for? Breaking and entering? Possibly. Stealing? Probably. Betraying a social contract—something like violating the right to expect law-abiding behavior from acquaintances? Uh…check.

Probably angry Mayans cursed people for a lot less.

So maybe A.B. wanted me to steal something. That was my forte, after all.

❖

By lunch, I had my report: "Codices. The plural of 'codex,' those books they had."

I was sitting at the table, and he was curled up on the floor with his back to me. No one would ever have guessed what we were doing. That is, on the off-chance they guessed we could do it.

"Go on."

"First of all, they were covered with jaguar skin." I made my voice as threatening as possible.

"Death doesn't frighten me, girlo."

"Oh. I guess not." You just couldn't faze the creature. "Well, moving right along, they were written on a paper the Mayans made out of bark that had a special coating to make the writing show up, and they were organized in pages, like an accordion. They were also decorated with all kinds of gorgeous pictures by a very high-born class of scribes, who were members of the nobility. There was even a royal librarian."

"Spare me the sociology. The books themselves?"

"All right, all right. There are only four surviving ones. Most were burned by the Spanish."

"And what was in them?"

"You mean in the ones that still exist? I don't know. Regular Mayan stuff, I guess. Astronomy and pyramid-building, maybe. How to wage war and grow corn—that sort of thing."

"Really? Did you find any mention of the last Great Cycle?"

"Huh?" He'd caught me by surprise. "What's that?"

"The one that ends in 2012."

"Oh. When the world's supposed to end." I was "chewing on it," as he might have said, but I must have looked a little nervous.

"Now, now, no need to panic. We have time to figure it out—and to prepare for it, if need be."

My brain was working overtime. "Hey, A.B., wait a minute! If it wasn't in one of the books we have, it's got to be in another. They must have written it down. What it's all about, I mean. Why they ended the calendar there."

"Really?" He was messing with my head, but I didn't see it yet.

"Yeah. In one of those books. In a codex." I sighed. "But the Spaniards probably burned it."

He had that canary-feathers look again, that smug-as-a-slug expression that made me want to swing him around by his hateful monkey tail. *Why's he so proud of himself?* I wondered. And then it hit me—what the whole Mayan history lesson was all about. "That's The Assignment, isn't it?"

He just sat there, blinking.

"We're going after the codex, right? The one that has to be there—about why they think the world ends next year—and how it ends." The importance of it was dawning on me. "Because if we knew how, maybe we could stop it. Like, maybe it's a meteorite, or a Death Star, and we could, like, just colonize the moon or something."

"The Alpha Beast works for Gaia, not your benighted species."

Suddenly I realized how small I was thinking. "Oh, right. Yeah, save the world—not just…uh, us. We're more likely to mess it up. Hey, maybe it's a nuclear explosion! Maybe we'd *have* to have world peace, because…"

"Does it occur to you that you're babbling?"

"That's it, right, A.B.? We're gonna time-travel back to Mayan times and cop the thing."

He flicked his tail, "Oh, I don't know. Your Spanish is really quite passable. And your shoplifting skills were never in doubt. Perhaps we can simply liberate it from the conquerors."

"The conquerors?"

"Cortes and that lot."

"Huh? You know that won't work! Because of the curse. Sonya saw a Mayan curse me."

"Human, think! Cortes was one man—who else was around then? In the New World?"

"Uh…Mayans?"

He didn't answer. But sure they were there, maybe even including one who was extremely angry. With me.

CHAPTER XIII: TACTICS OF MAGICAL COMBAT

I was confused. "Hold it, A.B. Mind if we backtrack a minute? Just because the Mayans thought the world ends in 2012—"

"Might have thought that."

"Just because they might have thought that, how do we know it really means anything?"

"That's the point, Soldier—I thought you had it. We don't know if it matters. But if it does, can we really afford to ignore it?"

"Uh. Not if you're a Planet Guardian, I guess."

"Right-a-mento. Now, first of all—how do we find out if there even is a book?

"Wait a minute. You're the Alpha Beast. You mean you don't know?"

His shoulders came forward in what looked exactly like a kitty shrug. Guess he'd been talking to humans so long he was starting to pick up our body language.

"The Alpha Beast is not psychic."

And then another shoe dropped. "But the Ozone Rangers are. Is that your point? You want me to get my friends to figure this out for you?"

"That could help." His voice was as smug as if he'd won a contest. "The time has come to unveil my..."

"Exalted presence."

"I was going to say, 'my identity.'"

"Hoo boy, that's going to be an uphill sell."

"I have no doubt you will find a way, Soldier. Shall we repair to the athletic field? With the rest of the school?"

Oh, yeah. Time for the punishment I'd brought on the whole school. AKA study hall with the Alpha Beast. Talk about your captive audience.

As we walked, he talked. "Shall we begin your magic lessons?"

"Huh? Magic lessons? You mean, for the Thing? I didn't know I had to know magic."

"Magical combat, student. I believe I've already mentioned that."

I sighed. "I can hardly contain my light-fingered little self." I was being sarcastic, but actually I was kind of excited. Maybe real witches did more than burn incense and chant.

"All that's perfectly good," the Beast said. (I'd forgotten I had no secrets from him.) "Would you care to hazard a guess as to why they chant and burn incense?"

"Probably not."

"It's quite simple—all magic is focus, or rather is achieved through focus. Those things improve the focus."

"Oh, crud. I seemed to have misplaced my Nag Champa."

We were having this perfectly civil conversation, and all of a sudden the Beast went crazy. For the first time since I called him "kitty-cat," he used the Guardian Voice, the one that melted your toenails. *"Focus, Soldier!"* he roared. *"Focus now, or your tour of duty is canceled!"*

"I'm focusing; I'm focusing." I was focusing like a maniac.

"This is the Simple Secret of Magic: 'As above, so below.'"

"Huh? You already said that. Sonya said it again last night."

The creature flicked his tail—not his shrug flick, his impatient flick. It made me nervous.

"What do you think it means?"

I couldn't think. I was too nervous.

"Simply put, it means the mundane is a blueprint for the magical, or vice versa."

"Gee, that clears it up."

"Focus, Soldier! Remember what I said before—about magic being energy?"

I did, vaguely.

"If you change what you might call the smaller picture, you can use that energy to change the divine, if you will. The larger picture. Listen, Novice—"

"Hey. It's 'Soldier.'"

"I shall use the terms interchangeably according to your progress."

I was stung, but I didn't let him know it.

"Listen," he continued. "Do you know the old lightbulb joke—the one that inquires how many therapists it takes to change a lightbulb?"

"Sure. The answer's 'One, but the lightbulb has to really want to change.'"

"Well, recast it. How many witches does it take? That is, if the lightbulb's a thousand miles away?" He didn't give me time to think, "Never mind. Here's the answer: One, but she has to really want the lightbulb to change."

"I don't get it. It seems more like she'd have to know how to do it."

"Now we're getting somewhere. She would. But since she's going to do it by using energy, she's got to use an enormous amount of energy."

"Ah. Focus. Like what we do in the Rangers meetings."

"Correctarini. Even the candle is a focusing device. So focus first, then will. Magical will. Our witch will do what it takes to change that lightbulb; she will do anything to change it."

I thought, What's your point, puddytat? And realized too late he'd know I was thinking it.

"My point, Human, is you better start changing what's available to change."

Uh-oh. Should have known he was going there. "My attitude, you mean? Hey, I have changed it. Haven't you noticed?"

"Chew on it, Soldier. Work with available materials. That's the Fourth Tactic of Combat, by the way. And a perfect illustration of the Simple Secret."

"Huh?"

"Combat exists on the mundane plane—'below,' if you will. Yet the same tactic applies on the magical."

"Wouldn't that be 'As below, so above'?"

"The Simple Secret is always expressed in the reverse."

He pranced daintily off the field, leaving me still walking around and around, working off my punishment with the rest of the school. What happened to the days when they just made you write "I will not kick the principal in the nuts" a hundred times?

Okay, I wasn't focusing. What on Earth did he mean by available materials? I didn't have any that I knew of—they wouldn't let me have any.

But maybe I would soon. Maybe Cooper really would bring a phone to the Rangers meeting that night. I'd call Manny Diaz exactly as advertised. And then I'd call my family and after that maybe Jace and Morgan.

Jace and Morgan? Huh? Did I really want to speak to them? Oddly, I couldn't work up any enthusiasm for it. Somehow, my previous life seemed so…mundane, as the Beast would say. I liked Carlos so much better. And Sonya was really growing on me, even Julia, who might look like a mall rat, but look at the stuff she could do.

The only problem was the person from whom hostility radiated like the hideous color of her aura, never mind that I'd saved her life.

The one I shared a room with.

❖

Cooper not only came to the meeting without the phone, but also without the computer. And with a kind of lame explanation: "I could only get it for two days."

"Well, what about the phone?"

"I already gave the guy all my contraband."

I was curious. "What kind of contraband was it?"

"The best kind, Pinkhead. Lincolns and Jacksons."

Oh. Money. If I'd known I'd needed it, I bet I could have smuggled some in too. I had to hand it to him.

"Oh never mind." I could fingerton a phone. It was what I did. "Everyone knows what I'm here for, right?"

Everyone shook their heads except Carlos, which made me think what a strange little group we had going. Except for Kara and me, it was like we were friends, like we were becoming more bonded every day, but we hardly knew a thing about each other.

"I'm like, a master thief. I can get us a phone. I don't know why we never thought of it before."

Kara's notebook suddenly rose above the table and sailed toward my nose. I ducked, but didn't make it. It swiped the top of my head.

"Crap, Kara! What the hell did I ever do to you?"

Silence. Not only on the part of Kara, but all around. Appalled silence.

"Okay, I'll get the phone and I'll make the call, but I've got a price."

"Sure you do," Cooper jeered.

"Tonight's meeting is going to be all about me."

"Isn't it always? Even when it's not?" Since we'd gotten the curse off him that one brief time, I'd started seeing Cooper very differently. If you looked at his eyes when he said stuff like that, they just looked sad, like something so much smaller was trapped in that huge cloud of energy. Something fine, something good. Or maybe they were just attractive eyes.

I ignored him.

"Why should we do that?" Julia asked.

"Because I'm getting the phone and I'm making the call. And because I need something for myself. And also because I need something for someone else. Something really important, that may affect us all."

"Not may, Novice," the Beast intoned. "Does." He stood up and stretched in Cat Position Four, Yoga Kitty, his front feet out like a pair of oars, his big yellow butt up in the air.

"All right," Julia said. "That qualifies as new business. What do you want?"

"I'd rather go into trance first." That was so Kara might be calm enough to refrain from throwing things.

Julia brought out the candle.

When we were deep into our trance, she turned the meeting over to me. "I have an enemy," I said. "Not the person who cursed me. Someone my own age. I need to know how to solve the problem."

The minute I'd said the words, I felt a huge rush of malevolent energy from Kara's direction. Carlos, who was sitting next to me, said, "Woo! Did anyone else feel that?"

No one answered.

And once I gave myself up to the trance, I wished I hadn't. After a few moments, I asked people to open their eyes, but I didn't bring us out of the focus and I didn't bring up our roots. I had the feeling we were going to need them.

"Look, I'm sorry I started this; there were things I didn't know." I glanced at Kara, who had shrunk down into her chair and even, it seemed, shrunk within her skin. She looked like some tiny, withered vegetable; something you'd see at Vons and pass right over.

"Wait a minute," Julia said. "This is important." She glanced at Kara. "You okay?"

No answer.

"Anyone else get that this is about Kara?"

No one answered. But it was clear that everyone had and no one wanted to talk about it. I was trying to get up the nerve to do it myself when the first book flew. It come off one of the shelves and hauled itself like a rocket in the direction of the table, catching the Beast squarely in the rib cage.

He yowled like a jaguar, but either Kara was unaffected or couldn't stop herself. The next one caught Cooper, who yowled like the Beast himself, and then it was a snowstorm of books, all flying in all directions, all of us scrambling to keep from getting hit, no one succeeding. But not for nothing did we live in earthquake country. We seemed to make a collective decision to do what we'd do if the ground started shaking.

As one, we pushed our chairs back and dove under the table, an act that had its own set of complications. For one thing, the chairs crashed with an even louder racket than the flying books were making. We were in imminent danger of being discovered.

For another, we were now bashing into each other, in my case into Cooper, with whom I butted heads somewhat painfully. We both sat back on our heels, rubbing respective temples and looking quite accidentally into each other's eyes. His, as I might have mentioned, were beautiful; green and soulful and sad. When I looked at him in that moment, they were something else as well. They were mischievous. Laughing. Even, I could have sworn, kind of delighted, probably at the absurdity of the situation. I did a sort of mental double take.

It was like I was looking at a completely different person from the oily olive one I knew, at the cheerful lime-green person who had to be in there. And a very weird thing: I was starting to like that person. In spite of the constant insults.

Suddenly it was dead quiet, the last book, apparently, having flown off the shelves. The door opened and Evelina stomped in, outraged. "What is going on in here?" And then, as she took the situation in: "Why are you all under the table?"

Julia scrambled out, assuming her presidential duties. "Uh...we had a little, um, telekinetic incident."

What had I just heard? The head Ozone Ranger had just revealed the deepest secret on campus to a faculty member?

Crawling out, my eyes on Evelina's face, I saw the corners of her mouth turn up. "New members, I see. Well." She looked at the chaos around her. "You people must be getting good. Is everyone all right?"

"Um, great," said Julia. "Wonderful."

"Just be careful, will you, or they'll close you down. I'll make up something for the librarian." And, to my complete amazement, she left without another word.

Carlos and I spoke as one: "What was *that*?"

Julia shrugged. "You can't get a room without a faculty sponsor."

"Huh?" said Carlos. "You and your psychic friends just..."

"No, we didn't just anything. We rode the ozone first."

"Oh."

"And we found Evelina would be the most receptive faculty member. As it happens, she comes from a long line of Mayan shamans."

"What?" The Mayan Connection again. Something about all this was seeming less than coincidental.

Julia either didn't hear or didn't care. "Listen, is everybody okay? I kind of fudged that one."

"Just fine," Sonya said, "'Cept Kara's missing. And Jag."

"Well, I'd be missing too if I were Kara, but omigod, Jag! He sounded really hurt." She glanced at me to see how I was taking it. Everybody knew the Beast and I hung together.

"Oh, he's fine. I wouldn't worry about Jag. He's probably the one who took out Abuela's mugger."

Everybody looked at me kind of sidewise, like "how mean can she be?" but I wasn't wasting sympathy on the Beast, who'd after all given me an assignment and then deserted. Too bad then, they'd have to learn about him another night.

"Why don't we see if we can get these books back on the shelves?" I said, and then, hearing the odd way I'd phrased it, ran with it. "Wait a minute. Maybe we can do what Kara does. Maybe we could just float them up there. Anyone want to try?"

Of course everyone did.

So we grounded again and tried it, picking a tattered copy of *Catcher in the Rye* to focus on. Since I'd had the idea, I was leading the meditation. We had our eyes open and we were looking at it. "All right now, on the count of three, let's move it an inch along the floor. Just an inch, that's all." But before I could even start counting, the book began to slide.

"Who's doing that?" Sonya blurted. But we ignored her and kept moving the book, which had now traveled a good three inches, only stopping when it hit *Pride and Prejudice*.

"Let's make it levitate. One...two...three...*lift*!"

The book lifted. And just not a little bit. It came a good five inches off the floor, plenty for Carlos to pass his hand underneath it, and the rest of us to still see air between it and the book. No doubt that made us lose focus because suddenly it plummeted, causing Carlos to say something rude in Spanish, but the rest of us didn't miss a beat, just jumped up and started yelling and high-fiving again, like we had when we made Cooper human for five seconds.

My head was spinning like the kid's in that old demon movie. I really could not believe what we'd just done.

Julia, who'd jumped up in the general hilarity, sat down with a plop. "We're actually getting good at this stuff. Imagine if we'd had Kara here!"

"Kara!" Sonya said. "Better go."

"No, wait," I said. "We've got to talk about her, and put these books back. We're meeting tomorrow, right?"

"I think we should meet every night," said Carlos. "I can't get enough of this." He got up, as we all did, and began shelving books— the old-fashioned way.

"Also, we've got some really important stuff to do. You guys don't know the half of it."

"Oh, yeah," Cooper said. "Like what, Miss Allaboutreeno?"

"I think tomorrow's soon enough for that. When Jag can be here."

"Poor cat's prob'ly lyin' wounded in a ditch," Sonya said. "How can you be so mean about him?"

"Trust me, he's no poor cat." I shoved *The Origin of Species* onto a shelf and *Breaking Dawn* right beside it. Funny, I thought, a book about evolution next to a book about a girl who wants to be a vampire.

"Okay, about Kara. I think something awful's happened to her. There's a reason she can't get on with her life. Anybody else?"

Yep, Everybody else.

"Well. What now?"

Nobody knew.

CHAPTER XIV: THE UNLEASHING

I had a history essay due, and I decided to do it on the Spanish Conquest—that way I could kill two birds with one stone. Boy, did I have stuff for A.B. by the time I got out of the library. Once again, we met during the afternoon parade around the courtyard.

"I've got one word for you, pussypaws: Cozumel."

"Go on," said His Fuzziness. He was in Cat Position Three, Beachfuzz, lying on his back in the sun with his feet all stretched out, looking for all the world like a dead cat—or at least an innocent cat. His famous tail was still for once.

"Are you quite comfortable?" I said.

"It's no wonder so many cultures have worshiped the sun," he said. "You simply cannot beat it for thoroughgoing delight."

Me, I was hot; and so were the hundred or so kids I'd sentenced to this afternoon ritual, most of whom would have been calling me names if they were allowed to. "Speak for yourself, kittybumpass. I could worship a soft drink right about now."

I went back to the Spaniards. "You've heard of Torquemada, right?" The famous torturer who gave the Spaniards such a bad name in human rights circles.

He got up, stretched out his front paws in Yoga Kitty, and plopped back down. "I see you've been boning up on the Spanish Inquisition."

"That's why they burned all the books; destroyed all those New World cultures. Because they were such 'good Christians.' See why I'm not such a fan of God?"

"Not a fan of the sun?"

"Huh? The sun?"

"Have you been listening, Soldier? Plenty of cultures thought it was God."

"Well, not the Spaniards. They went with the old guy with the beard. And if you weren't with them on that, you might get burned along with the books. Oh, but the Mayans and the Aztecs—guess who they thought was God?"

"Enlighten me."

"Cortes! The explorer. No, really, they did. They had this god called Quetzalcoatl, who was light, and predicted to appear in the year Cortes came to Cozumel. The Plumed Serpent, they called him. Cortes must have been blond, huh? And maybe he wore a feather in his helmet. I don't know about the serpent part, but he did turn out to be a snake—they mistook him for a god, and he cleaned 'em out."

"You did good work last night, Soldier."

"You keep getting off the subject. Whatever happened to focus?"

"I'm not off the subject." He was in Cat Position Five now, The Sphinx, and making about as much sense as the one with the riddle. "Do you know what you did in there?"

I didn't want to think about it. "Freaked Kara out so bad she turned into Carrie."

"I beg your pardon?"

"It's a movie, peachfuzz. About a really, really unhappy girl who happens to be telekinetic. Anyhow, she didn't even sleep in the room last night. She hates me. I feel really bad about it."

"I wouldn't if I were you," he said, and his kitty-voice had a dry sound to it, like an old-time British actor—David Niven, maybe. "You really don't know what you did in there, do you?"

He started grooming himself. How he could lick fuzz and talk at the same time I really had no idea. I thought about it. "Uh-uh," I said finally. "Enlighten me."

"You changed the energy in that room."

"Are you kidding? I changed the *weather* in there. 'Cloudy, with a chance of bookfall.'"

"You almost did magic. Very elementary magic, of course. Only a precursor, really. But it's a beginning. Yes indeed. A very, very small beginning."

"What in the name of Quetzalcoatl are you talking about?" But even as I was speaking, I got it. "Oh, wait. Change! That's it, isn't it? You said I changed something."

"Well not exactly a lightbulb, but you're getting there. Look, Soldier, what's the Simple Secret of Magic?"

He couldn't trip me on that one. "'As above, so below.' How dumb do you think I am?"

"Well?"

"Well what?'

His ugly eyes turned into nasty slits. "Do I really have to spell everything out for you? Look, you changed. You actually did something different. That would be the 'below,' correct?"

"Why not the 'above'?"

"Focus, Novice! If you're the 'below,' then the 'above' is…"

"Kara?" I ventured, thinking that made about as much sense as worshipping Cortes.

"The energy, Novice. The energy! You unleashed something."

"Well yeah. Ojai's first bookstorm. How could that be good?"

"Chew on it."

Work with available materials, he'd said. My life? I thought again. It was too weird for words. But just when I thought I was getting it, he was over it.

"Very well. The library report. What, exactly, happened in Cozumel?"

"It's one place Cortes landed. It was well past the Classic Mayan period, though—I don't even know if they had any books then."

"They did."

"Okay, but you've got to remember that every Mayan site was really a city-state. We have no way of knowing that's where the codex would be—the one we want, I mean."

"Are you always this negative? I had the impression you were a burglar."

"I am," I said, my dignity ruffled.

"Well, how can you know there's something valuable inside when you go into a house?'

"I take my chances. Okay, I see where you're going with that. Cozumel is where the Spanish were, so if we're going to try to get the codex from them, we might want to go there. It's in the Yucatan, quite a bit east of here."

"Yes, drat the luck. It'll make for a bumpier ride."

"Beg pardon?"

"One of the vagaries of time travel is that it gets more difficult if you have to go to a place other than the one where you start out."

"Oh. Well. I don't know if I'm into that right now."

"Hold the focus on Cozumel. And one other thing. You know that thing you did last night—that unleashing thing?"

"Uh-huh." I preened.

"It's only magic if you intend to do it."

❖

Well, I did what he said—I chewed on it. And right after the afternoon hike, I skinked into another dorm, one that wasn't in the remedial unit, and fingertoned an iPhone. Easy-peasy—people are so trusting. Some guy had just left one lying on his bureau, along with his charger and headset. Hmm. Very nice. Maybe I'd keep it.

Okay, first on the agenda: Manny Diaz. Oh, man, this was great. I just searched the Internet until I had him—hey, look at that, he was a sportscaster in L.A. now! Unbelievable. Sometimes it seemed like the worse people acted, the more they got rewarded. But for me, this was beautiful. All I had to do was call the TV station where he worked.

Okay, then. No time like the present:

"Mr. Diaz, please."

"May I tell him who's calling?"

Good question. I had an answer, all right, but it could easily be the wrong one. "Mr. Allingham's office," I said.

"Just a moment, please."

About half a moment, actually. And then a staccato, furious, slightly accented voice thundered in my ear: "What the f—k do you want, life-trasher?"

"This isn't Bertrand Allingham," I said. "I'm calling for Mr. Cooper Allingham." Significant pause. "Bertrand's son."

The voice that came back was entirely different. Alert; deeply interested. "Oh, yeah? How's the life-trasher's son doing?" There was a lot of malice in that voice. "Lemme talk to him, why don't you?"

"Mr. Diaz, you of all people know I can't do that. Cooper can't say what he means—and what he does say you wouldn't want to hear. And you know exactly why."

He yelped. And then: "Outstanding! You mean the goddamn thing worked?"

"The curse you put on him, you mean? He's just a kid, Mr. Diaz.

A really nice boy whose life you systematically wrecked. He's not Bertrand Allingham. He's somebody who never even knew about you, much less hurt you."

"Well, how the f—do you know that?"

"I figured it out."

"What the f —you talkin'?" He sure was large on the f-word. (though not on the air, I suspected).

"I'm one of a group of psychics working to help Cooper." I was trying my best to sound grown up. "We've ascertained that he's under psychic attack and that the attack came from you. The safest method is to remove the curse yourself. If you fail to do that, we cannot be responsible for the consequences."

I was making this up as I went along, but so far Manny seemed to be listening, at least. "Consequences to the kid? What do I care about somebody else's kid? Know what that kid's old man did to my kid? He saw his father disrespected by everybody, you get that? The whole world, you understand?"

"No. I don't mean consequences to Cooper. I mean to you."

"What the f —you talkin'?" he said again.

"What goes around comes around, Mr. Diaz."

"Well, it ain't coming to me. I don't do no spells. I hired the best *babalawo* in Los Angeles County for that shit. He can worry about it his own goddamn self."

He hung up. Okay, Plan B then. Whatever that was. But I had the beginnings of an idea, spawned by my completely empty threat. But what was a *babalawo*?

Back to the Internet. Damn, it was good to be connected again! I really, really wanted to keep that phone. But even more, I wanted to make Level Three and I was gaining on it. If I was caught with contraband, I'd probably get busted back to Square One.

Reluctantly, I skinked back into the dorm I got it from and returned it.

❖

A.B. had certainly picked the right word. I'd unleashed stuff I hadn't counted on, in my own mind, at least. Up till now I'd been afraid to ask about Haley, but now I was actually feeling kind of hopeful. I thought there was something we could do.

If we could just do it in time.

Mom would think I was crazy and jerk me out of school if I told her what I thought, so I wrote to Dad at work.

> *Dad, how is Haley? Listen, you were right about this school. I'm learning stuff here they don't teach you at Santa Barbara High. I can't say too much now, but I think Haley's under psychic attack. Do you know what that is? I had a dream about you and Mom that makes me think there's a curse on the family. LISTEN, DAD, I AM NOT CRAZY! Can you consult a babalawo? Do you know what that is? Well, yeah, I guess so, considering your field. I know for a fact that babalawos can curse people (don't ask me how I know), so maybe they can remove curses too. Dad, anything's worth a try, right?*
>
> *While I'm here, how is Curly? I sure miss her a lot. Every night I sleep with that great Curly dog you and Jamie got for me."*

(That and a big fat dangerous hairball—but I didn't mention that.)

> *Hey, am I getting any letters from Jace and Morgan? I really miss them, and I sure wish I could know what they're up to these days. If you ever get to the point that you think you can send their letters on, I wish you would. Just so you know, I'm up to Level Two again—I guess you heard about that unfortunate incident with the principal—it was a misunderstanding, that's all. But I'm doing great now. I've got a lot of points toward Level Three.*

❖

I wrote to my mom too: *Hey, Mom, I really like this school. I'm doing great but I can't wait to come home.* Stuff like that. I also did what A.B. told me to—I kept my focus on Cozumel.

Here's what I found out about it: There were four surviving ones—the Dresden, the Madrid, the Paris, and the Grolier, which was found in a cave in Chiapas a few years ago. The first three are thought to come from Chichen Itza. So it looked like A.B.'s idea was right. There ought to have been plenty more before Bishop Landa lit his bonfire. Because here's what happened—most of the Mayan books were destroyed, not by the "Spanish" as such, but by one man, Father Diego de Landa, a Franciscan who actually wrote down quite a bit about what we now know about Mayan life, but who destroyed most of their books in a giant fire in front of his monastery.

I reported to A.B. right before the meeting. He was curled up on Kara's unkempt bed, Kara having pretty much stayed away since the Affair of the Flying Books.

"So why didn't he burn them all?" A.B. asked.

"You're asking me? I wasn't there."

"Weren't you?"

"You mean I was?"

"Maybe. If we go back."

"That's too deep for me, A.B. If we go back, I've already been, five hundred years ago. Therefore I should already know the answer. Does that mean we're not going? I mean, we didn't?"

The monster grabbed my wrist with his tail, something he hadn't done since that day in the library. "Don't be difficult, Human. And read Stephen Hawking."

"Okay, okay. *A Brief History of Time*, here I come. When are we going, anyway?"

"As soon as you learn a few things. What would you like to work on?"

"Oh, let's see. How about energy?" Maybe I was being a little sarcastic, but only a little.

For once it sailed over the Great One's head. "And what would you like to put your energy toward?"

Actually, I'd been giving that some thought. I mean, if you were going to just break down and believe in magic, you might as well put it to good use. "How about invisibility?" I said. Boy, did I have a use for that.

"Oh, elementary. Invisibility. Are you quite sure you don't want to try something a bit more difficult?"

"Hey, are you messing with me?"

He was. He licked his fat neck to hide his stupid smug face. Okay, maybe nothing sailed over his head. But I was kind of disappointed.

"You mean we can't work on that? That's like, Lesson Forty-Nine or something?"

"We can work on it. Even you can master it—probably before the weekend."

I was excited. "Really?" If I were invisible, think what a great burglar I could be. I could realize my life's ambition of becoming a glamorous hotel jewel thief. Even better, I could walk in and out of St. Joan's at will.

"Where would you go, though?" the cat said.

Busted again. "Just get out of my head, okay? Are you going to teach me or not?"

"It's quite simple really. You know what a glamour is, Soldier?"

"What do you mean 'a' glamour? Sure, I know what glamour is. It's like sequins and stuff."

"Magically speaking, a glamour is a simple spell—i.e,. a simple use of energy—that makes someone think he's seeing something he's not. That's why the term is used with regard to female appearance. Women use cosmetics, undergarments, what-have-you to glamorize themselves—in a word, to create an effect outside reality."

I was starting to get his drift, and I didn't like it. "So I'm not really going to be invisible, more like, um…"

"'Beneath notice,' I think."

Well, it was better than nothing. "Okay, fine, how do I get that way?"

"Simply apply the Main Maxim of Magic—Put Energy on It."

"Uh…I don't think you taught me that one yet."

"All magic is focus, Soldier. What do you think focus is?"

"Well, psychic ability's focus too. But I don't guess you mean that."

"The two are not unrelated. For magic, you must devise your own spell, using available materials. You might begin with metaphor."

Metaphor. That was sure a word that came up a lot.

I decided to sleep on it. For now I had a Rangers meeting with two big reports to give.

CHAPTER XV: PLAN B

Still no Kara at the meeting, but Sonya was there. "How is she?" asked Julia.

Sonya shrugged.

"Hmm. You've got to know. You're sworn to secrecy, right?"

Another shrug.

"Look, here's the thing. You work with psychics, you can't really have secrets from them. We have to talk about this."

Sonya held up both hands, palms out. "I know, I know. She jus' stubborn."

"And scared. Listen, I need to talk to her alone. I have some stuff to tell her—she's not alone in this."

"She won't do it."

"Okay, not just me. Reeno and I and you—all of us together. Tomorrow, after dinner and before the meeting. Your room."

"She's not gon' do it."

"Look, we need her in here. But we can't have this…this…energy block in the club. I move that she does it or she's out."

"Second," said Sonya, totally shocking me.

"All in favor, say aye."

The motion was carried unanimously. All righty, then. Remind me never to cross Julia. But I knew she was right. We had to work together, to actually trust each other. Stuff was at stake and we were all in too deep to play games.

Speaking of which: "Okay," I said, "I have the Manny Diaz report. Plus yesterday's unfinished stuff."

"Stuff?" sneered Cooper.

"You know what I said to Manny Diaz? I actually told him you're a nice boy."

"Shows how dumb you are."

"The suspense," said Carlos, "is killing me."

"Okay, everybody, Plan A—getting Manny to remove the curse—isn't going to fly. Manny Diaz is a Class A assweed douchebag cigarhead."

Carlos looked puzzled. "Cigarhead?"

"Julia hates penis words."

"Dickhead. Gotcha."

"First of all, the guy landed on his feet. He's a sportscaster, still playing a little exhibition ball, all is forgiven, all's forgotten. For him. But he's not willing to extend that courtesy to Cooper."

"He actually admitted cursing me?"

"Oh, yes. He was really proud of it. Except he didn't do it himself. He hired a *babalawo*, which is a Santero priest kind of thing. Manny's Cuban, I guess. Santería's this Cuban kind of voodoo deal."

"How do you know that stuff?"

"I had an iPhone for about five minutes." I thought wistfully back to those precious moments. Why on Earth had I returned it?

"Anyhow, Manny won't remove the curse. So I had this idea—it's kind of like a psychic karate move. You know, where you use somebody else's energy against them? Think we could bounce that curse back to Manny?"

Sonya spoke up. "But that's mean!"

"Trust me," I said. "He deserves so much worse." And I outlined my idea.

Sonya and Julia looked at each other. Julia said, "Think it'll work?"

"Not without Kara," said Sonya.

"We can't afford to lose her, then," Carlos said. "You guys better make it good tomorrow."

"All righty, then. Moving right along." I took a deep breath. I was about to say some of the most outlandish stuff that had ever come out of anyone's mouth. But it had to be done.

"Everybody remember that Mayan stuff we talked about?"

"Yeah, The 2012 thing."

"The thing is, I might somehow be involved in that. Remember the curse? And how somebody said the only way it could happen would be if I time-traveled? Well, I think maybe I did. Only I haven't yet, if you can follow that."

"Technically you already have," Carlos said, "if you went backward. You just haven't left yet."

"Uh, Houston calling Earth," said Cooper. "Could somebody please speak English here?"

I took a deep breath. "What if I told you there was a kind of… being called a Planet Guardian? And these beings are supposed to see that the world doesn't end. And other stuff."

"You mean like an angel?" Sonya said.

"That was my first guess too. No, definitely not an angel. More like a Ninja for Gaia."

"For what?" Carlos actually scratched his head, but I think that was just coincidence. He probably had an itch.

"Oh, that's his word. It's another name for Earth."

"Who in Gaia's name is 'he'?" asked Cooper.

I squirmed. "See, that's the complicated part. I know one of these things. These guardians." I cleared my throat and spit it out. "I know a Planet Guardian. I can talk to him."

"Getouddahere!"

"You know the freaky thing about that? So do you."

Cooper said a word that I am far too polite to repeat here.

"Look, I'm gonna tell you all about it, but do you mind if we do a little demonstration first?"

"Sure," Carlos said. "Shoot." He looked as interested and benign as Cooper looked bored and malignant.

"Someone in here is not who he seems."

"Reeno, for heaven's sake," said Julia, "we all know that about Cooper."

"It's not Cooper." Everyone looked at Carlos. "And not Carlos either."

"Well, that does it for the he's."

"Not exactly. Meet my friend, the Alpha Beast. Shake hands with Julia, A.B." I held my breath. One thing the Alpha Beast did not do was take orders. But maybe, just maybe…

Sure enough, pretty as somebody's cute little pet, he stood, marched to Julia's end of the table, settled adorably into Cat Position Two, and offered her a paw.

"So? You taught the kitty a trick. Good for you."

Without further prompting, A.B. stood, flipped his body, and with that monkey tail of his grabbed both of Julia's hands, pulling them together, locking them in kitty-cuffs.

"Hey! That hurts. Tell him to let go."

"Julia. Have you been listening? This thing looks like a cat, but it's not. Did you ever see a cat with a prehensile tail? That could handcuff you? I can't make him let go. Talk to him yourself—and be nice if you don't want to lose your face."

Julia said, "Um…Mr. Kitty? Could you release me, please?"

A.B. growled and hissed and (I gathered from her screech) squeezed harder.

"He doesn't think that 'kitty' thing's respectful. A.B., can she call you A.B.?"

The Beast nodded. By that I mean he bobbed his head up and down, just like a human. He never did that. A collective gasp went up from the table.

"Mr. A.B.?" Julia said. "Could I possibly have my hands back?"

He let her go, leaving her rubbing a couple of no doubt very sore wrists.

"Hey, cool!" said Carlos. "We can talk to him?"

"Oh, sure. He understands English and…Hmm, I don't know… A.B., what else?" He told me.

"Thirty-seven other languages, none of which, unfortunately, is ancient Mayan. But the problem is, he can't speak back, except through me."

"Hold it," Cooper said. "We're supposed to believe you and that stupid-ass furbag communicate telepathically?"

Well, sure A.B. knew about the curse and how Cooper couldn't help it and all, but he's the Alpha Beast. He didn't mess around with Cooper's hands; just wrapped his tail around his neck and started squeezing. Cooper's eyes bugged. He began clawing at his fur-sheathed neck and making strangling sounds. "A.B., he can't help it, okay? Can you give him a break?"

The Beast unfurled his appendage. Of course I knew the whole thing was a big performance—he was just giving them a crash course in Attributes of the Alpha Beast—but judging from the horrified faces he could probably have taken it down a notch.

Cooper said, "Thing felt like a steel cable." His neck was red.

"A.B. says he's sorry." But he hadn't, and I wasn't escaping either. What happened next was both painful and strange. And quite memorable. Actually, one of the most amazing sights I ever saw in my life.

I was sitting with one hand resting lightly on the table. First the Beast stepped on it. And then, in one mighty motion, he hoisted himself on it and gradually, like a fishing line, sent his tail up like an antenna. It was an acrobatic feat no real cat could possibly manage (or would want to)—all three hundred pounds of him balanced on one paw. And that paw on the delicate bones of my hand.

When I yelped loud enough to be heard in Cozumel, the Beast was kind enough to hop off. That's right—hop. He hopped lightly—okay, not so lightly—off my hand, and maintained the pose for a good five seconds before folding gracefully back to Egyptian Temple Cat. No one said a word during the performance. We all just sat there stupefied, wishing for iPhones and cameras, at least in my case.

"Cat Position Ninety-Two," I said to A.B., as he basked in the outbreak of sudden applause. But not surprisingly, he didn't deign to answer.

"What," said Carlos, "was that?"

"Well, he didn't really say he was sorry about Cooper. I made that up to be nice. But the Alpha Beast is not nice. He wants you to know that. And he wants to make sure you understand that anything I say comes from him actually does come from him. Is that about it, A.B.?"

And once again the Beast nodded.

"Wow," said Carlos.

"Hold on," Sonya said. "Hold on." We held on until she said, "My angel say that thing for real!" She looked like she was about to flee.

"He is, but he won't hurt you. That was just a show to let you see who he is. Right, A.B.?"

This time he not only nodded but, swear to God, he stood up, splayed his front paws, and lowered his head and shoulders in a perfect kitty bow.

"Wow!" said Carlos again, this time joined by Cooper. And once again, spontaneous applause burst out. A.B. preened. Literally. Licked his paws and washed his face like your favorite little Snugglepuss.

"So. What's the story?" Carlos was looking at me as if I were the most brilliant scientist who ever built a rocket. What a beautiful guy! Why are all the great ones gay?

I flicked a glance at Cooper. He was looking at me too. And truth to tell, the look on his face was pretty interested. But interested in the Beast, probably.

"'There is only one Alpha Beast on any continent at any given time,'" I began, quoting His Beastliness, "and it's a very long time. In fact, its existence gave rise to what A.B. calls 'the primitive notion that a cat has nine lives. The Alpha Beast has not nine, but 999,999 lives, of which he uses 999 per year. He needs every single one and does not expend them carelessly.' I'm quoting here."

"Hey, wait a minute," said Sonya. "You know when got Jag buried? That time when you kicked Hal…"

"Don't remind me."

"They buried him 'cause they thought he was dead, right. Was he really dead?"

"Did you happen to see the bullet hole in his side? That Hal said must be a wound from the crowbar? People see what they want to see."

"Or," she said, "what they tiny minds can handle."

"Right." And then I took them through the whole thing about the kitty militia (AKA Planet Guard), the Universal Mandate, how A.B. calls himself a killing machine, the entire tedious *megillah*, even the part about how I was his "handmaiden" because the poor kitty had no actual hands.

"Wow," said Carlos for about the tenth time. "Does he have any other weaknesses?"

"Good question. A.B.?"

The Beast didn't answer.

"He's not answering."

We waited.

And then finally, he said, "I am mandated to tell the truth to those who help." I repeated the answer.

"Well, yeah," Julia said, "I can see how that could be a disadvantage."

I was getting a weird, uncomfortable feeling. "So, A.B., truth or dare here. Anything else?"

"Ah, two more. I am not permitted to harm children in any way, even by threatening." I filled the Rangers in.

"Oh, gosh darn," Carlos said, "That Gaia's such a beotch!"

"And I am rendered insensible by certain substances."

"Such as?"

"Alcohol, marijuana, any morphine derivative, cocaine, and heroin." Again, I spoke for him.

"Oh, well. Join the crowd."

"Also tranquilizer darts."

"Bummer!" I said. "Okay, listen up, everybody. I think it's pretty rare for A.B. to reveal himself to so many people at once, but he needs help with this project he's got going."

Julia nodded. "The 2012 thing."

"The end of the world as we know it," said Sonya.

And then I went through the whole thing about the book that might or might not exist and how it might or might not be in Cozumel, ending up with, "He wants us to take a psychic look at it."

Julia looked sober. And a little bit scared. "This is a great honor," she said.

"A.B., did you have to hurt her that bad?" I asked.

"Certainly, Student. She is now mine to command." All righty, then.

Julia got out the candle and off we went. Once she had us grounded, she said, "Reeno, you want to do the honors?"

I did. I had an idea for a visualization that I thought might work. Also, I wanted to try something new—talking while in trance. "You are in a Mayan town," I said. "And in this town is a palace, built like a pyramid with hundreds of steps. Start climbing the steps…up…up… breathing harder now…"

I let them catch their breath and then I took them into the palace library. "Here, there are many scribes working on important works of scholarship. They wear sarong-like garments with no pockets. So they tuck their pens in their headbands. They're working on books called codices, made of bark paper. Each codex folds like an accordion, and some fit into their own boxes. When you ask your question, the proper scribe will light up. Here is your question: Who is the royal librarian in charge of books about the calendar?"

I let them find the librarian and then I said, "Pretend you are in a reference library in your own hometown. Go up to the librarian and ask him for the book that explains why the calendar ends."

Again, I waited. And then I said, "Anyone getting anything?"

"Yes!" Sonya said. "I got thrown out. They all ganged up on me and started yelling. So I ran and they chased me."

"Aha!" A.B. said. "That would seem to indicate the book exists."

I translated for him: "The Beast is taking that for a yes on the book. Anybody else?"

"I *know* it's there. I saw it," said Cooper. "But the same thing happened to me. I guess it's kind of secret, because one of them took one of the boxes and tried to hide it. But I got a glimpse. Those boxes are round, did you know that? And covered with fur."

"Jaguar skin," I said, hoping A.B. would at least twitch. Naturally, he didn't. "That's what the boxes looked like. Did you notice anything else about it?"

"No, That was it."

"Okay, let's go back into the library. Since this is your vision, let it be a week earlier. You haven't yet alienated anyone here. Find a scribe—any scribe—and find a way to ask what city you're in and what year it is."

I let them sit with it. And I sat with it. But somehow the answer didn't come. Images did—amazing images—but they didn't narrow it down.

Since I didn't have any information at all, this was like saying, "Who am I going to marry?" Somehow, the psyche doesn't seem able to just pluck words out of some great cosmic database. It doesn't deal in words. If you said, "Am I going to marry Mike or Frank?" and you knew what Mike and Frank looked like, one of them might light up. But you can't just give it an abstract problem. It's got to have symbols to work with.

"Anybody get anything?" I asked.

"Incredible stuff," Julia said. "All these weird painted buildings and thousands of people in huge courtyards…but you know what? Not a single street sign."

"I saw a soccer game," Cooper said. "Only it wasn't really soccer, it just looked like it."

I nodded. "The Mayans had a ball game. Who else?"

Everyone, it seemed, had noticed the screaming lack of decent signage in the Late Classic Period—if that was even when it was. We didn't find out the date, either. "Why don't we try it a different way?" said Sonya. "Why don't we ask what path to take to get there?"

"Okay, great." And so we did that. My path led to a gorgeous sandy beach, but that was all I could get.

"I see a man," Sonya said. "One of those Spanish dudes—you know, with the helmets. Conquistadors."

"Cortes?" I was excited. "Could it be Cortes?"

She shrugged. "I don't know. Just a Spanish dude."

"I'm seeing a woman," Carlos said. "She's speaking Spanish, but all broken up. And then she's saying something else, kind of in gibberish. She looks...I don't know, I think she's black. And she looks kind of period...but I don't know what period."

"Oh. My. God. That's got to be Doña Marina. A translator for Cortes, not Mayan at all. She was given to Cortes as a slave.

"And the beach must be Cozumel. I think we're getting different pieces of a picture. And I think what it means is, we have to go to Cozumel and ask the only known person who can translate the question!"

"Very fine, Soldier! Excellent work," A.B. said, or so I thought. But he never said anything like that.

"Would you mind repeating that?" I said.

"I said that was very nearly half-decent, girleen." He jumped off the table and curled up on the floor.

When we had eaten our PowerBars and come out of the trance, I said shyly, "Did anyone notice what we did this time? We talked the problem through while in trance. What do you think of that?"

"Means we gettin' good," said Sonya. "I see a big difference since you late-breakin' musketeers joined up. Psychic powers increasin'. Too bad Kara's missin' out."

Kara. Right.

"Ask A.B. what he thinks," Carlos said.

"I already did. He said it was stellar work. 'Absolutely top drawer,' I believe, were his exact words." I was taking a helluva chance, but no steel cable tail rose up to contradict me.

CHAPTER XVI: RECESS!

I woke up the next day with a snarl of spaghetti where my brain should have been. So much to do! I glanced at Kara's bed, which was still empty, and as big a mess as usual. Kara never made her bed. You don't get points for that and she seemed to be on some kind of negative campaign not to get points.

Okay, there was Kara. There was Cooper's curse. And Haley's curse. Right. And school. Making the clowns happy. Then there was the time-travel thing. No question about it, I was going to Cozumel.

I want my mama! The words echoed in my brain, I didn't really think them. That was just what you were supposed to think in these situations. No sense whatsoever wanting my mama, I was never going to get her. When I needed a parent, I better be content with my dad. But the thing was, I had an overwhelming need for a kind parental presence; it had been nibbling at me for days. In fact, it was the reason I'd asked A.B. to teach me invisibility. I wanted to see Abuela.

I don't know why; maybe I needed to reassure myself that she was really okay. Or maybe, deep down, I wanted the thing moms usually provide but mine didn't—the sense that all's right with the world, everything'll be all right no matter how bad it seems. And the feeling kept ratcheting up. This morning, the need to see her was like a craving for chocolate. I couldn't really think about anything else.

Okay, then. How was I getting off this campus? I was going to have to do it undetected, and the only way to do that was to be invisible. Work with available materials, A.B. always said. So what did I have?

For openers, I contemplated metaphor. Everything depended on how you looked at something. People thought A.B. was a pathetic stray cat, but he'd wasted two guys a few weeks ago. He was the vampire they were shaking in their boots about. He was the werewolf mothers warned their kids about. He looked exactly like himself, but he was still invisible.

I mean, not to the naked eye. You just couldn't see who he really was.

So if I were going to be invisible, maybe I could…what? I thought about it. Could I sneak out with the cleaning staff? Get a mop and bucket, focus like a maniac, and just go?

Uh-uh. Because I couldn't be in two places at once. They'd miss me if I wasn't at school.

So what I had to do if I wanted to get out of there, even for a little while, just to see if I could, was look like something I wasn't. And I had a really great idea. The perfect metaphor.

I wasn't about to try it till I had a witness, though. I didn't know what A.B. was doing, but I knew he'd turn up sooner or later.

So I did my little assignment (as opposed to the Big One). I tried to hack my way through the jungle Stephen Hawking called a book.

At first the only words I could even understand were "the" and "and." So I skipped to the chapter on wormholes and time travel. In it, I found a couple of sentences I could sort of, more or less, just barely work out. This one, for instance: "The laws of science do not distinguish between the past and the future."

Good. Maybe that was all I needed to know. So if the laws of science didn't recognize a difference, maybe there wasn't one. But it seemed to be something Hawking was mentioning only in passing. He did seem to think that at some time in the future it ought to be possible to build a time machine, but that didn't help—A.B. wasn't using one. Hawking said if you could warp space-time, you might be able to create something called a wormhole. That didn't help either, but it did explain that phrase they're always using in movies—"warp speed." So that's what it was.

The best thing about the chapter was when Hawking said, okay, maybe it was possible, but if so, then why hadn't anybody come back from the future to tell us how to do it? He really had a point there.

"I assure you, my dear Soldier," said the Jag-voice, "that someday a time machine will be built."

As usual, he plopped onto my library table and hunkered there like a vast, peach-colored loaf of bread. He was in Cat Position Eight,

Chicken Kitty, with his feet tucked under him like he was laying an egg.

"Well, if isn't A.B. Where have you been?"

"Giving you 'space,' as they say in your world. You used it well, I hope."

I gestured. "Well, I read the book."

"I see. Well done, my little human. Well done. And understood it, I suppose."

"Not exactly. But Hawking raises a very good point about the future."

"And what do you think the answer is? Why *hasn't* someone come to explain how time travel is done?" Evidently he didn't expect an answer. "Simple," he continued. "What do you think Planet Guardians are for? For one thing, to guard against such a travesty. Don't you simply adore the way Hawking talks about 'the laws of science'? So brave; so very, very brave. And so thoroughly clueless, as your generation puts it."

He was so smug.

"Not that there aren't 'laws of science.' Insofar as humans understand them. But the Laws of the Universe supersede and override them. Science is just a crude human way to try to understand things. Not to be confused with the situation as it actually is."

"Why'd you make me read the freakin' book, then? The answer isn't even in it."

"The answer is quite in the Horatio category."

"That's something from Shakespeare, right? Can you refresh my recollection?"

"'There are more things in heaven and earth than are dreamt of in your philosophy, Horatio.'"

"Oh, yeah. I think I've heard that one. So I give up, Sandy Claws—how do you time-travel?"

"All right, listen up. You have to take a thought loop."

"Terrific! You just take a thought loop."

"Indeed. Every moment in time is connected to every other moment in time by a simple loop, called a thought loop because it can be traversed at the speed of thought. Time travel is elementary once you know how to attach to the correct thought loop. Unfortunately, at this juncture, only Planet Guardians have access to them. However—

and here's the crucial part—if a human is touching any part of the Guardian's body when he time-travels, she can hitch a ride."

"Uh—" I had questions, but I didn't get to ask them.

"The difficulty," the mad scientist continued, "is that each loop is connected to one place only. Make sense?"

Yep. That part did. "So if we went back to 1492 on the thought loop we're standing on, we'd still be right here looking at that those hills out there—not at sea with Columbus. Is that it?"

"Precise-a-mento, Traveler! You've been promoted again, did you notice? You're really doing splendidly."

"Thanks, Kittycurls. I can't tell you what that means to me."

"By God, I wish I could sigh. Sarcasm in teenagers didn't really begin until about fifty years ago—are you aware of that?'

"Great new invention. Must remember to patent it. So here's the question—how do we get from here to wherever we're going?"

"Ah, yes. The same way we got to Santa Barbara—bumpily. You see, here's where cosmic strands come in. You do recall those from Hawking?"

"Strings, not strands. Some kind of rubber-band thing."

"I suppose that'll do. Strands are similar. Once in the thought loop, we can get a cosmic strand to anywhere—provided we know where to grab it—that will permit a detour. However, it rather shakes up the kidneys."

"Rawther." I couldn't resist mocking him.

But did he care? Moving right along, he said, "I trust you've figured out how to be invisible."

It was like he could read my mind. Which he was probably doing. "I figured out how to get off campus, but it doesn't involve eye of newt. What would you say to hair of cat?"

"I should say it's a readily available material—should the Alpha Beast decide to be generous."

I told him my idea.

"Not a bad start, Traveler," he said. "Inventive, yet obvious." He actually stopped his incessant grooming to think about it. He touched my arm with his paw, in that gesture he said was a nod. "Yes. I very much like it. What do you plan to do once you're off campus?"

"I'd like to go see Abuela."

"Ah. That I approve of. Take the hair." He wrinkled his fat face like a kid eating fish eggs. "And make it snappy. The Alpha Beast is not a pet."

He let me stroke him till a handful of fluff brushed off in my hand, and for a second it really was like having a pet, a great furry love ball, like Curly. But I forgot he'd hear me think that. He snorted, disgusted, and ran for his life.

Me, I ran for a bathroom, but not for the usual reason. First I took out one of my contacts, and then I proceeded to put a spell on it. Maybe it wasn't the most professional spell in the world, but if the Beast had any kind of point at all, I could at least load it up with that thing he called "energy."

See, the Mayans used what's called "sympathetic magic," and I figured I could convert that idea to the twenty-first century. In Mayan times, a rain spell was pretty easy—they just emptied pots of water onto a fire, probably, I figured, chanting something while they did it.

I might not be David Copperfield, but I could sure make a contact lens disappear, which could be a metaphor for me disappearing and eyes not seeing, both at once. I dropped the lens in water and made up a rhyme telling it what to do:

Eye within Eye,
Listen—hear now!
Where you go, go I
I now take the clear vow.
As you are transparent,
I'm not now apparent.

As we move through the town,
Our profiles stay down.
As you are not seen,
I'm no longer a teen—
I now become
The Queen of Unseen!

Honestly. The things I go through for a little freedom.

I took the lens out of the cup, palmed it, and left. I was walking quietly and minding my own business when Rachel, the Level Four with the sappy lavender aura, came barreling toward the bathroom and smacked right into me. And I was walking down the middle of the hall, in plain view. No excuse for it. "Ow, dammit," I blurted. "Watch where you're…"

I stopped in mid-sentence, realizing I'd just sworn. If she reported me, I'd get two consequences, and I was seven-eighths of the way to Level Three. A seriously bad break.

But she didn't register any of it. She was looking at me like I'd grown a tail. "Reeno? Where'd you come from? I didn't even see you."

"Oh. Sorry," I said. "You're not hurt, are you?" Sweet as a chocolate churro. I could afford to be. Maybe I was going to get away with my little outburst.

And more to the point, I seemed to be invisible.

Now, people who don't believe in magic—like me, half an hour earlier—might think it happened because Rachel was in her own little dream world. And maybe it did. But it sure gave me an idea how the thing could work. Which gave me confidence; which may be what makes the world go 'round.

I slipped the contact into my pocket and made a big point of rubbing my eye in Spanish class. In about a nanosecond, my eye was totally red, angry, inflamed, and tearing like mad, due to being full of Beast fuzz. It was totally killing me! If A.B. was kind of a Beast of Beasts, maybe it followed that he had fur like a Sasquatch. It felt like somebody was scrubbing my eyeball with a Brillo pad.

I watched alarm spread, like a coat of sunscreen, from one side of the teacher's face to the other. "Señorita Reeno! What's wrong with your eye?" She sounded panicked.

Trying not to pass out from the pain, I said, "My eye? I don't know, it's been hurting lately—I thought I was getting a little infection, but I didn't want to say anything."

"Oh, *pobrecita*! Don't worry, we have very good doctors here."

For a moment, I did worry—I thought she meant we had doctors on campus, but all was well. Apparently what she meant was, in the past certain boarding school princesses had whined about small-town doctors. Can you imagine? I mean, when you're in someone else's town you can at least be polite.

Here's the beauty of going off campus—you have to have an escort, but you don't have to wear your uniform. That's nine-tenths of invisibility right there.

When I went back to change, The Beast was sitting on my bed. "What, pray tell, is a Sasquatch?"

"It's a mythical beast like you, only Californian. Bigfoot's another name for it. By the way, my eye's on fire."

A lot he cared. "Don't forget to take your contact with you—the one with the charm on it." He leapt to the floor and minced away.

But good thing he reminded me. I took the contact out of my khaki pocket and wrapped it in a fold of my T-shirt, my real, uncollared, non-uniform T-shirt that I hadn't even had on since I took it off on the first day of Bad Girl School. *Reeno rules!* I thought as I strode out to Hal's office to meet my escort. I felt powerful. I felt like myself for the first time since Dad brought me here.

"Forget powerful. Start feeling invisible," said the Jag-voice. The Beast was lolling in the hall in Cat Position Six, Jabba the Cat.

"Go chase a squirrel, kittten-witten."

But I hunched a little bit and kind of shuffled to the office, slipping in like a little ghost. I was probably there a full two minutes before Hal looked up from his paperwork. "Ah, Reeno—didn't see you come in."

"That's okay. I'm kind of invisible today." Hey, fake it till you make it. Who knew? It might work.

"That eye looks bad, honey. Rachel's going to take you to Dr. Alvarez. Here she comes now."

I'd lucked out. Rachel had recently made Level Five, so I guess they wanted to give her a little responsibility. She and I weren't exactly best friends, but one thing I knew about her—she was susceptible to my "glamour."

She didn't even talk to me on the taxi ride to the doctor's. Just like I was—you know—invisible.

I had a plan, once we got there. I figured Dr. Alvarez would call me in, leaving Rachel in the waiting room, and then he'd let me out through a different door from the one I entered. I'd still fetch up in the waiting room, but since I was invisible, I'd be able to sneak out without Rachel knowing, go see Abuela, then slide back in and claim I'd just come out of the inner sanctum. That is, if I decided to come back at all.

The first part went perfectly, especially when the doctor took that industrial-strength fur out of my eye. Boy, was that a relief! After that, it was dicey. I had to go out the same door I came in, and walk right past Rachel without her knowing—a real test of my glamour.

But as it happened, luck was with me—or else the glamour was working more magic than I counted on. Rachel was dead asleep and snoring when I glided past her.

Just like that, I did it. I was free!

I could have just caught the next bus to Puerto Vallarta, but I really did want to see Abuela. So I simply bumped into a prosperous-looking man, lifting his wallet in the process, to get the money for a taxi. "Excuse me," I said sweetly, but he acted as if he hadn't even heard. Excellent.

For once, though, I did feel bad about taking someone's money—Sonya's influence, maybe.

I took a good look around me, breathing free air on a free street and trying to get used to the idea. It was my first time out in the world in a a couple of months, a really long time to be in one small place. It was also more or less my first look at Ojai. At first glance, a little bit hokey, a little bit pokey.

But the town was happening, or so it seemed to me after all those weeks of confinement. Everything seemed to be going at a terrific pace, especially the traffic, which was as loud and relentless as a jackhammer. There was so much to see—shops and restaurants, and people rushing like they were in New York—and hear—traffic noise and manic chatter—and so much to smell that it was pretty bewildering, almost too much to take in. So many people on the street, so easy to run into them, even if you didn't need their wallets.

After all those weeks of wishing for the real world, now I had it and it was a little disappointing. For about half a second, I missed the peace and quiet of St. Psycho's, but I got over it, no fear. I got more and more used to the action with each passing minute, and by the time I found a hotel, I was a citizen of the world again.

I went in, got a map, and asked directions to the hospital. Before I left, I looked at the floor, squealed, bent over, and pretended to find the prosperous man's wallet. I turned it over to the desk clerk, thinking he might or might not return it to the man, but if he didn't, he probably needed the little bit of money I'd left in it.

Next, I asked for the ladies' room, went in, peed, and, turning to wash my hands, found myself looking at my reflection for the first time in months. I almost screamed. Because staring back at me was a freak with three inches of brown hair at the roots and a unibrow. I was weeks behind on my roots when I came to St. Joan's, which I could just about

get away with, but that last half-inch made me look freakish. And my
eyebrows! Without benefit of plucking, they'd had completely grown
together! How had I failed to notice this?

Oh. My. God. I wanted to go hide.

But, looking closer, I thought my unibrow had a certain Frida
Kahlo glamor (as opposed to "glamour"), and anyway, there was
nothing I could do about it. In situations like this my dad always says,
"It is what it is." I decided it was.

So I shrugged it off and went shopping. Since I didn't want to turn
up empty-handed, and Abuela lived for her sewing, I found a hobby
shop that sold needles and good embroidery thread. I helped myself to
some really nice stuff while the shopkeeper helped another customer.
He didn't even look up to ask if he could help me; didn't seem to notice
me at all. I was in such a good mood I left a little money, anyhow.

By that time, I was so full of myself I figured I might not even
have to pay the taxi driver, but this time the spell worked to my
disadvantage—I stood out in the road with my hand up in the air, but
the first taxi passed me by as if I weren't even there. Finally, I caught
one that had stopped to let someone out. I was beginning to see where
the phrase "worked like a charm" came from.

Abuela was asleep when I walked into her hospital room, and I
figured the way things were going, she wouldn't wake up unless I set
off a fire alarm. That was okay, I figured—I just wanted to see her,
make sure she was all right.

But I was shocked by the way she looked—so small, with her eye
all swollen. I was planning just to leave her my little gifts and leave,
but her good eye flew open. *"Hola, Reeno,"* she said, as if she'd been
expecting me.

"Hola, Abuelita," I said, blinking away the embarrassing tears
that had come out of nowhere.

By now, my Spanish was good enough for a simple conversation. I
showed her the embroidery materials. "I think I brought you the wrong
gift," I said sadly. "With that eye, I guess you're not sewing much."

Her hand flew to her face, and she winced as she moved. "Ee's
nothing," she said, seeing my look of dismay. "Just my cracked rib."

"Oh, Abuelita! I'm so sorry."

"No, *niña*, no. You can help me. They say my left eye will not see
again. But it will; it will! You can help me heal my eye."

"Me? But I'm not a doctor."

"I need to make a potion."

"A potion?" What was up with this place? Was everyone into magic?

"You must get me something I need."

"Anything, Abuela. But I can't bring it to you—I may not be able to get out again."

"I can wait until you can."

"But I—"

"I need only one thing. Tears from the eyes of a princess."

What?

"A real princess, you mean? Like the daughter of a king?"

"Good-bye, *niña.* Hurry now." And once again she closed her good eye.

Tears from the eyes of a princess. She had to be delirious. What were the chances of a princess getting sent to St. Joan's?

I got a taxi at the cab stand and went back downtown to the doctor's office. My luck was holding: Rachel was still asleep.

I shook her. "Rachel! Time to go."

She jumped. "Oh! Reeno. You okay?"

"Much better," I said.

"What about your contact?"

"He's ordering one from my doctor at home. My dad'll just stick it in a letter or something."

"Oh. Good." She seemed nervous about something.

I decided to be generous about it. "What's the matter?"

"Uh...I wasn't supposed to fall asleep."

"Don't worry about it. I won't tell anyone."

"Thanks," Relief flooded her face. "And by the way, thanks for not running away."

I laughed. "Are you kidding? Then everybody'd have to walk around in circles again. They hate me enough as it is."

We were in the cab when she said, "Nobody hates you, Reeno."

A.B. was waiting for me, his monkey-tail flicking like a whip. It relaxed the moment I walked in. "Welcome, Traveler. I wasn't sure you weren't going to live up to your name."

"And travel, you mean? I thought about it, but I'd never get service at a restaurant, being invisible and all."

"A word of caution, girlarama—that spell is good for only about twenty-four hours. You'll have to work it again if the need should come up."

I nodded, preoccupied. "A.B., something funny happened. Abuela—"

"Ah, Abuela. How did you find her."

I shook my head. "Not good. Not good at all. They say she'll be blind in one eye. And that's the funny thing…"

"The Alpha Beast does not laugh. The Alpha Beast kills."

"Not that kind of funny. She asked me to get something for her—so she can make a potion. Something really, really hard to get. Like impossible. What's up with that?"

His ears stood up like a bat's. I'd never seen that before. "I really couldn't say."

"Oh, come on, A.B. Thinks she's, like, a little out of it?"

"How should I know?"

"You know everything."

"Wrong, Human. I see most things. I hear almost everything. But I do not know everything. There are more things…"

"Yeah, yeah, yeah. I have to get her some princess tears. Tell me the truth—do you think that's a sane thing to ask for?"

"I think, if I were you, I should keep my eyes open for royalty."

"So. Do you think a JAP counts as a princess?"

"I don't think I should bank on it."

"That's what I thought you'd say. Listen—whatever happened to fighting lessons?"

"Tomorrow, Soldier. You have enough to do today."

CHAPTER XVII: MOMARAMA

He wasn't kidding. Next up was Kara.

At the appointed hour—after dinner and before the Rangers meeting—Julia and I descended on Sonya's room, where we found the two of them sitting cross-legged on the floor and reading the Tarot. "Uh-oh," Sonya said, "I think I see visitors in your future."

"Oh, great," I said, "you didn't tell her we were coming."

Kara's face was a stormy sea of boiling emotions, her face working involuntarily, muscles twitching and jerking just beneath the surface. She was fast unfolding her legs. Call me psychic, but I knew she was going to bolt if we didn't stop her.

I dropped into a squat and put a hand on her knee, causing her to jump about a foot. Her leg tensed so hard it felt like A.B.'s. "It's okay," I whispered. "You're going to be okay. Somehow, some way, we're going to get you away from that witch."

Her mouth dropped open in a gasp and her eyes filled. Julia had dropped to the floor as well. "We know, Kara. We saw what you've been through."

She was shaking her head silently, as if this were the last thing she wanted to happen, and scooting on her butt toward her bed, away from Julia and me. She looked as if she expected to be raped and pillaged any minute.

And finally I got it. She was embarrassed that we'd witnessed what she must see as her humiliation. "Kara, listen. You know what visions are like. I literally saw a witch. I don't even know what your mom looks like. All I saw was a crone in a black dress and a witch's hat. And she was chasing you. Something…I don't know what…but something about the vision told me it wasn't a one-time thing. Maybe it was the expression on your face—kind of like what I'm looking at now. I know you're scared, but you don't have to be. We're not going to invade your privacy. We just want you to know you're not alone."

"I saw you tied to a post," said Julia. "Like…well, like Joan of Arc or someone…and she was whipping you."

"You're crazy! My mother wouldn't tie me up."

I had to note that she hadn't said her mom wouldn't whip her.

"I want to tell you about my mother," said Julia. She was looking down at her hands, the fingers of which were interlaced in her lap, but constantly opening and closing, fidgeting, hopping about like small animals she couldn't control. I could see this was no easier for her than for Kara.

"She didn't let me go to school, didn't let me have any friends, didn't let me out of the house. I had to stay in my room for two days, with no food except peanut butter sandwiches, just for reading Harry Potter!"

Silence. Dead, stone-cold silence. What do you say to something like that?

Finally, Sonya said, "What was up with that?"

"Harry's *demonic,* that's why! Mom joined some church that thinks *everything's* demonic. Even school."

"Omigod," I said. "Like in *Carrie.*"

Nobody said anything. I guess they hadn't seen the movie—if they had, they'd have known Carrie's mom was a total lunatic. So I said, "What about your dad?"

"He couldn't stand it. He left us. And then I couldn't stand it. I ran away. And lived on the streets for two years till Dad found me. You know why I'm here? Because I couldn't make it in school at all. I'd never been, so I didn't have any idea what to do. I acted like a five-year-old because I hadn't been around other kids—I mean kids who lived in *families*—since I was five. I used to throw tantrums and get up on the desks and yell at the teacher."

Sonya put her arms around her, and just held her for a while, the rest of us being quiet like little mice. Disoriented, totally stunned little mice.

And then Julia, perfectly put together Julia, proceeded to lose it. She screamed first, to let us know the dam was breaking, I guess, and then she cried for a while and when she quit, she was still shaking, but she wasn't finished. "So, Kara. Whose Mommie Dearest wins the Joan Crawford Cruelty Contest?"

I just sat there with my face hanging out. Finally, Kara said, "But—how'd you support yourself?"

"Found kids to stay with. Begged. Slept in doorways."

"I'm so sorry," I said. "Julia, I'm really, really sorry." I reached out to touch her hand, but she pulled it away.

This was the girl I'd condemned as a mall rat? I'd imagined her shopping with her silly friends, all of them smoking in the rest room and giggling like retards while throwing their spoiled little lives away. When all the time she'd been freezing cold on the street, begging to get enough money for a Coke and a BLT. And now she probably dressed like she did as camouflage.

"Looks like it's up to you, Reeno. Let's hear about your delightful relatives."

I didn't know what to say. I understood that this was all part of a process to help Kara through whatever was muddying up her aura, but at the moment my mom didn't seem half bad. "My mom isn't so bad." I paused, thinking how to tell this. "She just doesn't have time for me, that's all. I mean with Haley getting worse and worse all the time. But I don't know—it doesn't seem like it was always like that. Can I tell you about my name?"

"Uh, sure," said Sonya, who was probably the only one who wasn't preoccupied with her own problems.

"See, my mom gave it to me," I said. "She doesn't know it, but she did." Tears flooded my eyes, but I didn't care. Right now I just didn't care. Let them escape, like the blood in my dream; let them flow like Yosemite Falls.

"When I was a little kid—a real little kid—back when I still thought nothing could hurt me, and every day was an adventure, my mom was nice to me. I mean, maybe she wasn't all that nice, but little kids trust their parents because they're their parents and because they're all they've got. They don't know any better.

"In those days, my dad used to come in and wake me up in the morning, and when I'd come down to breakfast, my mom would say, 'Well, look who's up? Hi-ho, Deboreeno!' and I'd say, 'Don't call me that, it's not my name.' It was, like, this game we had. I secretly loved it that she called me that. It was her special thing for me." I looked around to see if they were getting it, and they weren't. They were sitting there like three big question marks—one white, one brown, one black.

"Well, it was the *only* thing. See what I mean? That's the only good memory I have of my mom. After Haley got sick, it was like she was on my case all the time, and I couldn't do anything right, and I was always wrong and crazy and everything. But I wanted her to be a good mom—the nice mom I remembered! So I called myself Reeno to remind me. And now it makes me so sad because…"

"Kara?" Sonya said, "Kara, what is it?"

I guess I'd been doing what Julia had done, more or less stared at the floor as I talked, but now I looked up. Kara was sitting there with big fat tears rolling down her face. "My mom never called me anything nice. Not ever! Not even once! But I called her something—Reeno just reminded me, because it was, like the same thing. I used to call her Momerino."

Julia said, "And you're crying about that?"

"I'm crying because one day when I did it, she just…slapped me. For no reason. And said, 'Don't call me that—I'm nobody's Momerino. I'm gonna wash your mouth out with soap.'"

Sonya said, "Ewwww."

We were all quiet, thinking Kara's mom was probably tied with Julia's for America's Craziest Maternal Unit.

"You know how sick soap can make you?"

"You mean she actually did it?" I blurted.

"I never told that to my dad, or my school counselor, or anybody. And guess what else? Not even to myself. Because my mother's crazy, and you can't go around saying your mother's crazy. Because nobody'll believe you. They'll say you're just trying to get attention. You just can't say it.

"She did beat me. You were right, Julia. And she'd shut me up in a closet, and the basement, and sometimes she didn't, like, she didn't even *feed* me for a few days while I'd be in the closet and…oh, God, I can't talk about this." She was sobbing and slobbering the whole time she was talking.

I suddenly had a revelation. "That's why you never get any points. Because you don't want to leave here until you're a major. You don't want to have to ever go back."

She glared at me, trying to lock eyes, as if daring me to steal her dream. Suddenly I understood what button I'd pushed with her. "That's why you never forgave me, isn't it? Because I leaned on you about not making points, and you *couldn't* make points. Oh, God. I get it now. I'm so sorry."

She kept on glaring. This wasn't going to be an instant fix, ending with a tearful group hug.

Julia said, "Where was your dad in all this?"

"Same place he is now. In Colorado with his second family. He dumped us when I was seven and never looked back."

"But don't you ever see him? In the summer, at least?"

"My mom says…"

"What?"

"She told me he didn't want me…that he gave up all…I don't know…rights or something." It was funny, but even as she spoke, I could see her beginning to doubt it.

"But your mom's crazy, right? And meaner than Cruella deVil. Did you ever think she might be lying?"

Once again she gasped, getting it. Realizing she might have a safe harbor out there somewhere.

"You've got to talk to your adviser," I said. "They've got laws about this stuff."

"Nobody's going to help me." She sank down into herself and her voice was barely audible. "You have no idea how sane she can sound. Nobody's going to believe me. I'm not talking to anybody, okay?"

"Not okay," I said, getting to my feet. "If you won't, I will." I meant it too. I left and was halfway down the hall in search of Evelina when I heard her calling my name.

"Reeno! Wait, Reeno!"

I let her catch up with me. "You don't have to. I'll do it."

I went with her, just to make sure she really meant it.

Chapter XVIII: Remedial Phys Ed

So once again she missed a meeting. And it was a good one! The one at which we began to put my curse-removing plan into action. For that purpose, I arrived with my most prized possession—my Curly look-alike dog, which I put in the middle of the table.

At first we did some levitation practice, finding him even easier to fly than books.

We got him a foot in the air even without Kara!

"Whooo, this is fun!" said Carlos. "But now what?"

"Let's see if we can steer. Everybody! Over to Cooper."

The stuffed dog leaned in Cooper's direction, but didn't seem to be really moving until Sonya said, "What's his name?"

"I don't know. I call him Curly, after my real dog."

"Come, Curly," she said, "Curly, come." The dog moved toward her, two inches, three…but that was all she could manage. Curly just hovered. But, hey, at least we were keeping him up.

"Huh," said Julia. "Must be a slightly different way to use energy."

"Or maybe I'm jus' good," Sonya said.

"Let me try it," Cooper said. "Here, Curly. Come, you mangy furbag." The dog didn't move at all.

We all tried it to see who was best at it and it turned out to be Julia. Okay, that was information.

We moved onto the next stop—once again getting the curse off Cooper and into the dog instead of the astral basket we'd used before. Damn, it was a slog! That toxic slime of an aura was like superglue. This time we were onto its tricks, though. Once we had it in the dog, Sonya and Carlos together were assigned the task of keeping it there, while Cooper, Julia, and I worked on building a psychic shield around Cooper.

"Make it strong, make it tough, make it out of carbon steel," I was saying. "Make it an inch thick. Now two inches. Wrap it around twice. Pay particular attention to his back. Plug up any holes. Now add another layer—make it uranium this time." I'd heard once that they make tanks out of that. "Wrap it two more times…"

We were so involved with what we were doing that we didn't notice Sonya and Carlos until suddenly Sonya said, "Carlos, you faggot moron! What the hell!"

As one, we turned to stare at her. She looked terrified. Carlos looked stricken. "It got away," he explained.

"Oh, Lord, I'm frickin' possessed!" Sonya screamed. "You f—ktards!"

The more her mouth moved, the more her face became a tragedy mask. "At least," said Julia, "we know it's possible to transfer it. Okay, Sonya, here's what we're going to do. We're going to build shields around Carlos, Reeno, and me. Then we're going to transfer the curse to the dog, and seal it in. Do you hear me? I don't care if it takes all night. We are going to find a way to *lock that curse in that dog!*"

Sonya looked dubious. "I don't get a shield?"

"We'll build it after…uh-oh." Julia had just realized what I had—that Sonya had uttered a whole sentence without an insult in it.

"You ignorant moron retard *jackasses!*" came out of Cooper.

Julia sighed. "I guess shield-building should be our new focus. Sorry, Cooper and Sonya. This was a royal screw-up. But we're all tired. Let's try again tomorrow."

When I woke up the next morning, Kara was in her own bed. "How'd it go?" I asked.

She nodded, like someone pulling herself together to get up the nerve to speak. "Good. It went okay. Did you know that when teachers find out about abuse, they're legally bound to report it to the authorities?"

"Sure. Why'd you think I wanted to tell Evelina?"

"Well, I didn't know. Guess what?" She sat up in bed and I saw that her transformation was almost as pronounced as Cooper's had been. "She's calling my dad."

"Omigod, you're almost *yellow!*"

"What?"

"Your aura's clearing up."

"What the hell does that mean?"

"It was muddy before. That's the only way I can describe it. You're looking so much healthier—in a psychic sense, I mean."

"Oh." She blushed. "Hey, you want to go to gym together?"

This was my first class of the day and though I was vaguely aware Kara was in it, we'd certainly never walked together.

"Sure." I got dressed, noting that for the first time Kara made her bed and tidied up. The day was starting out great. I was even up for calisthenics, which was how gym always started, rain or shine.

I should have suspected things were about to go awry when I saw the Beast. He usually doesn't turn up till afternoon.

Lola, the teacher who leads the exercises, always goes, "Let's start with neck rolls!" in this great hearty voice, which usually cracks her up. I had no idea what was funny till someone told me it was what Jane Fonda used to say. I'm still not sure I get it.

But there I was, rotating away, when the Beast walked across the yard in front of Lola, talking a blue streak as if we were alone in an elevator. "Some things are worth fighting over; some things are not."

"So what else is new?" I shot back.

"Tactic Five is this: Choose your battles."

In my head I reviewed Tactics One through Four:

Fight smart, not strong!

Know your enemy.

Never underestimate your enemy.

Work with available materials.

Okay, so now I had five. "Choose my battles," I repeated.

"Now let's streeeeetch!" Lola chimed, "Reach for the sky, ladies. Let's open up those rib cages!"

"Usually, you fight over everything."

I reached for the sky. "I do not."

"Since that subject is not worth fighting over, I shall ignore it."

"And how'd it get to be your point? I thought it was mine."

We straightened and reached for the sky again.

"Hear me, Student. Choose your battles."

"Tactic Five. Fine." Once again, I went butt-up.

"Tactic Six: Choose your opponent as well."

"Now juuuuumping jacks!" Lola sang.

I spread my feet in a potent leap and popped them together smartly.

"In other words," he continued, "don't fight if you can't win."

"Got it."

"One, two, threeee," Lola warbled. stepping up the pace. The monster was oblivious. He was pacing like a sentry, barking out his little rules as if lecturing to a class. I was the only one who saw what was coming. "Now, kiiiiiicks!"

"Lola! No!" But I was too late.

Her right leg lifted like a rocket, her foot having neatly hooked the Beast under his blubbery tiger-pouch. As her leg reached its zenith—nearly at her robust melons—he sailed over her head, and in fact over the nearest building, some thirty feet behind her, and disappeared altogether.

"Field goal!" I yelled. I was seriously amused.

Fortunately, my little wisecrack was drowned out by all the squeals and screams and "oh my Gods" that surged through the air like so many bird songs. I was about to holler, "Hey, Lola! Don't you brake for animals?" when I suddenly realized everyone was looking at me. All concerned and sad, thinking I'd lost my sweet little fuzzy buddy.

I could have had a total laugh-riot out there, completely cleared out all the tension, if I hadn't had to act all sad and upset and brave. Thinking fast, I screamed "Jag! Omigod, Jag!" like I'd just seen a car crash. And all of a sudden, I noticed we really did have a problem, and it wasn't A.B.: Lola was on the verge of collapse.

She was still standing out on the field, going, "Oh no, oh no, oh no oh no," which you could barely hear because she was holding both hands over her mouth. I ran over to her, yelling, "Somebody get Hal!

"Lola, it's okay," I said, and put an arm around her. "Jag's a really tough little kitty. He'll be fine—cats have nine lives and really, it wasn't your fault. It was just an accident, because you love your work so much, and you were so into it. You'll be okay. Lola? Lola!"

She'd started screaming, just these loud, hysterical screeches, and she seemed to be sinking. There seemed only one thing to do, and that was help her down to the ground as gently as I could, and hold her. "Breathe deep," I said. "Come on—you've got to pull out of this." I may have spoken the least bit sharply, because all of a sudden she looked at me as if she might have a grain of sense somewhere behind her wild eyes. I hugged her close and patted her.

"I wouldn't hurt an animal," she whimpered. "I'm not that kind of person."

"Well, of course you're not. And you didn't. It was really Jag's fault—he got in your way."

"He's just an innocent little pussycat."

Oh, brother. Trying not to roll my eyes, I said, "He'll be okay. I promise."

"He won't. You'll be so lonesome without him. I know how you love that cat." She started sobbing like she was the kid. I was just about at the end of my resources—not to mention patience—when Hal came running, followed by a gaggle of Upper Levels, fluttering like a flock of incompetent birds.

"Reeno, I'll take over" he barked. "Why don't you and, uh"—he surveyed the crowd and picked out someone he thought was my friend—"why don't you and Kara get Evelina and try to find Jag?"

I moved aside while he took over the care of the still-sobbing Lola, and made my way through the sea of sympathetic eyes, all of them in the heads of innocents who thought the Alpha Beast was a fluffy little pet cat. Pretending stoic heartbreak, I joined Kara and put on the mask of a woman about to do what a woman's gotta do—claim the body of a fallen comrade and bury it.

Evelina was just arriving on the field. By now, the whole school knew what had happened and the teachers were turning out to help the fragile bad girls get through the terrible tragedy that was probably going to set us back weeks in our brainwashing.

"Come on," she said to Kara. "Reeno, you don't have to come if you don't want to. I mean, it could be upsetting. He might be badly hurt." She bit her lip, thinking he could be worse than badly hurt.

"I have to," I said bravely. "He might need me. What if he...you know...died and I wasn't there?" I paused and whispered, "I'd never forgive myself," wondering if I'd gone too far.

Three women on a mission, Kara and Evelina and I strode out through the gate, walked down the road, and knocked on the door of the cottage that housed the school's nearest neighbor. It was pretty hard to keep a straight face while Evelina explained to the bewildered homeowner that there was undoubtedly a badly injured cat in her backyard, suffering from an accidental launching during a morning exercise session. The woman seemed terrified, probably because she figured we were all drug addicts and social misfits.

But Evelina finally talked us into her yard, on the condition that we go through a side gate instead of the house. I fully expected to see A.B. sitting placidly on his haunches, daintily licking his paws, but, actually, he wasn't in sight.

"Jag?" I called. "Kitty kitty kitty?"

Silence.

I saw the other two exchanging glances, wondering if I was going to get hysterical like Lola. What I had to do was protect the Beast's identity. I had no choice but to feign despair.

"He's not here," I pronounced, mock-horrified.

"He must be," Evelina said. "Maybe behind that shed."

Maybe on the roof, laughing at us.

But I followed her obediently to the shed and peeked around it. At the far end was a peachy-looking rag. Even knowing what I knew, I couldn't look. I gave a little squeal and turned away. Kara, eyes like golf balls, put a protective arm around me, which was a first and then some. Only Evelina, being the designated adult, strode forward, her mouth in a hard, determined line.

I saw her kneel down, put out a hand, and draw it back covered with blood. And then she started sobbing. "Oh, Jag," she blubbered. "Oh, my poor, poor Jag."

After a moment, she came back and announced sadly, "We can't help him, Reeno."

I saw that her hand was lacerated. "He hurt you!"

"It's nothing," she said, as Kara went through her pockets, searching for a tissue to stop the blood. "His mind's gone. Injured animals sometimes attack, you know? It isn't their fault, they're just so frightened."

Kara was unconvinced. "If he's alive, there's a chance—we have to get him to the vet." She raced for him before I could stop her.

Great. Next, she was going to be bleeding. Silently, I pleaded with the Monster. "Get it together, A.B. Evelina never hurt you. You're just mad because I made fun of you. But Evelina is not me. She didn't deserve that. You touch Kara and I'll...I swear to God, I'll let them take you to the vet." It was an empty threat, of course—I wasn't about to be responsible for what the Beast would do to anyone who jammed a thermometer up his butt.

The voice that answered wasn't his. It was old, and weak, and kind of desperate-sounding. "Help me, girlina. Keep these bloody humans away from me."

Like I wasn't one. But this was no time to get my feelings hurt. I had to save Kara's fingers and face. "Kara, wait—let me!"

But I was too late. She screamed as if Freddie Krueger was after her, and come to think of it, there was similarity. But when she returned, pale and shook up, at least she wasn't bleeding. "He went for me—I couldn't get close. Oh, man, Reeno, there's blood all over. He can't live; we have to put him out of his misery."

I didn't even answer, just marched in to do my duty. A.B. was spread out on the ground like a blanket, facing outward, eyes closed. Blood smeared the top of his head and his bottom looked more or less soaked. As I approached, he reared up, bared his razoroid teeth, and opened his mouth in a hiss from hell. Involuntarily, I jumped back. "That's what I did to Kara." The voice was his own again. "So she wouldn't notice my ear's missing. Find the bloody thing, will you? And my tail."

Oh, boy, this was sweet! The mighty Alpha Beast forced to seek help from a lowly bad girl. I'd probably have giggled except for the effect that would have had on Kara and Evelina.

I looked up and saw that the tin roof of the shed had a jagged edge. He must have slid down it, and snagged on it, shearing off a few body parts in the process.

"Lie still and let me check you out."

He didn't answer, but on the other hand, he didn't move. His tail was well known to be as tough as a steel cable—how on Earth could he have cut it off? I checked his rear end first.

He hadn't, of course—but he had a deep gash that was still bleeding.

"Tail present and accounted for. What are you, a hypochondriac?"

No answer.

Evelina yelled, "Reeno, are you all right?"

"Good kitty," I said, cursing myself for a hypocrite. "You just lie still now. Gooood boy, Jag-cakes." And then I yelled to Evelina, "I'm talking to him. I think he's calming down a little. Could you just give me a minute with him?"

I started crawling around on my hands and knees, searching for the missing ear.

"What on Earth are you doing?" Evelina called.

"I lost my contact, but don't worry, it probably didn't go far. That's a sweeeet kitty."

"A.B., talk to me," I said in my head.

The Beast said nothing. Had he bled to death while I was crawling around? That was certainly going to screw things up. Finally, I found the ear, clinging by a film of blood to a Coke can someone had thrown back there. Gingerly, I peeled it off.

"Okay, I've got it," I said silently. "What now?" Out loud, I said, "Now you just take it easy, kittykins. Everything's going to be fine."

"Shmush it back in place," he grumped, definitely not dead. "And make it snappy. I'm getting blood in my eyes."

A severed ear is a delicate thing, like a papery apricot with a thousand tiny veins running through it, tissue thin and slimy with blood. I had to look at it pretty close to get it properly positioned, which was fairly disgusting, but I wasn't about to puke now that I was playing the hero. After some maneuvering, I finally got it right, a fact that became instantly obvious—the thing reattached like a piece of Velcro. "Got it, A.B. Now what?" a part of me said, while another went, "Tell me where it hurts, kitty-boy. Will you let me pick you up now?"

"No!" he shouted. Or rather, said, in the I'm-the-boss-of-you-voice. "Whatever you do, don't pick me up. Get something under me, like a stretcher. I've got three broken vertebrae, which won't heal for another few minutes. By then, those two'll probably euthanize me and I'll lose another bloody life."

"Which would be pretty hard to explain when you come back. Look, I need help for this. Could you meow piteously, please?"

Obediently, he began to make little kitty whimpers. I kept my back to the humans, pretending to stroke the poor, broken little thing. I'd noticed that Evelina was wearing a blue shirt over a tank top, which ought to serve the purpose just fine. "I think I've got him stabilized," I called. Like some veterinary paramedic. "Evelina, can we use your shirt for a stretcher? And can you help me get it under him?"

But it was Kara who brought the shirt over. "Evelina's kind of falling apart," she said, and turned her attention to the patient. "Oh, poor wittle thing. Does it hurt, Jag?"

He replied with an unholy growl.

"Sweeeet kitty," I said, meaning, *shut up, A.B.!*

We bore him back in state and ensconced him in my bed, since he spent so much time there anyhow. Hal was hovering, as well as a couple of teachers. "I think he's going to be fine," I said. "He's just in shock. We need to bandage that tail, though."

They all looked sad, as if they knew I was just deluding myself, but Hal went to get the first aid kit, and I loved it! Here was Reeno Dimond, bad girl extraordinaire, giving orders to the principal.

A.B. made a show of malingering for a while, even pitifully licking Lola's hand when she came to make sure she hadn't mangled him beyond repair, which was big of him, considering what he could have done.

And me? I basked in glory. I even got called to the principal's office. Hal started out slow. "Reeno, you did well out there. I'm going to tell you, we were all impressed. You really showed grace under pressure, which is what guts is, did you know that?"

Guts is or guts are? I thought.

But I grinned modestly. "Well, I've been around a lot of sick animals. My uncle used to have a farm where I went in the summer. But that didn't mean I didn't pray this morning—I've been around that kind of thing too. My dad's a minister, you know."

"Everyone noticed how well you handled yourself with Lola too. And Evelina says you've been showing a lot of progress. She feels you're really maturing."

"I don't think I can actually take any credit, Hal. The other kids set such great examples, you know? I watched them and I just, you know, kind of realized it was time to make things right. I feel good about it, I really do. I feel like I'm finally on track."

Oh, boy, was I full of it.

But Hal said, "Well, we're inclined to agree with you. The staff and I have decided to bring you up to Level Three."

I'd been hoping for that, but now that it was here, I really couldn't believe it. "For real?" I blurted.

Hal winked. "For real."

I jumped out of my chair and pumped my arms. "Yes! Level Three! Phone calls here I come! Can I call my dad? Now?"

Believe it or not, Hal was really enjoying the show. You could see he liked being the good guy for a change. "No, but he can call you. I'll tell Evelina to e-mail him right away."

Pumped? I'm here to tell you! I felt so good I was sorry I'd lied about praying. And there was one other thing I was sorry about—that cheesy field-goal crack. When I finally got back to my room—later that day, after lunch—A.B. was sleeping like a horse. (Some cats sleep like a kitten; not A.B.)

He woke up blinking, a rare thing for him; he usually went for the paralyzing stare. But right now he looked so cute I reached out to stroke him. And naturally, he dodged my loving little hand. "When will the human learn? For the twentieth time, the Alpha Beast is not a pet!"

"Sorry. You blinked. For a minute there, you looked almost like a normal kitty-cat."

Like he cared. "I hear congratulations are due."

"Yes! Level Three!" I pumped my arms again, and then it occurred to me I hadn't been thinking about it—so how could he know?

"Fluttermouths were here," he explained. "They happened to mention it in between calling me Jaggy-pooh and Kitty-Baby. It seems they actually felt you deserved it—apparently having missed that merciless remark you made upon my becoming airborne."

"A.B., listen, I need to apologize for that. I knew you weren't going to die—I just didn't know you were going to hurt."

"Only my dignity suffered, Novice. Injury is a way of life in my line of work."

"You're demoting me again?" It made me smile. "It got to you, didn't it? The 'field goal' thing."

"Don't be absurd. Hurt feelings are not in my repertoire."

"Well, all the same, I'm sorry. But it was so funny—I mean, you were so busy playing the Nutty Professor, you never even saw it coming."

He flicked his completely healed tail, still sporting its unnecessary bandage. "Didn't I?" He put his head on his paws and closed his eyes.

Didn't he?

What did that mean?

"Wait a minute. You mean you got in Lola's way on purpose? So I could save you and they'd promote me?"

"Congratulations, Student; let us leave it at that. By the by, do you happen to remember a thing I said out there?"

"About fighting? Sure. You only gave me two more. Choose my battles and don't fight if I can't win. Tactics Five and Six."

"Do you have anything to add?"

"You sound exactly like a teacher. 'And you, Ms. Dimond—do you have anything to add?'"

"Do you, Ms. Dimond?"

"Well, yeah. I guess. I should probably pick the right time for battles too. Like, maybe not when I have my period."

His tail did a total flamenco dance. "That is Tactic Seven. Henceforth, you will please refrain from discussing bodily functions."

I laughed. I was in a great mood. "Knew that would get you."

"Could you focus, please? Three more points. Tactic Eight: Prepare for your battles. Understood?"

"Too late for a black belt—but, yes. Understood."

"Tactic Nine: When possible, pull a hustle. Are you familiar with the concept?"

"Beastie-boy, you are talking to the old-movie queen of the universe. I happen to have seen 'The Hustler' six times." I shrugged to show him how simple it was. "You just act incompetent and the opponent underestimates you."

"Indeed. Particularly useful for an attractive young woman."

"Attractive! Aren't we mellow today."

"Tactic Ten, and third most important: If you need help, call for it."

"Sure, backup. Like in all the cop movies. See, one thing I never liked about *Fargo*, she just walked right into that nuthouse, pregnant and everything, without even calling for backup. Stupid, stupid, stupid. Believe me, A.B. I wasn't born yesterday. First sign of trouble, I yell."

"And what will you yell?"

I stared at him. "Yell was a figure of speech. It doesn't matter what I yell—because nobody'll hear it but you, right?"

"Wrong. Telepathy won't work if we're too far from each other. We shall have to rely on vocalization."

I thought about it. "How about 'Here kitty, kitty, kitty'?" I smiled sweetly, majorly amused at myself.

I could see he wanted to do his usual curled-tail pranceaway, but he couldn't without blowing his cover—injured cats just don't flounce out of rooms. I was raising my eyebrow, mocking him a little, looking right in his evil amber eyes, so I never saw it coming—he smacked me across the face with that anaconda he called a tail. Well, really! I sighed, not about to let him know how much it stung. "You win, A.B. How do you want me to call you? Holler 'mayday'?"

He put his head back down, closed his eyes again, and murmured, "Serviceable," he said, "but hardly original. 'Field goal,' I think."

Can you believe that? Just when I thought he had no sense of humor.

CHAPTER XIX: HISTORY LAB

The whole rest of the day I had butterflies, waiting for my dad to call, knowing it probably wouldn't be till night, but hoping anyhow. I even skipped the Rangers meeting, although it was Kara's first one since the bookstorm, and sure enough, I was right.

Evelina summoned me at nine thirty.

I raced to her office, sandals flapping, and grabbed the phone from her. "Dad? Dad, how are you? Dad, I miss you so much! How's Haley and Curly? And Mom! I haven't heard from her in weeks. I was just starting to get worried."

"Oh, Curly?" He sounded way too hearty. "Curly's just great. She gets cuter every day." He kind of paused, like somebody getting their nerve up—not sure whether to go on with the small talk, or just get to it.

"Curly's fine, but what? I hear a 'but' in there, Dad."

"Congratulations on Level Three, baby. Great timing—I was going to call you anyhow."

My stomach turned over. "But you can only call in an emergency."

"Honey, there's just no easy way to say it. I'm afraid I have some really really bad news."

It had to be about Haley. But surely she wasn't...she couldn't have died, they would have called me.

"Yesterday, Haley went to sleep and we couldn't wake her up."

Oh, God, it *was* the worst! "She...died? Dad, are you telling me she died?"

"No, no, of course not! We'd certainly have...I mean...let's don't even think about that. The doctors say it's a coma, honey. We're hoping she'll come out if it."

I could almost hear the words he hadn't spoken: *But we're not getting our hopes up.*

"Dad?" I could her the tears in my voice. "Dad, I need to come home!"

"No, baby, you don't. Haley won't know whether you're here or not. You need to be exactly where you are."

I thought about that. If Haley's illness was really a curse, he was exactly right. And he spoke almost as if he knew it. "Why do you say that?" I asked.

"Because you really can't do anything here. And I just have a strong feeling that where you are is where you should be. A strong *intuitive* feeling."

Intuitive. Why had he emphasized that word? "Isn't 'intuitive' another word for psychic?" I asked.

He laughed. "No, I didn't mean it that way. I just meant I feel it in a big way."

"Well, Dad, let me ask you something—did you ever think I might be psychic?"

"Are you kidding? I've always thought you were psychic."

What was this? "You did? Why didn't you tell me?"

"Because—" He stopped dead; I could feel him searching for words. "Well, because your mother didn't want to go there."

Of course. I brushed it off. "Well, look, Dad, I'm pretty sure I am. And those dreams I used to have—remember how vivid they were? I dreamed about you and Mom. You know what postcognition is?" I surprised myself. I was really taking charge here. "It's when you know what's happened in the past. I think I had a postcognitive dream about how you got engaged."

"Huh? What?" I don't think I'd ever before heard my dad at a loss for words.

"Dad, tell me something—it's important. Why did you and Mom adopt Haley instead of just, you know, getting pregnant?"

"Because we…because…"

"Because Mom didn't want to have children? Was that it? Because Haley's illness runs in her family and…"

"We knew it was safe to have *you*, Deb," he said. "Don't think for a minute…"

"That isn't where I was going with this. I know it only affects the oldest child. Listen, Dad, did it ever occur to you it could be a curse?"

Silence. A long silence. And finally he spoke. "That's what your mom's relatives call it. The Family Curse. Like something in a horror movie, she always says. She doesn't believe in it."

"Wow." Even now, with her own child in a coma, she didn't believe in it.

"Yeah," said Dad. It was weird how clearly I could see him, his jaw twitching a little, taking off his glasses, absentmindedly sticking the earpiece in his mouth. "What was that?" he said.

"Nothing," I said, but it was something. I'd had to suppress a sob. "Can I talk to Mom?"

"Deb, got a little more bad news. Your mom's not doing all that well. She's pretty depressed about all this."

Well, surprise!

"She doesn't want to *talk* to me?" I knew she didn't like me that much, but this made me feel really bad.

"No, it isn't that, honey, she doesn't want to talk about…you know. And she knows she'd have to with you. So I called while she's at the hospital."

It seemed late for that. I wasn't sure I believed it.

"Actually," he said, his voice sheepish, "she's pretty much at the hospital twenty-four seven."

I could imagine. My mom was so used to controlling things. It had to be the hardest thing in the world for her, a doctor and pretty much a dictator, not to be able to do a single thing for her own desperately ill child.

"She sleeps a lot when she's home," Dad said. "I'm trying to get her to go on medication. I don't…I just don't…"

He sounded close to tears.

"I just don't know what's going to happen if Haley…if anything happens…"

"Dad, listen to me! I'm going to solve this. Understand me now: Haley's going to be okay."

"I appreciate your trying to cheer me up, Deb, but you don't have to be the brave one here. You're just a kid."

Evelina was tapping her watch. I could finally have phone calls, but there was a twenty-minute limit. "Dad, they're giving me the signal. *I promise* you I will solve this. Gotta run."

I hung up before he could answer, before he could say again that I couldn't do it, I didn't have to do it, I was too young to do it. I wanted to end on a note of finality: On a promise that had to be kept.

I kept the tears in until I got back to my room. Thankfully, Kara was still at the Rangers meeting and A.B. was out slaying dragons for Gaia. So I could cry as hard as I wanted.

Sometime in the night the *thump* of a twenty-pound feline shook the bed like a minor earthquake. I didn't always feel the Beast land in bed, but that night I must have been sleeping very lightly.

"A.B., I've been waiting for you."

No answer.

"How is getting the book going to help Haley? I mean, if we don't get it, I don't get cursed."

"Novice, you *are* cursed. One way or the other, you're going to do it. When we go back, it's always going to be 1492—or whatever. It's only when we leave that's in question. As to how that helps Haley, I can't say exactly. I can only say that you can't remove a curse until you know what it is."

"But we do know. It's…"

"We do not know the specifics. As in, 'you are cursed *unless*…' 'you are cursed *until*…'"

I hadn't thought of that. It was such a revelation I would have sat up in bed if I could have moved, but he pretty much had me pinned.

"Let's go now. Let's go yesterday."

"Why the sudden urgency?"

"My dad called. Haley's in a coma."

"Ah. The situation is urgent. However, I beg you to reconsider. At the moment, you appear to be wearing pajamas decorated with pink bunnies. Is this really the way you wish to meet Cortes?"

"Uh…probably not."

"Tomorrow then. Nighty-night." He turned himself into a Fur Grenade.

I must have been really tired. When I woke up the next morning, I was still trying to make it sink in. That this was the day we were going to get the book.

This was it.

But I wasn't ready. I wasn't worthy. It was all a fantasy, anyhow. Just something to get me through.

A.B. was in the sink when I went to brush my teeth. "This is real, O'Neal. Three hours till blast-off." He hopped down and skittered off.

"Come back here," I commanded.

Did he listen? Ha.

Three hours! Three centuries, as far as I was concerned. Uh-uh. No could do. I couldn't go to class and act normal. That took too much focus. It had to be now, but there was something I didn't get, and for once I had time for breakfast before gym, which was good. A.B. hadn't been out to the field since his unscheduled flight.

I found him lapping milk in the dining room. "A.B., I've got a question. How long are we going to be gone?"

"You're not thinking things through, Novice. As long as it takes, of course."

"Fifteen minutes? Half an hour?"

"What does it matter? Days, maybe. Months. You have something better to do?"

"Well, meanwhile, what happens to my life? I can't just come waltzing in here next Christmas and say, 'Excuse me; I had an errand.'"

"Don't be absurd. We'll come back a split second after we leave. We could leave right now, stay away two centuries if we like, and when we get back, for all anyone will know, I'll still be trying to have breakfast with a human asking silly questions. Blink of an eye kind of thing."

"Oh."

"That's the beauty of time travel—you have time on your side."

"Well, I'm not going on an empty stomach—can you meet me at my table?"

He didn't deign to answer, but I was munching granola when he sidled up.

"A singularly appropriate day," commented the Monster.

"Why, A.B.? Are you into astrology?"

"The simple fact is, you're ready. You've seen the dark side."

"The dark side of what?"

"Life."

"Oh. You mean that thing about Kara's mom?"

"And Julia's. I may have mentioned that my line of work is particularly dangerous and violent. Do you happen to recall that?"

"Sure, kitty-pie. You're a regular pussycat bogey-man."

He grabbed my wrist. "Today of all days, you will take the Alpha Beast seriously."

"Believe me, I do." I had cereal all over me. "I was just joking around."

"What I meant to say is this: you will see some things that are distinctly not pretty. The Novice you were a scant few weeks ago would have cracked under pressure. The Student you were two days ago might still have clutched. Today, my little girly-q, you are a Warrior."

"Who, me?" Maybe it *was* real, Lucille. I about fainted.

"Yes. But one thing is as yet undetermined. We know we have to go to Cozumel, thanks to your little social group. But when, exactly, will we be arriving?"

"You're asking me?"

"Indeed," he said. "When did Cortes land there?"

I started to panic. This was the last thing I expected. "I need to hit the library."

"Blast-off in one hour. I shall meet you there."

"Uh…you want me to cut gym? I just made Level Three—they'll bust me back."

"Does it occur to you that this is possibly more important?"

I charged over to the library. I had only an hour to learn everything there was to know about what I was getting myself into, only enough time to skim, but I thought at least I had the dates and players right by the time the Beast arrived.

He stretched out on the table like he was planning a lazy afternoon in the sun. I'd give him points for cool, but when you're nearly a thousand years old, I guess it comes easier.

Me, I was bouncing off the walls. "Okay, A.B., here it is in a nutshell. In late February of 1519, when Cortes went to Cozumel—which is actually an island off the Yucatan Peninsula, by the way—he saw plenty of books. There's also a rumor that he's the one who took the Madrid Codex to Spain—that the Cortes family kept it for three centuries before it surfaced. That's one of the four surviving books, you recall."

"I recall."

"Cortes left Cozumel at the beginning of March, so any time in the last week of February ought to be good."

"Very well then. Let's give him time to settle in. Shall we make it February twenty-seventh?" Cool, did I say? He was Orange Ice.

"Okay, Orange Ice." Offering my hand, I tried to match his tone. "Blast off."

He flipped his snaky tail into my outstretched hand and that was it: No pause, no preamble, no "good-bye cruel world"—just the universe dissolving, the head-splitting noise, and the falling, falling into eternity…plunging more or less down a pitch-dark hole that felt like rolling down a flight of stairs, except that there was nothing to touch—no body, no stairs—and it hurt! It seemed a thousand times worse than last time, and it lasted at least the five hundred years we shed. And then the familiar grinding noise punished my ears, and we were on a beach.

Anchored offshore was a fleet of boats that looked like pictures I'd seen of Columbus's three—Cortes's little armada, I realized. Goose bumps broke out on my arms.

It was a beautiful beach, with lots of surf, maybe the prettiest I'd ever seen, and really different from the ones in California, which are always cold even in summer. This one was warm, and stretched for miles, with a little breeze coming off the clear, crystal water. The sand was white and so inviting I had an uncontrollable urge to step out of my sandals and wriggle my toes. You really appreciate little things after a few months in Bad Girl School.

"Put me down, Traveler. You know I hate to be held."

For a moment, I'd almost forgotten I had Catzilla in my arms. And how delicious the moment had been!

"Do it, Human."

I loosened my grip and let him leap. Which was pretty amusing because his precious paws sank an inch or so into the sand. One at a time, he freed them, shaking the sand off. "Ugh! Let's find terra firma."

For the first time, I looked behind us and saw the city from another galaxy that turned out to be a Mayan town.

"Shall we go there?" I said, and A.B. answered, "Just so long as I don't have to walk in this accursed sand."

We found a pretty good path, tree-lined but deserted, which we took, and then a weird thing happened. I couldn't help it, but I found myself dancing like the Tin Man and belting, "Follow the Yellow Brick Road." I hadn't been in such a good mood since sixth grade.

"Be quiet, can't you?" the Beast said. "Haven't you ever heard of a sneak attack?"

"But, A.B., this is a once in a lifetime thing. It's...enchanted!" And I swung into a chorus: "Follow, follow, follow, follow..."

"Quiet, before it's too late!"

And that was when the three men and a woman stepped out of the woods and began walking toward us, two of the men short and tattooed, the other wearing sailor's clothes about five hundred years out of style.

The woman was darker than the others.

Now, I'd read that the Cozumel Mayans were shy folk who slipped off and hid when the conquistadores first arrived. The Spaniards had to coax them back in order to buy goods from them. So surely these people weren't dangerous.

On the other hand, the men suddenly started shouting and elbowing each other, looking at me in a distinctly familiar way.

"Male bonding," I said nervously. "You can't get away from it."

"Warrior! Don't underestimate your enemy."

They were nearly upon us now, and one man broke from the group, one of the Mayans. He got up in my face, saying something I didn't get, but there was a look in his eye I did.

"A.B.," I quavered. "Do you understand Mayan?"

"He said, 'nice rack,' girlkin. You don't need Berlitz for that one."

"I was afraid of that."

Sweat popped out in my pits. I waved at the Spanish sailor. *"Buenos días, señor,"* I called. "Could you please tell your friend to go f—k off?' My Spanish was really coming along.

"Make love?" the Spaniard said. He turned to the woman. "Tell my friends she wants to make love."

"Did I ever mention," A.B. remarked, "how much I truly despise profanity?"

"Well, you just converted me." Sweat dripped into my eyes, but I was trying to match his cool. I went over my fighting lessons in my head—Fight smart, not strong! But that could only work if I *was* smart.

Choose your battles. Well, I'd blown that one. Choose the time for your battles. Likewise. Never engage an unworthy opponent...and certainly not a superior one. Too late to interview the guy.

I'd just flunked Fighting 101.

And then I remembered about available materials. I had a knee, the first Mayan had a groin—and he'd felt perfectly free to cop a generous feel. What was there to do but ram his equipment up his male chauvinist spine? I'd had practice at this, and despite the totally unfair punishment, had been quite pleased with the effect. It worked just as well the second time.

"Die, pig!" I yelled, for good measure. The guy fell down moaning and rolling around, which made the woman and the Spaniard burst out laughing.

But the second Mayan must have felt he had to protect his buddy. He got this look on his tattooed, flattened face that I can only describe as very unfriendly. I was about to turn and run when he passed one hand over my head, grabbed a handful of my hair, and spun me around like a Barbie doll so that I faced away from him, toward the Spaniard and the woman. I didn't actually see it, but I could tell from his bloodcurdling scream—and their petrified expressions—that the famous Planet Guardian had finally been moved to action.

I flipped back around and wrenched myself free, to find A.B. going up in the man's face—and believe me, only the Alpha Beast can make that phrase truly come alive. He had his paws wrapped around the pony-tailed head, claws biting into the guy's scalp, and his razor teeth were tearing out chunks of face as if he were eating an apple on a deadline. The Mayan man was trying to fight him off, but A.B. twirled his tail around the guy's right wrist and pried it off him, using his back feet to peel the skin off the left one. I actually felt sorry for the guy.

But not very.

I grinned at the Spaniard. "Abandon ship, sailor," I said. "Or you're cat food like your pal."

He didn't need to be told twice. Apparently, the woman—who must be Doña Marina—understood Spanish as well as he did, because both of them pivoted and burned shoe leather, which was the good news—the bad was, they were running toward the Emerald City. I had a nasty feeling we were going to be famous by the time we arrived.

I turned back to my fuzzy defender. "Okay, A.B., that's enough," I said. The man was now on the ground, kicking and screaming in pain, the cat still covering his face, working on his eyes. The second Mayan, the one I'd kneed, seemed to have recovered slightly. He was crawling toward the battle, but slowly, either out of fear or because his balls were killing him.

"Behind you, A.B." I yelled, but the Beast was way ahead of me.

He used his tail like a whip, flaying the guy's face with one stroke. I looked on in amazement—he'd hit me with that tail and now I realized it was just a love tap. "Gentle as a kitten" was not a phrase that applied here.

The man jumped back, touching his face and staring in horror at his bloody hand. He spat his two front teeth out on the ground. For the moment, he was pretty much in shock, but he was about to get a second wind and I was going to have to get the Beast's back. The problem was, I wasn't sure how.

"Stay out of it, Novice," a familiar voice said. I was crestfallen at the demotion.

A ripping noise tore the air, and A.B. lifted his head toward the crawling man, his jaws dripping blood, more blood pouring out onto the road—from the first man's throat.

"Aiiyeee!" the second one hollered. "Aiyeeeeeeeeee!"

I figured that was Mayan for "Time to kiss my ass good-bye."

For some reason, the Beast opted for mercy. Instead of springing, he flattened his ears and hissed, giving the man enough time to struggle to his feet and start galloping.

CHAPTER XX: A TRIBE IS BORN

I gaped in horror at the dead man lying in the road. Yeah, I knew he was dead, but I felt like I should take his pulse, just to be sure.

"Leave him alone," the Fiend said. He was washing his face in that cute kitty way, rubbing it sweetly with his paws and licking them clean. Only it was human blood he was sucking off them.

For the first time, I was afraid of him. "A.B., we have to talk."

"There's nothing to discuss. I told you how I work."

"You didn't have to kill him," I whined. "A simple maiming would have been awesome."

"Once started, I fight to the death. The Alpha Beast is as much a predator as Mommy's sweet little mouser—as precisely engineered a killer, and as merciless."

"Are you going to eat him next?" I asked sarcastically.

He was unperturbed. "I had a few nice bites."

"Omigod!" I almost wanted my mommy. "What am I doing here?"

"I so thoroughly wish I could sigh properly! This is the part I hate worst. You train them, you explain to them, you prepare them, and they still go soft at the first kill. I told you what I was. You knew I killed the men who attacked Abuela. You heard the vampire stories yourself." He stopped grooming, his peachy fur still faintly pink with blood. "Listen up, Warrior! The Alpha Beast is not a pet!"

"Okay! You're the devil in a fur dress. I get it."

His cable of a tail coiled round my wrist and tightened. "Has it occurred to you that I just saved you from rape and murder?"

"They wouldn't have raped me. I'm only fifteen."

"Do you realize how absurd you sound? Here, a fifteen-year-old girl is a probably already a mother of two or more."

"Okay, but they might not have killed me."

"They would have." He freed my arm and resumed spiffing up. "Have I lived more than nine hundred years for nothing? They would certainly have killed you. Perhaps the other woman too."

"But they couldn't. She's the—"

"Thanks are in order, Novice."

"I guess they are. Okay, thanks." I couldn't fight what he was any more than he could.

"Well. Thank you for not falling apart. You did well, Soldier. You showed grace under pressure. Not a bad first encounter."

He was switching ranks on me so fast I could hardly keep up. Okay, so I'd acted like a Soldier, not a Warrior, which was good but not great. That much I got. I was a Novice for doubting him on the execution issue, but what about the other time I was a Novice? When I wanted to help him.

"That was nothing," the creature said. "I was only annoyed about the singing."

The singing. There was something about that.

"Get it out of your head, girlfellow. It was poor strategy, but it did not cause this, understand? This man's blood is not on your hands. He saw someone weaker than himself and he tried to crush her like a moth. The human condition in living color. End of story. Let's move on, shall we? Do I look all right?"

"You look fine." We proceeded once more down the Yellow Brick Road, this time without the childish clowning around.

More with quiet dignity, I like to think—two Warriors out to conquer the enemy, whatever it might be. And I had a really bad feeling it could be an entire city of outraged Mayans.

A.B. must have thought so too. "Shall we review the Tactics of Combat?" he began. "Somehow, I fail to remember 'When in doubt, go for the groin.'"

"That's my contribution," I said cockily. "I've got it down really well."

"I know you've got it down, Traveler. But you might consider using your imagination now and then. Tactic One, as it were."

"Oh, yeah. Fight smart. It's pretty hard to think fast in these situations."

"You could take a trick from my fellow felines. Have you ever seen a kitten face down a German shepherd?"

"Sure. They just arch their backs and fluff out their fur." I snickered. "Works with majorly dumb mutts."

"Whereas you should never underestimate your enemy, also don't overestimate him. Tactic Eleven, and second most important, is this: When all else fails, bluff."

"Awesome, Wise One. But you know what? I really hate it when all else fails. Also, I kind of like to know what 'all else' is. Would you happen to have a plan for when we get to Oz over there?"

"No doubt something will present itself." No doubt the voice of experience again. Something certainly did present itself. In fact, someone did—an entire party of Mayan men in ceremonial costumes with feathers down their backs to their booties.

"Oh, help, A.B., we're probably about to get our hearts ripped out! Do you think it hurts?"

"Maybe they'll give us some of that fermented chocolate to ease our way to the other side."

"*My* way, Orange Ice. *You're* not going there, remember?"

"Look at them—I don't think they mean any harm."

They were smiling and beckoning in a welcoming way. "I've read," I said, "that it's considered an honor to be sacrificed. They probably think they're doing us a favor."

"You know that term you girlaroos use—chill? Can you please perform that simple operation?"

"Easy for you to say, Mr. Thousands of Lives. I think I forgot to ask something—how many assistants have you lost over the last millennium?"

"Is that a serious question?"

"Is this a serious situation?"

"Pah! Hardly a handful."

"Uh-huh—how many?"

"Two or three hundred. No more."

"I feel tons better. What are they doing now?"

They were lowering some sort of appliance to the ground—a sedan chair kind of thing. They seemed to want us to ride on it.

"Calling us a taxi, I think. Upsy-daisy." He said the last part as they lifted us into the contraption.

"A.B.," I said, "what do you think this means?"

"Let's wait and see, shall we? Meanwhile, can't you smile and wave or something?"

So I did a fair imitation of Queen Elizabeth as they carried us through the streets. I tried to take the Beast's advice and chill. *Deep breaths, Reeno, make like a yogi,* I coached myself.

It did change the focus, I admit. I mean, I thought, If I have to die, I'm sure going out in style. These guys had tattoos from Salvador Dalí-land. And the hats! Wooo. Drag queens of the world, eat your hearts out, I said silently. There couldn't be enough birds in all of Latin America to make those things—no wonder we had so many endangered species.

And that only covered our escorts. The people of the town were out in the plaza, in finery varying from jaguar and feathers to simple cotton work clothes. Up close, the buildings were breathtaking—much larger than they'd seemed, and elaborately carved as well as painted.

Everyone was chanting, like in my dream. Oh, good, I thought, maybe they'll just pierce my tongue and let it go at that. I clutched A.B. like a teddy bear, and for once he didn't try to rip my arms off.

There was a stone in front of a temple like in the dream, for their sacrifices. And they set me down near it. Next to it, in fact. Then someone in a jaguar cape and the snappiest chapeau on the plaza pulled me out of the taxi, but gently, as if politely helping a lady. Someone else made a grab for A.B., but he gave them the hell-hiss and wriggled away, landing on his haunches at my feet. Acting like he was the king instead of Cat-Man.

Without further ado, the Mayans began to strip me for the sacrifice. Cat-Man reached down, pulled my polo shirt out of my pants, and popped it over my head. I was about to pull the old knee-trick, but then this loud, "Ooooooh" went up, and everybody bowed. Got down on their knees and touched the ground with their flat foreheads.

"What's going on?" I yelled, and not just in my head. I really screeched out, waving my arms like a hysterical two-year-old.

At this, they lifted their heads, and A.B. said, "They think you said to get up."

"Well, who's giving the orders here? I could have sworn it wasn't me."

The Cat-King—and I don't mean the Beast—stepped forward and gave a short speech, whereupon the rest of them got up and began to dance.

A.B. said, "They're performing for you."

"Ever the optimist." But it really did look like it.

"They seem to have mistaken you for someone else."

"Just don't mention I got their pal killed."

"Pretend it's a school play. Be who they want you to be."

So I smiled and waved, and generally acted grateful, and then the king made another speech. I couldn't understand a word, but I liked his voice. He had what my dad would call a "nice persona." A good aura.

But that didn't mean I needed him to help me into the next world.

I was scanning for possible escape routes when the dark woman from the road appeared, along with the man I'd kneed earlier, escorted by four other men in quilted pants and jackets. They carried spears.

"The people are honored by your presence," the woman said in Spanish.

"You're Doña Marina, aren't you?"

She didn't even blink. "I am, Goddess."

Goddess! Well, that was more like it. I'd be the last to contradict her. But there was something funny about all this. It was like a scene from a bad Tarzan movie. Kind of cheesy and screwed up. In the real world, people just didn't go around worshipping strangers—especially kids in khakis and polo shirts. Puh-lease.

However, this was no time to ask questions.

The spear-carriers made the prisoner kneel, and suddenly I realized what they were doing. They weren't going to sacrifice me—they were going to sacrifice him. In my honor.

"Doña Marina, tell them"—I was thinking fast—"tell them I can't thank them enough for all the hospitality, but today I showed mercy to this man, and I cannot take him now. Not that I'm, not, like, majorly grateful, of course."

She spoke to the crowd in Mayan, but it didn't seem to go over. Disappointed little murmurs spread through the crowd like boos at a baseball game.

I said, "A.B., is this about to turn ugly?"

"Would Meryl Streep let it turn ugly? Act, Soldier!"

Soldier. Not even Student. I must be flunking drama.

I felt a little better when the soldiers jerked the man up by the hair and took him away, but things got a lot worse when they came back with a little boy. "Then they will give you the man's son," said Doña Marina.

Oh, boy.

"Look, Doña Marina, I'm in a really great mood today. Could you please tell the king he has a special place in my heart? I'm really crazy about the guy—and all his people too. Tell them because they're, like, big-deal favorites of mine, they don't have to give me anybody. Really! They can have all my blessings free of charge until the end of their days."

She nodded, expressionless. Very professional. But as she began to speak, the crowd started cheering. The king broke out in this great big filed-tooth smile and put an arm around my shoulders. Which was really weird because I was standing there in my bra.

"And the Oscar goes to...Reeno Dimond!" I said to the Beast.

"Aren't you forgetting something?"

"You mean the book? Something tells me it's the wrong time to bring it up."

I waved and blew a few kisses, and then Doña Marina translated a grateful little speech the king made, and I said, "Ask them if they'd like to see me again tomorrow."

She asked. They cheered. It was like being Homecoming Queen.

"Very well," I told her. "Tell them I shall return. Meanwhile, I wonder if they could give my shirt back and could take me to Cortes?" I indicated my taxi. "In that, preferably. Oh, and order one up for yourself. I need a witness to this little episode."

So commanded the goddess, and it was done.

Except that they brought me a much better shirt, one of those cool embroidered jobs they seemed to specialize in. Much better for a meeting with a historic figure.

Perhaps I should mention here that I may have taken a liberty or two regarding my fluency—my Spanish was still kind of in the pidgin stage, but it would be boring to write down all the words I got wrong and the times Doña Marina had to say, "Do you mean...?" and that kind of thing. The point is, I could make myself understood and what I meant to say is what I wrote, and I'm pretty sure that's how the Mayans took it. Do we understand each other?

A.B. snoozed in my lap the whole way back to the beach, all tuckered out by his murderous afternoon. I spent the trip composing little speeches to Cortes, who had been informed that we were on the way, and thus had come ashore in a dinghy. He'd had his men plant four poles in the sand and drape a blanket over them to serve as a little shelter where we could talk. On the whole, he didn't look thrilled to see us, but I kind of liked his looks. If he usually wore sailor's clothes, he'd changed out of them, into the kind of knee pants and puff-sleeved tunics you see in those old Spanish paintings. Like pictures of Columbus. He had a plumed hat and everything, which might be why the Mayans made that plumed-serpent error at first. Couldn't blame them, I thought. Anyone who mistook me for a goddess ought to be a lot more impressed by this dude.

I for one sure was, and I really couldn't afford to be.

I screwed up my courage, what there was of it, scrambled out of my taxi, stood up, and offered to shake. But he wouldn't do it—perhaps women didn't shake in the Middle Ages. So I had to content myself with a polite *"buenos tardes."*

"This is the woman," Doña Marina said.

Woman. So I'd been demoted. Very ungood.

"And is that," the explorer said, "the animal who so severely frightened my sailor?"

"Your sailor," I said, "was lucky to escape with his life. Not to put too fine a point on it, señor, but he and his two buddies tried to rape me up there."

"Is that so, little one? Pedro and Doña Marina tell quite a different story."

Doña Marina? So much for sisterhood. But I forgave her. I figured she had to live with these people.

But that "little one" simply wasn't doing it for me—once you've tasted goddess-hood, you expect slightly better from mere mortals. "I don't believe," I said, "that we've been properly introduced. You are the famous Hernan Cortes, of course. My people know of your accomplishments and exploits, and we salute you. I am Princess Deboreeno Diamondino of the Zigaloo tribe of Norte Americana. I have been sent here on a most important mission."

Okay, it was a dumb speech, but Meryl Streep could have made it work. My acting career was barely thirty minutes old. But I wasn't exactly prepared for what happened. This man I'd spent half my Bad Girl career reading about—and let's face it, the Spanish might have plundered, but you had to be a little impressed—this famous explorer laughed in the princess's royal face. Didn't just laugh, took off his hat and beat his leg with it, having a good old belly-whomper at my expense.

I was pissed. You just don't treat a princess like that. "Perhaps the conquistador," I said, "is amused by my accent. I apologize for my poor Spanish, but we Zigaloos speak much better English, which we learned from a shipwrecked sailor a century or two ago." I switched to my native tongue. "Would you prefer to continue the conversation in English?"

He looked confused, so I pressed my advantage, "'Four-score and seven years ago,'" I said, "'our forefathers brought forth on this continent a new nation, conceived in liberty and dedicated to the proposition that all men are created equal.'"

Of course he couldn't know the Gettysburg Address, which wouldn't be written for another three hundred years, but I wanted him to know I really did *habla Inglés*. I figured he didn't and it might make me look smarter.

I was right.

But it only made him mad. "The English haven't sailed to the Indies!" he huffed.

I shrugged and switched to Spanish again. "Their ship was blown off course. You know—like the Spanish Armada, that other time?" But of course that hadn't happened yet, either. To cover his confusion, he said, "What is Norte Americana?"

"Nice little country north of here. We don't get down here much, but I've come on a very important mission, and I really need your help."

He held up a hand to stop me. "What kind of tribe sends a mere girl on an important mission?"

I'd figured that one out on the ride over. "Like I mentioned, the Zigaloo, señor. You see, among the Zigaloo, the women are the leaders—the rulers, the soldiers, the artists, the explorers. We do all the important stuff, and the men are more or less our slaves. It's an extremely advanced civilization."

CHAPTER XXI: THE FOUNTAIN OF LIES

He was turning red.

"Oh, it's quite true. Ask Doña Marina—she saw how respectful the Mayans were. In our own little way, we kick a lot of sexist butt in these parts, and if you mess with me, my mama the queen will cut your fancy Spanish liver out."

Okay, okay, I didn't really say the last part. Instead, I followed up with, "My mother the queen, who particularly admires you and happens to be a world-class babe, sends her compliments and asks me to invite you to visit us. Her Spanish is really a lot better than mine, and the royal *cocinas* are renowned for miles around. Also, she's very forgiving and would probably only torture that rapist Pedro for an hour or two."

I was banking on the old saying about the way to a man's heart, and I do think he loosened up a little at the mention of the royal kitchens. "And the animal?" he said.

"Ah, the animal. Can it be that news of the cats of the Zigaloo has not reached your ears? They are the secret of our success in battle. We herd them, señor. The tiny ones, like the scruffy specimen at my feet, serve as our infantry, and the larger, like jaguars and cougars, are our mounts. Like your...horses." I made the last word a sneer. "Except, of course, they're much better in battle than horses, because each cat is as much a ravening foe as the bloodthirsty Warrior Woman on its back. We wear green in battle, with our arms bare, which are tattooed with fearsome serpents"—at this point I did a little show-and-tell—"and we dye our hair startling shades of red. The mere sight of a Zigaloo army has caused many a brave regiment to retreat in terror."

"I can believe that," said the great explorer, or something pretty close. I was wearing him down. "Doña Marina?"

"In his speech to the city," she said, "the Mayan king did mention that the goddess rode a jaguar in her previous appearance. And of course, there is the hair." If I thought I'd managed to make the word "horse" sound like "turd," you should have heard what she did with "hair."

"Very well." The great man nodded. I figured my lying skills were getting right up there with my thieving ability. "But, surely, Princess, you haven't traveled all this way just to invite me for a home-cooked Zigaloo meal. What, exactly, is this mission of yours?"

The tricky part was coming up. "I'm looking for a manuscript."

Cortes looked frankly bewildered. I could see that Doña Marina was a bit in the dark as well, but her confusion had a hint of slyness to it. She knew something I didn't.

"Know your enemy," A.B. warned. I'd almost forgotten about him. Okay, I had to find out what she knew.

I said, "You know about it, don't you, Doña Marina? Suppose you tell the conquistador."

So at that point she took over. It was a beautiful thing. I felt as if I'd accomplished a verbal martial arts move—somehow managed to use the enemy's strength to my own advantage. "The Mayans," she said, "call the princess, not Deboreeno Diamondino—it's probably too much for their primitive brains to absorb…"

"Hold it right there!" I said. "There's a lot more to the Mayans than meets the totally retarded European eye. They're brilliant astronomers and they have this incredible calendar…"

A.B. gave me a look that said this was no time for consciousness-raising. I sighed. "Never mind. Go on."

"They call her Jaguar-Snake Woman, because of her tattoos. They recognized her by four signs—first, the snakes themselves, then the hideous two-colored hair, and the tacky unibrow. Zigaloo women apparently don't pluck."

Involuntarily, I raised my hand to the fuzzy space above my nose. I remembered looking in the mirror on my trip to town.

"And the fourth sign?" Cortes asked.

"The murderous feline." She glanced at A.B., catching him preening his whiskers, and shrank back a bit. "They say that the woman appeared out of nowhere in Uxmal during the reign of King Palak, bearing wonderful gifts that made the entire town delirious with happiness."

No wonder they loved me. It sure explained the Tarzan scene. (Also, it explained how to say Uxmal, which I knew about from my reading—it's "Ooshmall.")

"But she betrayed them," Doña Marina continued. "She repaid their hospitality by attempting to rob them."

"I don't understand," the great man said. Neither did I, but I was glad I hadn't asked for the book in the city that day—they might not have taken kindly to it. "Why would they revere a thief?"

"Because she—or her ancestor, one presumes, has since passed into legend. She has become a goddess in their eyes." She shrugged. "The story is merely a story now. Whatever she may have stolen is of less importance than the legend itself."

"After all, it was four hundred years ago," I said. "That's a long time to hold a grudge."

But there was something vague about the way Doña Marina told the tale—that word "attempting." And I didn't know how to ask for the specifics without betraying myself as an impostor.

Cortes addressed me. "What was the object your ancestor was supposed to have stolen?"

"Not my ancestor," I said. "Me. I removed the item myself."

That was Doña Marina's cue to say, "Oh, no, the book wasn't stolen, it was merely an attempt"—if she knew for sure. Because that was the missing piece: Whether or not I'd succeeded in my mission. But she didn't say anything—only looked at me as if I'd gone crazy.

Cortes said, "What do you mean you stole it? As you point out, that was over four hundred years ago."

"Perhaps," I said, "you've heard the legend of the Fountain of Youth? It's true."

See, I knew the legend from reading up on the *conquistadores*. Another one, Juan Ponce De Leon, had plundered his share of New World gold, but he'd never found what he really wanted when he set sail in 1513—a magic spring that had the power of restoring youth. Given that that was sixteen years earlier, I figured Cortes had to have heard of it.

"What I stole," I said, "was a book that tells how to find it."

He did a satisfying double take. "You are four hundred years old?" he asked.

"Four hundred thirty-three, to be exact. We found the Fountain of Youth, but the Mayans still have the important book—the one that says where the gold is."

If we hadn't already been on the ground—Cortes's men had spread a blanket for us—the famous explorer would have had to sit down. He looked like a cartoon character with dollar sign eyes. "Back up for a minute. You're telling me the Zigaloo have the secret of eternal youth?"

"My friends say I don't look a day over three hundred. But, see, when we got the book, we got something else we didn't bargain for—it tells about the other book; the one with the map to El Dorado. That's the book I came for this time." Now, El Dorado was a mythical land of gold the Spaniards also tried to find, but in later expeditions. I wasn't entirely sure how time-travel worked, but for a moment I wondered if they heard about it from me.

However, the look on the conquistador's face said the legend had already made the rounds. He was suspicious, though. Shaking his head, he said, "Princess, Princess. You expect me to believe a thing like that? If the Mayans know the way to El Dorado, why don't they just go there and take the gold?"

I was ready for him—all that library time was paying off like crazy. "Because it's too far away," I said, "Think about it. They don't have wheels or sails. How are they going to go all the way to Colombia to get it?"

"Colombia?"

"A land many miles to the south—named for your Christopher Columbus."

He raised an eyebrow. "How are *you* planning to get there, Your Highness? Ride that kitty over there?"

"Please, señor, give my people some credit. We have ships that make your little boats look like bathtub toys."

He looked puzzled. "What is 'bathtub'?"

Uh-oh, a misstep. They probably didn't have bathtubs in 1529. But then I remembered that the Moors in Spain took ritual baths. "Civilized people," I said, "have pools for washing their bodies. Our seers say they exist in Spain."

"Civilized! The infidels use them."

"Whatever. The point is, we've got a totally happening navy. You really shouldn't mess with the Zigaloo."

Cortes stroked his beard, thinking. "Well, then. If I'm supposed to believe your little fairy tale, why didn't you come back sooner for the El Dorado book?"

"The stars, dude. On our continent, we don't make a move without asking the royal astrologers. The stars say that *now*"—I emphasized the word—"is the right time."

He was buying it. Oh, man, was he buying it. I almost felt sorry for him, having to decide between eternal youth and a lake full of gold and jewels. But I guess he figured he couldn't defeat the amazing all-female Zigaloo army: He went for the gold. "And this book," he said, looking way crafty. "Why are you telling me about it?"

"Doña Marina," I said, "do you read Mayan?"

"I can't even read Spanish. I'm illiterate."

"Well, there you have it, señor. Nobody you know can read the book, even if you could get it. Oh, sure, you probably think you could torture some poor scribe into doing it, but haven't you noticed? The Mayans aren't afraid of pain or death, either one. They're not going to translate it for you."

I could see him about to huff and puff, so I held up a hand. "Wait. Our great seer, The Sibyl of Minneapolis, tells us that El Dorado won't be found for hundreds of years. Now, we Zigaloo can wait. Time is seriously on our side. But Mamma Mia, as she is known, also mentioned that the Spaniards have been known to burn a few books. How about that, señor? You haven't destroyed anybody's library, have you? Because I'm telling you, don't. The book's there, and. in time, it'll give up its secrets. So treat the Mayan books like sacred objects. Maybe you'll find it, maybe I'll find it, but if it gets burned, nobody wins. *Comprende?*"

I was pretty satisfied with that little speech. It wasn't getting A.B. and me any closer to the end-of-the-world text, but maybe I'd just saved the Dresden Codex.

"And also, I want to make you an offer. Do you know if the Mayan king has a daughter?"

A.B. was livid. "What the almighty devil are you doing, Human? What's that got to do with anything?"

I said I'd tell him later, I was busy.

"Yes," said Doña Marina. "A girl about five or six. Apple of his eye."

"The prophecy says that a little girl will lead us to the codex—the daughter of the ruler of Cozumel. Tomorrow, I want to go back to the city and fulfill the prophecy"—I turned to Cortes—"but I need a translator."

"I see," the explorer said, "and what do I get out of the deal?"

"Exactly what you want. A chance to steal the codex."

"What?" He'd heard me, he just couldn't believe he had.

I nodded. "Fair is fair. After we leave the city, take it if you can. But remember two things…" I paused.

"Yes?" Boy, was this guy eager.

"First, the prophecy says I will prevail."

He nodded. "Fair enough."

"Second, you'll have to get past Sweetie-Fluff here." I petted A.B., who had obligingly crawled into my lap like mama's precious little boy-cakes.

"Ah," said Cortes, trying to conceal his embarrassing childish glee. "That is the difficult part."

"Think it over. You can decide in the morning."

"That won't be necessary. You're on."

Uh-huh. Big surprise. (But of course, he didn't really say, "you're on"—I hope I don't have to keep explaining that a) my Spanish is so lousy I hardly know what he did say and b) I have a legal and current poetic license.)

Cortes was thrilled, but I was in agony. Most people would probably think the words "cat" and "apoplectic"—as in "about to have a stroke"—don't belong in the same sentence. They would have no idea of the pain I was currently enduring from Sweetie-Fluff's claws digging into my thighs to show his displeasure. He didn't let up, either, while I negotiated the next few arrangements with the great explorer—no, we wouldn't like to sleep on his boat, thank you very much, yes, we'd very much appreciate some food if he could send us some, and no to a couple of guards to protect the royal butt. (This last was at A.B.'s insistence; I had no idea why, I just wanted to get those claws out of my legs.)

When the Monster and I were finally alone, he went ballistic on me. "Are you out of your mind, Novice? We have the information we need: We know we didn't get the book here because we know we went back to Uxmal to get it. Ergo, we have to go back to Uxmal. We have no reason to stay here. Why the bloody devil do you want to go to the Mayan city tomorrow? Do you realize how many lives it could cost me?"

Yada, yada, yada, meow, hiss, yowl, yada.

Except for the wounds, I was pretty much enjoying myself. "Oh, hiss-hiss, yourself," I replied cockily. "We have to go: I made a promise to Abuela. I have to get the tears of a princess—and face it, no matter what I told Cortes, we both know I'm not one. So where else am I going to find a princess? Bad Girl School? This is my only chance and you know it. By the way, can you make a little girl cry?"

Like I didn't know the answer.

I could swear he softened up when I mentioned Abuela. But he had to save face—I mean, snout. "They'll try to kill us," he grumbled.

"No, they won't." I told him my exit plan. "Besides, we have to at least ask for the book. Otherwise, we won't—"

"It's not here. If it were, we wouldn't have gone to Uxmal."

"But how can we know unless—"

"I am not making that child cry," he said. "It's unethical. Besides," he said, and I could have sworn he was the least bit sheepish, "it is forbidden."

"Oh, right, I forgot. Okay, I'll pinch her or something. By the way, isn't there one more Tactic of Combat? Think it's time to let me in on it?"

"The Twelfth, last, and most important Tactic of Combat is this: It's not over till it's over. Chew on it."

We slept on the blanket Cortes had left for us and sometime in the night I woke up feeling crowded. I pushed at my sleeping companion. "Move over, A.B.," I said aloud. Nothing moved, and I realized that the thing crowding me was big, a lot bigger than A.B., and it didn't like being pushed. A warning growl shook the ground. "Field goal!" I yelped silently. "A.B., wake up. Field goal already!"

"What is it?" the familiar voice snapped.

"We're not exactly alone here. I think I might have about five seconds to live. Could you do something, please?"

"What is it?"

"There's something big in bed with us. And it's growling."

"Oh. That's Jose." He said—or rather thought—something I could hear, but it wasn't in English or Spanish or anything I recognized. The thing got up and moved a respectful distance, then plopped itself down in Cat Position Two, the Egyptian one, looking at me with mean green eyes.

Jose had spots.

"Omigod! He's a jaguar."

"He's our babysitter—remember when I told you about the Planet Guard? The all-feline backup? Jose and Paco came down so I could get some sleep."

I looked around for Paco, who was about twenty feet away, curled up like the Fur Grenade that ate Cleveland. My heart started to slow down a little. "Uh, okay. But I have to pee."

"More information than I need, Soldier. Do what you have to do."

"These guys won't hurt me?"

"Don't be absurd. Jose will escort you."

Have you ever tried to pee on a beach with a jaguar staring at you? "Jose, could you turn your back, please?" I entreated silently.

But I guess only the Alpha Beast speaks Human. The jaguar either didn't hear or didn't care.

After that, I slept like a cub in a cave, Jose on one side and, eventually, Paco on the other, and A.B. at my feet. If any Spaniards were prowling, I hope they saw us and crossed themselves.

The guards were gone the next morning. And soon it came to pass (great myths always start this way) that once again the fabled Jaguar-Snake Woman and her darling pet, Sweetie-Fluff, went into the city to greet the people.

Only this time they had a sixteenth-century police escort, complete with flying flags, strutting soldiers, and a famous explorer in a plumed hat.

The king made a welcoming speech, the beautiful goddess made a thank-you speech (through Doña Marina, of course), and then I asked to meet the princess. She was this adorable little kid with a bead hung over her nose so she'd be a cross-eyed grown-up, and I honored her by letting her hold my precious Sweetie-Fluff.

Of course, I knew I couldn't lose. The Beast wasn't going to chew her hand off, he'd already mentioned that. So there was nothing he could do but let her pet him and stroke his cute little ears and call him Cuddles in Mayan. But when I tried to take him back, she stamped her royal foot and said, "Princess keep the kitty!" or something close to it.

"Okay, A.B.," I said, "this is your cue. Hiss, big-time. Give her a nip."

But he just snuggled deeper into her arms, and even mustered a purr. A purr! I didn't know he had it in him.

"Kitty's going home, now," I told the girl, and lifted him out of her arms. Whereupon she screwed up her little face and started to cry on cue. Unceremoniously, I dropped the monster, produced a tissue from my pants pocket, wiped her winsome mug, and stuffed the tear-soaked tissue back in my pocket.

"How about I give you my shirt instead?" I said. "So you have something to remember me by."

Now, here's the thing—parents are the same anywhere, anytime. Naturally her dad was thrilled with the bribe. He was all, "Sure, kid, wouldn't that be a great thing? A shirt worn by the goddess! Like, you know, a magic shirt!"

And she bought it.

So I had them bring me back my polo shirt, and then I had to change in front of everybody (which I did with extreme dignity) and then I picked up Sweetie-Fluff, and I said to Doña Marina, "Tell the people I love them very much, and I will be sorry to leave them. But before I do, I have one tiny request. Could the princess, please, take us to the Book of the Great Cycles?" (Of course I didn't know the name of the one A.B. and I wanted, but I figured that was as good as any.)

The king's eyes flashed furiously. "Hrrraaaaah!" he said, and something else. Then he made a sign to his soldiers, the ones in the quilted armor, who started toward me from their station across the plaza. I didn't need Doña Marina to tell me what was going on. I seemed to have said the secret word.

"He says she's an impostor," Doña Marina said to Cortes.

Well, I really hated to leave on a sour note. I raised my hand for silence, clutching A.B. with the other. "Tell the people," I told her, "that the book is safe. And tell them also"—I pointed to Cortes"—to beware the foreign devil!"

I pulled A.B.'s tail, and he grabbed a cosmic strand for St.

Psycho's and there we were, doing the time-travel polka again. I tried to holler *Adios, amigos*, but you really can't do two things at once. I like to think maybe they heard it, though, like from a tunnel in the distance.

Not counting the two rapists, I really liked those people.

Chapter XXII: Zeroing In

"Idiot! Fool!" The Beast fumed.

We were back in the dining room, and I was once again eating granola. "Guess that's even worse than Novice, huh?"

"That was unnecessary, Human. I told you the book wasn't there. We wouldn't have had to go back to Uxmal if it were."

"But, A.B., we didn't know that we got the book in Uxmal—Doña Marina only said we *attempted* to steal it. I was just trying to find out if we made it. Because, you know, why go to Uxmal if we didn't?"

"But we did go, Novice. That means we *must* go. We can't change history. Really! 'Beware the foreign devil,' indeed. You couldn't resist warning them about Cortes, yet we know Cortes—"

"Hey, he wasn't as bad as some of them. Maybe he got away with less stuff because I warned them."

"And maybe the two of us scared the wits out of him…"

"So he tried less stuff. I'd sure love to think so. Okay, okay, so we'll go to Uxmal. Meanwhile, I've got to go to English."

And off I went, but I was suddenly so exhausted I fell asleep in class. After a somewhat embarrassing takedown by the teacher, which you would have thought would have woken me up for a month, I still hadn't recovered. Thinking I must be getting mono, or possibly African sleeping sickness, which is completely fatal, I finally went to Evelina for an infirmary pass. (Which was handy because I got to claim I missed gym because I couldn't move.)

The nurse couldn't find anything wrong, but thought I might be catching something and sent me back to bed on grounds of looking awful. By afternoon I still couldn't get up. A.B. sat on my chest, crushing my lungs and heart. "A.B.," I managed to gasp, "I think I'm sick."

"You're not sick. Time-traveling takes it out of you. You'll feel okay in a few days."

"Listen, I'm sorry I was stupid. I'll try to improve. I swear."

"You did well, Traveler." He took a load off my chest, his elephant paws thumping on the floor like four telephone books. I went back to sleep in my clothes, feeling in my pocket for my princess tears. They were there, dried up but still there, on that tissue in my pocket. The clowns let me sleep another day, and by then I felt about halfway back to normal.

However, near-total exhaustion did not keep me from the Ozone Rangers meeting that second night. A.B. was there well before me, of course.

"Hi, everybody? Did Kara tell you? A.B. and I went to Cozumel!" (Of course *she* knew—we were speaking now.)

"Woo-hoo!" Carlos yelped, sweetly, but in a way that I could tell he already knew. "How was it?"

"Amazing! I'm a goddess. Wait'll you hear the Legend of Jaguar-Snake Woman."

So I spun the tale for them, in such precise and vivid detail that I could see they didn't believe a word, not even Carlos. Looking around at their doubting faces, I decided to just…give up. Who cared if anyone believed me? "Not buying it, huh?" I said. "Okay, listen, it doesn't matter. Let's just get on with the meeting."

Whereupon A.B.'s tail lassoed my wrist in a death grip and yanked me to my feet. "A.B., what the hell?"

Cooper stood, balling his fist. It was so sweet. "She's full of shit, but let her go, Ape-cat!"

While I stood there in agony, A.B. talked to me.

I translated. "Um…he says I'm wrong, it does matter." And guess what? My voice wasn't mine, it was his! That British, half-Cockney, Michael Caine *male* thing.

They all screamed, even the guys. Sonya stood up so fast her chair fell on the floor, and backed up against the bookshelf. I swear if she could have turned white she would have. Kara actually did.

A.B. let me go, and I could see that already my wrist was purpling up. Stunned, I said aloud, "A.B., what was *that*?"

"That was nothing, Student. Just a trick. It is imperative they understand this is real. Tell them to focus." Then he told me what to do next.

"The great and powerful Oz…" I began, but he was in no mood. He grabbed Kara this time, holding her hostage. "A.B. let her go. I'm sorry. Okay, let's try again. The great and powerful Alpha Beast says this is real, O'Neal. And for reasons best known to his Fuzzy Highness, he wants to make sure you get it. He says we should focus and listen up…"

So we lit the candle and I led them through a short visualization more or less describing what I felt when I time-traveled. And then I said, "Let it unfold."

What happened then was A.B. showed us a movie. Wow! I have no idea how he did it, but it was like he projected the whole trip to Cozumel on the backs of our eyelids. I got to see myself with Cortes and Doña Marina, and sleeping with the jaguars, and tricking the little Mayan princess, and everything. Of course I was a little embarrassed that Cooper and Carlos saw me in my bra, but who really cared? Even Meryl Streep does nude scenes.

When the lights were back on, and everyone had dutifully exclaimed, we compared notes to make sure we'd really all seen the same thing. As it became clearer and clearer that we had, people started to get more and more weirded out. Finally, Julia, eyes sort of halfway cut at A.B., as if she were afraid to drop her guard, even for a second, blurted, "But…what does he *want*?"

A.B. said, "Traveler, give me your voice!"

"Uh, everybody hang on. He says he wants me to channel him again." And then I said, or rather A.B. did, but it came out of me: "We are talking about preventing the destruction of the planet, my innocents! *This is real, Lucille,* as my apprentice would say. Please do not disrespect the Alpha Beast. If you wish to help Reeno Dimond and me, decide now. Are you in or out?"

"Wow," I said. "My throat hurts." But what I was really thinking was, *Did he just call me his apprentice?*

"Slip of the tongue, slip of a girl," the Beast said.

"Well, that was helpful," said Cooper. "What does he want us to *do*?" And then he had to go through the dread tail-bracelet torture. Finally, the Beast said, once again in my voice, "When we go, we will need you to send energy to Uxmal."

"Huh?" said Carlos, Cooper, and me together. But Sonya, Kara and Julia nodded in understanding. "Oh, is that all," said Julia. "Piece of cake."

"We will need it on a consistent basis the entire time we are in Uxmal."

"Well? How long will that be?"

"That remains to unfold. Possibly weeks."

The three original Rangerettes said something like, "Plfff!"

Carlos said, "Could someone clue us in about this energy-sending thing?"

Julia said, "Well, there's nothing to it, really. When someone needs some—like when they're sick or hurt or something, we just focus on sending a piece of our energy to them. Or maybe the universe's—who knows where it comes from? Anyhow, it's like, I don't know, cosmic vitamins or something. A booster shot to keep them going." She paused. "It's easy for a few minutes. But I can't imagine how we could keep it up for a long time."

I was excited. "Hey, did I say why we went to Cozumel so suddenly? I got kind of desperate—Haley's in a coma. Could we send her some energy?"

Julia said, "Oooh, sorry to hear it. But sure. We're barely started here. Wait'll you see what Kara taught us. In fact, let's do that first. The way we usually do it is try to generate energy first, so we have a good supply on hand. Do you know what I mean?"

"Not exactly."

"Well, the work we're going to do with Cooper and Stuffed Curly will get our adrenaline going. Then we can chant a little to generate some energy and we can send it off to Haley. Make sense?"

"Not too sure."

She nodded. "Just trust me. More new business? No. Okay, then: LET'S RIDE THE OZONE!"

Weirdly, everyone shouted the last three words with her. It seemed like a new group tradition—a lot had happened in two days.

Julia put the Curly dog in the middle of the table, lit the candle, and we were off. "Okay, Reeno, watch this. I mean, don't just watch, help us. Let's levitate Curly."

Almost the moment we started to focus, the doll lifted into the air—and kept rising! It was easy too, not just some three- or four-inch thing, accomplished by focusing so hard it strained your neck muscles. That thing *floated*. And kept floating until Julia said, "Top of the right bookshelf," whereupon it did an immediate one-eighty, headed to the appointed shelf, and plopped itself down.

"Yes!" Cooper made a fist and pumped downward with his elbow.

I settled for a simple, "Zowie! How the hell did we *do* that?"

"It was mostly Kara," Julia said. "Kara, do you mind demonstrating?"

"Sure." Kara had gone from French's to something like sunflower gold—in other words, she was almost radiant. And she was in her element now. She nearly glowed as the stuffed toy left the shelf and floated slowly to the one on the opposite side of the room.

"Now let's put it back," Julia said, and with all of us on it, it practically flew. "See? She can do it by herself, but with all of us on it, what we gain is speed. We tried the other way too—just us without Kara—and we actually can't raise it more than a couple of feet."

"Yet," said Carlos, and Cooper gave him a fist bump.

"Really, really impressive," I said. "but a quick question. Any luck with the other thing?"

"Oh, you mean the curse?" Julia laughed. "Hey, it's only been two days." Pause.

"But…yessss." She drew the answer out, to tantalize me—and also out of pride, I thought. Something was happening here, something like the sum being greater than the parts. Maybe each of us was psychic in our own way, but when we got together, we got stronger. You might expect that, but we didn't just get a little bit stronger—we got a lot stronger. Almost exponentially stronger.

I wished A.B. and I could take the whole group with us when we went to Uxmal. But that would probably look suspicious. And anyhow, no one at Cozumel had mentioned the others were there. So they must not have been.

"In fact tonight," Julia continued, "we're going to make the transfer."

"All right!"

First we floated Stuffed Curly back to the table, and then we built tough, thick shields around ourselves (all except Cooper), the whole group working on each person's shield until it was penetrable only by bullets, and even that might be in doubt. (Or so I imagined.)

And then we did make one for Cooper.

After that—and here was what the group had figured out in my absence—we slipped it off and put it aside, like a piece of physical body armor, so that we could pop it back on at a second's notice.

Then, to my amazement—and appreciation—we made one for the Curly dog! And popped it off for a quick outfitting as well. Brilliant!

"We tried it last night," Sonya said, "but we forgot to close it up, you know? Shoulda put feet on it."

"Hey, wait, I've got an idea. We could eliminate a step. Let's make a new shield for Curly, only with a hole in it for the curse, so we can leave it on him…hey, wait, here's a better idea. Forget the hole. Let's make it a door that we can leave open while we do the transfer, then snap shut without having to build a whole new piece of shield."

"Could be worse," said Cooper. "Could be a lot worse, Jaguar-Snake. Maybe there's a reason we let you in here."

Jeez, the curse must be weakening—he was finding ways to make insults sound almost like compliments.

So we made the new piece of toy body armor—that is, astral toy body armor—and turned to Cooper. Once again Sonya and Carlos were assigned the job of keeping the curse in the dog while Julia, Kara, and I pulled. We'd just started tugging the thing off when I thought of something. I'd forgotten how sticky it was. "Hey, hold it."

Everyone opened their eyes, clearly annoyed.

"Before we do this, let's turn his shield inside out and see if any of the curse is sticking to it."

Julia said, "Whoa. Yeah, let's do."

And so we did, each person working in his or her own mind, turning an imaginary shield inside out, and removing icky, sticky pieces of psychic slime and storing them in the toy animal. An onlooker would have thought we were crazy.

"Only crazy," A.B. said, "for thinking it imaginary. You do have an onlooker, girlie-poo."

All righty, then. The thing was real. Good, because the curse damn sure was. It might not look like some sort of cross between chewy algae and half-digested beef, which was how I saw it, in fact it might not look like anything, but it was definitely real.

And the shield must have been too, because it had lots of little curse-specks sticking to it, like so much toxic lint. Curiously enough, we all finished de-cursing it at the same time, and then we turned back to Cooper.

This time the curse didn't seem so stubborn. In fact, seemed to come off almost like a wetsuit stuck on with astral Velcro, more of a peeling than the mental jackhammering we'd had to do before. But it was really stubborn Velcro, and the wetsuit split and splintered over and over, and each piece had to be pried off and stuffed in the dog.

Just when I felt the job was done, Julia said, "Ready?"

We all were.

"Pop his shield on."

We astral-Kevlared Cooper.

"Now slam that door!"

We slammed. I could have sworn it closed with a "thunk."

"Seal it shut! Now!"

I started out with astral sealing wax, then I put grout on top of that, and some putty and a good coat of epoxy. After which I poured cement on it. And for good measure, I mixed up another batch and poured it over the whole shield.

"Whoa," Sonya said.

Carlos said, "I feel it too. I mean, I don't."

"What?" Julia asked.

"It stopped resistin'. Think it's in there to stay."

"Woo-hoo!" Kara hollered, which was by far the most animated I'd ever seen her, and then, for the first time during the procedure, I looked at Cooper. "How do you feel?"

He smiled. "Great! Fantastic. You guys, just in case anything happens and I can't talk again, I really, really have to tell you how much I appreciate this. You're the greatest friends anyone could ever have and I just"—his eyes started to water up—"I just wanted you to know."

We were quiet for a second and then Carlos said, "I didn't think it was possible to talk that fast."

Cooper's eyes lit on me. "Especially you, Reeno."

Me? Why? There must be some reason; I should ask what it was, but I couldn't get the words out. I felt a sudden warmth spread to my cheeks. What, I wondered vaguely, is *that* about?

"Let's keep working, people," Julia said, "while we're hot. We can talk after the meeting." She looked at me. "This is the part where we send Haley some energy. Listen up, newbies, the principle is something like you might see at a pep rally; or maybe a revival meeting. People with a common focus create energy."

"In church," Sonya said, "you know how people put their hands up when a Gospel choir sings? Y'all ever do that? Makes your palms and fingers tingle. That's when you can actually feel it."

"Ohhh." I had a sudden memory of doing that at a rock concert.

"Now what'll we chant? Or sing?"

The most rousing song I knew came, not from a concert, but from the movie *Casablanca*, the scene in which they sing the French national anthem. "I don't guess anybody knows 'La Marseillaise,' do they?"

Cooper said, "I do," but no one else did. So "La Marseillaise" was out.

Sonya said, "Le's just chant her name, why don't we? That way she'll be all we can think of."

"Sure," said Julia, and we started chanting, "Haley! Haley! Haley!" We kept it up for a long time, maybe a good five minutes, eventually holding hands and swaying in a circular motion, I have no idea why, we just did it.

"Keep chanting," Julia said, "but begin to form the energy into a ball. Imagine where Haley is—just down the road in Santa Barbara…"

Whoo. I was beginning to see what this was all about. I could *feel* the energy, it was there, all right, the room did feel like one in which people were cheering for a team, or singing hymns, even applauding after a particularly rocking concert—there was that excitement, that electricity, that *focus* on a common cause. And toward the end of the chant, I could see the energy too. It was blue at first, and wispy, and then it grew yellow, and then orange, like a fire; it was this hot, roaring, *live* thing contained in the circle we'd made when were joined hands. I was getting light-headed.

"Get ready to send it…okay now…on the count of three. One"—the orange cloud coalesced into a blazing, shimmery, exuberant ball—"two"—the ball began to rise above us— "three." It shot through the wall with what I could swear was a great "swoosh."

"Swoosh," said Sonya, clearly having heard it too. I closed my eyes and focused on getting it to Haley.

As one, we dropped each other's hands and fell back in our chairs. "Everyone tired?" Julia chirped. "That was fantastic, Rangers. Tonight I brought whole PowerBars for everyone. I think we're gonna need them."

As we munched, Kara thought to ask, "How do you get these, anyhow?"

"You'll never guess."

"Oh, just tell us. We're too tired to guess."

"Our faculty adviser supplies them."

Evelina? A faculty member was supplying contraband? That was almost as strange as…well, as the whole off-the-charts evening.

Cooper said, "Anyone else seeing colors?"

"Yeah. I am," I said.

Sonya shrugged. "Don't worry about it. Jus' means you're a little stoned." She paused. "Jus' don't operate any heavy machinery."

"Listen," Carlos said, "what are we going to do with that damned dog until we can make the drop?"

"Think we gon' have to work on that shield every night," Sonya said. "Maybe more. Sooner we do it the better. We gotta find out Manny's schedule."

"I'll do it," Cooper said. "With pleasure. Why don't we just put the dog back on the top shelf? Then we can take him down whenever we need him."

So, tired as we were, we floated the thing back up; but it wasn't easy. Was it the curse that made it heavier? Or we just exhausted? We wouldn't know till we tried it tomorrow.

I slept like a dead woman.

CHAPTER XXIII: CHOCOLATE HELL

D ad called early the next morning. Which terrified me. I spoke
even before he could. "Is Haley okay?"

"What? Oh—sorry to scare you. Thankfully no bad news. But
it's funny you should ask. She seems a little better. Her breathing's
stronger, and she's stirring a bit. She isn't leaking at all today."

I breathed a sigh of relief.

"But your mom's not that great."

"What? Mom?" My mom wasn't the sort of person things happened
to. She usually happened to other people.

"I know it sounds crazy. She's always such a rock. But, Deb, she's
completely overwhelmed. She collapsed last night and they admitted
her to the hospital. Don't worry, it's not that serious—I mean, not a
heart attack or anything. But they're keeping her for observation."

He paused. "It couldn't have come at a worse time, because I have
to go to San Francisco for the weekend. Anyhow, the point is, we've
had to hire a full-time nurse to stay with Haley—your mother doesn't
trust the hospital—and I've given her your number in case…well, in
case we need you to come home right away. The school knows and
they'll bring you."

My heart speeded up. What he meant was, in case it looked like
Haley was going to die; in case I might only have one chance left to see
her. I understood what he was trying to say—but not say—and I could
feel tears pricking my eyes, starting to cloud my vision. But there was
something I *didn't* understand.

"Dad! Are you telling me Mom's so out of it she can't even dial
the phone?"

"Um, no, baby, I'm not saying that. Not because of the fainting thing—or whatever it was. You know what I bet? I bet she forgot to eat and had a low-sugar attack. You know how she can be. She just has a lot on her mind."

What he was saying was Mom might forget me; that he didn't trust Mom on the small matter of her younger daughter any more than Mom trusted the hospital. Well, okay, that wasn't news—but it still made me feel bad.

"Okay, Dad, I get it. But who's taking care of Curly?"

"Your buddy Jace is. You know how she's always liked him—so I phoned and asked if he'd like to take care of her. I thought it would be better than boarding her."

"Dad, that's so sweet! To think of Curly like that."

"I'm taking her over right now. I have to leave for the airport in about an hour. By the way, Jace said to tell you hi."

That was nice. I wish he could have said the same for Mom.

Usually A.B. didn't turn up till around two o'clock, but I needed him now! How to get him? Oh, yeah, we had a system, but it involved making a spectacle of myself. Oh, well. No alternative.

I went out in the middle of the quad and hollered as loud as I could: "FIELD GOAL!"

Too late, I saw Cooper walking toward me, waving. Oh, God, this was embarrassing. But he had such a cute smile on his face. Could this be the same kid? "Field goal?" he said. "Is that some kind of signal or something? Because, see, there's no actual game going on. Unless maybe it's an astral game. Yeah, that could be it. Are you seeing something I'm not?"

As sad as I felt, he had me laughing. He was funny! Who knew?

"Bingo. It is a signal. If A.B.'s too far away, telepathy won't work, so I have to actually yell for him. 'Field goal' is his idea of a joke—something about the way Lola kicked him that time."

"Ha! An assassin with a sense of humor."

"Whoo. Assassin's right. How about the way he took out that Mayan, huh? Did it make your blood run cold or what?"

"You actually saw him do that, right?"

"Yeah. My first murder."

"You're something, you know that? I'd have been reduced to whimpering." He smiled at me like he thought I really was something.

"Oh, no, you wouldn't. Things were happening much too fast." I smiled back at him.

He was still smiling. What was happening here was that somehow or other, we'd wound up kind of staring into each other's eyes, and as I've mentioned, Cooper had really pretty ones. To tell you the truth, I felt kind of woozy.

All of a sudden, with no warning, his eyes got all wet. "Reeno, I can't believe we're having this conversation. I mean...that I can actually...I just can't believe I was such an asshole and you guys..."

It could have gotten all sticky and gooey there if A.B. hadn't suddenly appeared. He gave Cooper a big old "Wowwwwwrrrr!"

To me, he said, "This better be good, Human. Tell your little boyfriend to run along."

My little boyfriend? I may have blushed. I looked up at Cooper, but he was way ahead of me, looking so amused you'd have thought he overheard us. "Sounds like Cuddlekins wants you all to himself. Catch you on the flip side."

I think the Beast was starting to like him—he didn't try to strangle him or even give him rope burns.

"What's so important it couldn't wait till afternoon?"

"A.B., my mom's in the hospital. This thing with Haley's breaking my whole family down. Listen," I blurted, "if the Rangers can remove Cooper's curse, we can do Haley's. And we need to do it now. You could help us—we could all hold on to you and we could time-travel to Santa Barbara—"

"Slow down, Novice. First of all, I can only accommodate one passenger at a time. Three at the most."

"We could do it in shifts!"

"Second, the trivial psychic attack upon Cooper is a child's prank compared to the centuries-old malignant, virulent, and, not to put too fine a point on it, *lethal* one levied upon your family."

"So?" I threw back my shoulders defiantly. "We're getting really good."

"Novice, hear this. The Alpha Beast will not be responsible for unleashing that thing upon the planet! Try it and I will stop you."

Okay, that was that. I didn't doubt he'd stop us if he was going to speak in that tone of voice. But I couldn't help resenting that he was so willing to sacrifice Haley.

"Oh, please, girlo. There's only one thing that can save Haley, and it's not some bunch of admittedly talented but nonetheless amateur psychics. *That codex has to be returned.*"

Huh? He'd never said that. "What are you talking about?"

"It must be retrieved to prevent the 2012 disaster—if indeed the disaster even exists. We don't know that it does. But it most *certainly* must be returned to remove the curse. Only you can remove it and only by stealing the book—which you have already stolen. So we know you *will* steal it. The only variable is when."

"What are you talking about? How do you know this stuff?"

"Seers have seen. More powerful psychics than you have interpreted the curse."

I was outraged. "Why didn't you tell me this? And if they're so powerful, why couldn't they see where the book was in the first place?"

"This is new information, based on your own group's considerable achievement. I've so far avoided telling you in an effort not to further raise your stress levels. But now I believe I must be clear: *The book must be returned to its rightful owners before the curse can be removed.* And it obviously cannot be returned until we actually have it in our possession."

Suddenly I was plain tired. "You mean we have to time-travel twice? Once to get it and once to return it?'

"Certainly not, Student. By now succession will have occurred."

"And that means?"

"There will be heirs."

That was a relief. I didn't think I had more than one time trip in me in the near future. "Okay, fine. In that case, we need to go to Uxmal *now*! Today. Before lunch."

A.B. cocked his head in the adorable way a normal kitty will, a move I'd never seen him perform. On him, it looked slightly ridiculous. "Student, how do you feel?"

"Feel?" That was the last thing I expected. The Alpha Beast inquiring about my welfare? What was this? "What do you mean how do I feel? I feel…" Well, when I thought about it, not so hot.

"As a rule, it takes days to recover from time-travel that spans centuries. If we go now, you could short-circuit."

"I could *what*?"

"You could end up in a coma like your sister. Although you might manage a short hop."

"A short hop? What good would that do? Where would we go on a short hop?"

"Off-campus, I should think. Have you thought about what we're taking?"

"Run that by me again?" And then I remembered what Doña Marina had said: Jaguar-Snake Woman came "bearing wonderful gifts that made the entire town delirious with happiness."

"Oh, yeah. We need some cool presents. I guess. Are you sure she didn't just mean our fabulous personalities?"

"Reasonably." He yawned.

"Hey, I've got it!"

"Just like that? You've got it?'

"I haven't spent months in the library for nothing. But give me another hour. I think I read something good once. I just have to find it."

In study hall, he announced himself with the usual leap on my table. "Well? Did you find it?"

"Listen to this: 'So I presented to the king a little wine which I had with me in a bottle, which he esteemed above any treasure: for wine, they will sell their wives and children.' This English guy wrote that in 1569—claimed it kept him from being eaten by Mexican cannibals."

"Pah! An exaggeration, surely."

"About the cannibals? Probably. But the point is, the Mayans loved their pulque, right? It comes from the maguey plant, like tequila. So what about some fancy tequila?"

"You know little about tequila, Novice. They could probably brew it as well as Mr. Cuervo, whoever he may be."

"Well, then—oh, yeah, I've got it!" I was getting excited. "How about chocolate liqueur? Even though they had fermented chocolate, which by the way, they probably drank to dull the pain of all that blood-letting, I'll bet anything they didn't have crème de cacao. Wow! That stuff's really good."

"You're too young to know that."

"My parents let me taste some. They're crazy about it. Hold it, I'm not finished. How about other chocolate stuff? Everything you'd get in a movie theater, maybe. Milk Duds, chocolate-covered raisins—hey, and Godiva candy, and chocolate syrup. Think about tortillas and chocolate syrup. How cool would that be? Hey! Heath bars. Chocolate truffles. Chocolate ice cream? Uh-uh. Too hot. Brownies! Bet they've never had brownies."

"Your idea," said the Beast, "is not without merit."

I had another idea. "Of course, there's one other thing the Mayans loved: jade."

"You're thinking, perhaps, of robbing an Asian art museum?"

"No, but my mom's got a real nice pin thing, a whaddayacallit—brooch."

"I hardly think it will compare with what the Mayans already have."

"No, it's good. My dad's parents were missionaries. They got it in China a long time ago—I think it's an antique. Anyway, it's all carved and stuff. What do you think?"

"Perhaps."

"Look, I've got a really great idea—my mom's, like, paranoid about getting her purse snatched. She never keeps more than one credit card in her purse, and she switches around. She keeps the others in a desk drawer at home. We could buy chocolate with them, and lift my dad's booze. And the brooch, of course. Omigod, we have to go now! I mean tonight, or maybe tomorrow. While Mom's in the hospital."

"Your father won't notice his own daughter? And an unusually handsome cat?"

"He's in San Francisco. And Curly's at Jace's. It's perfect. If the credit cards aren't there, I'll think of a way to steal the chocolate. We can go to different stores if we need to—see, I know where everything is, and how to find stuff.

"But wait—where'll we keep the stuff? Can you put a glamour on a grocery bag full of chocolate?"

"Leave that part to me. It will require two trips—actually two trips each time—but one will be such a short hop you might manage."

I didn't like that word "might." I was about to say something, but he did his famous pranceaway before I could open my mouth. Okay, fine, that gave me time to work on my plan.

A.B. didn't show his conceited self till the meeting that night, which was mostly just practice for our next amazing exploit. Afterward, while everyone was gathering up their things, he said one word: "Ready?"

"Ready for what?"

"Santa Barbara, of course."

"What, now? We're going to Santa Barbara now?"

"I asked you, Student. Are we?"

"Let's do this," I said, clenching my jaw against the bumping and grinding ahead. He gave me his tail, and we were out of there.

Next thing you know (if you didn't count the pain and the noise) I was standing in my old bedroom, clutching A.B. so tight he forgot himself and spoke aloud. "Yowrrrrr!"

"What's that?" someone said.

I froze. No one should be there.

"It would seem," A.B. said, "that we miscalculated." He dropped onto my bed, and then to the rug without a sound.

Everything was quiet for a while. And then another voice said, "Something outside. Cat, I guess." The voice seemed familiar, but it was very low. I couldn't even tell if the speaker was a man or a woman.

"I think they're on this floor," I said. "Let's check it out."

My room was dark as a closet, but the hall was faintly lit, and the light came from Mom and Dad's room. I crept along the corridor, flat to the wall, A.B. on the other wall.

I peered around the door frame and saw that the room was lit by a single candle. There were two people in it, Jace and a girl I'd never seen before, with a shaved head and a pierced lip. The light glinted on the stud in her lip, and it was ugly. She was holding up a picture of me that Mom kept on her bureau. "This is your old girlfriend? Seriously lame."

Jace looked at the picture. "Yeah, she's kind of a dog, but she taught me some pretty good stuff."

Baldy was just fascinated by that picture. "What did you see in her?"

He shrugged. "Hard up, I guess. She was the only girl who ever paid any attention to me. Anyway, forget about her. Let's just get the stuff and leave."

I couldn't believe this was happening. Jace knew no one was here because my father had told him! He'd betrayed my dad's trust and mine. And not only that, he was dumping me for a chick with no hair on her head. (Not that he was ever my boyfriend.) I looked her up and down, and what I saw almost made me lose it—something light green pinned to her black T-shirt.

"Easy," A.B. said. "Easy."

I went over the Tactics of Combat in my head—know your enemy; pick the right time; when in doubt, bluff. Those were the ones that came to mind. Okay, I didn't know the girl, but this was the right time, no question; I had surprise on my side. And I was really good at bluffing—I'd had plenty of practice on Cozumel.

I wondered if I could manage a reverse invisibility spell. "Be large," I told my body. When I stepped into that room, I felt about the size of the Statue of Liberty. I held out my hand: "Give me the brooch, Baldy."

She screamed like she'd seen a ghost. Jace turned around, his face white in the dim light. "Reeno! What are you doing here?" He looked like he was about to puke.

"Interrupting a burglary in progress. What does it look like?" I turned to Baldy. "Give me the brooch."

She quit screaming and started yelling. "She can't be here! She's in Ojai."

"I said give me the brooch. Or I'm going to take it."

I guess the Statue of Liberty thing didn't work. Baldy launched herself at me, knocking me down before I had a chance to brace. A.B. jumped on her back and dug in his claws, which started her screaming again.

"Shut up!" Jace said. "Be cool, man. You want the cops in here?"

A.B. wrapped his tail around her neck and tightened it, which did make her shut up. When she started gagging, I said, "Are you going to give me the brooch?"

"Uch! Uch!" she said, which I took for "yes," since she tried to nod at the same time.

"All right, Snookums," I singsonged. "You can let go of Baldy now."

The Beast sprang off her and parked himself in front of Jace, growling like he thought he was Cujo.

Baldy rolled off me and managed to get to a kneeling position, staring me in the face. She had guts, I'll give her that. "My *name* is Tabitha."

I sat up. "Give me the brooch, Baldy." I held out my hand again.

"I don't have any roach! Are you crazy? We're not doing drugs here, we're on a job."

Jace sighed. "She means the jade pin, stupid."

"Oh. Well, why didn't she say so?" Her voice had a high, whiny quality; it was really grating. Her fingers went to her boob and she started to undo the clasp. I stood up, dusted myself off, and held out my hand, silent, till she plopped it in my palm. I stuck it in my pajama pocket and addressed my former good buddy.

"Jace, I really didn't figure you for a two-timing turdball. But just for the record"—here I turned to Baldy—"I never was his girlfriend. He was just a kid whose daddy had lock picks." It was true. The most attractive thing about Jace had been his dad's locksmith business. He'd always had a crush on me, but I'd...well, to tell the truth I'd played him. Suddenly I realized I'd never do that to one of the Rangers. What had I been thinking?

"Liar!" Jace yelled, and he tried to jump me, but A.B. climbed up on his chest and dug all eighteen claws in.

"Aiiiyeee!" Jace hollered, and I said aloud, "Off, Snookums."

You'd have thought he was Lassie the way that cat obeyed when it suited him. He hit the floor with a thud, leaving Jace staring in amazement at the blood seeping through his T-shirt.

"That's no normal cat!"

"No kidding."

"What is that thing?"

A.B. threatened him with a growl.

"Watch out, he understands English," I said sweetly. "That thing is a Mexican Fighting Cat. We have a whole herd of them where I've been."

"I never—uh—heard of anything like that."

"There's a lot of things you never heard of, Horatio. This school where I've been? It's no average everyday school. They're doing top-secret research there, little kiddies. That Bad Girl thing is a cover."

"Gimme a break!" Jace said. Tabitha was respectfully silent.

"Snookums, do me a favor, will you? Leave Jace alone while he repairs the damage here, okay?" I nodded at an open pillowcase on the floor, next to a flashlight. "You've got it in there, right? The rest of Mom's jewelry?"

"Look, Reeno, I know you never liked your mother. I thought you'd want me to…"

"To what? Come in here with some bald chick and steal my mother's jewelry? Oh yeah, and insult my picture? Tell me, Snookums, would I like that?"

Snookums growled.

"Put it back, Jace, and I'll tell you what you're going to do next. Meanwhile, Baldy, you call Morgan on her cell phone and tell her to get her butt in here."

Baldy stammered, "I…uh…"

"Look, I know you've got a cell phone and I know she's outside in the car. This is my crew, remember? I designed the whole program. Call her."

Baldy hit the phone. "Morgan? Yeah, everything's okay, but we've hit a snag. Reeno's here. Yeah, Reeno. Could you, uh, come in for a minute?" She paused. "Yeah, I know that's not how we do it, but she…"

I snatched the phone out of her hand. "Get your butt in here, Morgan. Or I call nine-one-one." I kept the phone and said to A.B., "Guard these two while I let Morgan in."

I did the Statue of Liberty thing again and opened the door to a distraught Morgan. The little gray cat from next door ran in with her. "Oh, hi, Rosebud. The more the merrier. Morgan, you're a Class-A sleaze case."

"It was Jace's idea. He said…"

"Yeah, yeah. Get upstairs."

We started up, "What are you doing here, Reeno? We thought you were at school."

"Obviously. Look, I'm not going into detail, but I'm here on a mission. I work for the government now and…"

"You what?"

"I was recruited, igmo. Thief, spy—I have talent, what can I tell you? That school thing's a cover."

"Bull! You ran away!"

We entered Mom's room. "Oh, really? Have you met my kitty? Do a trick for her, Snookums."

And to my amazement, not only Snookums, but sweet little Rosebud, performed a dance. They jetéed into the air simultaneously, executed double somersaults in opposite directions and landed, one on Jace's head, one on Morgan's, not even clawing, just balancing perfectly.

"Nice!" I said, whereupon they hopped to the floor, stood up on two legs, and came back down to four in a perfect bow. "Bravo!" I yelled spontaneously. It really was impressive.

"Did you ever see cats like that?"

"Uh—"

Jace said, "That's no Mexican Fighter—that's just Rosebud, from next door."

"What I'm trying to tell you, Snookums is a genetically altered specimen from our lab. Among his other talents."

"What other talents?" Morgan asked.

"Show her, Baldy. Lift up your T-shirt." The fight was gone out of Tabitha. She whirled and raised her T-shirt to show her mangled back.

"Foiling burglaries," I said.

"Don't mess with him, Morgan," Jace said. "That cat's bad news."

"As I was saying, among his other talents, he can actually summon and command other cats. Right, Rosebud?"

"Meow!" said Rosebud, doubtless on a signal from A.B.

"By the way, Snookums, did they behave themselves while I was gone?"

A.B. growled and jumped up on Jace's right leg, like a dog. He clawed at the pocket. I held out a hand, "Give, Jace. Down, Snooks."

Sheepishly, Jace reached in his jeans and took out my mom's diamond stud earrings.

"For Baldy?" I said. "She'd look better in a pair of fishhooks."

"Anything else, Kittykins?"

A.B. actually shook his head in the "no" gesture. Full of surprises, that cat.

"Okay, are you people convinced?"

No one said a word. Meaning they were convinced, all right—convinced they were in a nightmare about a crazy woman.

"Good," I said. "Now you're all going to help me carry out our mission. Who's got money?"

"I do," Tabitha said.

"Put it on the bed. Who else?"

"You're robbing us?" Jace whined. "That's low."

"Yeah, right. Give it up."

Jace put his money on the bed.

"I don't have any," Morgan said.

I said, "Search her, Snookums." A.B. ripped off her jeans pockets. A ten-dollar bill fell out. "Okay. Punish her." He jumped onto her chest, wrapped his tail around her neck, and tightened it till I said, "Enough."

I was glad he didn't really hurt her. I'd seen enough blood for one night, but Morgan was the only one who hadn't seen what he could do. I didn't want her thinking she could get away with something later.

"Now, crew, I'm going to tell you about our project. It involves aliens."

"You mean, like, illegals?' Jace said.

I gave him a withering look. "I mean, like, UFOs."

"Right," he said in a neutral tone. Maybe these guys weren't buying it, but that was no reason not to spin a story. Combat Tactic Nine: "When possible, pull a hustle."

"Guess what about aliens? The E.T. kind."

They looked obligingly blank.

"There is certain evidence to show that they are planning an invasion of Earth within the next six months."

The crew didn't even react. I was crazy and they were going with it—end of story.

"And there is further evidence that they can be easily stopped. They happen to be vulnerable to an ordinary, everyday substance, easily obtained by anyone on Earth who can get to a supermarket."

"Beer," Morgan said. "You want us to buy you some beer." She sounded supremely exhausted.

"Chocolate."

"Chocolate," Jace said, as in, "humor her."

"We are now going chocolate shopping."

"Oh, sure." Baldy was getting bold again. "The whole government ran out of chocolate and they've sent you to Santa Barbara to get some. To fight the aliens. I mean, if they can get it anywhere, why would they want to come here? And why would they send a kid ?"

"That information is classified. Give me my mother's brooch, please."

"I don't see why the hell I should."

"Snookums?"

Casually, the Beast sank his teeth into her ankle, all the while doing his Cujo impersonation.

Well, how hard should it be to get a cat off your ankle? I guess that's what Baldy was thinking, because she tried.

The fool.

A.B. grabbed her hand with his tail and pried it away, squeezing hard enough to make her yell, "Okay, okay!" And she did it.

Speaking telepathically, I said, "Okay, A.B., what can Rosebud do?"

"She's authorized to maim, but not to kill."

"Can she take care of Baldy?"

"Easily."

"Okay." I spoke aloud to the humans. "Here's the plan. Morgan will drive Jace, Snookums, and me to Celebrity Vons while Rosebud guards Baldy here. Tabitha, you make one move and that little gray kitty jumps up on your bald head and takes off your scalp. Understood?"

"She does and my parents sue!"

"I've heard if you get really bad scalp damage, your hair won't grow back. Want to look like that—only scarred up—for the rest of your life?"

She pouted, but she shut up.

"Jace and Morgan—throw your cell phones on the bed." When they had obeyed, I took one, scooped up all the money, and said, "Let's go. Morgan first, Jace second. Anybody gets out of line, and I call the cops on Baldy—or else sic Snookums on you two, whichever I'm in the mood for."

Nobody spoke on the way to Celebrity Vons, which is called that by the locals because it's in an area where a lot of Hollywood people live. Since everybody in the neighborhood is more or less loaded, I figured it ought to have the best goody selection in town.

When we got there, I took the car keys from Morgan, leaving her and Jace with A.B. Then I went chocolate shopping. Mmm boy, it was a kid's dream—I got every kind of fancy chocolate bar, not to mention Snickers and Almond Joys and Three Musketeers, and little packs of mini candy bars, and candy kisses, and chocolate syrup, and Oreos, and peanut butter cups, chocolate chips, and then, for good measure, chocolate chip cookies. My best score was a chocolate almond torte

I found in the bakery section. I hated to be the one who brought tooth decay to the Mayans, but maybe they had good dentists. One thing I knew, it was never smart to underestimate them.

Morgan and Jace were pretty scratched up by the time I got back to the car. Some people just don't learn.

"What happened, A.B.?" I asked when I'd loaded my groceries.

He was sitting in the storage area under the back windshield, contentedly removing the blood from his coat. "That monstrous boy-child came at me with a tire iron. Really, Human, I can't see how you stand these people!"

"What, Jace? Jace tried to hit you?"

"They both did, actually."

"You cowards," I said aloud. "Attacking an innocent pussycat!"

Jace looked shaken. "Innocent! That thing's Beelzebub in disguise."

"You thought he was just a cat, Jace. No matter what I told you, you still thought he was a regular kitty-cat, maybe with a few tricks. Otherwise, you'd have left him alone. I just want to tell you—" I struggled to figure out how to put it.

"Yeah?" he sneered. "You want to tell me what?"

"I am just so majorly, completely, totally disappointed in both of you." I kind of hated the way I sounded, sort of like Mom and Dad when they were mad at me. But it was true. "Disappointed" was the only word I could think of to describe the way I felt.

I wasn't even particularly mad. I just wanted to cry. And I sure wanted to get rid of them. It was tempting just to send them on their way when we got back home but I needed them to help me unload the chocolate. We took it up to the bedroom, where we found Tabitha asleep with Rosebud, apparently not having done anything stupid or violent. That made me like her better.

"Okay," I said. "You three can go. I'm keeping your cell phones, just in case. Just get out of my parents' house and out of my sight. Rosebud, see them out, will you? And thanks for all your help."

"Mrowwww!" said the gray cat, and ran down the stairs, the three humans clattering at her heels.

I was pretty sure what they'd do next, so I moved fast. I had the perfect carrying case for the chocolate—a multicolored Guatemalan duffel that Mom had gotten in Los Angeles. The designs on it may or may not have been Mayan, but they were close enough. You could really pack a lot in there, and I started by visiting the pantry and rounding up a bottle of chocolate liqueur, and some brandy to mix with it; then some tequila I saw. The Beast didn't know everything: I really couldn't believe that in eleven hundred years, distilling techniques hadn't improved.

I nestled Willie Wonka's entire chocolate factory around the bottles and, just as I was zipping up, I happened to notice the flashlight the wannabe burglars had left in Mom and Dad's bedroom. How cool would that be at midnight in a Mayan city? I threw it in, along with one other thing, and then the knock came. I looked out the window.

Uh-huh. Two police cars had arrived with no lights and no sirens—with or without cell phones, my ex-friends had ratted me out. "Let's go, A.B.," I said through clenched teeth—and this time the clenching had nothing to do with the discomfort of time travel.

Wisely—now and then the Fiend actually can be wise—A.B. said nothing until we'd completed the second leg of the trip back to Bad Girl School.

The first ended in a cottage of the type the Mayans have been building for centuries and possibly millennia, except without the thatched roof. And there were other clues that this one was contemporary. One was the length of this leg of the trip (barely noticeable); another was the presence of a large flat-screen television. "Leave the bag on the floor," A.B. ordered. "It'll be fine here."

"Where," I asked, "is here?"

"Later. I need to get you home."

And indeed we were back in the Rangers meeting room in about a second. Everyone was still packing up and the Curly dog, which was beginning to give me the creeps, was back on its shelf. The only difference was, I had two new things in my pocket—the brooch, which I hadn't wanted to leave in some stranger's house, and Morgan's cell phone.

I thought the phone might come in handy—and so might Morgan.

❖

Later, when we were in bed, A.B. said, "You handled yourself well, Traveler. Well, with one small exception, which can wait till tomorrow. Even the Alpha Beast was impressed."

"Thanks." I tried to give him a friendly cuddle, but he resisted. "You know what I was worried about? I was afraid you were going to kill them."

For the first time since I'd known him, he laughed. I didn't even know he could do it. "Kill them? Pah! They're a grain of sand on the beach of crime—why the devil would I kill them?"

"I don't exactly know what your standards are."

"Whatever they are, Student, I can assure I wouldn't kill your friends in your parents' house in front of you. What kind of fiend would do a thing like that?"

He cracked me up. But all the same, I felt my teeth unclench as well as a few odd stomach muscles when I realized I could ask about something I'd been really concerned about. Smiling, I said, "I'm glad to hear it, kitty-muffin. I suppose that means you wouldn't—"

"Kill Julia's mother? Or Kara's? No, I would not. But only because of you. Student, do you understand that? No doubt they deserve it by my 'standards,' as you call them. However, you'd feel guilty for the rest of your life if I did. I would never permit my servant to suffer."

"Thanks so much, Your Majesty."

"Nonsense. It's simply inefficient."

I got in a little ear scratch before he could jerk away. "What a little sweetums kitty is."

CHAPTER XXIV: COUNTDOWN

The next morning I woke up feeling clobbered, but nothing like when I traveled five hundred years. If I'd been at home I'd probably have stayed in bed, but I had things to do, and anyway, I knew I was going to be out of it for a week after the trip to Uxmal, so I didn't want to miss any more time than I already had. The point here was to get points, and I couldn't do it in bed.

So I dragged myself out of bed, whipped up a glamour while I was grooming, put it on the brooch, and slipped it into the back of my top drawer. I was kind of dreading breakfast because I knew the Beast would be there, and I knew exactly what he was going to say, but there was really no avoiding him. As he'd pointed out on so many occasions, that was the beauty of being a cat; you could come and go as you pleased and no one even noticed.

I was safe during gym, I was pretty sure of that. He hadn't showed up on the field since the incident of the kitty-rocket. I thought it was because of the bad memories, but after what he'd told me the night before, I thought it might actually be because he felt bad for Lola.

Imagine! He wouldn't kill my friends in my mom's house in front of me! Is that the sweetest thing? For him, it was like sending a valentine. So I'd begun to think he might have something resembling feelings, but I still knew he was going to give me a hard time that morning.

He didn't look up from lapping milk. But then he never did.

"You're mad at me, right? About making up the alien thing?"

"Naturally, I was going to ask you what the very devil you thought you were doing. If you must lie, Student—and face it, sometimes we must—then the best lie is the easy lie. Why on Earth did you have to go into all that gobbledygook?"

I was ready for him. I had a really good reason. "You know how I've known Jace all my life? When he was a little kid, he was a UFO freak. He probably barely remembers it now, but grown-ups never forget."

"How, exactly, does that apply?"

"You just have to trust me, kitty-kiss. I had my reasons."

"Very well," he said, and bounced off the table.

As usual, he turned his retreating tail into a question mark. I was getting kind of used to it. If you want to know the truth, I was actually starting to think it was cute.

Dad called from San Francisco that night, just like I knew he would. Because once Jace and Morgan had called the cops on me, I figured they weren't going to stop there.

"Reeno, I just had to make sure you were okay," he said. "Your buddy Jace called today and said he saw you in Vons last night."

"Dad! You know that's crazy. I'm here, not there. How could I be two places at once?"

"He swore it was true. He said you told him some crazy story involving secret missions and extraterrestrials. He thought you'd escaped and gotten on drugs."

"You know I don't do drugs."

"Well, sure, but—"

"And you know I'm here."

"Um, I—"

"So why would you believe Jace? You know he's always had that UFO thing going. When you really think about it, who has more access to drugs, me or Jace? And by the way, why would I be in Vons and not at the hospital? If I ran away from this place, it would be for one reason only."

"I'm sorry for doubting you, Reeno. I just had to check it out."

"How's Mom?"

"Cranky. I just talked to her. That's probably—"

I interrupted him. "Dad! I just thought of something. Jace is a burglar, you know?"

"You never admitted that."

"Well, I'm admitting it now. He knows you guys are gone, right? Because he's taking care of Curly."

"Where are you going with this?"

"Well, the house is sitting empty and everything. It's a perfect target."

"It's funny you should mention that. The police got a call about a prowler there last night."

"I hope nobody got in."

"I'll get Clarice to check it out." The next door neighbor. Rosebud's mom.

"Oh, good," I said, but I wasn't too happy about it. Because I'd suddenly remembered I'd left Jace and Tabitha's cell phones on the bed in Mom and Dad's room. They'd be traced, and the two of them would go down. It was as simple as that.

I got off the phone fast, kind of sobered by the idea that I might have just sent my best friend and some strange girl to jail. Okay, neither Jace nor Morgan were my best friends anymore. For one thing, they'd burgled our house—*and* they'd tried to get me thrown in jail—but I sure wasn't happy about it. I could have been happy that Morgan was out of it, but I didn't know for sure she would be—one of the others might rat her out.

One thing, it made me think about how easy it was to get busted.

Did you ever hear adults sit around and talk about the totally dangerous things they did as kids? How they drove drunk or stoned or went home with a guy they didn't know, or hitchhiked in Afghanistan? This is the kind of thing your parents hope you won't hear, of course, but sometimes you do. Sometimes they think you're asleep.

Or maybe they're not your parents and you're in the next booth at a restaurant; or maybe it's even on television. They say what they did and then they take a quick sip of their drink and cover their face and they sometimes turn red, and say, "Omigod, what was I thinking? How on Earth could I have ever been so stupid?"

And you think, "You got away with it—what's the problem?"

Well, that was the way I was beginning to think about my life of crime. Like I was my parents. Like I couldn't believe I'd been so dumb and gotten away with it. By the time I got back to my room, I felt like I was getting old before my time.

Like I was completely losing my nerve.

Jabba the Cat was lounging in the doorway. "Risks are what makes a hero, Student. Just not stupid risks."

"Hero," I said. "I like the sound of that. Isn't it time I got promoted again?"

He galloped down the hall, sounding like a herd of buffalo.

And for some reason, I realized that, for the first time, my dad had called me "Reeno" instead of "Deb."

❖

At the Rangers meeting that night, Cooper, having temporary custody of someone else's iPhone, reported on Manny Diaz's schedule. "It turns out he's one of those general sportscasters, meaning he doesn't cover just baseball, which is lucky for us, since it isn't baseball season. Right now he's covering the Lakers, whose schedule"—he held out the phone so we could all see—"is posted online. How cool is that? All we have to get is get to a Lakers game, and we've got him."

"After Uxmal," A.B. said, twitching his tail to let everyone know he was talking.

"A.B. says after Uxmal," I told them.

"Roger," Julia said. "And now—LET'S RIDE THE OZONE!"

For the next few days—until Uxmal—we had two main chores: practicing moving Cursed Curly with our psyches; strengthening its shield; and sending energy to Haley, which would also be practice for what the group had to do while I was in Uxmal.

First, we floated the dog down from its shelf, but rather than submit to our collective will, it dropped in little stutter steps, sometimes resisting. It felt heavier somehow.

And then when we actually had it on the table, we could see that it was starting to look worn, its white plush turning slightly gray. Or was that me?

"Hey, is this thing a different color or not?"

Puzzled looks all around.

I felt a weird prickling at the back of my neck. "Guys, I hate to tell you this, but I think that thing's developing an aura."

"Yow!" said Carlos. "What do you think that means?"

"Could mean the curse gettin' stronger," Sonya said. "Maybe 'cause we compressed it."

"I think it might mean it's trying to get out," Julia added. "And maybe about to succeed."

Neither was a good option. So we went into the dog itself and compressed the curse yet again. Then we built a second shield for it—within the dog. And after that, we reinforced the outside shield.

"Something else about that dog," Carlos said. "I don't like it anymore. It doesn't seem like a cuddly kids' toy. To tell you the truth, it's creeping me out."

"Yeah," Cooper said. "I kind of get why nobody could stand me when I had that thing on me."

There was something sad and sweet about the way he said that—like remembering innocence lost the hard way. *I can stand you now*, I thought. And hoped he couldn't read my mind like A.B.

After we'd done the shielding we noticed the toy was much easier to steer—at first—but then after a few minutes all our work seemed to get worn down.

Julia said, "The thing is definitely getting stronger. Wonder when we can go, anyhow?"

Cooper checked online with his liberated iPhone. "There's a Lakers game Thursday. Think we could aim for that?" He looked at A.B. as if expecting the Beast to speak to him. Like that was gonna happen.

A.B. was silent. Big surprise.

"I just thought of something," Cooper continued. "How are we going to do this, anyhow?"

"I've been thinking about that," I said. "I think I can get us a ride. But we might need Lakers tickets. How do we do that?"

Julia said, "Why don't we steal a credit card and buy them online?"

"We can't," Sonya said, "that would be immoral!"

Julia, who almost never lost it, sighed in exasperation. "Sonya," she said. "did it ever occur to you you're a prude? What the hell did you do to get in this school, anyhow?"

Sonya shrugged. "Same as y'all. 'Cept instead of seein' things, I heard voices. They thought I was crazy."

"Why didn't they send you to a shrink instead?"

"Uh…" Sonya smiled mischievously. "Could be all those drugs I did 'cause I felt so bad about bein' crazy."

"To get back to the matter at hand," Carlos said, "I think we could do that credit card thing. Because the person whose card we used would just report it stolen—and then he wouldn't have to pay for the tickets."

"But somebody would," Sonya said.

"You know what?" I said. "I've already got really bad morals. Why don't I just do it and—"

"Wait," said Cooper. "They didn't confiscate my checkbook." He grinned evilly. "Guess they thought there was no place to use it. Why don't I just get someone in the dorm to do it and then reimburse them with a check?"

"Problem solved," Julia said. "Moving right along—how do we get out of here without being seen?"

"Easy," I said. "We make ourselves invisibility cloaks. Only not exactly like Harry Potter's. There's this thing called a 'glamour'..." Quickly, I explained the concept and taught them how to do it. By the end of the evening, we hardly noticed each other.

(Okay, kidding, but we made a lot of progress.)

❖

I was desperate to get to Uxmal, but I couldn't get a word out of A.B. Nor did Dad call with news of Haley, which I took to be a good sign. At least as good as we could hope for.

Another day went by and nothing happened except that I continued to feel better, a fact A.B. must have noticed. Finally, at the meeting that night, The Great One spoke:

"We leave tomorrow. From this room. Tell them to gather at the usual time—with plenty of food and drink—and be ready to seal themselves in here for at least two days."

I told them.

"Huh," said Carlos.

"Double huh," Sonya said.

"What is it?"

"Well, if we gon' send you energy for two days, and you come back a split second after you leave, then when the two days come in?"

"Yeah," Carlos added, "how would that work?"

"A.B.?" I said aloud. All was quiet as he answered.

"This time, of course, we'll return on their schedule. In other words, if it takes us two days in 'real' time, we'll come back in two days. If two weeks, then at the end of the two weeks."

I relayed the info.

"Damn," Carlos said. "Damn damn damn! I thought we were going to find something out about how time travel works."

I thought about it. Pretty clever of A.B. to deflect that one. I guess we'd all hoped that. Because, after all, I was about to steal a book to break a curse that wouldn't exist if I hadn't already stolen the book several centuries ago and couldn't be broken unless I did it in the near future. It was the kind of thing that would keep you awake if you let it.

Most of the rest of the meeting—aside from shield-building, telekinesis, and energy-sending—was taken up with talk about how to get supplies for the Uxmal session.

It was finally decided that they could all use their newfound glamour techniques for food and drink stealing. But meanwhile, since the discussion was heavy on fantasies of food that I wasn't going to be eating, I kind of let my attention wander, something I seldom did in a focus.

I was kind of in a state of psychic limbo, maybe more receptive than usual. All I know is that I heard another voice—definitely not A.B.'s voice—in my head. *I need to talk to you*, it said. *After the meeting.*

Startled, I met Cooper's eyes. *Huh?* I telegraphed back, really talking mostly to myself.

To my embarrassment, he didn't react at all, only dropped his gaze. But I could have sworn he turned ever so slightly pink.

I'd probably imagined the whole thing, but just in case, I made an excuse for Carlos, with whom I always walked back to the dorm—(just had to check out a library book) which I went ahead and actually did—and when I went outside, Cooper was waiting for me.

"Carlos already left," he said. "I told him I'd walk you home."

"Cooper, listen, did you…um…send me a message? To meet you after the meeting?"

"You mean write you a note? Or what?"

"I mean telepathically."

"Whoa." He drew back, startled. "Um…yeah. Yes, I guess I did. But I didn't know you'd actually get it. You know how sometimes you wish you could tell someone something, but you just can't get their attention? So you send them a telepathic message just because?"

I laughed. "Yeah. But it never works."

"Guess I should be more careful."

"Yeah. It's spooky."

"Bears looking into." Well. Definitely time to leave *that* subject, but neither of us knew how.

We were standing on the library steps shifting from one foot to another, a little embarrassed, marking time, really, a conversational situation I can never stand. So I finally just blurted, "What did you need?"

"Huh?"

"What I got was, *I need to talk to you.* What's up?"

"Oh. Well. I was hoping to walk you back."

I looked at him quizzically, sending him my own telepathic message: *Could you be more specific?*

But he didn't seem to get it. "Okay," I said. "Sure. Let's walk."

So we walked, chattering awkwardly about the importance of high-energy high-carb snacks, such as Ho Hos and doughnuts, for the impending energy vigil. The subject couldn't have interested me less, but I didn't know how to get on something more substantive.

This time Cooper was the blurter. As we neared the dorm, he said, "Listen, I've never gotten a chance to say I'm...um...really sorry about Haley and that...you know...we're all rooting for her."

This was a boy? Talking to me like this?

"And I wanted to say something else. Remember the first time we met?"

"Um. Not sure."

"Think back. It was your first day and you asked me for directions."

"Oh, yeah. I think you insulted me."

"Big surprise. But before that..."

It was the strangest thing, but I really could remember something before Cooper had opened his mouth that day. He'd looked at me as if...

"I was trying to send you a message," he said. "I didn't know I was psychic, but I was still trying to communicate with you. Telepathically."

"But why?"

"Because I couldn't talk to you. You know, because I couldn't talk to anybody. So I was trying really really hard to tell you I knew I was about to completely gross you out and I was sorry because..."

"Because what?"

"Guess it didn't work, huh?"

I smiled. "No, but we seem to be getting there." Omigod, I was flirting!

Taking the cue, he instantly abandoned whatever incredibly sincere thing he'd been about to say and just settled for, "You are without question the weirdest chick I ever met in my life."

"You are so sweet!"

"Yeah, right. Well, I wanted to apologize for that day."

"That's *all*? You've said much worse stuff to me since then."

"Well, a couple of other things. I wanted to thank you for, like, making it possible for me to rejoin the living."

"It wasn't exactly single-handed."

"And for going to Uxmal."

I grimaced. "Only under duress. Wish me luck."

"Well, see, that's exactly what I want to do. Because you know what's the luckiest thing you can do before you take off on something like that? You need to go out and get a good-luck kiss."

Uh-oh. I hadn't seen that coming. I wondered what colors I was turning. "Well, I was going to," I said, "but I wasn't sure where to find one." And then, bold as anything, I turned up my face, and he leaned closer, the lime-green of his aura washing over me. His energy felt warm and so...enticing.

How is this done? I wondered. Do I...or does he...?

And next thing you know, both of us had our arms around each other—don't ask how it happened, I think it was some kind of magic—and his lips went on top of mine and I closed my eyes, and...

Mmm, boy. So *that* was what a kiss was like.

When we stopped and breathed, we were still so close together it kind of shocked me, still looking straight into each other's eyes, still feeling strangely dazed and woozy. Or at least I was. It was kind of wonderful, maybe the best part.

"You'll be okay now," Cooper said. And then he whispered, *"Bon voyage!"*

CHAPTER XXV: GRAND ENTRANCE

How was I supposed to sleep after that? How was I even supposed to feel? Because the way I felt was complicated—kind of syrupy delicious and maybe a little scared. Did I like this boy? Yes! I thought, I've always liked him, even that first time he mentioned, when he insulted me on sight. I'd pulled for him, rooted for him all that time we'd worked to un-curse him, but I'd kept Cooper himself—the real boy under all the oily olive mask—at a distance. Still, I wasn't kidding when I blurted out to Manny Diaz that he was a "really nice boy." In my heart, I knew that. (I'm psychic, right? Of course I did.)

When I repeated it to myself, it didn't sound romantic, but the kiss? Definitely romantic.

"Reeno, would you go to sleep?" Kara said. "Do you suddenly have restless leg syndrome?"

"Sorry. Nervous I guess. About Uxmal."

"Oh, hell. Close your eyes and listen." She spoke softly and slowly. "You are in a beautiful place that only you know about…a place in the woods with a soft floor of moss…a perfect place for the best nap you ever had…"

Yow. Even Kara was being nice to me. I guess what she did was technically hypnosis, which is just another kind of trance. At any rate, it worked. Kiss or no kiss, I got a great night's sleep, zombied through my classes, and ended up at the Rangers meeting exactly at the appointed time, with Mom's brooch in my pocket.

I was the first one there—except for the Beast, of course, who was always so punctual you'd have to question whether he ever left if you didn't see him everywhere else. Except, oddly, not in my bed the night before. Could he have been giving me privacy to contemplate my personal conflicts?

Naaah. It just wasn't him.

"You underestimate me, Traveler."

"Ah. Awake, I see. Just testing. Listen, about Uxmal. Can we arrive a little outside the town—in the village where the poor people live?"

"Certainly. May I ask why?"

"I've got a plan." I told him what it was and, to my amazement, he seemed to approve: "As plans go, it will do."

"And one more thing—how am I supposed to know the book when I see it?"

"You will."

He could be such a know-it-all. "I will? That's all you have to say?"

"You will."

I shrugged. "Okay, Fuzz-button. I will."

That was all we had time for before everyone arrived with contraband sandwiches, sodas, and who knew what else—Ho Hos and doughnuts if they had their way. We were all on edge and nervous, like people waiting for a plane or something. I needed to get out of there.

"Ready, A.B.?"

"Not merely ready. Impatient."

"Okay, everybody," I said, "A.B. says this is it. Wish me luck."

They did—loudly. But I heard two words under the din—or perhaps I only imagined that Cooper whispered them once again:

"Bon voyage."

"Watch this, everybody!" I grabbed A.B.'s tail and we were off.

❖

We arrived almost immediately in the same Mayan hut where we'd left the Guatemalan bag, and once again, there seemed to be no one home unless you counted a fluffy little calico cat. "Say hello to Spot," A.B. said.

Aloud, I said, "Hi, Spot—how you doing, girl?" The cat let me pet her.

Then I got to work getting the little mini candy bars out of the bags, unwrapping some of them and leaving some in their paper and foil wrappers. I emptied all the chocolate kisses into a pile, leaving most of them in their foil, and made sure all the cookies and things were good and handy.

A.B. fluffed up his fur while I worked and Spot watched in Cat Position Eight, Chicken Kitty. Finally I rolled up my sleeves so my snakes showed, grabbed the bag, said to Spot, "Don't wait up," and reached out for A.B. "Let's go."

A.B. said, "Next stop, Uxmal." And before you knew it, we were boogying back eleven hundred years and I don't know how many miles—falling down, down, down the stairs of time, hitting each one, it felt like. And there must have been thousands of them. But I was used to it by now. I just hung on to the cat and the bag and tried to keep breathing.

When we landed, it was late afternoon on a bright sunny day. We were on a path near a little thatch-roofed village where not a lot was happening, except women making tortillas and taking in clothes that were drying on bushes. Some kids playing too. Very quiet and peaceful, much like a Mayan village would be today, according to my reading, the men still in the fields, everyone else getting ready for dinner.

A.B. and I touched down far enough away that no one could have sworn we hadn't simply come around a bend. We stayed on that path, me carrying the bag, both of us relaxed, just a girl and her cat having an afternoon walk. Perfectly ordinary except for two things—I looked about as Mayan as Cortes did, and no one here, if I understood correctly, had ever seen a domestic cat before. The Mayans had several kinds of dogs (one of them barkless), but so far as I knew, they didn't keep cats. These people knew all about jaguars and pumas and ocelots, but a little orange fluffball? Uh-uh. And who doesn't like little animals?

So I was counting on A.B. to do his nice-kitty impersonation and charm the little Mayan kids into eating out of my hand. I hoped their mamas hadn't warned them about taking candy from strangers.

Sure enough, pretty soon we had an adoring circle of admirers—or at least A.B. did. The kids all pointed and giggled, and A.B. let me pet him so they could see what that was about. A few dogs arrived, all huffy about this strange new animal, but A.B. lost no time showing them who was the alpha animal, which amused the kids no end.

He had a lot of nerve telling me to "act" in these situations. That cat was the Johnny Depp of felines. You would have thought from his performance that day that his name really was Sweetie-Fluff or Snookums. He let the kids pet him and he rubbed his head against them, and he even purred for the second time in our acquaintanceship.

And then when he pretty much had them in love with him, I opened the bag, took out a piece of chocolate, and ate it. You can imagine that that got their interest. I took out another and held it to the nose of the nearest kid, a naked little boy about four, I guess. "Um," he said, or maybe it was "yum." And then, "Cacao." Well, it sounded like that, anyhow. The Mayans used the cacao bean both for money and to make chocolate, so I was pretty sure the kid had identified the scent. I gave him the candy.

You should have seen what happened next. He popped it into his mouth, and his eyes brightened up like headlights. Such a look of bliss crossed his sweet little face that you'd have thought I'd handed him an entire hot fudge sundae.

Shouting that word again, "Cacao!" (or whatever it was), he grabbed for more, but I held back.

By now the other kids had caught on. I doled out a few more naked pieces. Then I unwrapped a chocolate kiss, to show them how, and gave the kiss to one of the kids. But to my surprise, another grabbed for the foil wrapper. I was afraid she'd put it in her mouth, and then I'd be in trouble with the moms, who were starting to gather. But she turned it over and over instead, examining its shininess, feeling its tinny texture, finally tearing it and rolling it into a little silver ball.

This was wonderful news—now I had twice as many gifts as I'd thought.

And by now, we had a really good crowd—dozens of kids, and maybe a dozen moms, some of whom tried to talk to me. I told them politely that I didn't understand their language, which they seemed to get, and then offered chocolate. Adults or not, even they went nuts for it. Not only that, they wanted to pet the kitty-cat. I was the most popular kid in the village and I'd only been there twenty minutes.

"What do you think, A.B.?" I asked. "We doing okay?"

"You mean if you don't count the petting? I've spent hours grooming this fur, and now look!"

"You look good," I said.

I pointed toward the Great Pyramid, the tallest building in Uxmal, and said "Palak." The king's name. "I have gifts for Palak."

Of course all they got was the name, which I probably

mispronounced, but they seemed to catch my drift. They fell into step both in front of us, leading the way, and behind us, protecting our rear, and we marched on Uxmal.

The more we walked, the bigger the parade got. Some of the men were returning now, and the women chattered to them like birds, describing the amazing taste treats they'd experienced, not to mention the soft little kittykins, so like a jaguar, yet so tame and loving. (You can sure fool some of the people some of the time.) I passed out a few more chocolates, to keep the goodwill going, and the men were as enthusiastic as the rest of their families. Everyone was very polite, not grabby at all, perhaps due to the intervention of little Kitty-Cream Puff when someone got pushy. He was doing a pretty good job of teaching them what cats were like.

When we got to the gates of the city, I didn't even have to do any work. The villagers explained in their strange language (strange to me, anyhow) that the weird snake-woman had gifts for the king. All I had to do was cross a few palms with silver—silver-wrapped kisses, that is—so the soldiers could see what I had for their glorious king. And boy, were they into it! These people were chocoholics on a major scale. And they hoarded the foil like money.

Once they were converted, the soldiers more or less took over. They conferred among themselves, and must have decided to send the king a messenger, because one of them took off at a gallop. Then they surrounded us importantly, making the villagers bring up the rear, and we continued our march, more or less in the manner of a Roman triumph, I fantasized, but without the laurel wreath. More and more citizens, many of them better dressed than the villagers, joined our procession, and it was a beautiful thing—a girl, a candy store, a pussycat, and about two hundred chocoholic Mayans.

At Uxmal, the Great Pyramid towers over palaces that archaeologists now call the Governor's Palace, the House of the Turtles, the Nunnery Quadrangle, and the House of the Magician. I'd seen pictures of the ruins, but of course none of it looked anything like the photographs. For one thing, all the buildings were gorgeously painted and carved in ways that more or less made you want to sit down and stare at them for a week or two. For another, I couldn't really tell from the books which one was which. All I know is that the king came out of his palace and stood on the steps, surrounded by about fifty people, some men, some women, some children, all of them dressed in amazing feathers and embroidery and jaguar skins and jewelry. I didn't know if they'd dressed up just for little old me (after the messenger came) or if they always looked like that.

If the Mayan city at Cozumel had seemed like Oz, the Uxmal spectacle was like something from another planet. Triple wow! Was this thing a treat for the eyes! The costumes from Hollywood on drugs, the magnificent buildings, the funny thatches atop the amazing architecture, the art covering every inch of everything, and—how can I say this?—the peacefulness of the whole scene. It was magnificent and incredible and beyond imagining and yet, it was so—like, sweet. Like these were just people living the way they lived, maybe getting dressed up for a visitor, yet completely comfortable in their splendiferous surroundings. This was the most impressive thing anyone from my century had ever thought of seeing, and it was everyday stuff for them.

"Call me Horatio," I said to A.B. "This is a little outside my philosophy."

"Even for the Alpha Beast," he said, "it's a bit on the grand side." It was the humblest statement I ever heard out of that furry little brain.

I knew from Cozumel how the Mayans greeted each other at the time of the conquest. What I didn't know was whether it was something they did four hundred years earlier. But I tried it anyhow—I touched the ground with my hand, and then I touched my head.

The royal party wasn't about to do that, because for one thing, it was probably beneath their dignity, and for another, they'd have fallen off those narrow steps. But some of the people on the ground did the same thing in response. So I figured I'd managed to say hello.

CHAPTER XXVI: THE KING AND I

The king said something that may have been "Welcome," and I said back that I was happy to be there and I had gifts for him. After that, one of the soldiers took my bag for me and two others escorted me up the steps, A.B. scampering ahead like a scout.

When we were face-to-face, Palak and I, I bowed, figuring that ought to be a sign of respect in any culture, and it seemed to go over pretty well. He smiled and opened his arms, a gesture that must mean "welcome" anywhere you go. From down on the ground, he'd seemed huge, but he was actually shorter than I was, and surprisingly young, maybe in his twenties. He had a handsome, flat face, with filed teeth, but a nice smile, anyhow, and, you know what? He seemed like a good guy, like the king in Cozumel—not grand or snotty or anything; just nice. And extremely curious about the strangers who'd turned up in his city.

The fact that he was young was good. It took away some of the intimidation of meeting a king. Palak seemed less a royal personage than a kid fairly near my age. I thought about the reverse of that—there might be an outside chance I'd seem like an adult to him. That had to be good.

His wife, in fact, may even have been about my age, even younger. Fifteen and a queen! It was a little weird to think about, but I was going with it.

Palak and his entourage took me into a palace room hung with tapestries and feathers, where the soldier set my bag down. Torches were burning in there, and the smoke was pretty bad. There were windows, but they were small, and the room was dark even though it was still daylight. Mats were spread on the floor to sit on, and Palak signaled that

I should have a seat, but nobody wanted to sit right away—everyone wanted to pet the kitty, especially the kids. Everybody was laughing and chattering in Mayan, so I laughed and chattered too, in English and sometimes Spanish, just for variety. No one had a clue what anyone else was saying, but we were all trying to show goodwill. That much I could tell.

I showed the kids how to scratch A.B. under the chin and behind the ears, which he permitted and even pretended to like, lifting up his chin for more like a normal cat. Some kid pulled his tail, and instead of killing her, he did the Halloween-cat thing to show his displeasure, puffing up to twice his size and making everyone go into gales of laughter, which must have caused him to put them all on his hit list. But he didn't say a word. He really took his job seriously.

Finally, when we were settled, someone brought water in clay cups, and pumpkin seeds for munchies, along with some little dried tortilla bits. They were pretty good.

When there was a lull, I took the brooch out of my pocket and gave it to Palak. Well, he just loved it—ooohed and aahed, and passed it around to all the adults (the kids still being occupied with the cat) and finally, gave it back to me. I unfastened the clasp and pinned it on him. "For Palak," I said.

He looked really surprised and said, no, he couldn't take it, and tried to get it off; but he couldn't really work the clasp. I said with my hands that I really wanted him to keep it, and he kept saying what seemed to be no, and I kept insisting, until finally he sent one of the women to get something. She brought him something small, which he presented to me—as an exchange, I figured.

It was a small jade carving of a man. Palak placed the carving in my hand, with a little speech that probably explained that it had magic powers or something. I really, really wanted to know what he was saying, so I looked around for A.B. to see if he had a clue, but a kid had him in her arms. She was carrying him out of the room.

I wasn't too comfortable with that. "A.B.," I said, "you okay?"

"I'm miserable, thank you. Carry on, Student."

Carry on. Well, what was next? First, I figured I had to thank the king, so I told him how much the green man meant to me and that it was a symbol of peace between our two tribes and that I would treasure it always, and he nodded and smiled as if he understood every word. Which, in a way, I guess he did. We were developing a way of communicating by hand gestures and the way our voices sounded, and by what would seem like the thing to be saying, even if we couldn't translate word for word.

I figured it was about time to bring out the booze. So I reached in the bag and cracked open the chocolate liqueur, figuring that ought at least to taste familiar. I asked with my hand for Palak's cup and poured him some. He indicated that I should pour some for myself, which I did. Then I signed for him to drink, but he said, no, I should drink first. I didn't know whether the "after-you" routine was for politeness, or if he was trying to make sure the drink wasn't poison, so I figured the safest thing would be to assume the latter. I showed him how to clink cups and then I held up mine, chirped out, "Cheers," and what do you know, he said, "Cheers" back, loud and clear.

I took a sip, nodded to show it was good, and waited for him to drink. He didn't look as if he wanted to. I took another sip and pulled an ecstatic face that made everyone laugh. His wife couldn't stand it any more. She just had to have some. Impatiently, she took the cup from him, and tasted.

It was like watching that little kid who first tried the chocolate. Her eyes glowed like a pair of stars. I really thought she was going to swoon right there. "Hey, Palak, you've got to try this," she said excitedly. Okay, it may not have been exactly that, but I'd bet fifty dollars it was pretty close. So Palak tried it.

And I thought I was about to see a grown man cry. He looked like he'd just seen the face of Jesus in a pizza. Omigod, was he a happy man! He took another sip, smacked his lips, turned to me and said, "Fabulous beyond compare!" or something like it.

"The pleasure's all mine," I replied, slurping up some more. Then Palak passed his cup to his right-hand neighbor. "Cheers," he said to her. I waved my hand in a circle, to show that I wanted everyone to have some, and Palak sent for more cups.

While those were being brought, I dug out the brandy and tequila, but I didn't open them yet. After everyone had tasted the chocolate liqueur, I produced my fanciest treat, the chocolate almond torte. It was now a few days old, and I prayed that it wouldn't be too stale, but I figured even if it was dry and powdery, it would still taste good. The Mayans probably didn't have the recipe, so they'd think it was supposed to be that way.

I asked for a weapon I saw in a soldier's belt, a knife with a blade made of obsidian, the volcanic glass the Mayans used for sharp objects. Reluctantly, the soldier gave it to me, and I cut the cake. This time I didn't even go through the "after-you" thing. I made sure to taste it first so I'd know if it was still good, and it was, frankly, totally great—dense fabulous chocolate more like a candy bar than a cake, with a hint of orange. I invited Palak to try it.

"Cheers!" he said, popping a piece into his filed-tooth mouth. Once again, everyone had some and nearly fainted with delight.

Things were going rather magnificently if I did say so myself. After that, I gave everyone a little sample of chocolate candy (with similar results) and made my largest attempt at communication. I waved toward the city, then pointed at the rest of the chocolate, and told Palak I wanted to share the goodies with his people. I wasn't sure if that was protocol, or if he was even going to get what I meant, but he did, right away, and he was all for it.

Things were going even better.

Palak had someone blow this horn-type thing made out of a shell to gather the people. Then we all went outside again in a sort of mini-procession. We walked down those steps together, the king and I, almost all the way into the plaza, and when we were ten or twelve steps from the bottom, Palak told the people something, probably something like, "This crazy snake-woman has brought us some really great stuff. Bon appetit, and you can thank your generous king later."

Then we started throwing chocolate into the crowd.

Oh, man, it was pandemonium! Adults and kids alike acted like it was a day at the circus. Some of them just stuffed their faces, after which they rolled around on the ground in delight (well, not really, but you get the idea), but a lot of them examined the little paper-wrapped bars for a long time before carefully peeling off, first the outer paper layer, then the foil layer, examining each strange substance with awe and (it seemed to me) curiosity about how they could put it to use. I stopped a few minutes to show some of the kids how to fold the foil and make rings with it, which could then be fashioned into chains for cool jewelry. They started doing it with the ordinary paper too—it didn't have to be silver to be fun. One man, dressed like the scribe in my dream, got excited out of all proportion—he went around collecting the papers, even bribing people to get them, so he could write on them, I gathered. Nothing was wasted here.

Even though we had a lot of bounty and we were obviously

willing to share it, once again it was like the scene in the little village. Everyone was polite, no one pushed or shoved; and people who caught candy shared it with their kids and friends. The Uxmalites may have been just naturally polite or they could have been on good behavior in front of the king—but I thought the first, since they'd been so nice in the village. These people seemed so gentle it was hard to believe the stories of human sacrifice. (I was definitely going to come to believe, but so far, so good.)

That night was like a fiesta. By now, it was a beautiful twilit evening, and the temperature was just right, around seventy, maybe. If you want to know, it was about the best time I ever had in my life, and not just because of the power of giving something away—I enjoyed being with people who were having so much fun and who seemed so comfortable with themselves. And I was thrilled by the beauty of it. For one thing, I'd never seen so many stars. I knew why, of course. In a city with streetlights, you can't see stars—in our world, you have to go out in the country. Here they were in your face. Aside from that, though, there was that great, painted city, and the beautifully embroidered clothes, and Palak himself. How often do you get to hang out with a king? Especially one with incredible fashion sense?

When we had given out most of the candy (saving some, of course, for the royal *niños*), Palak said, "Why don't we go have a well-earned drinkie-poo?" (Or the Mayan equivalent.)

And once again, we trudged up the stairs, Palak and me and Mrs. Palak and all their merrily chattering pals. Once again, we took our places in the dark, beautiful room, smoky from the torches. I may not have mentioned it when I wrote about Cozumel, but the Spanish didn't smell so good. I'd read that they weren't fond of bathing, but apparently the Mayans were. They smelled good, and the room was perfumed with incense. I was slightly drowsy, probably from the alcohol I'd consumed, but if there was one thing I couldn't do, it was get sleepy. From now on, I'd have to take tiny, almost imperceptible sips, or just pretend.

For the time had come, I thought, for the serious banishing of inhibitions. Jollity above all must prevail. Somehow I had to find what I was looking for and put the fingerton on it.

I was busy opening the cognac and tequila bottles when another guest arrived, as unexpectedly, I gathered, as I had. A handsome older man, maybe the father or grandfather of Palak, came in, looking as if he'd traveled a long time. The king got up to welcome him, and so did the others. I rose as well and was duly introduced. Again, I touched the ground and then my head, which made everyone smile with approval.

A long time passed while Palak told the story of the Snake-Girl and the Pussycat, and then the newcomer had to taste the amazing chocolate drink and the remains of the torte. But there was a near disaster when the king reached to his chest to show him the jade brooch.

Somehow, it had come unclasped and fallen off.

Immediately, everyone started scrambling around on the floor, trying to find it, and I saw a great opportunity. Once more, I reached into my bag of tricks, brought out the flashlight, and turned it on.

Well, that was almost better than chocolate. Everyone had to touch it and try to figure out where the fire came from and marvel at the bright, clear light. It was Mrs. Palak who found the brooch, which Grandpa (who'd have been called *Abuelo* a few centuries later) duly admired, and then the queen pinned it playfully to her bosom, which Palak let her get away with. Abuelo turned to me with a question about the flashlight. Trying to figure it out, he turned it full on me, and gasped with surprise. Carefully, he examined my snakes with the light. Then he spoke excitedly for a while, and there was some wise nodding before Palak once again sent someone to get something.

While we waited for the messenger, to come back, I turned off the flashlight and very carefully repacked it. I could have sworn Palak watched with envy, but I couldn't be sure. I did think he was sorry to see it go, though.

It was the scribe, or royal librarian, who came back with the messenger, carrying with him a round box covered in jaguar skin. I'd seen pictures of these, and my heart skipped a beat. This was the kind of box in which the codices were kept.

Pulling open the box, the scribe showed me the first page. On it was painted a picture of a woman with exactly the same tattoos that I had. Her hair wasn't two-colored, or even pink, but she definitely had my snakes.

Okay. A.B. had said I'd know the right book when I saw it, and if this wasn't it, I was the uncle of a scribe-god. (Scribe-gods being monkeys.) Here I was, looking at the codex, and A.B. was nowhere in sight! If he had been, I could have just asked to look at the book, grabbed his tail, and that would have been that. But the little beast-face had chosen this particular moment to go play with the kids. And kids were like Kryptonite to him! What was he thinking?

So back to Plan A. After much admiring of the codex, I asked Palak if the scribe could join our little cocktail party. Anything to keep the book in the room. Everyone seemed to think that was a fine idea (especially the scribe), so we sat down to another merry round of drinking. I let my hosts taste the brandy, which they liked somewhat less than the chocolate stuff. But then I showed them how to mix the two, and that met with major approval.

After that, I brought out the tequila, and we had a good old time mixing that with various things and throwing it down. Food was brought in, which we ate, and which I'm pretty sure was good. But by now the fun had gone out of it for me. All I could think of was how to find my little fuzz-bucket and get back to the twenty-first century with my heart still in my chest.

When everyone seemed well in their cups, I made a bold move. Maybe too bold. I simply asked for the codex. I pointed to it, and then to myself, raised my eyebrows in a question mark, and mimed putting the book in my bag.

I guess I broke protocol. Because the room went silent.

This couldn't be good.

They weren't going to give it to me, and now they knew I wanted it. So I quickly backed off, shaking my head, crossing my fingers in front of my chest, anything I could think of to show them I was just kidding. Palak was silent for a while and then a tiny miracle occurred. He began to nod.

He pointed to the book, and then to me, then to the bag, then to himself. And I got it. He wanted to trade.

Nodding happily myself, I took out the flashlight and offered it. Palak reached for it, obviously thrilled, as if unable to believe the wonderful thing was really his, and then, ceremoniously, he handed me the codex.

I bowed about a thousand times to show my gratitude, and the awkward mood was finally broken when the king raised his cup and said, "Cheers!"

While Palak ordered the lamps put out so we could party by flashlight, I stroked the fur on the codex box, feeling pretty smug about myself. I kept the book close beside me in case I had an opportunity to make a quick getaway. Which currently seemed unlikely.

And I didn't know why. I'd done my job—where on Earth was A.B.? I thought of asking for him, but then rethought it—maybe, after such an awkward exchange, this wasn't the time. So there was nothing to do but party on.

But I still wasn't into letting down my hair. I wasn't used to alcohol, and I'd never done anything this important in my life. I absolutely couldn't let down my guard. So the party got a lot less fun as time went on.

Have you ever been with your parents when they were drunk? Or with any bunch of drunks when you were sober? You know how it makes you want to read the dictionary, or some package labels, maybe? Well, imagine being with a bunch of drunks whose language you can't speak, and who'd think nothing of ripping your heart out if you made a wrong move.

I had to sit there and smile till my cheeks hurt and laugh every time my hosts did, and try not to fall asleep from the alcohol I'd had, and count backward to keep from dying of boredom, and belly-breathe to keep from dying of fright, all at the same time. Now that I had what I wanted, and the hours kept passing with no A.B., my palms were sweating buckets. He'd never disappeared on me before.

To make matters worse, I didn't like the way Palak was looking at me—and I noticed he kept touching me when he talked. If I had to worry about being groped by the king, I was going to blow my circuits.

In spite of all that, everything might have gone fine if my stupid ex-friend Jace had remembered to change his batteries. You're supposed to do it before every job, but he was really bad about it.

It must have been around midnight when the flashlight gave up.

Chapter XVII: Night of the Living Jaguar

How do you explain about batteries several hundred years before the discovery of electricity? In a foreign language, to an entire royal court that's, like, totally wasted?

Here's the thing about royalty—they're like anybody else when they've had a few too many. When the evening starts to go sour, things can go one of several ways. People can get mad; or they can panic; or they can completely fall apart and get hysterical. If you've got a whole bunch of them, all those things can happen.

They did.

Suddenly we were swallowed by total darkness, with no matches and no light switches. The only way to get light was to find fire somewhere else and bring it in to relight the lamps. Palak started shouting orders, one of which apparently was to seize the betrayer immediately—because someone did.

A couple of people—one man and one woman—started crying, probably under the impression I was a demon with a big nasty ulterior motive. A few others just screamed, I guess thinking the end of the world was coming, and I was causing it.

Once I was in the totally rough hands of a soldier, and someone had fetched a torch from another room and relit the lamps, Palak started yelling at me and shaking the codex in my face. He was communicating brilliantly. I knew perfectly well he was saying I was a cheat and a thief and I'd sold him an inferior magic light in return for a valuable sacred book and I ought to die for it.

Me, I wasn't doing nearly so well.

All I could really do was shrug, and show him the button that turned on the flashlight and try to make him understand that it wasn't my fault.

Like that was going to fly. Even I could see how lame I looked. And still there was no A.B.

If I ever needed backup, this was it. "Field goal!" I hollered silently. "Field goal, A.B."

Then I started yelling out loud, "Field goal! Nine-one-one! Hey, Fuzz-bottom! Field freaking goal!"

So much for backup—he didn't come.

Two soldiers hauled me off and threw me into a tiny, dank, totally dark hole that could only be called a dungeon. I felt around to see what was in there, and nothing was. It was about the size of a large closet, with a wooden grate over the top. I figured this was probably my last night on Earth, and I tried to be peaceful, to somehow prepare for myself for death, but if you want to know, that's a lot harder than it sounds, even if you know how to meditate. I was trying to do belly-breaths, counting them to calm myself down, but my heart wouldn't stop thrumming. It was like a hammer in there.

But belly-breaths will do it every time. Finally I was thinking about nothing, nothing at all, which is pretty much where I wanted to be, when I heard a loud, angry yowling, like a wild animal somewhere in the distance. It *was* a wild animal, and I knew its name.

A.B. was in trouble.

Well, big surprise. Why else wouldn't he have come back to the chocolate party?

I tried to talk to him: "A.B., like, I'm here in this nasty dungeon, awaiting sure and certain death. What's up with you, by the way? Hey, if you're not too busy, *field goal!*"

Nothing.

"Yo! A.B.! Field goal, okay?"

Dead silence. He must be too far away to hear.

But I knew what had to have happened. The Alpha Beast needs humans for only a few things, and one of them is to open doors. Therefore, A.B. had to be behind one. The royal brats must have tossed him in some kind of kitty-dungeon.

So much for instant rescue. He wasn't coming, at least not now, but there was always morning. I remembered the Twelfth and last Tactic of Combat: It's not over till it's over.

Okay, then, it wasn't over. Prepare for your battles. That was another good one. There was only one thing I could do to prepare for battle and that was to sleep. That ought to be good in any case. If I was going to die, at least I could be wide awake for it. I'd more or less missed being born, and if the fat lady was about to sing, I didn't see why I should miss that too. And there was always the outside chance I was going to get out of this. Very outside, of course, but hey, Haley was still alive. Hope sprang eternal. The tough had to get going. That kind of thing.

So I curled up and breathed myself to sleep.

The thing about a palace, a lot of people live there and they have to get up and have breakfast and dress the kids and stuff—all the things that happen on a smaller scale in a regular house. So it gets kind of noisy first thing in the morning. After a while I woke up to more or less regular morning sounds. People walking around, cleaning up from last night, kids chasing each other, guys sharpening knives for the day's sacrifices.

I thought about dying nobly. With dignity. People were always doing that in stories. The least I could do was give it a shot.

These people worshiped lots of gods, particularly the sun god. If I was going to be offered to them, I ought to get to know them a little bit. So I thought about dust to dust, which was a phrase I knew from Dad's church, and becoming one with nature, maybe my atoms joining the others in the atmosphere, and wondered if I could just somehow think of it as beautiful.

Something I'd learned about the Mayans—some people saw their culture as evil. It was a politically incorrect thing to think, so it wasn't said much, but I'd run across it. I'd met plenty of Mayans by now, and I didn't think they were evil—really, really different from us, but not evil. They just had their own ways of thinking about things. So I tried to think Mayan.

If I'd been one of them, I'd have been happy about being sacrificed. I wasn't really into that, but I tried to see it the Mayan way and what I came up with was that I hadn't always done the best I could. But I could start now. Even if I only had a few minutes to live. I thought that if I were Mayan, I'd be a lot braver than I was because I'd know that I was going to die eventually, and I'd just accept death as a part of life. So I'd either die properly, or I'd use every skill I ever had, and I'd pull off the best escape you ever saw outside of a movie. Whichever it was going to be, I wanted to really do it well.

The only thing, I felt totally awful about never seeing my mom and dad and Haley again.

I hope this doesn't sound too morbid. Because it wasn't. Honest. Whichever way it went, I just wanted to put my heart in it.

Uh-oh. Heart. I wished I hadn't gone there.

It wasn't that long before they came to get me. But by the time they did, I was calm, and centered, and dignified, and maybe a little bit noble. Whatever was up, I was ready for it.

Prepared.

Two soldiers I'd never seen led me down the steps of the palace, and out to a plaza where half the town was gathered around an altar with one of those big carved stones behind it that the books call stelae. (I could never figure out how to pronounce this.)

Palak was already there, and most of my drinking buddies from the night before. They were dressed as grandly as ever, so maybe they hadn't been gussied up just to welcome me the day before.

There was a lot of incense, and fire, and speeches. Especially speeches. Talk, talk, talk. And then more talk. Finally, Palak's wife knelt and began pulling a thorn through her tongue, the same way I had in the dream, and Palak stood over her, just as my dream-husband had, and everything was quiet except for some drums.

It was early morning, just after dawn, and it was really beautiful. Peaceful, like this was the way things were supposed to be. And I understood that, for them, it was. Mrs. Palak was perfectly fine with what she was doing—giving herself to the gods (though that was a concept I personally had a little trouble with). I thought of it more as letting the molecules and atoms of her blood rejoin the earth and the air. I felt tears come, but they weren't for her. I was moved by the beauty of the thing. No kidding.

It has to sound crazy—we're so different now!—but take my word for it, it was beautiful.

When she had pulled the rope with the thorns entirely through her poor, ragged tongue, the drums got louder, and two men stepped out of the palace. They carried a pole with an animal hanging from it, front legs tied together, back legs tied separately. Uh-oh, I thought, Cat Position Nine—Captured Tiger. It had to be A.B., but I didn't get it—he was the Alpha Beast, for heaven's sake!

How in the name of the sun god had he ever allowed this to happen? I knew for a fact that no two guys with a couple of ropes could ever do that to him if he wasn't drugged or something. I was hoping for the "something."

I tried to talk to him, but he was still too far away.

He was the first to make contact. "Warrior, are you prepared?"

"Does the Pope wear a dress?" I said. "And by the way, do you have a plan, by any chance?"

"Naturally: To get the book and go home."

"Just when I'm having such a good time."

"Observe. It's going to get ugly."

"Yeah. Tell me about it."

"Remember the rules." The rules of fighting, he meant. He hadn't called me "Warrior" in a long time. It made me feel kind of good.

When they had laid him on the altar, someone handed Palak one of those obsidian knives, maybe the one I'd used to cut the cake. The drumbeat was very slow now, and everyone was silent. Palak approached the altar. He was about a step away when A.B. broke his bonds, flipped to his feet, and morphed into a jaguar. I'm not kidding. One minute, he was a precious little fluff-puff, the next he was this huge, furious jungle cat.

A lot of people screamed.

He even scared me. And he sure scared Palak, who dropped the knife and took off running.

So much for dignity.

But the soldiers seemed to be pretty well trained in the Tactics of Combat. About forty of them rushed him with spears, and murdered him right before my eyes. Dropped him right there, with about a million wounds, before he could take out more than four or five of them.

Okay, so they'd killed him. He'd said things were going to get ugly.

But, all things considered, "dead" didn't mean anything in this case, right? In a few minutes, he was going to shock the bejeezus out of everybody by getting up with all his wounds healed. I was totally psyched for it.

Tactic Seven was pick the right time for your battles—like not when you have your period. And probably not when your backup was temporarily dead. I tried to calm down and wait for him.

But the trouble was, they didn't give him a few minutes. Palak, probably humiliated by his unmanly retreat, bounded up, cut A.B.'s heart out in about three strokes, and held it high, bleeding and steaming, in a triumphant salute to the people, who all started chanting, working themselves into a trance.

Not the king's right-hand men, however. Four of them rushed forward with knives, made a few well-practiced incisions, and peeled A.B.'s skin off.

Right. They did.

They cut his heart out and skinned him right in front of me.

The four guys held up the bloody skin, and the people kept chanting. Then along came the royal garbage detail, and threw his carcass on the fire.

I was kind of wondering if all bets were off. I mean, could he come back if he didn't have a body?

The butchers were still holding his skin high when it began to blow up like a balloon. Palak continued the heart-salute, his eyes closed in ecstasy. But all of a sudden A.B.'s heart popped out of the king's hand like he'd squeezed it too hard. It landed inside the jaguar skin, and (I presumed) commenced to beating immediately.

Because A.B. was back! Jaguar A.B., that is, once again snarling, rearing, but covered with blood, and ten times scarier than in his last life—the one he'd left five minutes ago.

Nobody even screamed. They were frozen in place, too terrified to move a muscle.

"Tell them to look around them," A.B. said.

He sure had it right about timing. You could have heard a feather drop at that moment. Whirling, I waved my hand in a circle, crying: "Look around you, Children of Uxmal. Check out the rooftops, subjects of Palak!"

They hadn't learned English overnight, but if someone points, everyone else will look—it's just human nature. And here's what we all saw: jaguars.

Jaguars that covered the city like wallpaper.

They were on top of the Great Pyramid, all over the Nunnery, and the House of the Turtles, and every other building in town. They were sitting in the trees, and marching into the streets like the Great Kitty Cavalry I'd lied to Cortes about.

Only, these babies weren't figments of my imagination.

Can you imagine seeing something like that? If I thought the city was the most gorgeous thing I'd ever seen, I was a babe in the woods. You haven't lived till you've seen a few hundred jaguars invade a city.

No one moved; no one uttered a sound.

Even the drums had stopped.

A.B. sailed gracefully off the altar. "Time to go, Warrior. Hop on my back and hang on to my ears."

"But you hate to have your ears touched."

"Hang on to my ears, girlahini!"

I mounted, snared ear, and boom! I was riding a jaguar. Now this is not as romantic as it sounds. You would not believe what a bony back a cat has, but that's another story.

Everyone was still transfixed, unable to believe what was happening. I was focusing like crazy just on staying aboard, but I had to give directions. Thank the sun god I didn't have to move my mouth to talk or I couldn't have said a word—my teeth were clicking like castanets. "A.B., I had the book last night. It might still be in the party room. Everybody was pretty much out of it when we left."

He didn't answer, just flew up those steps, while everyone else waited to be mauled to death by marauding jaguars. But the marching jaguars didn't attack. They sat down in Cat Position Two, becoming a silent army of furry guards that no one wanted to mess with, even people who usually thought of jaguars as clothes.

There were still plenty of people in the palace, and as we entered, they scattered, yelling in Mayan, probably something like, "Run for your lives. The apocalypse is now!"

Two or three servants puttered in the party room, picking up dirty cups, but posing no immediate threat. The good news was, the codex was there too, forgotten in the alcohol haze of the night before. The bad news was, so was the royal librarian, who'd apparently come to retrieve it. Ignoring both the cleaning staff and the scribe, A.B. tried to grab the book in his jaws, but it was almost too big for him. He had to make an adjustment to get his teeth around it, and during the second it took, the librarian drew a knife and rushed us.

A.B. lifted his face from the floor, the book in his teeth, just in time to get a knife in the eye.

I knew what was going to happen next. We had the book and we were leaving.

But in the split second before we did, I wondered what would happen if A.B. lost one of his lives while time-traveling. Could even the Alpha Beast come back from that? And if not, would I tumble through time for eternity?

Let me say this: It totally seemed like it.

But after a season or two in hell, all three of us landed in the little Mayan hut where we'd stored the bag with the chocolate, the knife still in A.B.'s eye, the librarian still clutching it, the book still in the jaguar's mouth, and me still on his back, frantically gripping ears with my hands, flanks with my knees. Spot remained exactly where we'd left her, contemplating the joys of rodent torture in the laying-hen position. At the sight of us, she swung immediately into Cat Position Seven— Halloween Cat—back arched and fur fluffed.

I was pretty shaken. "A.B.? You okay?"

"Get this damnable librarian out of my eye!" he snapped back.

I slid off his back and tried to talk to the scribe, but the poor man was in shock. No matter what I said, he continued to sit perfectly still, eyes wild, totally paralyzed. I finally had no choice but to put my hand over his and pull the knife out of the Beast's eye.

"Better," A.B. said, and dropped the codex.

For a second, the only sound was Spot's hissing and snarling. "Would you please shrink?" I said. "Spot's blowing a gasket. Why didn't you tell me you could do that jaguar thing?"

"Shape shifting," he said, "is the technical term for it." And he proceeded to demonstrate the process, turning back into a fuzz-pumpkin.

Instantly, Spot dropped her back and let her fur droop, but the scribe had a meltdown. Panicked, he slid on his butt to the far wall, whimpering like a crazy person.

"Oh, for heaven's sake," A.B. barked. "Pour water on him."

I had a better idea. There had to be a flashlight around somewhere— this was a house, right? I located a little utility area and rifled drawers till I found one, along with an unopened pack of batteries. I brought the two items into the living room, demonstrated that the light was in good working order, took out the batteries, showed that it no longer worked, then inserted the new batteries and turned it on again. "Got that?" I asked the scribe.

He looked at me like I was the devil. He wasn't going to be himself for a while, but I figured nothing I could do was going to make it any better for him. Surely they had a potion for this where he came from. So I pried open the fingers of one hand, closed them around the flashlight, put the extra batteries in the other, and said, "We're square, okay? One book, one flashlight. I'll throw in the extra firepower. A.B., take him home, will you?"

"With pleasure," the Beast said, leaping into the man's lap. The guy's mouth opened in a big "O," like a scream, but no sound came out. "Now click those heels," I told him, "and say 'there's no place like home.'"

I must have blinked. I don't remember looking away; all I knew was that suddenly the man was gone, but A.B. wasn't.

"How'd you do that?" I asked.

"The same way I always do it. I delivered the package, and came back a split second after I left. Bet you never even noticed I was gone."

Right as usual.

But I had a question. "Listen, how come you couldn't just do what you just did when you were in the pit—time-travel out and carry on as usual?"

"Good, Student. Excellent question. I might have gotten away with it. But it's never good to do that when you're out of your own time. We knew the legendary Zigaloo princess Deboreeno Diamondino had successfully stolen the book four hundred years before we met those chaps at Cozumel, did we not? So we had to be careful not to do anything to alter the outcome. I couldn't run the risk of changing history, or we might not have gotten the book at all. Worse yet, might not have gotten back—or you might not have. What if I'd left the pit and found you guarded by someone who killed you when I arrived to effect the rescue? With time travel, you simply have to let events evolve as they do—or rather as they already have. So I had to do it exactly the way I did it the first time."

"But how did you know you didn't time-travel out the first time? You're not going to tell me you remembered, are you? Because I know you couldn't have. If you had, you'd have changed history by not doing it."

"Don't be absurd, girlette. I knew, of course, what decision I'd have made. Because I'd always have made the same one."

All righty, then. I may have sighed. "No doubt, Mr. Wiz. So how was Uxmal?"

"Getting back to normal. The Guard was just leaving. Bit of bad news, though. In the interim, Palak seems to have cursed your family."

"Palak! That backstabber! We had a deal, dammit—I sent back the flashlight fair and square."

"I presume we weren't fast enough. And apparently Mayan curses can't be rescinded."

"Oh, well. It's not like we didn't know about it. Your eye looks better. What happened last night?"

"I fell into the evil hands of spoiled brats. The royal monsters locked me up."

"Excuse me, but you're the Alpha Beast."

I was messing with him, of course. I knew this was a sensitive point. But all he said was, "I *loathe* working with children."

"Yes, but—"

"I'm supposed to be smarter than they are. I know. Could you give it a rest, Human? How did I know they were going to throw me into a pit and pull a grate over it?"

"Oh. I was in one too. But here's the thing—why didn't the servants let you out? I heard you complaining—why didn't anyone else?"

"Have you any idea how much noise you people were making out there? You couldn't have heard a plane crash."

Speaking of which, I was starting to experience major jet lag.

"Well, I feel like I've been in a war. Can we go to bed now?" But then I remembered something "Wait. What should we do with the codex? We have to return it to break the curse. The curse! Hey, we did it, A.B.!" It had suddenly dawned on me what this could mean. "All we have to do is find the owner."

"Done."

"Huh?"

"This is the home of a Mayan shaman."

"So we just…leave it?"

"Exact-a-mento."

"So, like, the world's saved and everything?"

"Mission accomplished," he said. "Let's go home."

Emboldened by my Jaguar ride, I grabbed an ear for the road, which earned me a gentle love tap—the kind that leaves bruises. So back to the tail.

And in seconds, we were back at Ranger Central, which now smelled like stale popcorn and nervous kid sweat. Kara and Carlos were dozing. Everyone else was focused on the candle, sending energy as promised. I was touched.

And I suddenly got why A.B. had thought it was so important. I wondered if, without it, he'd so easily have reincarnated himself after death by skinning. If he'd taken five minutes more—even three—we'd both have been permanently dead.

"We're baaaaaaaack!"

In the pandemonium, Cooper and I found each other's eyes, and I could have sworn his were a little misty. But that's impossible; he's a guy.

CHAPTER XXVIII: RANGERS' NIGHT OUT

I slept the clock around. We got back about noon and by noon the next day, Kara decided she should call Evelina. I woke up to find her leaning over my bed, one hand on my shoulder.

"You okay, *chica*?"

"I'm just really tired. You know our psychic club, right? We've been working on a project that kind of took it out of me. Did everybody lose points for missing classes?"

She shook her head, sitting down on the bed. "I handled it. Everything's good." She gave me a little pat. "You did a good job, *mija*."

"Uh…and that means…um…what?" How could she know?

She smiled. "I have my sources. And also…your back."

In my half-asleep state, it took me a minute to figure out what she meant. Could she really have said she had my back? Wow. Good to know. "Thanks. Can I ask you something? There haven't been any calls from my family, have there?"

She shook her head so sadly that I could tell she knew a lot that I hadn't told her. "I'm sorry, Reeno. I'll let you know the minute they call."

Well, hell. I was just supposed to get up and go to class, like everything was normal? Uh-uh. No. "Could I just go on sleeping for a while?"

"Sure."

I slept till early the next day, roughly forty hours. A world record, I figured; and I still felt like I'd run a couple of marathons.

I looked at the alarm clock—whoo! I seriously had to get going.

First, I dug out Morgan's phone, the one I'd stolen, and speed-dialed the number under "Mom," hoping she hadn't yet left for school. "Hi, did someone there lose a cell phone? I found this phone I'm calling from and…"

Evidently her mom was the impatient type. The next thing I heard was, "*Morgan!* Somebody found your phone." And then Morgan came on the line.

"Hi, Morgan, it's Reeno. You want this phone back? Good, 'cause I need a ride to the Lakers game tonight."

The stuff she said next seemed to be in some strange language, best translated thusly: "#$%^U(U^E$@%*^#%*!"

"Hey," I answered, "did the cops pick up Jace and Baldy? Because, the funniest thing, I noticed a couple things about this phone. First, you forgot to erase the texts Jace sent you about the hit. Second, this thing's got video of my house on it. Hellooo! How amateurish can you get? The minute I leave, the standards fall all to hell."

"Give me a break, Reeno. Last thing I'd do is take video of a hit. How dumb do you think I am?"

"Oh, I must have forgotten. Maybe it was me that took that video. After you left."

Actually, I hadn't thought of that, but she didn't have to know.

"And then there's the texts," I said. "An elementary burgling no-no."

"I was gonna erase those," she said, her voice decidedly sulky. "But somebody stole my phone."

"Bummer. But it could be a learning experience. Maybe next time you'll follow procedure." I paused for a long time, drawing out the tension, and then I said, "So. You wanna go to the Lakers game or you wanna go to jail?

And then I paused for more profanity.

"Uh-huh. Good. We're in Ojai. Yeah, I said 'we.' Sure I meant Snookums. I never go anywhere without my kitty-fluff. Snookums and six humans, including me. Bring your mom's mini-tank. Huh? Well, steal one."

I hung up, absolutely confident we were going to see Morgan at the appointed time and place. The tiny texting faux pas aside, she was a thoroughly meticulous criminal. Much more talented than Jace.

Next, I made sure Cooper had the tickets, and got messages out to all the Rangers—we were meeting at three p.m., usual place, to finalize plans, pick up the Curly dog, reshield both ourselves and it, and get our glamours on.

A.B. must have been with me at least some of the time I was sleeping off the time jaunt, but we hadn't had a chance to talk, and I had some really big questions for him. Imagine my horror when he wasn't in the Rangers room. What was this? How were we supposed to do this Lakers thing without Snookums to keep Morgan in line?

But he arrived! He was waiting by the car when we got there. "Somebody," he sniffed, "had to put a glamour on this monstrosity." Meaning the SUV, not Morgan, I assumed. And he was right to think of it. I'd barely noticed the tank myself. With the glamour on, it registered as "visiting mom car," rather than "ginormous suspicious vehicle."

And in our glamours, I hoped, we looked like well-behaved kids going to dinner with someone's parents in a completely authorized fashion.

As opposed to "Red Alert! Remedial Unit Runaways!"

Morgan was cool as Orange Ice behind the wheel, only she was more like Platinum Ice. She wore black as always and, as usual, looked like some dangerous blonde from a spy movie. And trust me, dangerous was exactly what she was. We'd met when I skinked her house. She was older than me, already sixteen, and she was so nice to little, trapped me, just talking instead of calling the cops. But she had a little agenda of her own—she wanted me to steal stuff for her.

Well, no problem. I wanted her to drive for a kickass crime crew. So we struck a deal. Or, as some might say, I made a pact with the devil. She was a great criminal, but you couldn't trust her. As experience had shown, she didn't have your back.

"Hey, Morg," I said. "How's it going?"

She held out her hand. "Give me my phone."

I picked up A.B., knowing he wasn't going to resist. This was an acting op and I'd long since realized he lived for them. "Snookums," I said, "'splain things to my good friend Morgan."

"Wowwwwwwrrrrr," the Beast explained, in a voice that should have had a glamour on *it.*

Even some of the Rangers had to hold their ears.

"Shall I translate? He said you do the job, you get your phone."

She turned from the window and stared straight ahead. "Pile in, everybody," I said, but when Carlos climbed in with the dog, she drew the line. "Ewwwwww. What *is* that thing? No way that thing's going in this car."

"Huh? It's just a stuffed dog."

Cooper pulled at my sleeve. "Reeno. You're just used to it. But that thing's toxic, trust me. We started fighting while you were gone, and finally figured out it was the dog. We had to renew our shields every couple of hours. Finally, we just put it out in the hall."

"Oh. Well, what if it makes her run off the road or something? How are we going to do this?"

"I know!" Sonya said. "Let's put a shield on her too."

Julia nodded.

"Okay, Morgan, a little ceremony first." By now, we could go into our focus just by closing our eyes and collecting our thoughts. She must have thought we were praying, poor innocent babe. But it worked. Once we'd shielded her, you could see her muscles relaxing, her jaw untensing. "Better?"

She looked at me suspiciously. "Is this school some sort of religious crackpot thing?"

"I told you. It's government. And don't ask who these agents are. If I told you I'd have to kill you."

She didn't crack a smile, just kept staring. "Where are we going?"

"Didn't you believe me? To the Lakers Game. Cooper even got you a ticket." Obligingly, Cooper slipped her a cardboard rectangle.

"Where the hell is the Lakers game?"

"Staples Center, of course. You must not be a basketball fan."

"I'm not. How am I supposed to get there?"

I turned to the backseat. "Oh, Agent C.A., when you got the tickets, did you have a chance to MapQuest the destination?"

"Roger that," he said, producing the printout. "Located in downtown Los Angeles, on Figueroa Street, Staples Center is easily accessible from several major freeways." I stifled a giggle. He had to be quoting from the Staples Center website. Cooper had plotted out this hit every bit as carefully as Morgan used to plot the hometown ones.

"And I'm supposed to park there?" Morgan said.

"Agent C.A.?" I asked.

"There are three thousand three hundred parking spaces at Staples Center with more than sixteen thousand others available within a seven- to ten-minute walk. Anything else, Commander R?"

Hey, that was a better rank than A.B. gave me. This was starting to be fun!

"Yeah," I said. "Tell her to shut up and drive."

"Ma'am," he said, "I'm going to need you to shut up and drive."

Excellent. We heard not another word out of Morgan until we had parked in one of the more than 3,300 available parking spaces and entered on Eleventh Street, the entrance nearest the press box, which we knew to be above the upper concourse on the west side. The problem was, we figured, the general public probably couldn't get into the press box. So what we had to do was get Manny Diaz out of there.

We'd thought of yelling "fire," but decided against it.

Yelling "jaguar," however, had merit.

On the drive down, I explained the plan to darling Snookums.

"Not in a thousand millennia," he answered sweetly. "Not if a hundred of my lives depended on it."

"Well, actually only one does," I said. "They can only shoot you once. This isn't like that other time—you're not going to be tied up. You can just time-travel out of it when you're ready. And you have to admit you do kind of owe me—for saving the world and all. Plus, doesn't the Alpha Beast have a mandate to stop any evil he hears about? Can you really be responsible if we don't get that curse out of circulation? Besides, you'll get your picture in the paper."

I truly think it was the last argument that won the day. The Beast had more ham in him than Wilbur the pig.

But he did have a question: "How exactly do you propose to enter the arena with your delightful tiny pet?"

"Three options, Mr. Whiskers. You can put on a glamour and sidle in like you're the official stadium mouser, you can time-travel in, or…"

"Yes?"

"There's always Carlos's backpack."

"Wowwwwwrr." He actually spoke aloud.

In the end, he chose time-travel. It had far more dramatic appeal, and you know how His Ninjaness loved the limelight.

❖

Here's what we knew from the website: The press box was accessible only by a stairway on the upper concourse and by a particular elevator near the press room on the event level. And from that press room, you could take the stairway to the private media entrance, which we figured, on this occasion would be serving as the private media exit. And once on the upper concourse, we figured, anyone leaving the building would still have to use that elevator, so why not just board it in the first place?

Thus, we planted ourselves in front of it, all but A.B.

When things started happening we had to keep close to the door of the press room. But we just had to see the show. So at first we watched the game.

Things were along in an entirely sportsmanlike way until…well, until, for one split second, a harmless orange cat appeared in the middle of the court and then, before you could blink, it morphed into a jaguar the size of a couple of large mastiffs. Seriously—I've looked it up. A male jaguar can weigh 350 pounds, and when A.B. was a jaguar, he was flamboyantly male. I mean, *cojones* the Lakers could play a game with. So 350 at least. In the middle of the court.

"There's an animal on the court!" screamed the announcer. "What *is* that thing? It's some kind of a leopard—it's a leopard! There's a leopard on the court!"

Meanwhile, Lakers and opposing team members alike were busy scrambling for safety, not to mention anyone else who happened to be on the court. Except for the photographers, of course. Nothing ever scares photogs, and in this case at least, they were perfectly safe. A.B. was not about to let his Oscar op go undocumented.

"I think it might be a—it is! Actually, it's a jaguar, not a leopard," screamed another announcer. "It's…it appears to be washing its face."

He was right. A.B. had plopped himself down in the middle of the court in Cat Position Two (Egyptian Temple Cat) and was now proceeding to lick his dainty paws and rub them adorably all over his big spotted face. I looked up at the monitors, to make sure he was getting his close-up.

Yes! Beautiful!

Meanwhile, people were starting to stand up, wondering whether to be scared or enjoy the show. But the first announcer quickly made that decision for them: "Ladies and gentlemen, don't panic! DO NOT PANIC!"

Which of course was the signal to panic. People started streaming for the exits.

A.B., in an effort to keep the lid on, went into Cat Position Five, The Sphinx, and then rolled over into Beach Kitty, doing his best to look non-threatening.

Meanwhile, uniformed men began to converge on the court. A.B. licked his paws some more, and probably would have purred if anyone could have heard him.

"We have a message from security advising everyone to stay in place, the situation is under control. A team of experts from the SPCA is on the way, Meanwhile, sharpshooters are in place, but the chief of security asks everyone's cooperation in an all-out effort NOT TO FRIGHTEN THE ANIMAL!"

Nonetheless a near stampede was occurring. People were practically stepping on each other's heads to get to the exits. Screams, yells, catcalls (excuse the pun), whistles, and profanity billowed in delicious cacophony throughout the arena. Not the least of the screamers were hollering at other people to get out of the way so they could take cell-phone videos.

"Target arriving!" Carlos yelled. He was out of the energy loop, his job being to act as our personal commentator, also to distract or encourage Manny as necessary. I turned around in time to see the elevator doors opening, various broadcasters debouching, nearly all clutching cordless microphones.

"And theeeeeere's Manny!" Carlos hollered. Kara was clutching the Curly dog, her face a rigid mask of focus. "And a one," yelled Carlos, "and a two, aaaaaand *threeeeee!*"

On "three," Kara let go, the signal for all five of us to focus on flying it straight up. Carlos moved closer to Manny (who I now saw had a blue-gray aura) and we moved closer as well, guiding the dog with our energy. But suddenly some civilian saw Cursed Curly flying low over everyone's heads. "What the hell is that?"

The various broadcasters all tried to answer at once, to solve this new riddle, and I could hear Manny saying, "It looks like some kind of...stuffed toy. Folks, a stuffed dog seems to be...well, floating above us, but we're not sure..."

Carlos yelled, "Watch out, Manny! *Catch!*"

Well, of course that fired everyone up. All the broadcasters wanted to be the one to catch it, but Manny, after all, was the ex-baseball player in the bunch. And one more thing—Cursed Curly was going right for him if the Ozone Rangers had anything to do with it.

"Contact!" Carlos yelled. Manny had dropped his cordless mike and opened his arms. The stuffed dog was no longer floating, but downright *hurtling* into them.

"Bull's-eye!" He'd caught the dog.

Like lightning, we pulled off its shield.

"Hey," we heard Manny yell, "what the f—k was that? This is nothing but a f—king stuffed toy. What the f—k was that all about? Get out of my way, turdface. Give me that!" The last sentence was meant for Carlos, who had politely picked up the mike and held it out to the poor distressed broadcaster, who wrenched it rudely out of his hand.

"Hey, you're on the air," Carlos said, as in "One, two, three, testing."

"I don't give a f—k if I'm on Mars. This is the worst f—king clusterf—k in the history of broadcasting!"

Yes! Success! Psychic Tourette's!

I gave Manny a good squint. No doubt about it—no longer blue-gray. He was a bilious shade of oily olive. I had a feeling this was going to be his last broadcast.

I turned back to the court to give A.B. the high sign before somebody tranquilized him, but he was way ahead of me. One second he was there, the next he…just…wasn't.

"What the hell?" the announcer screamed. "The animal is…gone. Where did it go, for God's sake? How did that even happen?"

The rest of the Rangers high-fived on that one, but guess what Cooper and I did instead? Something we shouldn't have, in public. I don't know, we just couldn't help it.

Guess our secret was out.

CHAPTER XXIX: YOUTUBE IS FOREVER

Poor Morgan. I doubt she'll ever be the same. A.B. certainly won't. Not only did he make every major news show that night, he was on every front page in the country. But those things are ephemeral. YouTube is forever, and A.B. had already gone viral by the time we got back to Ojai. Now he can watch himself over and over again for the next nine hundred years.

Me? I was going crazy. I absolutely couldn't believe the clowns still wouldn't let me call my family! I fell into such a fit of despair I slept for another two days.

And then on Saturday, Evelina woke me up. "Guess what? You have a visitor."

"My dad?"

She nodded, smiling, and disappeared. But I wasn't smiling. If Dad had come instead of calling, it could only be with bad news. If Haley was better, why not just call? Why show up?

I shoved A.B. out of bed. "It didn't work!"

"What didn't work?"

"Oh, never mind. It's not your fault. You're not superhuman, you know."

"I'm not?" he asked. I'm pretty sure it was a serious question.

But when I stepped onto the quad, it wasn't Dad who came running to hug me. It was Haley. Haley, *running*, her aura a brilliant pinky red!

Objectively, I knew it was Haley; she was the only Chinese sister I had who looked like that. And the man with her *was* Dad, the radiant woman at his side being a mom I hadn't seen for years. But my brain just couldn't take it in. I stood rooted to the spot, unable to run to meet her, to move at all, until I actually held her in my arms. And then I tried to squeeze the life out of her. She was so skinny!

But so beautiful. Her complexion glowed, her cheeks shone pink, her eyes flashed with life and energy. I didn't know what to say. I think what came out was, "You're so…back!"

Dad and Mom had caught up with us by the time I found my tongue. I squeezed them like a grizzly as well, and Mom said, "I am too, Deboreeno. We're both back!"

Dad was trying to explain. "The doctor says it's the fastest recovery he's ever seen in his life. Absolutely unexplained by medical science."

"She woke up from the coma—when? Early this week," Mom said.

"Feeling *great*," Haley supplied.

"Two pints of blood later and…this!"

"Well, the blood plus a burger and fries," Haley said.

"So, Mom," I said, "you think the family curse is finally broken or what?"

Mom glanced at Dad, vaguely irritated. "Who told you about that old myth? Give me a break—this is medical proof the whole thing's garbage. Haley's illness was a rogue virus."

"Could I just ask one thing? What night was it exactly? That she woke up?"

The parental units looked at each other.

"Um, Tuesday, I guess," Dad said. Uh-huh. The day I was in Uxmal. "Because they said she could come home in two days, and Thursday night, we were in our own family room, watching the Lakers game together. We had popcorn and everything, but the game got canceled."

"I heard about that. Something about a leopard in the stadium?"

"Anyhow," Dad said, "want to go have breakfast?"

"For real? I can go off campus?"

"You can spend the whole day with us. We got you a family emergency pass. The school agreed it was the biggest emergency they've ever had here. In a good way."

Mom handed over a suitcase. "We even brought you some clothes."

"Great, I'll go change. Haley, come! I want you to meet my roommates."

"You have two?"

"Well, one's not exactly human."

But of course the Beast was gone when we got to the room. Any time he sensed a bout of possible petting, he was so out of there.

I shook Kara awake.

"Reeno, for God's sake, can't you…?"

"Kara! Kara, I want you to meet somebody."

She took one look at my sister and whispered, "Haley? Is this Haley?" And then she threw the covers off, leapt out of bed, and started hugging Haley and crying. Crying! Even I didn't do that. "Omigod, Haley, I can't believe it's you. I have to go get the others."

I touched her arm. "Kara. Wait. It's okay, there's plenty of time."

"Oh. Oh, yeah, there is. Well, Sonya anyhow. I'll be right back." And she pattered away in her Megadeth T-shirt, black cotton panties, and bare feet.

While I was dressing, Haley sat on the bed and asked cautiously, "What was up with that?"

"It's a story. The short version is, you've got a great little support group on this campus."

"Black magic isn't involved, is it? Because, somehow, I feel like this is some kind of miracle."

"Well, not exactly *black*. Kind of more…oily olive."

"Ewww."

Kara came back with Sonya, and while she was hugging Haley and welcoming her back from the dead, I rummaged in my top drawer for my princess tears and Palak's little carving.

"Come on, Haley."

"Y'all have fun," Sonya said. "Haley, remember one thing—you got the biggest fan club ever right here at St. Joan's. You ever want to run away, you just come on. The Ozone Rangers'll take you in."

As we walked down the hall, Haley said, "What was she talking about?"

"You wouldn't believe it if I told you."

"I would."

"Uh-uh, you wouldn't, but guess what, I will tell you. Just not today. And only if you'll support me when I tell Mom and Dad I have an errand to do."

She shrugged. "Sure. I'm in a pretty good mood. Hey, guess what. We've got another surprise for you."

As soon as we stepped out of the dorm, my other surprise came running toward me just like Haley had. Curly! The *real* Curly.

I wasn't sure what being with Curly was going to be like after hanging with A.B., but it was bliss. She let me pet and cuddle her, and she was so glad to see me I thought she was going to wriggle her butt off. And she didn't call me Human or Novice or any other demeaning names. She just licked me and loved me like a pet's supposed to and sat in my lap all the way to the restaurant.

And breakfast was…about two hours long. We had a lot of subjects to cover.

After Dad paid the bill, I brought up my question. "Listen, I know this sounds weird when I haven't seen everyone in so long, but I kind of need to deliver a gift to someone. Could we do that?"

Mom looked hurt. "I don't understand."

"When I first got here, there was one person who was nice to me before I made any friends, and she was our housemother. But she got mugged, and as a result she was hurt so badly she hasn't been back. I just need to see that she's okay. And take her a little something I got her."

Even Mom couldn't object to that. So Dad called Hal, found out where Abuela lived, and set the GPS. Her home was on the outskirts of town, in a little thatch-roofed cottage with a calico cat in the yard.

I knew that cat! Suddenly a lot of things started falling into place.

"Mrrrow," said Spot, recognizing me instantly. Curly tried to chase her, but she did her Halloween thing, thoroughly intimidating the poor pooch.

Abuela greeted me like I was her own granddaughter. Her eye was no longer bandaged, and I wondered if her sight had returned. "Not yet," she said, "but it will. I have faith; I know it will." She asked us all in for some juice, and I saw that although everything else looked exactly like I remembered, the codex was nowhere in sight. When I went to the kitchen to help her, I gave her the princess tears.

"They're a little dry right now," I said, "but they're there. And here's something else for you." I fished the little carving from my pocket.

She examined it carefully with her one good eye. "This is no tourist bauble. This is pre-Colombian."

"Is it?" I asked innocently.

"Where did you get it?"

I shrugged. "Found it—in my travels."

She hugged me. "You're a good girl, Reeno. My eye will heal now."

Did she know everything, I wondered? She was surprised by the carving, but A.B. had said, *This is the home of a Mayan shaman.*

Of course, I knew how A.B. knew about her—Spot was the informant. And now I knew why she could predict the future, and knew what would heal her. She had magical powers herself. And she must know that I did, because she'd asked me for something really hard to get.

But you just don't go around mentioning talking cats to sane people.

Still, I had to know about that codex. "Abuela, may I tell you a secret? I know about the Mayan book."

"Yes?" Now she was the one acting innocent.

"What's in it, Abuela? Does it really say what's going to happen in 2012? How the world's going to end, I mean?" So A.B. and I could start preventing it. It could be sunspots, I thought; or space aliens. We could go to the right scientists, maybe even time-travel to the future…

"I'm sure it says, *niña.* You did well."

"Well, what's next? I mean I could—"

"All I can tell you is this: It is in the hands of the right people."

I must have looked doubtful, because she said, "It isn't just me, you know. My granddaughter is helping."

"Your granddaughter?" What was she getting at?

"You know her."

Oh. My. God. "Evelina!" I burst out.

"She speaks very highly of you."

Before we left, she gave the carving to Haley. "Keep this with you," she said, "and you will always be safe. Whatever harm has come to you in the past will not recur. It's a magic charm given to me by a very good friend—a friend who's a powerful witch."

"A witch? I don't know…"

"A nice witch," Abuela said, and winked with her good eye.

When we left, I hugged her and said, "I love you, Abuela."

She said, "Come and study with me when you're ready."

Something about that made me anxious. *I already have a magic teacher*, I wanted to say. But of course I couldn't.

❖

A.B. was waiting when they took me home. "*Buenas noches, compadre.* How was your day?"

Polite conversation wasn't his style. It made me nervous. "What's this *compadre* thing? That's a new one."

"We worked well together, girlagig." That was more like it. Condescending. "You've earned the title. You have heart—no thanks to Palak, of course."

"Very funny, fuzzball. By the way, I delivered the princess tears. But Abuela wouldn't tell me what happened to the codex. So I was kind of wondering—did we save the world or what?"

"Be patient, *compadre*. It's only 2011. You'll find out next year." Seeing my glare, he said, "Very well, you deserve a straight answer. We did our part."

"Come on, A.B."

"Be patient. Do you know what H-men are? That's the name given to the Mayan shamans in practice today. Abuela is one, as you learned. And there is another, a very, very skilled magician, who works closely with the Guard. She will decipher the codex and cause the information to fall into the right hands when the time arrives."

I nodded. "Anybody I know?"

"Possibly."

Ah. "But whose hands? Politicians? Scientists?"

"Perhaps. Perhaps other members of the Guard. We can't know the solution until we know the problem. If a Cleveland-sized meteor is heading for Earth, all the scientists in the world couldn't stop it."

"Like the Guard could."

He flicked his simian tail. "Never underestimate the power of magic."

"Right. Okay, I get it—we did our part. It's out of our hands." I paused just for a beat, because I was excited. I tried to be casual. "So what's our next mission?"

"Yours is to graduate. Mine is for me alone to know."

I couldn't believe what I was hearing. For a moment I didn't speak at all, just stood there feeling as if he'd whacked me with his tail. "You're cutting me out?" I finally managed, my voice barely a whisper, hoarse with disbelief and loss.

"Our time together is over, *compadre*. It's been…jolting. Wouldn't you say?"

"Hold it! What about my lessons? Magic! Magical combat! We barely got started."

"There's only one lesson, little one." *Little one.* Like he was somebody's grandfather. He never talked like that. "There's the Simple Secret and there's the Main Maxim, but there is only one lesson. Are you ready for it?"

I was way too mad to answer.

"Magic is transformation—princess tears to healing potion. You understand the principle perfectly."

I was running out of arguments, so I resorted to whining. "But, A.B., you can't leave me alone with the ceiling spiders!"

"You have Kara. And your other friends." Well, I did.

I really didn't know what else to say.

He let me cuddle with him that night, but the next morning the ungrateful Beast was gone. Just like that. After all we'd been through together.

Okay, I know what he is. He's the next thing to the Prince of Darkness—a merciless fiend and a bloodthirsty monster; a callous killer and a ruthless assassin. But I miss him like crazy. Go figure.

However, I do not *need* him. As I keep telling myself. He's right, I have friends. Real ones this time, not fake ones like Jace and Morgan. And I have Haley back. And Mom. And a great dad and a great dog, and a potential magic teacher. And even, I think, a boyfriend.

A really great boyfriend. Cooper's a terrific person. Super considerate and a master criminal in the making. Once he figured out the check trick (get someone else to order something, then reimburse by check), he got us an official Rangers laptop. So now I can watch A.B.'s YouTube videos any time I feel like it.

But I still have this insane need I just can't shake. I have *got* to get a new tattoo the second I get out of here—a jaguar, in Cat Position Five.

The Sphinx.

Author's Note

There's a bit of real history in this book, but so far as I know no king named Palak ever ruled Uxmal; there was a Pakal in Palenque, though, and it may be no coincidence that "Palak" is an anagram thereof. The lady piercing her tongue with thorns is not a product of my disturbed mind, but a famous Mayan image. Cortes really was in Cozumel in 1519, and best of all, Doña Marina was a real person! But I've taken a couple of liberties here—Cortes didn't meet her until he reached the Yucatan Peninsula later that year, and, though she was indeed his interpreter, she usually worked with a second interpreter, a Spaniard who knew a bit of Mayan. Incredibly interesting woman, also known as La Malinche. Some of the palace details are made up—who knows what Mayan hors d'oeuvres actually were? However, with the help of an expert, I made an educated guess. What isn't made up are the twin passions for chocolate and jade.

About the Author

Julie Smith is a former journalist who began her career at the *New Orleans Times-Picayune* and then moved on to the *San Francisco Chronicle*, where she remained for fifteen years, absorbing gritty realism and (hopefully) street smarts, as careful preparation for a life of crime. Crime-writing, that is.

She's the author of 20 adult mysteries featuring three female sleuths and one neglected guy: a cop (Officer Skip Langdon, NOPD), a PI (Talba Wallis, poet and computer genius, also of New Orleans), a semi-amateur detective (Rebecca Schwartz, San Francisco lawyer), and a complete amateur (Paul McDonald, crime writer, also of San Francisco). The first book in the Skip Langdon series, *New Orleans Mourning*, won the Edgar Allan Poe award for Best Novel.

CURSEBUSTERS!, Smith's first YA novel, is also her first paranormal adventure. While writing it, she met a young male editor who gave her the quote she thinks most embodies the spirit of the book and her own philosophy as a YA author. It's this: "There's far too much emphasis in YA on the importance of girls getting the guy (or the girl— this is Bold Strokes here!) and not nearly enough on the importance of girls kicking ass." Smith deeply and firmly believes in the importance of girls kicking ass, an opportunity they're seldom afforded in real life—hence, every opportunity must be taken in fiction.

For more quality Young Adult GLBT fiction, look for the Soliloquy Imprint from Bold Strokes Books

Cursebusters! by Julie Smith. Budding psychic Reeno is the most accomplished teenage burglar in California, but one tiny screw-up and poof!—she's sentenced to Bad Girl School. And that isn't even her worst problem. Her sister Haley's dying of an illness no one can diagnose, and now she can't even help. (978-1-60282-559-8)

Who I Am by M.L. Rice. Devin Kelly's senior year is a disaster. She's in a new school in a new town, and the school bully is making her life miserable—but then she meets his sister Melanie and realizes her feelings for her are more than platonic. (978-1-60282-231-3)

Sleeping Angel by Greg Herren. Eric Matthews survives a terrible car accident only to find out everyone in town thinks he's a murderer—and he has to clear his name even though he has no memories of what happened. (978-1-60282-214-6)

Mesmerized by David-Matthew Barnes. Through her close friendship with Brodie and Lance, Serena Albright learns about the many forms of love and finds comfort for the grief and guilt she feels over the brutal death of her older brother, the victim of a hate crime. (978-1-60282-191-0)

The Perfect Family by Kathryn Shay. A mother and her gay son stand hand in hand as the storms of change engulf their perfect family and the life they knew. (978-1-60282-181-1)

Father Knows Best by Lynda Sandoval. High school juniors and best friends Lila Moreno, Meryl Morganstern, and Caressa Thibodoux plan to make the most of the summer before senior year. What they discover that amazing summer about girl power, growing up, and trusting friends and family more than prepares them to tackle that all-important senior year! (978-1-60282-147-7)

5/17D